# MURPHY'S FAVOURITE CHANNELS

*For Artsworld Television,*
*which is so good I still can't believe it.*

*Also for Julia Darling,*
*another living legend.*

# MURPHY'S FAVOURITE CHANNELS

John Murray

FLAMBARD

First published in the UK in 2004 by Flambard Press
Stable Cottage, East Fourstones, Hexham NE47 5DX

Typeset by BookType
Cover design by Gainford Design Associates
Printed in England by Cromwell Press, Trowbridge, Wiltshire

A CIP catalogue record for this book
is available from the British Library

ISBN 1 873226 68 3

Flambard Press wishes to thank Arts Council England
for its financial support.

website: www.flambardpress.co.uk

'These affairs of yours will end badly someday,' I said sadly.
'Never mind!'

Anton Chekhov, Agatha


Billboard outside an old picture house:
Coming next week *Kaiser Bill's Arse*. In two parts.

# THE AUTHOR

John Murray was born in West Cumbria in 1950 and now lives with his wife and daughter in Brampton near Carlisle. In 1984 he founded the highly acclaimed fiction magazine *Panurge*, which he and David Almond edited until 1996. He has published a collection of stories, *Pleasure*, for which he received the Dylan Thomas Award in 1988, and six novels: *Samarkand*, *Kin*, *Radio Activity*, *Reiver Blues*, *John Dory* and *Jazz Etc*. Two of these have been nominated as Books of the Year in *The Spectator*, *The Independent* and *The Observer*, and *Jazz Etc*. was longlisted for the 2003 Man Booker Prize.

# TWO SHORT NOTES

1. This novel has alternating 'terrestrial' and 'satellite' chapters throughout. The first gives a more or less linear account of the hero's life (and his terrestrial TV viewing) between 1957 and 2001. The second deals with a few concentrated days in November 2001, and explores them via his experience of his new digital TV. The relevant digital codes are given at the start of the book.

2. Murphy can watch 'Akbar TV' Arabic broadcasts with no difficulty as he read Arabic at London University (SOAS) in the 1970s.

# KEY TO MURPHY'S FAVOURITE CHANNELS

**103** Border Television (regional ITV serving Cumbria, South Scotland and the Isle of Man; also available as terrestrial channel)

**121** Talk TV (a small British input but principally US chat shows)

**156** Cwmri Digidol (Welsh language channel)

**187** Ireland's Own (broadcast from Dublin; light entertainment, music and documentaries)

**210** People Together (films about issues affecting local communities; produced by community groups)

**212** Health and Family Channel

**214** Date Me Channel

**215** Fashion First

**216** What Men Like (soft porn channel)

**232** Hobbies and Interests

**233** Science TV

**234** Geographical

**237** FSF (Fantasy and Science Fiction)

**240** Lifestory (a channel devoted to celebrity biographies)

**356** Culture Fix (devoted to the serious arts)

**555** EuroTV (news and documentaries from a European perspective)

**625** BBC Radio 3 (Audio channel; classical music, arts)

**626** BBC Radio 4 (Audio channel; arts, drama, news, current affairs etc.)

**636** Bible Channel (Audio channel; Authorized Version Bible readings)

**677** Akbar TV (Cairo-based news and documentary station; programmes broadcast worldwide in Arabic)

# 1

Flogger pressed his old man's face to the window and peered into the Franklins' sitting room. His quivering ears were very red with the cold and his nose was mottled purple. Those fleshy lugs stood at strikingly asymmetric inclinations to his head, the left at around thirty and the right at maybe thirty-five degrees. The back of his skull protruded in a tapering bullet fashion and one of his many derogatory nicknames was 'Turnipbrains'. He was hogging the window and so engrossed in what he saw he was neglecting to act as relay commentator to me.

'What size?' I asked him anxiously. 'How big is Wilf's, d'you think?'

'Twelve inches,' he said with authoritative contempt. Of course he was not exactly in the running himself, but that didn't stop him playing the unappeasable connoisseur.

'Is it?' I said wonderingly and hoarsely.

'Twelve,' he sneered. 'When even Willy Farish's is fourteen inches. And he's a wizened up, daddery old bugger if ever there was.'

'Oh?' I said, moderately surprised. 'You mean he's older than Wilf?'

But Flogger's thoughts were elsewhere. His glowing brown eyes indicated hero worship and he began to brag with a throaty excitement, 'Now my Uncle Derek from

Doncaster . . .'

I sniffed and curled my lips at this legendary uncle. Doncaster Derek was the one who had a brand new Alvis with leathered upholstery, and who took beach holidays in Cyprus not once but three times a year. He had once stood close to Billy Cotton in Scarborough. He had once touched Shirley Abicair's washboard in Leeds. He had once been at the same wild New Year's Eve party as Lonnie Donegan . . .

'My Uncle Dekko originally had one seventeen inches. But then last Christmas my Aunty Shona told him it wasn't big enough to satisfy her. She insisted Dekko get a twenty-one inch.'

I was so fed up with this Doncaster marvel, I couldn't restrain a little fertile exaggeration.

'My Uncle Dick in Tasmania,' I said smoothly, 'has one that's twenty-seven inches . . .'

Flogger turned to scowl at me. He was torn between the wish to assert the obvious, viz. that a specimen two-foot-three-inches long was an objective impossibility . . . and a wish to outdo me and my relative at all costs.

'Well,' he began very ponderously, 'I have another Uncle in . . . in . . .'

I said combatively, 'Oh yes? Where's that, Flogger? And what's he called?'

'Morton,' he said, more confidently. 'I've told you about him before. He's not really my uncle, he's my grandad's cousin, which makes him my great half-uncle. And he's Dinah Betick, so he has to inject himself with sugary water. He lives in ah . . . Dowdy Lid.'

'In where?'

'I mean in Delhi Dad.'

'You mean that he's an Indian?'

'Is he shite!' Flogger said, deeply insulted at the uncalled-for slur. 'Think I have a darky half-uncle? No, he's an Australian through and through.'

I ruminated for about ten seconds. I collected *Flags of the*

*World* bubble-gum cards and knew an inordinate amount about world geography for a seven-year-old.

'I think you must mean Adelaide, Flogger.'

'Yep. Daddy Lid alright. Well my Uncle Morton's is thirty inches.'

I decided to exploit this common antipodean connection and see how far Flogger could be trapped into collaborative fantasising.

'So when he has his telly on, this Uncle Morton has to balance on his head?'

'You what?'

'When your uncle is looking at his thirty-incher. He has to stand on his head on the sofa like that telly body Eileen Oojah.'

'I . . .'

'Australia's upside down, it's down under, everyone knows that. But of course they don't realise that they're all walking on their heads all the time. They've no idea from their own point of view. Because they're all doing it together at the same time, they cancel each other out like improper fractions.' Extrapolating boldly. 'It's the same as the time difference between us and America.'

'Is it?'

'Or like a dog not knowing that it's colour blind. Let's face it, you and me don't go around *feeling* and *acting* like we're ten hours behind America, do we? Let's face it, Flogger.'

'Ah –'

'They all think that they're the right way up like us. But of course the telly they're watching is only an electric picture, it's not real flesh and blood, is it? At first, when they switch it on everything on the screen is turned upside down. It's a technical problem that they have to get round. So to start with, until their Australian brains get adjusted, for the first few months of watching it, they have to squat upside down on the sofa watching the screen between their arseholes.'

Flogger cheerfully concurred, entirely at one with this alluring picture. 'Yes, Uncle Morton told us about that in his last Hair Mail. He says if you walk round Diddly Dad and look through the curtains, you'd see all these rows of great fat arses stuck up in the air on the sofas. And you'd wonder, if you weren't an Australian, what the bloody hell was going on.'

'It's great,' I said warmly and enthusiastically, 'what the telly does to folk. Isn't it?'

I began to elaborate a fictional South African relative who had a TV that filled an entire wall of his parlour, on the impossible lines of a cinema screen. Flogger and I were going to the village pictures that night, to see *Cockleshell Heroes*, and that was inspiring my imaginative baseline. But halfway through this entrancing fable, a vast and spreading figure loomed upon us. We flinched and started to bolt but the figure reached out an elderly hand and said in a placid voice.

'Roe? Humphrey?'

The designation 'Flogger' might have suggested violence, vigour and virile cruelty but the reality was his turnip head, the lop ears and that hideous Christian name. Forty-five years on, I have no idea why his soubriquet was Flogger unless it was faintly alliterative with his surname Farrell. As for 'Humphrey Farrell', it bears as much relation to the thing in itself, the reality of Flogger, as shallow denominative categories like 'An Ugly Little Boy' or 'A West Cumbrian Pit Village Kid'. And unlikely as it sounds, we will be probing more of this unfathomable epistemological mystery in the Franklins' sitting room before long.

'Come on in,' Mrs Franklin said, extremely friendly. 'Come on in and watch it. You don't have to gaze through the window at it.'

We hesitated then trooped in in sheepish excitement. Wilf Franklin was sat in his heavy old rocking chair gazing very earnestly at his twelve-inch telly. Wilf was in his late seventies and always wore a rough and fuzzy grey cap at a standard forty-five degree tilt. He also had a severe squint, and a manner that was both rough and gentle. I had never heard him raise his voice to any kid in the backs, even the wildest, even the maddest ones. I did some arduous mental arithmetic and calculated he was in his mid-thirties at the start of the First War, and touching retirement during the last one. It seemed to me extraordinarily galling that a squint-eyed pensioner should have a brand-new television, while the new unsquinting NHS generation incorporating Flogger and me should not.

'Look,' Wilf said in a thrilled voice, not even inquiring the cause of our visit. It was obvious why anyone, why the whole bloody village would want to be in his sitting room the day after this mighty purchase from Workington's Pow Street. Even the few other villagers who possessed a telly would want to compare notes on the picture quality, the quantity of snow interference, the toughness and robustness of the ancillary knobs. Volume and on/off were straightforward enough, but vertical hold and horizontal hold sounded confusingly like cross-buttocking Cumberland Wrestling where the prize was half a stone of Alston Sausage. And contrast, contrast – there was a far from black and white mystery! There were also those reckless village heroes who were currently contemplating acquiring ITV that was broadcast all the way from Glasgow. 'Commercial' television, it proudly dubbed itself, and its few Fingland subscribers obviously saw themselves as vicarious financial speculators. Undaunted by all that snow, the jumping picture, the signal so weakened by its progress across the Solway Firth it could barely take root on a distant West Cumbrian telly, they were prepared to fork out for a second aerial so that they could watch and sing along to the excellent commercials, even better than the novel programmes, including those vulgar American imports entirely unknown on the austere and hallowed BBC.

Wilf, being old, had only risked the one channel. Flogger and I refused the chairs Madge Franklin offered, sat on the floor, and watched the beautiful foot-wide box. We had been hoping *Watch With Mother* was still on, but it wasn't, and it was afternoon horse racing. For perhaps five minutes we simply imbibed the euphoria of the moving picture, the lovely joiner's shop odour of the tiny telly's timber casing, the breathless gabbling voice of a gentleman called Peter O'Sullivan. The horses were parading around the paddock, and in between shots of the favourites and the rank outsiders and the complete impossibilities there were these cards indicating whimsical names and incomprehensible figures.

Wayward Lad? Bird in the Hand? Dan's Delight? OK Corral? 5–1, 100–1. Why, I wondered then, and for many a year after, did the odds have to stop there? Why was it never a 1000–1, 1,000,000–1 and beyond, to infinity?

After five minutes of grey cards, grey faces and grey paddocks, we were both bored out of our skulls. I could read it in Flogger's bullet physiognomy that he was even more distracted than I was. However as an accredited TV authority he could scarcely display his painful tedium.

'It's a very good picture,' he announced magisterially. 'It's a very good picture, Mr Franklin.'

Because of his squint Wilf was obliged to admire his new pet from an oblique angle, so that it looked as if he was viewing it with his right ear. It was as if he was touchingly bashful of staring this twelve-inch prodigy straight in the eye. Wilf's ear was currently watching the 4.15 race upon which he had a five-bob stake. But this solemn praise of the new household deity, this votive offering even from a turnip-headed seven-year-old devotee, had to be politely acknowledged.

'Thank you, son. You never said a truer word. It is. It is a bloody good picture. We made damn sure of it. We made him put it on in the shop before we bought it. We weren't going to buy any old gimcrack doings.'

Flogger was the first to crack and he suddenly murmured that his mother wanted him back home for twenty past four.

Mrs Franklin looked rather perturbed by such an exact appointment. She offered us cake and Brothwell and Mills pineappleade but we demurred. Wilf meanwhile was angrily banging his sofa as his 25–1 called Curious Vision sauntered in last at Sandown Park. He looked at us boys mournfully and permitted himself to say 'hell's bollicks and bloody buggeration'. He muttered derisively about 'blurred' vision, never mind curious bloody vision, his own monstrous squint notwithstanding. Then, lifting up his dark black pipe, he shouted: 'Come back on Sunday afternoon, if you've nothing better to do. There's a great programme will make you two lads sit up. Talk about bloody exciting, Roe and Flogger.'

Flogger smiled gratefully at the dignified vocative. 'What is it, Mr Franklin? Which programme is that?'

Wilf tapped his nose mysteriously and his squint seemed to lurch periscope-wise around the back of his cap. 'Never you mind! Let it be a surprise. Three o'clock on Sunday. Provided you've not been shoved out to Wesleyan Sunday school, that is.'

The pictures was a weekly event and it took place in the Fingland Miners' Welfare Hall. The freestanding screen was provided by the Welfare committee, and the seating was rows of hard folding wooden chairs. The projectionist was an elderly and foul-tempered man called Horlick who drove through the eight miles from Aspatria, and who was pushed to explosive madness at least ten times every performance. The average age of his audience was perhaps nine, with a few listless and cosseted teenagers too feeble to attempt the proper cinemas in Workington and beyond. Though, tonight, there was an unprecedented and quite baffling event. A courting couple in their twenties had decided to brave the unbridled mania of these hundred crazed urchins, and had seated themselves demurely two rows from the rear of the hall. Even aged seven, Flogger and I could see that they were waiting for the lights to dim so that they could set to at advanced gum-sucking and other varieties of loudly amorous slurping.

The tickets were dispensed by a very gaunt old lady called Maisie Figgs who sat at a table and unwound them from a huge roll. Crisps and Underwood's pop could be obtained during the interval from a cramped upstairs room manned by ginger-haired teenagers called Sam and Tom. These palpably nervous snack vendors were identical twins. Both with obese porcine faces, they were strongly reminiscent of the Pinky and Perky puppets I had seen on my Aunty Winnie's gigantic twenty-one inch Dynatron last week. Their nicknames were Tweedledum and Tweedledee, and these gawky Alice characters had a subsidiary if vital function of berating the worst troublemakers when the lights were off. They were both anxious and sweaty at their policing responsibilities and were rightly afraid of certain of the Fingland clientele. It was quite impossible to distinguish Sam from Tom, Pinky from Perky, 'Dum from 'Dee, and nobody, not even their employer Horlick, addressed them other than as 'thee' or 'thoo' in the abrasive Fingland dialect.

Flogger and I were seated on the next to the back row. Immediately behind us were the hardest hard knocks, Death, Skunk, Middy, Bazzer and Blagger. Of course we wouldn't have opted for such vulnerable seating, but the hall was almost full and we had no choice. The first picture hadn't started, but already Skunk had spat on Flogger's hair before whistling and examining the slatted ceiling for architectural flaws. Flogger wiped away the glutinous saliva and looked hopelessly at Skunk. Skunk could batter every seven-year-old in Fingland and numerous ten- and twelve-year-olds as well. All Flogger could manage was to murmur chidingly in a theatrically maternal voice: 'Give over will you! Have some sense, Skunk please. Do please cut it out.'

Skunk looked derisively at old woman Turnipbrains. Skunk was half-gypsy and lived in an insanitary cottage next to a defunct pit reservoir. He smelt OK, though not like a skunk, more like a racehorse or a circus elephant. As thickset as an apprentice blacksmith, he leant across and growled: 'Else wat?'

'Else . . .' began Flogger. 'Else nothing, Skunk. Nothing honestly! But my Mam will go and bray us if you puke in my hair. She'll say that I've puked in my own hair.'

'Puke' was a versatile Fingland verb that could signify either vomit or salivate. It was actually pronounced 'poick' as in 'poikilothermic', which was highly apposite given Flogger's cold-blooded temperament. Skunk was pondering the brilliant oral gymnastics required for spitting in your own hair. He looked at dozy Flogger and remarked that Flogger's mother must be a poor judge of her son's pathetic limitations.

'No,' pouted Flogger, as if he were disputing on some ponderous committee. 'What she says is that I spit on my hand and rub it onto my hair. She reckons I do it just for badness and just to drive her mad. So she goes and brays buggery out of me every time you go and puke on my head. I tell her that it's you, Skunk, but . . .'

Skunk was very bored by this too discursive narrative and was impatient for the Three Stooges. He shut Flogger up by spitting full in his face and clattering both ears for good measure. At last the lights went out and the black and white film spluttered and crackled across the screen. The sound track followed effortfully in sync though in the comic context the time lag seemed to make no difference. The Three Stooges with their crazy haircuts roared into focus, and soon we were hooting at the absurdity of Mo being mistaken for a qualified dentist. Undeterred by the misunderstanding, Mo succeeded in wrenching the wrong tooth out of a screaming innocent pinioned in the chair. He treated his trembling patient with absolute smirking heartlessness and Skunk sat in dazed admiration of someone who actually made a fortune out of acting like Skunk. Encouraged by his role model, for the next two hours at considerate ten-minute intervals Skunk spat upon Flogger in the following manner. Across the hair five times, in each asymmetric ear four times, twice down his neck, on the apex of his bullet skull just the once, and in two cases, having courteously tapped him to gain his attention, he hosed Flogger's eyes with pineappleade saliva.

I had Blagger sat immediately behind me. I was spared the worst of Flogger's humiliations, because although I was no fighter, I was an indispensable footballer and could not be goaded too far. Blagger was altogether subtler in his torments, improvising on the lines of a playfully comic surrealist. Blagger a.k.a. Fingland's Luis Buñuel didn't spit on me, but instead blinded me both literally and artistically. He waited for every dramatic high point during *Cockleshell Heroes* (e.g. where the doughty naval saboteurs make their perilous underwater journey), then, just as it reached the most breathtaking moments, he put both hands across my eyes. Hence all the nodes of dramatic tension were edited from my enjoyment, and I felt as if I were being trained to endure a future existence where all of the troughs but none of the joys were on offer. Over the next forty years it often struck me that Blagger (Alfred Arnold) Baines had a hell of a lot to answer for . . .

But our sufferings were as nothing compared to Horlick's. When the film was at its most thrilling, as demarcated in my case by Blagger's blindfolds, the audience would show its appreciation by stamping wildly on the floor. However, should this stamping of two hundred prepubertal feet prove altogether too deafening, Horlick would promptly stop the film and incur an operatic chorus of hissing and booing.

'If,' he bawled at us, the veins on his head like the vivid striations of an anatomical cadaver, '. . . if you carry on any bloody more, I'm taking *Cockershell Eros* back to bloody Spyatri! I'm warning you lot for the last bloody time!'

By Spyatri he meant Aspatria and by Eros he did not signify love for his pintsized tormentors. When, as frequently happened, the projector broke down, the Finglanders not only stamped their feet, they began a rhythmic jungle chorus that sounded like discarded offcuts from a Johnny Weismuller movie.

*'Ooh, Orlicks!*
*Oo, Warlicks,*
*Wooh, Arselicks*
*Wooh, wooh, wooooooooooooooooooh!'*

Horlick could bear them dropping the aitch and even the corruption to 'warlick', the Fingland all-purpose designation for rascal or brigand. But to be called 'Arselicks' was more than any seventy-five-year-old Mafeking veteran could endure. He shook his hero's fist at us and roared: 'You little bloody bastards! You do this every flaming week! Week after week you awful bloody bastards!'

Horlick's more fluid policing system was to employ Tweedledum and Tweedledee to make torchlight searches for those making the rumpus. The film could stutteringly proceed while the ginger-haired monozygotes could flash their instruments in the offenders' faces. Of course in the pitch darkness 'Dum and 'Dee were only making inspired guesses, and were obliged to seek corroboration from their suspects. The formula used by the identical twins was identical and unchangeable, and is rendered here in the precise Fingland phonetics.

'Wuzz it thoo? Er *thoo*? Er *thoo*? Eh?' Extended admonitory pause. 'Noo, any mare ev it, an yer *oot*!'

Pinky and Perky were openly fearful in the presence of Skunk and Blagger and would never have dared to shine a light in their smileless sultans' fizzogs. Remarkably enough, no one was ever turfed out of the Welfare Hall, not even on the occasion Skunk made a lively bonfire in Flogger's hair with some purple Halloween matches. Like the breaks in projection and the haranguings from Horlick, the spotlight interrogations of Sam and Tom were a strategy that did not work but only relieved their irritations. Though in the last analysis they didn't even do that, and on the one hand they and their Aspatria employer were like fatuous parents who threatened to smack and never did, or they were like crest-fallen Beckett characters who kept on going on, even though neither the going nor the keeping on had any discernible point.

In front of us the courting couple were engaged in A-Level or possibly S-Level gum-sucking. Smarting from all of Skunk's poickings, Flogger found a certain distraction in watching these bizarre manoeuvres. The man obviously believed very little could be seen in the dark, but our seven-year-old pupils had accommodated enough to note that he was industriously massaging her buttocks. Impressed by this, as the lover removed his hand to light a fag, Flogger grabbed hold of mine and forced it to knead her sprawling backside. I gasped in bilious horror. The woman groaned. Incensed, I used my free hand to crack Flogger's lug and to my disgust felt Skunk's saliva.

Flogger squawked at the blow and whispered none too quietly, 'Look at him pestling away at her bum. Look at that, the dirty big get!'

Did he mean me, Roe Murphy, or the man with the glowing Player's? At that very moment Tweedledum chanced to be passing. He flashed his torch suspiciously and observed not mine but an adult hand re-employed on the woman's behind.

'Fuck off,' she hissed, outraged at Tweedledum, who instantly dropped his torch.

Blagger said, 'Yis, thoo fuck off, Coont Drackla!'

'Aye,' added Skunk. 'Fuck reet off, Belly Lug Horsey.'

At the end of the night, as the lights flashed on, it was the unchanging finale. The back door that was a fire door was forced open and the bawling vandals made their roaring exit. Before that they kicked over not one but every single wooden chair, a hundred and fifty seats that would have to be wearily restored by Tweedledum and Tweedledee. Then they raced off like victorious Boer cavalry across the Welfare backs, whooping and swearing as they vanished from sight.

The grieving Mafeking soldier shouted after them, 'This is every single bastard bloody week. You bloody little Fingland *bastards . . .*'

On the Sunday afternoon we had nothing better to do, so were back in front of the Franklins' twelve-inch telly.

Wilf said with a queasy, boyish excitement, 'It's on in five minutes. In the meantime, just sit down and watch the interval, lads.'

We watched the continuity interval. It was the famous film of a burgeoning daffodil, laboriously executed by Fifties time-lapse photography. A week later we would see a brilliantined potter whirling a pot out of wet clay. The bustling light orchestral accompaniment reminded us that the BBC stood for a cheerful though always sober and tirelessly educative bustle.

'What's the exciting programme, Mr Franklin?' asked Flogger with very twitchy impatience. 'Is it *Circus Boy* that my Uncle Derek likes? By the way, did I tell you that Uncle Dekko's is a twenty-one inch?'

Wilf smiled a little drily. 'Is it now? I don't like a telly that dwarfs a room personally. I like a TV but I like it to know its place. Eh, Madge?'

His wife said, 'No, it isn't *Circus Boy*. It's something much more exciting, Humphrey.'

Flogger flinched at that mortifying address. 'Oh? Oh is it?'

'Here it is,' said Wilf almost deliriously. 'Here it is, here it comes.'

The programme in question, the thing that had the old Franklins in such a joyous fever, was *The Brains' Trust . . .*

'*The Brains' Trust*!' I said stunned. 'It's *The Brains' Trust*, Flogger.'

*The Brains' Trust*? If Flogger had flinched at the word Humphrey, he turned grey with suspicion at the name of this programme. He might not be in the same 'progress' class as Skunk or Blagger, but Flogger certainly didn't put any trust in his or anyone else's brains . . .

'Look,' snorted Wilf. 'It's that Pullet lad again. He's a bloody brainy boyo. And Chud, old Chud, he knows more flaming words than any damn cyclepeedy.'

'Old Buck Offsky there,' said Madge. 'I bet that feller's read every flaming book that's ever been writ.'

'And Oar,' chorused Wilf. 'Jay A. Oar. That young bow-tied brainbox could talk away till his arse dropped off.'

'Phew,' gasped Madge. 'What a terrible bunfight it's going to be.'

As if stung by a wasp, Flogger shot up and announced, 'My Mam said I had to be back at –'

Madge pushed him back down reprovingly. 'Relax will you, Humphrey! I spoke to her about it at chapel this morning. She said you could stay here till bedtime as far as she was concerned.'

Flogger sighed and shuddered, then sank into a palpably anaerobic state where he became as inert as the pattern on the Franklins' carpet. Meanwhile the presenter explained that the 'trust' comprised four highly trustworthy brains; those of T.P. Pullett, T.S. Bukowski, C.T. Judd and J.A. Orr. All of them of course were supereminent Oxbridge dons and leading authorities in their respective disciplines of history, English literature, moral philosophy and logic. Without further ado, the spry presenter then read out the first question, one sent in by a regular viewer from of all places Keswick, up in Cumberland.

Madge exclaimed, 'From Kezzick! The question's a local one, Roe. Crikey, Humphrey!'

Flogger attempted to raise his eyes to the screen but they weighed like lead and he had to drop them. The arresting query that had been sent in by the searching Lake District viewer was: *Is it conceivable that in due course Mankind will know everything worth knowing?*

Wilf Franklin looked at me with a superior expression as if to imply it was he or at any rate his magic telly had thought up that monstrous poser.

'That,' he said tersely, 'is what I call a bloody *question*.'

J.A. Orr coughed and grimaced but grasped the nettle firmly. 'Well,' he said with a rat-a-tat donnish haste, 'when you talk about the business of "knowing", of course, it depends in the first instance what you mean by the term "knowledge".'

'It's true,' concurred Madge Franklin. 'Oar's damn well right at that.'

'Maybe,' said Wilf judicially. 'And maybe he's bloody not.'

'If,' continued Orr, 'like Immanuel Kant for example, we depart from a facile empiricism, it means that we are obliged to acknowledge the inevitable contribution made by the mind itself to this thing we call "knowledge". Whereupon "experience", which is clearly the forerunner and concomitant of such knowledge, might then be erroneously construed as the acceptance of the given, plus the formal structure which is disclosed in the given . . .'

I looked astonished at Madge. She was bashing her wrinkled fists together as she anticipated a bloody clash of jousting minds. Raising her hand to her mouth in mock alarm she warned me, 'Chud isn't happy with that . . .'

C.T. Judd took hold of J.A. Orr's nettle and immediately denounced it as stingless. He retorted with a glacial disdain, 'But I feel it perhaps rather foolish, Orr, to adumbrate anything quite so categorical at this preliminary starting point in our discussion. Moreover, and in all frankness, it might be forcefully argued that it were – how ought one put it? – egregiously meretricious . . .'

Madge hazarded, 'Old Chud has to be from Lancashire. He has a posh voice alright, but he's always saying things like "it were" . . .'

Now, aged fifty, I ask myself something that I couldn't have asked in 1957. Was it that Madge Franklin's empirical knowledge did not include a certain given? Namely that prickly SCR iconoclasts like Judd would resort to the resonant subjunctive mood whenever it seemed most tellingly appropriate.

'Surely,' continued Judd, 'it were, in addition, demonstrably fallacious to avouch, as Orr here would attempt . . .'

Pullett, always the urbane pacifist, interjected, 'Instead of these rather too frequently rehearsed mutual antagonisms, extended no doubt in characteristically playful fashion, mightn't we turn to some helpful theoretical preliminaries? May I? Thank you. Let me see. Perhaps I can usefully start with what Locke has to say about knowledge in his four chosen categorical forms. Namely and firstly, if I may address the listener, I mean the viewer, from ah Keswick. Firstly, Mr Wilkes, the identity and the diversity of ideas. Secondly, what is more or less accurately describable as relational knowledge. Thirdly and alternatively, the coexistence, without any necessary connectedness, of what we call those ideas. Fourthly and lastly, the so-called "real existence" of ideas . . .'

C.T. Judd struggled with his shapeless tie then seized back the wilted nettle and hissed, 'But surely, Pullett, after this bald recital of such a ludicrously categorical and hyperreductive quartet, it were a wholly nugatory . . .'

Wilf said with reverence, 'He used it last week, that nougat doings. Chud is my man, my winner, I have to admit. 3–2 favourite if he's a day. Look at all those bloody big words he throws. They're like coshes or clubs, they stun old Buck Offksy and old Pullet unconscious. Go on, Chud, give him it, go on man and flatten those specky young buggers!'

Suddenly there was a doubting and critical expression on Madge's old face. 'The only time,' she wheezed through the chronic heart and lung conditions that would carry her off in two years time, 'the only time I didn't enjoy it, *The Brains' Trust*, was when they had a flipping smirking young body on it. Professor Irene Minto I think she was called. She wasn't a patch on them, this upstart bluestocking lass. And you know what made me sure she wasn't, Humphrey?'

But Humphrey in his *Brains' Trust* catatonia was only listening to the hallucinatory echoes of his aching soul.

*'At least twice I could nearly work out what she was talking about!'*

She looked me challengingly in the eye and I exclaimed politely, 'Crikey, Mrs Franklin!'

'Eh? There was no damn point in that now was there, Wilf?

'No,' snorted her derisive husband, who would die next year in 1958 of coal-dust pneumoconiosis. 'Who's going to *trust* a person's brain when any bugger can understand it? Let's face it Flogger. Let's face it, eh Roe?'

# 2

*High Mallstown, near Longtown, North Cumbria, 11th November 2001. Lunchtime satellite viewing and listening.*

## 232

I was concentrating on a remarkably fuzzy-haired man who, if he were English, would probably have been nicknamed Zulu or Kermit or Max Wall behind his back. He had a broad palette, a spatulated knife, a variety of brushes, and was painting a snowy forest clearing which exuded a placeless and extraordinarily childlike calm. He was from the American Midwest and had a tender pioneer's burr, a friendly, tolerant and courteous intonation in his voice.

There was an old black shed in his snowed-up clearing, which he suddenly daubed and highlighted with a couple of touches of white.

'And if you want to make your snow on that old shed there look colder, you can add some blue to the white.'

He did so with two quick dabs and I shivered at the vividness of his cold.

'Bloody hell,' I snorted.

'It's real easy,' he said gently. 'Blue to white makes for cold. I guess you maybe noticed it's all of it easy what we're doing. Anyways, you just enjoy it, what you're painting out there. It ain't no damn exam after all. You just enjoy it, it's for pleasure, not to give yourself no durn ulcer.'

'No,' I said, enthused, though I was not painting anything myself. 'Durn right it is. And I won't.'

But I was caught in a powerful reminiscence. It had taken me a good five minutes to realise who this Midwest man was the living spit of. With that same fuzzy tribal warrior tonsure, curled and sprung like a woman's hairy wig. He had no specs like Davies but otherwise he could have been his twin. It was twenty years since I had last seen Samuel Davies wiping his glasses in that terraced house in Cambridge. He was our landlord and virtually the only one in the dignified university city who would take tenants who owned dogs. We had a beautiful mongrel that was a spaniel cross called Willy and as we had no children Willy was most definitely our four-year-old son. Davies owned about a dozen rickety properties in the seediest bits of the town, and was mortaged not to the hilt but far beyond and way above his amiable, always smiling head. He was not only easy about dogs, he was admirably tolerant of welfare claimants and problem sociological categories of all kinds. Unfortunately he not only accommodated the bona fide workless and the single mothers in their teens and twenties, but the criminal, the insane, and the downright dangerous. Samuel Davies, who wore very strong glasses for a lifelong myopia, did not care nor choose to see what lay underneath a brittle polished surface.

Because Borgue had a smooth dress sense and an ingratiating manner and a public-school voice, Davies allowed the ponytailed twenty-three-year-old entrepreneur (sundry odoriferous New Age products, oriental wall hangings, carpet imports from Afghanistan) to take the upstairs attic two floors above. After only a week Borgue was getting innumerable and intriguing nocturnal visitors, all of them looking tense and single-minded and all of them vanishing upstairs as soon as we opened the door. As our room was next to the front door and as Borgue never answered it, Jane and I ended up as virtually indentured below-stairs skivvies for this immaculate public-school hippy. Borgue was, it transpired, a major Cambridge heroin dealer with a sideline in the kitchen Liebig manufacture of hashish oil, and when we explained these worrying realities to Mr Davies he showed a genuine amazement.

'But Mr Borgue is ever such a polite young man,' he said by way of unarguable rebuttal. 'And he always pays his rent on the dot. I mean I've never had to ask him for it once.'

Davies stuck to these tender first impressions for the next six weeks. Finally as the dealing got ever more flagrant, the house was busted in the middle of the night by the Cambridge police, and Davies himself was interrogated for his possible connections with this Borgue of a dozen aliases. Thereupon his indignation knew no bounds and he intercepted all of Borgue's mail from his house and returned the giro cheques to the Post Office in person and pointed out to the baffled postmistress with the anomalous singsong Wigan (in Cambridge!) accent that the taxpayer's money, hers as well as his, was being spent on bloody heroin and hashish oil by this Borgue whose real name was Kirkcudbright. Was she aware, Davies asked her incensed, could the Wigan-exile lady credit, that all Kirkcudbright's deceitful aliases were actually *Scottish Border towns and villages* (what a slur on the likes of, say, Sir Walter Scott!) and that between 1976 and 1981 he had christened himself Borgue, Dalbeattie, Dalry and even Tim Haugh and Tim Urr as in the Haugh of bloody Urr?

Having got shot of Borgue, Davies introduced us to an exemplary-looking replacement who was found one day at the open attic door with his trousers down masturbating hell for leather, humming random snatches of the Sultans of Swing, and talking to the myriad clamorous voices in his head. Ironically Samuel Davies would do virtually anything for his tenants, including putting up a hundred feet of bookshelves and/or kitchen shelves gratis. Yet he would not protect them from proximity to the mentally deranged and the professional criminal. Why was that, my wife and I asked ourselves frequently and with numbed exasperation. Because at all costs he wanted his *rents*, he needed his hundred-odd rents averaging £100 per month to keep his mortgage hilts at a tolerable level. £120,000 per annum was, to be sure, only a bloody aperitif in the four-course meal that was his fiscally bloated existence. Meanwhile he was copiously rich and voluble in innovative theories pertaining to the science of housing. For example he daydreamed of building the perfect compact revolutionary urban bedsitter box, a self-contained womb not so much capacious as retro-minimal albeit perfectly functional. The fridge tucked away inside the folded bed, or was it the bed slammed away inside the folding fridge, or possibly the bed rammed against its will inside the non-folding fridge (save on eating Mr Murphy, save on keeping things fresh!). Samuel Davies had been watching too many telly documentaries set in Tokyo where certain ulcer-case businessmen lived in these handy-for-work microcubicles. Davies watched considerable amounts of TV in his very limited free time, and it was all of an educative and documentary nature. Hence he was also a Radio 4 man, and like all of that class of addicts could retail every single bit of last night's *Money Programme* down to every last paradigm calculation of every consumer hitch, glitch and itch. The presenter's name, he informed me, was Louise Botting, a wonderful trial in itself no doubt, as Mr Davies for one always jocularly referred to her as Radio 4's Loose Botty.

'When,' continued the Midwest man in his beautiful soothing burr, 'I do a painting, I tend to make up a little story to go with it. It helps to do it, and it makes the painting go easier. You try it. Or hell, shucks, you just do what you want. Just enjoy what you're doing out there, this ain't no test. Look at my shed here though, cos I've made myself a story around it. Here inside this black hut is an old, old guy who as you can see doesn't do a lot of repair work and maintenance on his property. He ain't awful houseproud this old bachelor guy. So this shed's a bit beaten up and I'll show this now with a bit of stippling. See. Ain't that too easy? And we'll give him a good long fence running alongside his old shed. First, though, I'm going to use the bevel on this knife to make a beautiful-looking path in the snow past the shed. Remember, too, to add some blue to the white to make your path look good and icy cold. Brrr. Too cold I reckon. The old guy inside the hut is staying put, we ain't going to see his nose poking out here today. I guess he's reading himself an old newspaper or doing his washing or cooking himself some food. Now we'll do some nice looking beat-up rickety posts for the old feller's fence. Remember the easy rule that as the posts go away from you they get smaller and closer together. Too simple. Listen, though, out there, when it comes to it, forget about the rules, forget about me the TV expert, you folks just enjoy what you're doing. And finally, to do these old wires on the fence here, you take the heel of the knife and just draw it across like so in one smooth movement. Ain't that just too darn ridiculously easy?'

And at the end of his lesson the caring and fatherly Wyoming man (the Samuel Davies that ought to have been but never was, choosing instead to be a myopic Cambridge Rachman without the violence) turned face-on to his viewers across five continents, and said simply and sincerely: 'Happy painting, you all. And God bless, my friends.'

### 677 (broadcast in Arabic)

A turbaned man in a vivid orange blouse who looked as if he was posing for an action-film publicity still. He lay sprawled on a bare hillside four miles outside Mazar i Sharif and beside him lay an unpeeled orange he was keeping to break his Ramadan fast tonight. He was a farmer who'd been shot by a dozen desperate Taliban troops, some Pashtun, some Algerian, some Chechen, encamped over the next hillock who had wrongly assumed he was of the encroaching Alliance.

The orange blouse and orange fruit seemed a tasteless cinematic apposition because they distracted from the rawness of the gaping bullet hole in his neck. He had lain dead for two hours before the Taliban retreated closer to Mazar and his body could be retrieved. His wife was now grieving over his body and addressing the camera as best she could through a full burqa. She told the TV journalist that she thought she was twenty-three and she had (once her *and* her husband had had, she sobbed) four small children. To observe a stricken wraith crying through a little hole in some swaddling shrouds is an eerie televisual thing. It was like watching a corpse trying to speak through the immurement of a tomb, like a tragic marionette telling of her epic, oriental fairytale grief. Though no one watching could actually see her flowing tears, they could feel her faceless painfulness a hundredfold. It was like the power of some child's drawing where the figures and the drama are only imaginatively suggested, the reality is simply as given, all done and finished and precisely as the child dictates. (At which point, without any effort, I thought about Judd and Orr on *The Brains' Trust* on Wilf Franklin's telly back in 1957. *It all depends of course what you mean by 'knowledge'* . . .)

The orange had rather a lot of grime on it, and it lay perhaps a yard from the clutched hand that hadn't peeled it and would never do so. The farmer seemed mordantly of little consequence now that he was unable to peel his dirty orange. The pity aroused by that eternal inability was quite unbearable. However when the news bulletin switched to central Mazar, the spectacle of the gibbeted corpses was so shocking I was completely distracted from what later seemed an equal tragedy for the farmer and his wife. I realised that in the news bulletin neither the orange-bloused farmer nor the black-burquaed widow had been given any *name*. We hadn't been told their surnames nor even their forenames. The only provisional descriptive category I had for them was Poor And Simple Peasant Afghanis . . .

Who knows? Perhaps the corpse's childhood Tajik nickname was the same or something similar to Fifties West Cumbrian Flogger's or Blagger's or Middy's . . .

The three men had been gibbeted for cheering at the sight of reconnoitring American airplanes, publicly executed only a few days before Mazar would be taken by the Alliance. If they could only have restrained their insolent cheers they would have lived to see their city in the condition they had been cheerfully anticipating. Now they had got themselves on prime-time satellite telly in at least fifty-five countries for the first and last time in their lives . . .

## 555

A weekly round-up from the Balkans, examining some current and recent troublespots. First a brisk five-minute documentary about the historical port of Durres in central Albania. The nearby beach resort might just be Europe's poorest country's answer to England's Blackpool and its golden sands. So far it has attracted rather few foreign holidaymakers, perhaps because of lingering associations. Ten years ago, we are reminded, in 1991, Durres made the headlines when the town was full of desperate mobs rioting to get on the boats to Trieste, Bari and Ancona in Italy. A long shot of the attractive Italianate harbour front, then we pan in on successively the Archaeological Museum, the former palace of the former King Zog, the Moisiut Ekspozita e Kultures Popullore, the Roman baths and the Ottoman Sultan Fatih mosque. Known by the conquering Romans as Dyrrhachium, under Italian imperialism as Durazzo, Durres was the capital of Albania from 1914 to 1920. The Turks, who had departed in 1913, had allowed it to dwindle into a dismal condition of shabby insignificance. Between the Romans and the Ottomans who took it in 1501, it belonged successively to Achaea, Serbia and Venice . . .

We now focus on an individual Durres troublemaker of 2001. There is a two-second still of an ironically smiling, badly dressed, intelligent-looking, forty-five-year-old man who went interestingly berserk here this time last week. He had walked up very uneasily to a busy kiosk which was displaying wristwatches decorated with the visage of the tyrant Enver Hoxha, dead and derided for some sixteen years. Though as poor as everyone else in Durres, this shabby little chap was nevertheless perfectly law abiding, thus giving the lie to the blood-feuding bandit stereotype of the modern Albanian male. The day before, he had sold his battered Italian scooter in order to purchase the entire stock of these Hoxha watches from the astonished kiosk vendor. He had carried them off and halted conspicuously on the steps of the Hotel Pameba, just so that everyone could enjoy an unhindered view of what he was doing. Then, taking off his hideous yellow Rumanian plastic shoe, he'd proceeded to batter to bits all forty-five images of the pitiless late lunatic.

*This is for your bloody Mao uniforms and for filling up our country with arrogant, swaggering Chinks.*

*This is for your senseless millions of completely pointless 'defensive' pillboxes.*

*This is for destroying all the churches and imprisoning and torturing all the priests . . .*

*This is for disappearing all those talented Albanian research scientists who couldn't achieve your ignorant, quite impossible demands. Not least because you wouldn't even let them correspond with a single foreign (other than Chinese) specialist in their chosen fields . . .*

*This is for the wife of one, my aunt, who went insane because her husband Mehmet Tafa, Albanian's finest molecular biologist, simply disappeared off the face of the earth one day in 1981. And no one, despite her obviously crazed and pitiful anguish, would even hint at where he'd gone. For the last twenty years Aunty Shemsie has sat pulling at her hair in a creaky old rocking chair, gibbering like an unhinged old monkey from dawn till dusk.*

*This is for doing precisely what Stalin did and for the fact you proudly venerated that awful monster and put countless leering busts of him all around our wretched country.*

*This is for the fact you weren't shot like the mad cobbler Ceaușescu, that you didn't die violently and humiliatingly by anyone's hand . . . !*

Meanwhile in a parallel incident in Fush-Kruje, a sixty-year-old farmer, Ilir Shehaj, grew so incensed at the sight of Enver's unrepentant widow Nexhmije being interviewed on Albanian TV, he simply would not suffer the purveyor, the innocent conduit, of such a hateful presence in his sitting room. The muscular old man, who boasted he could still drape a prize pig across his shoulders, picked up a ten-kilo sack of potatoes and flung it at the treacherous telly. The bag burst of course, but it burst along the wrong axis and both the Bulgaria-manufactured TV and Mrs Hoxha survived un-scathed. Worse, as well as the entire floor being carpeted with spuds, a good portion of the taties came ricocheting back and clattered the farmer Shehaj. One of them struck him pain-fully on the nose, as if it had taken lessons from a Tom and Jerry storyboard. Demented by which, Shehaj seized two brick-hard swedes the size of pumpkins, one in each hand, and flung them with venom at the grinning wife of Enver. Bingo! Ilir's telly shattered nicely, and with it smirking Nexhmije vanished from the Fush-Kruje farmhouse. Yet still far from satisfied, the crazed and choleric smallholder lifted up his kitchen clock manufactured in Istanbul in 1887, and tossed it in a spluttering rage at the screen. After that all four five-hundred-page volumes of Hoxha's profoundest consid-ered meditations on everything under the sun (*As I Uniquely See It*, The Will of the People's Press, Tirana 1955–1965), which had been used for decades now to prop up a lopsided farmhouse dresser. Even when the treacherous telly was a piti-ful mass of shards and valves, Shehaj kept throwing things at it and cursing the unbearable names of that man and his widow.

I catch the dying strains of the beautiful finale of the classical opera *The Muses*, composed by Jean-Baptiste Lully in 1666. As the Oiseau-Lyre CD fades away, the radio announcer reminds us that France's greatest seventeenth-century musician, the favourite of the court of Louis XIV, was actually born a Florentine. The immigrant musician was in his day celebrated for two things: the greatness of his musical genius, and the terrifying severity of his Italian temper. An unabashed homosexual who used to ballet joyfully alongside capering fourteen-year-old King Louis, Lully nevertheless deplored the immorality of those court nobles who fornicated so flagrantly with the divas of his Frenchified Italian operas. *Putain*, it put them off their decorous strides, and threatened to give them poorly controlled voices, so dissipated they were by their lascivious all-night grapplings and, *putain de merde*, thus compromising the gay Florentine's artistic reputation. As volatile and irascible as any Albanian Hoxha-hater, should any musician in his ensemble play a bad note or otherwise fluff their turn and humiliate Lully, the forthright Florentine would stomp across in a rage, berate said imbecile, then grasp his treacherous instrument and *smash it to shards* at his feet . . .

More often than not the stricken performer would burst into scalding tears of shame. Apropos which, the radio presenter jovially reflected, could any jobbing musician ever hope to improve as a result of this brutal pedagogic method?

## 187

A commercial also shown regularly on English TV, but here overdubbed with Irish accents. Three raucous twenty-year-old males in a cheap Dublin café are poking their fingers in mockery at a wobbly-legged old crock of an anthropomorphised mobile phone. The lads' lips do not move, but they are grinning extravagantly, and we are meant to imagine them saying what is a three-hander voice-over.

'Boys, but would you look at the desperate cut of your man there!'

'Musha, his old nibs is in a bad fettle right enough!'

'Personally, I've seen less rickety clockwork models from before the owld Uprising . . .'

Fourth voice-over in an exceedingly warm and cajoling Dublin accent informs us that if the said mobile cripple had been sent to the Mobile Infirmary Limited out in Dalkey it could have been given a nice pink or blue marbled case instead of the bilious grey it currently sports. Also a dashing new ring tone, wisha, come on now folks, a wide selection of excellent new ring tones from snatches of classics by the Dubliners all the way through The Pogues on to Hothouse Flowers and back again to Danny Boy, Ruby Murray and Daniel O'Donnell if you wish. Cut back to the cacklers at the table, and as the workhouse-grey crippled mobile on his shambly legs attempts to walk onto their table like a craven dog for a kindly pat, a jeering lad reaches out his little finger, flicks the useless old wreck in the guts, and sends him reeling onto the floor. These four confident Celtic tigerish children of the Eighties then cheerfully laugh their guts out at the dying cripple.

At this point, I cannot but reflect on the related events of the 11th of August 1999. This was the day of The Total Eclipse, you might recall, which in my case was haplessly eclipsed by something else. The only time I ever came close to homicide was occasioned by a mobile phone, two years ago in mid-August on a four-hour train trip from Carlisle to the capital to visit one of my ex-wives. Seated opposite a pin-striped software executive in his mid-thirties, I was trying to read a subtle historical novel by a compatriot of these jeering café lads, a very gifted Irishwoman called Kate O'Brien. This novel was composed in 1945 in a handsome little town called

Corofin, County Clare, and it dealt extremely movingly with the jealous revenge of an infatuated sixteenth-century Spanish monarch upon a one-eyed but beautiful noblewoman called Dona Ana.

The software businessman was called Geoff and indeed could scarcely have been called anything else. I knew his name and his profession because he wore a badge which identified him as such, and he was obviously on his way down to some metropolitan computer conference. At first I thought this Geoff had an excruciating earache when he regularly convulsed, then clutched his left lughole as if in unspeakable pain. That misperception lasted all of a tenth of a second (*it all depends what you mean by 'knowledge', Judd*) and then of course I realised he was part of the national, European, Third World, pan-universal electronic earache plague. Because from Faro to Mykonos, from Aceh to Bangui, from Carlisle to Calcutta, from Brampton to Buenos Aires, they were all in 1999 at the time of the Total Eclipse stopping dead like stricken mannikins in the middle of the street and clutching their afflicted ears. Then of course they would start to talk and improvise fantastically about their extremely trying, anomalously millennial condition. They would talk and talk and talk and would never willingly stop . . .

*Penrith*
Kev! Geoff. Yeah. I'm just currently as I speak leaving Ox and Ham. Nah. Nothin. No, I told him Wedsdy. He said he wanted it before Chewsday but he was edging his bets. Leafy tart, I says, none too gently to him. No, nothin really, but I thought I'd just ring. Cheesemite. Cheesemite Take hair. Take hair.

*Oxenholme*
Aye aye. Guess who? I'm ringing to tell you two things. Just that we're pulling out of Ox and Ham and . . . Confused? *You're* confused! Yeah, that's what I'm ringing about. It's

funny alright. Typical. I'm ringing to tell you it was actually Penwif before, it wasn't Ox and Ham. No, Penwif first. Lankyshire I think. I don't think it's Camria. The second thing is. Typical. I can't remember what the second thing is! But as soon as I remember I'll ring you back. OK. No, nothing really. It's just a bit boring on a long train journey. My laptop's getting sorted in Staines and I can't do nothing longhand. I simply can't do it any more. That's me for you. Anyway I like to have a little chat. Keep an eye on you. Hah. Take hairmite. Cheesemite.

*Lancaster*

Washersan. It's the firm spy what's ringing. To keep his eye on you and keep you on your toes, san. Just ringing to say two things. Firstly to say I still can't remember the previous second thing. The new second thing I was going to tell you was . . . What d'you mean? Two second things? Yes. Naw, leafy tart, leafy tartmite, it's straightforward enough. The second thing from the first phone call. No, sorry, I tell a lie, it was the second phone call. It was the second thing from the second phone call. Well this is the second thing from the third phone call at Lank–, nah the train's moved on. Lank something. Lank. Lankyshire? The second thing I had to tell you was. Paw. I've forgotten again. OK. Nothing really. But when we get to the next station I'll ring you to tell you about the two second things I forgot to tell you at the first and second stations. Paw. I tell a lie again, Kev. And it's me what's in charge of coordinatin communications training, innit? Eh? Aw, do leafy tart, just for once. Keeping me on my toes? Haw. No, the second and the third stations. Penwif, Ox and Ham, and wossname, Lankyshire. Take hair. Cheese. Simtayoomite . . .

By Preston I was bilious, by Wigan incensed, by Warrington incandescent, by Crewe half-insane. By Stafford, if I hadn't finally opened my mouth, I would have had to insert that sleek little ear trumpet up Geoff's immaculately pinstriped fundament.

'Excuse me!' I blurted.

I had to say it three times and wave my hands before him as he was still loudly chastising himself to Kev over his continued failure to remember the second thing he'd forgotten to tell him back at Oxenholme.

'Oh,' he said finally. 'Can I be of any help?' he added with fluent unctuousness, as if he had been on one his own customer-care seminars and had tutored himself as rigorously as anyone else.

'Yes you can,' I said. 'I mean no you can't.'

He stared very uneasily at the grey and bearded fifty-year-old enigma that was me. 'Eh?'

I leant forward disarmingly. 'Don't take offence at what I'm going to say. But I couldn't help overhearing you saying to your friend that you found long train journeys very tedious. I know this might sound a rather odd proposition altogether, but I was thinking perhaps that I might just tell you an interesting *story*, as a means of passing the time for the pair of us.'

Geoff looked startled to the point of terror. He blushed then paled, as if I had made a flagrant and disgraceful sexual overture. 'Eh? You what?'

'Surely,' I purred in a silky tone that I hoped would impress him as the last word in courteous deference, 'surely, when you were a schoolboy, you must have studied a few short stories where someone was relating a tale to someone else? Nine times out of ten, if you recall, they were both sitting opposite each other on a train? Remember the kind of thing for O-Level English? Ghost stories, macabre stories, mystery stories, all related in a railway carriage?'

'Ar . . .'

'If you did Russian A-Level, and you look to me as if you probably did it, Geoff, you'll recall that at least half of Russian literature is about some bugger talking to some other bugger on a train. Of course this was all in the days before TV and radio, and before the dear old mobile phone, which I noticed you've been playing games on in between talking to your colleague Kev?'

'Ye–'

'People don't change much, do they? They certainly got bored on long journeys a hundred and twenty years ago in Russia, travelling for days and nights across the utterly featureless taiga. You'd wonder how they coped without going mad with the tedium, wouldn't you? No Walkmans, no *TV Quick*, no Napsta downloads on their laptops. They had lap-*dogs*, or at least Chekov had one in one of his stories, which I recall I once read on a train between York and London somewhere back in 1979. As I say, in the old days they beguiled themselves by telling stories. This one I'm going to tell you, if you'll allow me, I promise you will make your eyes pop out of your head. In fact you'll find yourself down in London before you have time to text yourself with tomorrow's alarm wake-up.'

Geoff was shuffling stiffly in his seat and was obviously about to change carriages. He looked at me very anxiously, and said with a flush, 'You're not a Jehovah's Witness are you?'

I picked up my copy of the *New Statesman*. 'Jehovah's Witnesses have never been known to read this particular periodical. If you can find me a single Witness in the whole universe that reads the *NS*, I will give you a million pounds and my sixteenth-century four-bedroom farmhouse.'

He gulped, then gave me a rather sly look. I could see him making a mental note to pursue some enquiries via *Awake!* 'You're not trying to *sell* me something?'

I looked at him paternally. I gestured assurance and avuncular kindliness. 'Do I look like a double-glazing salesman? No, I'm just a local journalist from up north. I'm completely harmless, no axe to grind, nothing to sell, and I don't want to purchase your handsome little mobile either. I merely want to relieve both of our travellers' tediums. Perhaps I can even distract you from racking your brains about what you forgot to tell your friend in Oxenholme. Look, here's a simple and straightforward proposition. If you are bored or fed up after say one minute of my story, just lift your hand, nothing more, and I'll shut up and go back to my book and you can get back to ringing Kev. OK? In addition I'll immediately up sticks, shift carriages, and leave you here in peace, even though the only vacant seats on the train are among the smokers?'

The software man whispered something inaudible, and I waited for him to make a quick text to Kev announcing he was sat opposite a bearded nutter just outside Nunnoffin, no, he told a lie, it was actually Robby as in football.

'It's a true story and one drawn from my personal experience. None of it is invented or exaggerated I promise you, even though you might find this rather hard to credit. It all took place about thirty years ago, when I was in my early twenties. The very end of the Sixties, that is, when you were about three or four years old, Geoff. Do you mind me calling you that?'

'O–'

'Good. What I want to tell you about, Geoff, is that unforgettable occasion I set out one day into downtown Workington, West Cumbria, *to buy myself a pair of socks.*'

Geoff's jaw dropped open. His podgy hand twitched mesmerically as if it was trying to raise itself to shut me up. However my voice was by now so remorselessly hypnotic he simply could not move a muscle.

'I set out to buy a . . . no, I tell a lie, it wasn't a pair of socks. It was actually *three* pairs of socks!'

Geoff blinked like a doleful old seal. 'Three?' he echoed hoarsely.

'Yes. As I promised you, parts of this story are more or less incredible. I don't normally buy three pairs of socks in one go, only one at a time just like everyone else. What I mean is, I don't buy cheap bargain mixed socks, three for £3.99, or in the currency of the late Sixties I would never buy three for 12/11d off a market stall. I always treated myself to nice expensive shoes you see, so it would have been completely absurd to go cheapskate on my socks. Plus at the time being nineteen and in between girlfriends, I was feeling a bit insecure with regard to my – how shall I put it? – my personal image, Geoff. Man to man, Geoff, I felt I really needed to make some serious *effort* with my hosiery.'

I looked to him for some comradely masculine affirmation. I also sneaked a glimpse at his own socks, which right enough were perfectly matched with his immaculate suit. Geoff suddenly lifted up his mobile, perhaps to ring 999, then put it down sharply as I frowned and continued my tale.

'The reason for this multiple purchase was that I had had a splurge in a Workington shoesale, and had bought myself three lovely pairs of shoes for my nineteenth birthday. One pair was imported dark black Italian winklepickers. The second was buff-coloured slip-ons with ribbed lateral gussets. The third was a pair of Polish oxblood brogues with raised up ornamented eyeholes.'

Geoff's own eyeholes seemed to be raised up and moulded at this rather striking information.

'I was about to delegate the job to my mother, and ask her to buy me a pair of black, cream and red socks respectively, for the winklepickers, the slip-ons and the oxblood brogues. But then I thought better of it, and said to myself, buggerit, she might come back with a charcoal black instead of an anthracite black, she might bring me fawn or camel instead of buff socks, she might bring me a haemoglobin red instead of a proper oxblood match. So I stirred myself from my nineteen-year-old sloth, and caught the afternoon bus from Fingland, the village where I lived, into the nearest West Cumbrian shopping centre of Workington. I sought out the best gentleman's outfitters, which was in lower Pow Street and was called Twentyman and Son. It was a very old-fashioned shop with a dim electric light and a nice old gentleman proprietor Sidney Twentyman in a black suit in his mid-sixties I would say. After scrutinising the window display, I went inside, and as there were no other customers I walked straight up to Mr Twentyman. I explained carefully and at length exactly what it was I wanted: "I need the matching shades of socks for the buff gussets, the Milan winklepickers and the Polish oxbloods. It's tempting to be lazy and go for any old colour of sock of course. But as they were all very expensive shoes, even in the sale reductions, it seems worth the trouble to get the socks spot on."

'Mr Twentyman couldn't have agreed more. He assumed an extremely solemn expression. He said there were all sorts of men deluded enough to think that just because in the usual run of things only three inches of your socks show, nobody takes any notice of their appearance. Far from it, he assured me, quite the opposite if the truth be known. In point of fact, he asserted dourly, socks are an accurate litmus indicator of a man's personality. It's plain commonsense for example that cheap socks usually indicate a cheap sort of personality. Likewise worn socks, a worn sort of gent. Dull grey or dung brown institutional socks, a man who is prone to hopeless melancholy even if he doesn't know the cause. Bright and screaming pink and yellow bobby-dazzlers speak for themselves. Forgivable in a twelve-year-old boy but laughable, even dangerous, in the case of a grown man. I nodded sagely at what he was telling me, though I also noticed an irreverent not to say cheeky expression on his smirking boy assistant. This awkward lad was dressed smartly enough in a neat grey suit, but his hair stuck up in an odd Daffy Duck way and he sniffed a lot and picked his nose when he thought old Twentyman wasn't looking.

'"So," I resumed pleasantly as I turned back to the latter, "what would you recommend for the . . . well let's take the buff gussets first . . .?"

'It was at this point, Geoff, when we got down to the

names of the shoes, the descriptive categories, the handy abbreviations (buff gussets, Polish bloods, Italian winkles) that all hell was let loose so to speak.'

I paused and mobile-deprived Geoff, from his hypnotised if not traumatised state, managed to mutter, 'How exactly do you mean?'

'The old gentleman outfitter had a bit of a strange speech impediment, though I'm not sure that's an accurate way of putting it. When it came to speaking the usual run of words and sentences, Geoff, Mr Twentyman was as articulate as you or me. But it turned out that he had a strange and I would guess very rare verbal tic that caused him to spoonerise when it came to unusual juxtapositions of words.'

The software man blinked at me blankly. I puckered my lips a little, then explained as to a child that a spoonerism was where the initial letters of two adjacent words were transposed. Usually nonsensically, sometimes comically, occasionally inadvertently or deliberately obscenely. Geoff looked very interested at that last option, and asked me for some examples.

'Well aside from the familiar example of "pheasant pluckers", there's a women's theatre group I've heard of who call themselves "Cunning Stunts".'

'Eh?' said Geoff, still blank. Then after half a minute, 'Oh I see. Faw, the dirty little buggers!'

'Mr Twentyman wasn't so much a simple as an advanced spooneriser. When he couldn't get his tongue round a cumbersome duplicate of words, he would struggle away gamely at the impossible task, giving every possible variation, none of them correct. The odder and wilder his improvisations got, the more determined he was to get it right for his patient interlocutor! Sorry Geoff, I mean the person he was talking to. So for example, when I first of all said "the buff gussets", he tried to echo "buff gussets" in businesslike anticipation, but could he hell as like get his old tongue round it.'

Geoff frowned and took up the linguistic challenge himself. He said 'buff gussets' several times in a row without a hitch.

'It's child's play,' he murmured complacently. 'A bloomin child could say it. Buff gussets, buff gussets, buff gussets.'

'Quite. But not so for Mr Twentyman. First of all he said, "a colour match for your *Bug Fussits*", which was a fair enough lateral spoonerism. Of course his boy assistant with the springy hair guffawed immediately at his comical error. Mr Twentyman glowered at him, and addressing him as Wally, told him to go and sort some flat caps behind the counter instead of cackling away like a halfwit. Then he turned back to me and tried again: "Regarding your *Bust Guffits*".

'"Haw," again from tufted Wally who was playing at random card shuffling with the flat caps.

'"I mean, sir, your *Gust Buffets*!"

'"Haw," roared Wally quite helplessly. "Haw haw haw!"

'"Quiet you blasted young fool! And put the damn seven-and-a-eighths with the seven-and-a-eighths, not with the damn seven-and-a-quarters! Now then and I'm sorry sir. You want some matching socks for your *Bust Fuckits* . . . Oops! Damn! I mean your *Fucked Bussets*! No, I mean your *Bucked Fussets* . . ."

'"Gaw!" shrieked the tufted cap-shuffler. "Gawhawhaw-hawhawhawhawhaw!"

'Well,' I said to wide-open-mouthed Geoff, 'luckily the shop was empty apart from the three of us. But naturally I coughed and blushed for poor old Mr Twentyman, and he blushed and coughed even more.'

'I bet he bloody did,' gasped Geoff, 'And they wunt even have heard of customer care in Working Ham back in 1969.'

I smiled at this gratifying attentiveness and attempted a certain hilarious mimicry with the principal players in my story.

'"Gaw!" continued tearful, hiccoughing Wally, "No! Don't say any more, Mr Twennyman! Gawhawhawhaw."

'Wally's padded shoulders, Geoff, were shaking like a tractor generator. His Daffy Duck quiff was dancing and swaying like an elephant's howdah. Crazed with merriment at his dirty-mouthed and mortified old boss, he was scattering those flat caps all over the shop. Why, there was even a six-and-a-half mixed up with an outsize of a seven-and-seven-eighths!'

'No!' said Geoff genuinely intrigued and concerned by this terrible mercantile disarray.

'"Sorry sir," old Twentyman sighed aghast at that point. "Forgive me if you will. I'll get my stupid old tongue round it, if you can just be patient with me. Ahem. The recommended matching socks I suggest for your *Guff Buckets* . . . Damn damn damn for your *Gut Buckets*! . . . Damn damn damn, buggerit, for your *Gust Buffets*! . . . I mean your *Guest Buffets*! . . . I mean your *Breast Pockets*. No I don't sir, I mean for your *Best Corsets*."

'At this, Geoff, the lad with the sprung-mattress haircut was in such throes of mirth he did what many small infants would do. Some of his autonomic functions began to operate all too autonomously, and Wally the assistant began to *fart* as well as hiccup!'

My train companion started, then guiltily laughed out loud. In fact it was the first time he had expressed any amusement at my story, which presumably up to now he had deemed to be deadly serious.

'There was a definite danger,' I told Geoff with a worried face, 'that if Twentyman hadn't ordered him out of the shop, his hiccupping teenage trainee would have lost all control of his bowels!'

'Gaw,' said Geoff, impressed. 'What a bleeding how d'you do and all.'

I spent another forty minutes narrating my buff gussets epic to this wide-eyed software man. As for the Workington outfitter's struggle with the tongue-twister 'Milan winkles' ('willing minxes', 'mixed willies', 'Millie's winkies' . . . it got bluer and bluer as old Twentyman failed to get it right first time), relating this second epic took me a total of one hour twenty minutes. By Milton Keynes I had Geoff completely enthralled, but by the time we got to Euston I still hadn't got a quarter of the way through Twentyman's battle with the Polish oxbloods ('pissing rosebuds' was the cleanest spooner-ism that the poor old proprietor blurted out).

'We're here,' I said cheerfully to Geoff. 'London Euston at last! Phew. Doesn't the air feel different already? Didn't I tell you the time would pass like magic?'

But instead of springing to his feet and swiftly buzzing Kev to tell him he had reached his destination, Geoff stayed solidly in his seat. He had that same taut expression as an anxious two-year-old who must have his gripping bedtime story finished.

'No,' he protested pettishly. 'You can't just leave it like that! I need to know how it all ended!'

'Eh?' I said in an absent tone as I lifted up my *New Statesman*. 'Now where did I go and put my –'

I was hunting for my luggage and had lost all interest in my pinstriped listener. My ex-wife Fran had ordered me to get her a particular bottle of wine that could only be bought in one obscure off-license in the whole of South London as far as I could recall. I had no time for dallying with story-hungry software experts who thought Oxenholme and Penrith were interchangeable, as well as both being in some-where called 'Lankyshire'.

'Sorry,' I told him stiffly. 'But I have to rush now, Geoff.'

'Eh?' he said with a wounded indignation. 'No! Hang on! Wait a minute. Finish your story off properly! Finish off what you've gone and started . . . !'

I sighed like a captious old teacher at a peevish, more or less repugnant pupil. 'But it would take me another hour at least. We'll get shunted into a goods siding and dusted down by an industrial hoover if we keep on sitting here. They might even think we were a pair of third-rate loco-terrorists.

And before you suggest adjourning to a pub or a café, I'm sorry but I have to meet my ex-wife in exactly forty-five minutes, and she lives out in SE bloody 23 . . .'

Geoff looked terribly woebegone. His eyes were actually pricking with tears. 'Well you could at least summarise it for me, then! What happened in the end with poor old Twentyman? How did you get the right shades of socks that you wanted?'

'Eh?' I said in a careless, abstracted voice. 'Oh I wrote it all down on a bit of paper, of course. Buff Gussets, Warsaw Oxbloods, Milan Winkles. All he had to do was nod at each, and then trot off to his antiquated sock drawers. The old boy breathed a sigh of relief and burbled away joyfully after that. I suggest this shade, sir, he chuntered, or how about this one, and then, look here's my complete selection of buffs and near-buffs! He could manage the word buff on its own you see, but not alongside the word gussets. We had the whole thing sorted in ten minutes after that.'

Geoff blinked at me sourly. With an ugly expression he rattled his briefcase. 'Eh? You're bloody kidding! I was expecting a damn sight more interesting ending than that, I must say!'

'Really?' I said coldly. 'And how exactly would you have liked my West Cumbrian sock story to finish?'

'Well for example, couldn't you have helped him, Mr Twentyman, with his peddyment? That would have made a much better story, I reckon. Winning through against impossible odds, just like whatsisname the whatsit on that weekly thing on telly. That's what I'd have done in the circumstances. That would have been my approach, for what it's worth.' He surveyed me with a baleful scorn. 'Humph! But no! Ducking the issue and writing it all down was your solution! All over in ten bloody minutes as a result! Bugger that for a bloody lark . . .'

It was strange, I reflected, as I glanced disdainfully at his pinstripe suit, that Geoff went in for this unedited Walt

Disney moralising? Or perhaps it was not all that strange at all. I looked at him stonily and allowed my expression to convey the subtle truth of the matching sock drama as enacted in the remote provinces of thirty years ago. After all, my poker face implied, did I, even in my nineteen-year-old incarnation back in 1969, did I really look the kind who would go in for *gusseted slip-ons*?

A sudden painful intelligence dawned on Geoff's horrified features. I watched him clench his podgy fists in a surfeit of nascent rage.

'You made it all up!' he hissed, looking more or less half-insane.

I hesitated then admitted, 'Yes indeed. Yes. Fraid so.'

He gasped as if struggling with a pulmonary seizure. 'You *what*! You bas–'

'Feel shortchanged?' I smirked, as if the whole ridiculous business had nothing to do with me. 'Personally, I thought it was quite an attractive little rigmarole.'

He bawled at the top of his lungs, 'You bastard! You bearded bald-headed barmy bloody bollicking *bastard*!'

'Oh come come, Geoff,' I demurred. 'Oh come come come come come!'

The software expert lunged at me. His strong fat hands went tightly around my throat. That day was, as I have already mentioned, the day of the Total Eclipse, 11th August 1999. I realised this pregnant, possibly occult fact as Geoff's thumbs began to press brutally around my windpipe. I thought to myself with some sadness that this was a singular and rather inglorious way to go. Executed without a trial or a jury simply for making up a story about socks and buff slip-ons on a train from Carlisle to London Euston.

But then I was saved *literally* by the bell: '*Brr brr. Brr brr. Brr brr.*'

The purblind software man was brought back to earth as if by magic. Geoff's homicidal thumbs relaxed as if he were a programmed item of technology.

Saved by the bell, no less! By my attacker's mobile with its gorgeous and most welcome ring tone of *I Did It My Way*, as immortalised by Frank Sinatra. Sure enough an approaching double-decker bus or a team of foaming horses would not have stopped this man from answering his mobile phone. After all, it might have been something crucial, something ground-breaking, something mega, something altogether life or death, as far as Geoff and his invincible IT firm were concerned.

'Gurr!' I gurgled, as I panted for breath. 'Gurr! Hwrr! Gurr!'

On the day of the Total Eclipse, 11.8.99, my life had been saved by a mobile phone. And though of course I still don't own one myself, I have never ever been sarcastic about these marvellous objects since. As soon as Geoff let go of my tonsils I grabbed my bags and scooted hell for leather. En route to the carriage door I caught the intriguing gist of his calmly monotone conversation.

'What? Kev? Nah, Euston. Safe an sound. Nah. Quiet really. Nah noffin. Nah I just played games for free arse on the old mobile. Weird geezer opposite droning on but I just ignored him. Meet enough bleedin bores in my line of work without encouragin new uns. Leafy tart, eh! Cheesemite. Take hair.'

# 3

*Fingland, West Cumbria, February 1959*

On an icy Sunday evening Flogger was staring at Broderick Crawford and his painfully weary investigator's scowl. It was *Highway Patrol* and Flogger's very favourite programme. By now both our families possessed a two-channel television, but tonight we had opted to watch mine. We were tuned to Scottish ITV whose transmitter was at mythical Kirk O'Shotts, so the reception on a windy wintry night was capricious if not hellish. At one point a vital piece of illumination concerning a shopgirl's patently spurious alibi was obliterated by a K. O'Shotts hailstorm on our seventeen-inch Ekco. Personally I was very bored by a transatlantic cop show where it was all turgid analytic exposition after the event, and no action worth the name. For that matter there were no meaningful characters as such, there were just wooden actors who spoke their staccato lines in sullen Upstate monotones. In any case, the dramatic focus of this episode, a bank robbery committed a hundred miles down Brod's stretch of highway, was meagre stuff compared with the real events of this afternoon. Though we hadn't mentioned it to either my or Flogger's parents, a man had tried to *kill* us today up in Fingland Woods . . .

We had been up by the pit and the sprawling solvent works and had just skirted the colliery reservoir where Skunk and his family lived. Their damp, crumbling cottage had once been nicknamed 'Boggy', and in due course this had become its recognised postal address. As we passed it, I remarked to Flogger it should have been called Skunk Cottage or Skunk Mews. Ahead of us were Lord Teesdale's pine forests which spread for miles in all directions. They were full of defunct colliery workings, silted up pit drainage systems, hidden, seemingly prehistoric rock formations, whispering becks and stagnant ponds. They were a perfect paradise for two moderately imaginative lads, even for one called Humphrey who was always demurely gingerly about things like modest exercise, much less physical risk and objective danger.

'Look,' whispered Flogger excitedly as he saw a hovering, miraculous phenomenon. We stood there with open mouths and beating hearts at the moving spectacle. It was as if were watching the invention and the formal launching of the Archimedean screw or the first ever Egyptian pyramid.

A rusty old wheelbarrow full of glistening sulphur was being raised by pulleys as we passed the solvent works. Up above a lone workman was trundling it away to a nearby feeder. It was the very clumsiness of that dangling barrow that gave it an unlikely even startling heroism. A dizzy mountain of sulphur was piled up below in a rickety open shed. It looked so beautiful, that burning lemon-coloured hillside, that Flogger suggested we go across and roll in it. I stared at him and puckered my lips scathingly. I knew just enough hearsay chemistry to tell him that it would rot his clothes, make his teeth drop out, his balls drop off, his piss turn blue, his eyes go blind.

'Bloody hell,' whistled Flogger. 'In that case I *definitely* want to roll in the bastard.'

He set off at a mad run and was just about to nose-dive into the brimstone mountain when a man with huge sideburns stepped out from behind the shed. It was one of the older factory hands and he looked more intrigued than critical at the sight of an ugly little boy pirouetting towards the gleaming sulphur. At once Flogger changed his run up into a coy ellipse, and teetered his way back to me.

He mumbled disappointed, 'I'll roll in it another time. I've always wondered what it's like going blind. I . . . bloody hell . . . ugh! Roe have you gone and *shit*, you dirty bastard?'

He actually said, *hess thoo shit?*, with an excessively long 'oo' and a minute 'i' in the verb. It was the last word in dialectic and dialectical emphasis. It was his unarguable West Cumbrian West Cumbrianness, a philosophic nicety that would have impressed say J.A. Orr of *The Brains' Trust*.

The solvent works emitted frequent and substantial quantities of hydrogen sulphide all over the village. As well as being a hazardous chemical, $H_2S$ also stank of rotten eggs so that Fingland was regularly called Fartland by the inhabitants of Workington and Whitehaven. It was this that inspired Flogger to accuse me of shitting, given that the full-blown (so to speak) act of defecation was in the dialect often homologised with the lesser act of farting.

'Don't be stupid,' I said indignantly. 'It's that bloody factory back there not me. It turned my grandad's presentation 1917 All-Cumberland Knockout Bowls Tournament cup jet black. The silver in his cup reacted with that fart gas to make silver sulphide and it was as black as coal.'

Flogger snorted admiringly at such technicolor magic. He told me that tonight he was going to amaze his mother and request a half-dozen bowls of her notorious split pea soup, a mess of pottage which normally he loathed. Then, half an hour later, and after running up the stairs a few times to aid the process, he would fart all over the silver foil of a Kit-Kat wrapper and watch it turn as black as soot. He looked at me shrewdly. Would it really do that, Roe, he asked me doubtfully. Of course it would, I told him with a bumptious confidence. Why, I added glibly, I had done the same explosive trick numerous times myself.

We went by Skunk's cottage nervously. It was a pitiful slum to any adult eye, but to us with its proximity to the fly-blown reservoir full of minnows and frogs and discarded prams and old shoes, it was the perfect Fingland residence. We were very pleased there was none of his gypsy clan about, as Skunk and his brothers would have thumped us on the spot for trespassing. To encroach within fifty yards of his cottage was to infringe the quiet enjoyment of his property as far as Skunk was concerned. Instead of spitting in his ear, he would probably have submerged Flogger's head in the reservoir, and/or forced him to eat a tadpole.

After Boggy we passed the largest of three pit banks, a calmly magnificent black pyramid. Then we turned towards Tintack, which of Fingland's half-dozen woodlands was the very gentlest. It had the widest slowest becks and some very old deciduous trees as well as pines. There were alders, oaks and beeches, and there were hedges of bramble, rosehip and hawthorn at Tintack. It had a grace, an infinite gentleness, that always moved me to the roots. Neither Flogger nor I had a family car, so we had only a limited experience of the Cumbrian Lake District. Hence, despite the proximity of coal pits and stinking sulphides, the tenderness of that Tintack stream with its bent old oaks and bowed old alders was my first experience of natural beauty. Of course I had never communicated any of this to Flogger, as it would have been highly embarrassing. Instead I ventured to remark to him today: 'It's bonny here isn't it? Tintack is really lovely isn't it?'

'Eh?' said Flogger very suspiciously. 'Bonny' was a damn queer word and 'lovely' wasn't much better.

'I . . . I mean that it's great here. Eh?'

'Oh aye . . .' Suddenly he turned unusually pale and then a very curious shade of green. 'I . . . bloody hell, Roe!'

I looked the length of the country lane. It ended at a fenced field and the junction forked right for Tintack and left for Maryport. By the fork itself, about fifty yards off, like some quaint and timeless omen, stood a wizened, odd and unsmiling little man. He was about forty, he had a flat black cap, he was very tanned, and he might or might not have been a gypsy. He had no dog, or at least none was visible. He certainly ought to have had a dog, because he had a shotgun half-raised as if he was busy pot-shotting crows and starlings.

There was a strange hallucinatory second where I wondered why Flogger was quite so startled. After all, bachelor gunmen in the Fingland forests were a common enough phenomenon. If you had no car and no money and were in need of diversion, there was nothing to do here apart from walking or hunting up in the woods. I looked at Flogger, then looked back at the hunter, and saw what Flogger must have seen two seconds ago. The man's shotgun was raised and aimed at *us*, and at nothing else. It was very difficult objectively to make out whether it was pointed at me or at Flogger, and we later argued over who had escaped a violent death by inches. The rugged scowling little man looked as severe as a fairytale goblin or a lunatic. For an instant we froze like two terrified hares. Both our voice boxes had seemingly died. Flogger was the one who managed at last to croak: 'Fuck! He's gonner kill us, Roe! Run like fu–'

We tore off like two Fingland greyhounds. Flogger as a rule could run no faster than a puffing Pekinese, but today he sped on aerial wings. As we ran for our lives, the shotgun went off like a cannon.

Flogger shrieked, and went hurtling down on the ground.

'Ooh!' I whinnied in terror. 'Flogger! Flogger! Fuckin hell!' I halted and shivered then blurted out, 'Are you dead?'

I was only nine years old, but it was still a burlesque question to put to a corpse. Flogger was groaning very pitifully. I looked at his feet and saw the cause. He had tripped over a big stone and was badly winded. I grabbed his shoulder, pulled him to his feet, urged him to get running, then ran off gibbering. The dirt track down from Tintack is a very long one, and as straight as a Roman road. We were in fact sitting ducks for at least five hundred yards. The goblin's gun went off again, and Flogger screamed in horror.

'Ooh shitfuck!' he shrilled. 'Fuckshitooooowoogh!'

I am not at all brave in 2001, and was even less so back in 1959. Yet I steeled myself, and turned to see how far the gunman was behind us. I panted like Chris Brasher and sweated like an exhausted Caldbeck fox. The dwarfish madman was still at the crossroads but now he was blasting away with his back to us. He was aiming at a flock of starlings in an elm, and was a miraculously bad shot. At least half the starlings seemed to be coolly staying put, commenting loudly and ironically on his pitiful marksmanship. Perhaps it was this laughable lack of accuracy was responsible for his sudden homicidal fit? If he couldn't manage to hit crows and starlings, he would have a crack at two dozy little Fingland juveniles instead?

We ran as far as the sulphur shed. There were two old workmen idling nearby and that ugly little gnome wouldn't dare to potshot us here. As soon as we felt more or less safe, we found the matter uproarious. In fact we became completely hysterical. We sat down on a bench outside the shed and began to laugh like braying donkeys. The old workmen stared at us and tapped their Brylcreemed heads. We were chortling at Flogger tripping over a little stone and me thinking he was dead. What, we speculated, would I have told his distraught Mam? Humphrey's been killed by a gypsy, Mrs Farrell, and he hadn't even called him a gippo! At last we stopped cackling and briefly philosophised about death and its advantages. No more school, no more bullies, no bloody awful *Brains' Trust* or *Top of the Form* on telly, no halibut oil capsules, no fatty neck of lamb in our horrible Sunday tatie pots! Then we argued about which of us he had been aiming at, and why he might have been murderous. It was his nature, I said flatly, he was just bloody warped. Flogger, though no liberal, demurred, and suggested he was an escaped prisoner from Durham. I pooh-poohed him on the obvious grounds that sensible convicts don't draw attention to themselves by blasting away at starlings. Flogger scowled at my know-all piss-wiseness. But then, before our dispute could get any more heated, he suddenly beamed at me euphorically.

All this talk of criminals had reminded him that tonight on Scottish ITV it was his favourite programme *Highway Patrol*. His rapture was remarkably short-lived though, for he kicked the ground as he remembered something else. His idiotic father, he snorted, would insist on watching *What's My Line?* on the BBC. Those preening panellists all wore bloody dinner jackets while his stupid Dad had never worn a DJ in his life! All that deadly boring drivel with bald-headed magicians and titled diamonded ladies and moustachioed old goats called Gilbert. The boy called Humphrey sneered at the man called Gilbert. I frowned sympathetically at this painful disappointment. It is difficult these days to imagine a world without video players, but then inescapably it was so. There ought to have been regular murders over disputed channels, though as far as I know such things were very rare. I thought for a while, then invited Flogger Farrell to come across and watch our television instead. My mother openly admitted that she fancied attractive Eamonn Andrews, but she was out tonight at the Fingland WI. My Dad could obviously be encouraged to forgo the insidious young Irishman who presented *What's My Line?* . . .

At five to eight that evening *Highway Patrol* was reaching its finale. Flogger sat there entranced as if immersed in *Othello* and the RSC. Meanwhile my Dad was sharpening some tools with an oilstone in front of the fire and only half watching the telly. I was bored to death by Broderick Crawford but was amused to see our guest Flogger making himself sumptuously at home. He was sprawled the length of our new sofa, his scruffy head on a matching cushion, watching Crawford from a virtually upside down perspective. Maybe, I reflected, with all that extra bloodflow to the receptive brain, it improved a third-rate programme, that postural inversion?

What happened then smacks of the mad gunman, and

there is no real explanation for what suddenly took hold of me. Blame the restless destructive tedium induced by this new and potent addiction in the form of imported US telly. Blame the supine smirking complacence of Flogger reclining like a Fingland sultan on our brand new sofa. All that he needed was for a voluptuous odalisque to be pushing grapes into his open adenoidal mouth (an interesting alternative to the saliva that had been aimed into his lughole in a rather different cinematic context) . . .

I went through into the kitchen, filled up a beaker with water, and returned to the sitting room. Then I walked across to Flogger, and tipped it all over his head . . .

'BLAH!' Flogger hooted, catapulting off our sofa as if a tarantula had burrowed inside his ear.

My Dad gasped, 'What in *hell*! What the bloody hell!'

I laughed like a mad hyena, like a wild buffoon. Flogger's vast leap through the air at the watery shock had been wonderfully comic, really first-class entertainment. It would have made a perfect piece of theatre, or even perfect television come to that. It was funnier than Brian Rix and his falling trousers by several miles. In fact it was superior to any TV, as it was a kind of living telly itself. TV after all only meant 'seen at a distance'. Telly was just a perverted Greek preposition turned into something humorously homologous to belly or welly or jelly. Well I had seen something humorously homologous to Charlie Chaplin here in my own front room, and it hadn't cost me a single penny . . .

Flogger, justifiably enough, was itching to lay hands on me. But as the assault was in my house, and my father was there, he could hardly let fly with a vengeance . . .

My Dad waggled his oilstone and barked, 'What the hell are you playing at, you stupid bloody imbecile?'

I snorted but said by way of justification. 'I thought that it'd be funny.'

He roared, 'I'll funny your flaming bloody earhole! You've soaked the sofa, you brainless, gormless, half-baked halfwit! Just wait till your mother gets herself back from the Institute.'

Flogger had missed the devastating tail end of *Highway Patrol*, thanks to my fooling. So he complained at any rate, but in fact it was Kirk O'Shotts's fault not mine. In the last few minutes an arctic flurry of interference had obliterated everything including most of Crawford's deathless dialogue. The terrible reception continued as we watched the adverts, so that *Barry's Lemonade, Cool Clear, Sparkling,* voice-overed in rasping Glaswegian, had no accompanying picture. Ditto for *Pan Drops Peppermints* and *Lofty Peak Flour.* Still cackling at the excellent way I had doused him, I dabbed away at our soaking sofa as Flogger squeezed the water from his ear. Tomorrow, he whispered earnestly, at Fingland school, he would shove my treacherous head down the toilet bowl and shit upon it.

'Shit did you say?' I asked. 'Or sit?'

I never did find out. For then the queerest thing happened. There was an enormous, quite unearthly, rat-a-tat on our door.

My Dad said, much affronted, 'Who the hell is *that?*' The knock had been both brutal and hesitant, a highly unnerving combination. 'You run and answer it, Roe.'

No one ever came visiting us at eight o'clock of a Sunday, especially now there was a telly in every Fingland home. Always hungry for novelty, I walked to the door with a definite expectancy, thinking perhaps it might be a talkative young travelling salesman. For some unfathomable reason this impoverished little village was a favourite destination for these door-to-door desperados. Usually they turned up of a weekday morning, but perhaps one of them had boldly opted to change his hackneyed routine. I was always pestering my mother to indulge these theatrical heroes willy-nilly; polish, matches, dubbin, elastic bands, even if we had ten years' supply of each.

As I touched the doorknob I had the mad premonition

that that psychopathic gunman might have followed us here. It was a lunatic notion, right enough, and I tried to brush it off as my father roughly shouted, 'Get a bloody move on, will you!'

I swallowed as I opened the door. At once I suffered mountainous waves of petrifying shock. It was not the woodland killer, of course, but it was something just as bad . . .

An unbelievably thin woman, a complete stranger, was standing there. She was a very cruel phenomenon to confront on a village doorstep of a black winter night. The most hideous thing was the state of her right eye. The skin below it was pulled down in grotesque deformation, as if it had been pinned or sutured by an amateur surgeon. She must have been in some terrible fight, perhaps been given a drunken beating. Whatever had been done to her, it had almost put her eye out. Both it and its partner were very bloodshot. She was only middle-aged, but had monstrously wrinkled, grey and desiccated skin. Neither of my parents drank, but I knew the smell of booze, and it came off her like a miasma. I stared at her in blank terror, assuming she was some spectral nightmare. I simply could not credit that she was real.

'Son,' she began in a queer and cadaverous croak. 'Have you go–?'

I tore off quickly but with leaden feet. I was full of a depthless fear. I had just doused Flogger Farrell and been in an ecstasy of mirth, but now I was being punished by an indescribable phantasm at the door. I muttered to my Dad: 'There's a *woman* at the door.'

'Oh?' he said challengingly, as if I might be making it up. 'What woman is that?'

I mumbled in a low voice, 'I don't know. She looks very funny.'

He looked at me warily. I had just described a drenched Flogger as 'funny', and now here was something else was funny. He flung down his oilstone and went irritably to the door. After a long couple of minutes he came back shaking his head.

'Who is she?' I said, my voice distorted with anxiety. 'Who *is* she, Dad?'

'She was just a woman who was going round begging.'

'Eh?' I gasped. 'But one of her eyes was –'

'She was in a sad state alright. A tinker gypsy from somewhere, I think. Stinking like buggery with drink.'

'But why was her eye –?'

'I gave her two bob to get rid of her. Though it'll only go on booze I guess. She'd have stood there all day and all night if I hadn't.'

On the way to school, I was fretting obsessively about the one-eyed woman, not at all about the woodland killer. The hopeless marksman had already been assimilated as something farcical, but the thought of that vile and one-eyed gargoyle still had me shuddering. Hell's teeth, would she come begging at our house again, come staggering back tonight for example? Would it be me who'd be sent to answer the door again? I'd end up a chronic nervous case if I had to keep on opening up to blood-eyed phantoms of the night. Panic-stricken, I decided to have an armoury of watertight excuses for any more evening visitors. I had the skitters and I urgently needed the toilet for the next ten minutes; I was no use as a doorman because I had a cramp in both hands after wrestling with Willy the dog; no, Dad, that definitely wasn't a knock on the door at all, it was an explosion at the Fingland quarry . . .

That day, incredibly, we had another encounter with another gypsy. This third confrontation was in fact more Flogger's than mine, and instead of water in the lug it would involve something a lot less pleasant in the mouth. The term 'gypsy' in this case was a folklore hypothesis rather than a racial fact. She was called Karen Mavir, and she was as rough as a midget wrestler or a female pugilist. Like that woodland gunman she was very tanned in the face or as the villagers said 'varra swaarthy'. She didn't live in a hovel like Skunk's, but in the nearest equivalent, a row of miserable two-up two-downs called Tottergill. Tottergill Row had no bathrooms and no inside lavatories, but like Boggy it was worryingly close to the solvent works. Dick Mavir was a Fingland miner who had married Mima Stubbs, who came from God knows where, because he had met her on a stall at Maryport Fair, and subsequently at Workington and Whitehaven Fairs. She was a fairground traveller, meaning more or less a gippo, hence Karen and her little brother Billy must be likewise.

Billy Mavir was a farcical, jabbery ten-year-old who blinked incessantly as if always anticipating violence. Once after PE it had been discovered he possessed no underpants and that his trousers were decorated with prodigious faecal skidmarks. This caused an explosive playground hilarity and he remained a permanent laughing stock. Karen however was not only proud but as wild as a young bear. If anyone taunted her she lashed out first with words, then fists, or occasionally both together. No one but a suicidal fool like Flogger would have tangled with her over such a pointless bagatelle as an ancient battered yardbrush . . .

The skinny old caretaker Maisie usually left her brush and pail in the playground when she went off for her tea and cigarette. Maisie was admirably easy-going, and had no objection to some of the older girls playing with her implements, nor even doing a bit of handy sweeping and gratis caretaking. Strangely enough the gypsy Karen Mavir was one of her favourites, and it was tacitly accepted that she had absolute priority when it came to bagsing Maisie's brush and pail. No one would have dared to sub-lease these objects without Karen's express permission, because no one but an imbecile would have chosen to confront the Tottergill bruiser.

That imbecile was called Humphrey Farrell. This windy Monday playtime, God knows why, Flogger decided he would like to sweep the entire schoolyard. He advised me proudly of his bizarre Rumpelstiltskin intention, and I looked at him derisively. It was of course the enlightened Nineteen Fifties, when sweeping and skivvying were both regarded as feebly womanish, and when lairdly pre-pubertal gents like Murphy and Flogger would refuse to lift an indolent finger.

I sneered at him. 'What the hell for? Everybody will laugh like buggery.'

He sniffed with a senile sort of emphasis. 'Bollicks to that. I like to sweep things. In fact I wouldn't mind doing it as a full-time job.'

I blinked at him in astonishment. I realised that by irrigating his lughole last night I must have afflicted him with water on the brain. I shrugged at such idiotic obstinacy and warned, 'You'll have to ask Karen Mavir. If you don't, she'll go completely bloody crackers.'

Flogger assumed a pious bravado. 'Fuck that. Fat lot I care about a great stupid gippo twat like her. She's just a daft big shitey lass. She's just a –'

Without further ado, he strutted across the schoolyard and picked up Maisie's brush. Karen, who was leaning moodily by the back wall, observed him with tense amazement. She seemed almost immobilised for the best part of ten seconds. I stared at that remarkable expression. I also noticed an undeniable and inscrutable physical beauty. Karen Mavir might have been tough and fiery-tempered, but she was also strikingly fine-boned and quaintly oriental looking. She was like some glamorous, wary and misplaced young Turkish girl in this grey and dowdy West Cumbrian playground. At last she blinked from her trance, then bore down on this ludicrous thief in a bridling rage.

'Get your bastard stinking hands off that!' she bawled.

Flogger hesitated, stiffened and paled. He put his hands on his skinny hips and attempted a pedantic certitude. He intended his voice to be as rough as Brod Crawford's, but it came out as a high-pitched squeak, 'No I won't. Will I fuck as bloody like.'

That soprano shrill signified his true state of mind, but he could hardly back down in front of a girl. He was also squeaking because he still had water on his brain and it had percolated down to his voice box. It was *Highway Patrol's* fault, that laughable shrill. It was all the television's fault, in the last analysis. Worse still, and long before they started agonising about the deleterious effects of TV's violence, it would definitely be responsible for Flogger suffering a calamitous personal assault.

Karen grabbed hold of what had been sub-leased to her for ninety-nine years and a day by her best friend Maisie. Flogger pouted and displayed an absurdly pettish determination. Karen gave him a Romany scowl, a Turkish sneer, a Finland leer of disdain. The algebra, an appropriately oriental word, was simple enough. Despite his nickname, Flogger was a soft-as-piss milk-white little fool whose real name was Humphrey. He lived in the soft part of Fingland, not on the hard estate, but on the soft estate. Karen was from desolate Tottergill, a tough collier's lass, and though she blinked a lot less than her brother, she probably suffered his violence too. However if Karen had asked me, I could have advised her that although Flogger was soft he was exceedingly obstinate. For example if he'd decided to win a game of draughts, he would sit there for hours deliberating over a single boring move. As determined as any geriatric miser, he could make a single Rowntree's gum last for an eternity. Fishing for competition plaice or cod off the end of Silloth pier, he would clock there in the pissing rain, morning, noon and night if need be.

'Gizzit!' she roared at his sacrilege.

He squeaked at her, 'You can fuck right off! You can go and get fucked, as soon as you like.'

'I'll bloody well kill you! You bloody big string of piss!'

'Go on then! Go on! Go and kill us. And get yourself arrested for whammycide!'

Foolish words. Karen and he began a furious tug of war

with the yardbrush. Humphrey Farrell was obviously physically weaker, but his obstinacy lent a sort of strength by proxy. The numerous playground spectators were moved in complex, noisy ways. Karen being from Tottergill was a semi-outcast, but Flogger caught in the act of transgender skivvying was a damn sight more questionable category. Some of them started to cheer for Karen Mavir, an unprecedented novelty. Even then, aged nine, it occurred to me, and I had never even heard of Machiavelli, that allegiances are never absolute things but are conditional and variable. Everything depends on the circumstances and on the players. So true in fact was this universal, that I was suddenly startled to find myself amnesically shouting for *Karen* instead of my best friend Flogger Farrell . . .

It was probably my treachery that did it. Just as my water bomb had stopped him enjoying his favourite telly, so my thoughtless bellowing for Karen unnerved him so much that he lost his grip. Flogger looked at me cheering in disbelief. Karen saw her sudden chance and seized it. She gave a single ferocious yank and the yardbrush was instantly hers. A great roaring and a lesser booing went up from the crowd. Aghast, Flogger tried with one huge spring to seize his prize, the brush. He leapt in the air in much the same way as when doused in the lug. But Karen had lost all patience with this purblind fathead. She brought down the brush shank across his face, not with all her might, but with let's say eighty-seven-and-a-half per cent of it . . .

There was a loud crack and a collective intake of breath. Blood started flying along several elliptical arcs. Flogger Farrell remarkably did not cry out, neither then, nor even later when the shock had had time to settle and cease its anaesthetic effect. Karen looked momentarily surprised, then considerably frightened, and then the fear became a dull defiance as she saw how the storm clouds were gathering round her.

Blood was streaming stanchlessly from Flogger's nose.

There were also pools of blood all over his mouth. He had his hand raised carefully to his lips and in it he was holding half a front tooth.

I groaned. 'Oh bloody shite, Flogger. Your top front tooth. Oh bloody hell!'

Someone shouted that one of us should go and tell the headmistress, Snotty Messenger. Various fearful hypotheses abounded. Flogger would need a hospital, a blood transfusion, an ornamental coffin, plastic surgery, a new nose, a new mouth, a full set of dentures. Flogger stood there blinking and absolutely silent. He was a bloody sight, a terrible mess, yet still oddly tranquil, still immovably patient, and in his own way, for the first time ever, powerfully impressive.

I ran off to find a teacher. My intention was not to rat on Karen, but to stop my best friend bleeding to death. I had been cheering his enemy and now I had to redeem my treachery. I knocked and entered the staff room, where Miss Messenger was sipping coffee beside Mr Bill, Miss Bone and Miss Berry. The biscuits on the pale-blue plate were, I noticed, Rich Abernethy. I blurted it all out in an incontinent rush and I saw Snotty's face tighten with something like spite or anger, perhaps even relish.

'Bring Humphrey Farrell to me!' she snorted. 'Bring him here at once! And bring that . . . that girl . . . Karen Mavir!'

I stood there open-mouthed at this woman who had two, no three, Rich Abernethys grasped in her podgy fist. Snotty glowered at my feckless dawdling and repeated the imperative. I blinked and ran off panting to execute her orders.

'She wants to see you as well,' I said to Karen, and she tightened her delicate mouth with defiance.

The three of us shuffled into the staff room, and Snotty gulped at the sight of all that blood. Miss Berry who was trained in First Aid knelt beside Flogger with a sponge and gently and tenderly dabbed away. After half a minute it looked a great deal less horrific, yet still horrific. He had a large weal on his top lip, a wide bruise on his broad nose, and of course half a top front tooth missing. Though still, astoundingly, he bore that extraordinary patience and did not cry or complain at all.

'You little *fool!*' Snotty Messenger hissed at sullen and expressionless Karen. 'What on earth . . . what earthly *right* have you to attack anyone like that? Are you completely *mad*, girl? Look at that! Just look at the terrible state of his mouth! I hope you realise his poor parents would would have every right to *prosecute* . . . !'

Karen gazed down at the varnished floorboards and hunched her shoulders tight. Snotty was talking pure baloney of course, and in any case neither Flogger nor Karen had heard of the word 'prosecute'. However Flogger's father, Reg, was a newly-elected parent governor, and blustering old Snotty looked moderately stricken by the possible implications.

'His front tooth!' she grieved and shuddered with a tragic face. 'Humphrey has such lovely front teeth. Or rather he *had* such beautiful teeth, before you decided you had to maim him! Tell me, son, is it hurting very badly? Of course it is, my pet. It must be absolute agony. Look at what you've done to his poor face, you wicked and evil little ragtag!'

Or was it raggle-taggle, as in gypsy-o? I, who knew him better than most, had no memory of Flogger's photogenic dentition. His teeth had looked no better and no worse than anyone else's. At last, after another ten minutes' harangue, Mr Bill was ordered to drive the victim to his dentist in Workington. Miss Berry was delegated to walk up the village and inform poor Mrs Farrell, though, as a strategic precaution, only after her son had departed in Mr Bill's car. Before all that, however, we must witness an appropriate meting out of punishment. Snotty Messenger who was florid, fretful, fifty-five and obese, crooked a chubby finger at silent Karen.

'Come here!' she cried. 'Come here to me at once, girl!'

Karen went and stood in front of the spitting Gorgon, still maintaining her sullen defiance. She was ten-and-a-half, five feet tall, and better looking than everyone here by a factor of ten. She knew what was coming, just as she knew it many a time at home. The teachers were seated in a circle on hard school chairs, like a bunch of Christmas party gamesters. That ring of seats also looked like an amphitheatre where Christians might be fed to Roman lions. Mr Bill flinched as his stout superior grabbed the girl by the arm and upended her over her knee. Miss Berry, who never touched any of her class, averted her eyes and quivered. Miss Bone blushed at what was about to take place, and there was also considerable anger in her eyes. Snotty briefly seemed to ponder her various flagellatory options, then vauntingly lifted up Karen's dark blue skirt. I blinked at this remarkable sacrilege and began to sweat.

Unlike her laughing-stock brother, Karen at least wore underwear, navy blue knickers in this case. Miss Messenger thrashed her harshly perhaps half a dozen times. She was scarlet and panting by the end of this ferocious exercise, and Karen likewise was flaming when she stood up to right her skirt. The gypsy girl was blazing with shame of course, but also blazing with blood pressure. The blood had rushed to her head, just as it had to Flogger Farrell's when he'd watched our TV upside down last night.

Only when he observed Karen beetroot red did Flogger venture to show any signs of satisfaction. Otherwise he followed this punctilious administration of late Fifties justice with a more or less abstracted air. It was almost as if he'd been watching it happening on the telly.

# 4

*High Mallstown, North Cumbria, 12th November 2001.*
*Lunchtime satellite viewing and listening.*

## 212

A bearded, sleepy-eyed, forty-year-old child psychologist, Sef, from Santa Monica is working with a problem child called Tommy. The TV camera is not in Sef's professional clinic but is making a swift impressionistic inventory of Tommy's sumptuous home. Attractive shot of Tommy emerging from crystal blue swimming pool with head bent quizzically but humorously. Tommy is eight years old and is strikingly blond-haired, limply blue-eyed, altogether poignantly angelic. His mother Kelly is a computer science professor, who delegates much of the childcare to a listless black teenage employee called Marnie. Tommy's father Jeff, we are told, is a pre-eminent software tycoon who is rarely at home because he is obliged to travel the world, especially Western Europe, cheerleading other less responsible executives. There is a photograph of him on the desk in the sitting room where Tommy is being trained out of his problem by Sef. For no reason I can authoritatively put a finger on, I believe that the Dad is having serial affairs across Brussels, Berlin, Florence, Paris, Manchester (no, possibly not, conceivably *not* Manchester). Perhaps it is Jeff's absurdly alluringly teasing smile, for he looks like his namesake Jeff Bridges with perhaps a soupçon of the youthful Ryan O'Neal. Sef does not hazard the hypothesis, but I believe from my North Cumbrian armchair, surely Jeff the peripatetic pop ought to be here for comprehensive therapeutic wholeness. Jeff most certainly, plus for even more fastidious therapeutic verisimilitude, why not include Paris Monique, Berlin Brigitte, Florentine Carla, not forgetting Cissie from posh Didsbury or Stockport or Altrincham, if she be a part of the transglobal philandering?

Tommy's present problem is what? That he won't tidy his disgrace of a room, no more and no less. No matter what ad hoc or structured strategies a confounded and houseproud Kelly tries, from reproof to threats to penalties to punishments. Once, to her horror, she found herself slapping him when he refused to pick up his Gameboy paraphernalia, and, even greater horror, he slapped her back! Then of course she had to wallop him a great deal harder. Upset by these spiralling fisticuffs, she decided to contact Jeff in Verona, but of course her husband's mobile was switched off like it always was. Tommy's Mom, who has twenty-four people working under her at the university, insists that she is frequently at her wits' end.

*Sef:* It's a case, as always, in these child-parent potentially imploding conflict situations concerning family routine, of reinforcing the child's attempts at positive behaviour. So instead of using threats and punishments, you reward the child as you would a young animal you're training. With, huh, no serious disrespect to Kelly or Tommy, of course, by using that metaphor, I mean simile. OK, let's hear it from you, Kelly. You wish your kid to be more what, *specifically*, when it comes to tidiness around the house?

*Kelly (glazed looking):* More compliant, I guess.

*Sef:* Exactly. More compliant. More dossle. Right. So if you want your Tommy more dossle, I believe that you need to establish some working ground rules here. So let's say you go away right now, and delegate a room or a corner or shelf or whatever to put the stuff, the various items of kids' toys and junk. OK? Day by day you show your Tommy where to put it in its proper place, so whenever he shows the least compliance, the least dossle acceptance of your authority, ma'am, you reward him with appropriate rewards. Candies and hugs that is, they're the usual winners. (*Scrupulously, after a pause*) Or just hugs, I guess if you don't believe in stuffing a little kid with ca–

*Kelly*: But –

*Tommy (scowling)*: But that sucks!

*Kelly*: Oh? Bart Simpson here we go. What precisely sucks, honey?

*Tommy*: Hugs but no candy. I don't need the hugs.

*Sef (pensively fingering his beard)*: Of course for the reinforc–

At this point I almost choked on the Kit-Kat I was consuming. I had been overwhelmingly reminded of a subtly parallel situation with my own daughter Sassy when she was about half the age of Tommy. It was that adamant insistence by Kelly, the put-upon Prof, and Sef, the tranquil psychologist, on the advisability of imparting an adaptable 'docility' to one's offspring which set me thinking. Sassy aged three in 1979, and now aged twenty-five in 2001, was and is slightly less dossle than an anaconda or a grizzly. Sassy's name is comically onomatopoeic though not intentionally so. Her proper name is Sarah but at two she altered it by repetitive lisping and refused to be called anything else thereafter. Sassy-Sarah Murphy has from infancy to womanhood always demonstrated the undocile principles of absolute determination, inflexible stubbornness, an unflinching antagonism to moderation, calm reason, phlegmatic deliberation.

In this traumatic instance, I was not in fact training three-year-old Sassy, I was just trying to do something furtively and on my own. Very young children are of course obsessive imitators, compulsive helpers and sometimes a reckless danger to themselves. Sassy for example saw no reason why she shouldn't wield a hedge strimmer like me and poke her hand in the serrations to fish out the grass. Nor did she see why she couldn't clip her nails unaided like I did, drink eye-popping espresso coffee or take a hearty puff on my birthday panatella. It had got to the stage where I slyly hid from her whenever I was doing anything even remotely hazardous, repetitive or tedious. If I didn't, Sassy would vehemently insist on joining in, and my stiff refusal would lead to tears, anger, sulks, depression, not all of it on one side of the generation divide.

It was a cool summer morning in 1979 and I was busy cleaning the lavatory. It wasn't so much that I was virtuously refuting the stereotype of the idle male, as I was demolishing some vivid dun spatterdashes on embarrassing display in our toilet bowl. Last night I had consumed an incendiary carry-out jalfrezi curry, plus half a bottle of Moldavian red, and the controversial not to say explosive conceptual art was left for all to see. Fran my wife was at work, and Sassy as far as I knew was downstairs watching *Sesame Street*. TV, all too inevitably, was still central to the narrative picture, and Sassy was as glued to children's telly as I would have been aged three had there been a TV in our house back in 1953. As everyone knows, the Year of the Coronation was a record patriotic year for television purchase.

I was halfway through my cleansing when Sassy suddenly poked her head round the door. Or rather that was when I noticed her, but in retrospect I assume she must have been watching my curious activity unobserved.

'What are you doing?' she asked, frowning.

'Cleaning the toilet,' I said brusquely. 'I am cleaning up this stinky, stinky bog.'

'Why?' she asked, as she always did about everything. I hesitated over whether to discuss the encopretic effects of red-hot jalfrezis, madrases, sri lankas and vindaloos. But no, I decided cleverly, instead I would earnestly lecture her about the laws of lavatory hygiene and quickly bore the pants off her. With any luck she would buzz off to see Bert and Ernie and Big Bird, and leave me to my shameful task. But before I could say anything, she stepped a bit nearer and said longingly: 'Can I have a go doing that?'

'No,' I said quickly. 'No you can't. Don't ask me why, it won't get you anywhere, I promise. You can't because you can't because you can't. Suffice to say it's full of germs that can make you ill. They don't make me ill cos I'm a big man, but a small girl like you they will make really horribly sick and . . .'

I watched gratified as she walked off at my boring discursiveness. No raging insistence, no lunge at my brush (q.v. twenty-five years earlier the reckless schoolboy Flogger), no tears, no obvious contempt for the authoritarian father. For once she was being as dossle as they come, and I quietly counted my blessings as I finished off my malodorous task.

Time passed. Maybe ten or fifteen minutes. I walked downstairs and sat beside Sassy as she watched *Sesame Street*. The puppet characters Bert and Ernie were extremely funny, especially Ernie, and the two of us cackled away. Bert and Ernie were meant to be sprung-haired little boys but both had dopey old men's faces and dopey old men's quirks. Bert's hobbies were downright Beckettian inasmuch as he collected useless objects like bottle tops and paper clips. Ernie's speech, and by implication his mind, was so witlessly ponderously eccentric he had me in helpless stitches.

'You know,' I confided seriously to Sassy, 'this is nearly as good as Pingu.' Which was definitely the highest praise, the most stringent critical yardstick, I could think of. Pingu the Penguin, a German puppet animation series, was at least ten times funnier than, say, the top ten alternative and/or orthodox UK or US television stand-up comedians.

The adverts came on and Sassy stood up looking thoughtful. She announced that she needed a wee. Mm, I said abstractedly, still chortling at the memory of Bert and Ernie and thinking how crushingly unfunny the childrens' television was back in the Fifties. Muffin the Mule, Lord save us from his paltry antics; Andy Pandy, almost as bad; Mr Pastry, not a great deal sharper. Bill and Ben, the horticultural sprites who spoke gobbledeygook, were amusing without being hilarious. No, I mused, thank God for the Germans and the Americans, for their superior wits and their superior comic minds. I told Sassy to shout down for help with her toilet if need be. In her bumptious three-year-old's soprano she assured me that wouldn't be necessary.

Time passed. *Sesame Street* had resumed but Sassy had not returned. I knew I ought to go up to the bathroom, but Kermit the journalist's newsflash about this porridge-pilfering female felon called Goldilocks was so brilliantly scripted I stayed where I was cackling. I was halfway through a demented monologue by furniture-guzzling Cookie Monster when it occurred to me I really ought to stir myself. She was incredibly quiet up there, and she had never been known to neglect Part 2 celebrities like streetwise Kermit and importunate Grover.

Upstairs I beheld the following Hieronymus Bosch extravaganza. The bathroom door was flung wide open, and snorting Sassy had sorted herself and clearly finished her toilet. She had done what she had to do, had pulled up her pants, and was engaged in shall we say post-operative procedures. At first I could make no sense of what I saw, as she seemed to be flogging something to death inside the toilet bowl. Was it a louse, a rat, a mouse, an imaginary monster?

Her flagellatory instrument was the toilet brush. This brush was covered very vividly with a shredded wreath of pale pink lavatory paper. In among this wreath were some brown ornamental sausages, a.k.a. precious unreplaceable baubles in the form of my three-year-old daughter's miniature turds. I stared into the bowl and saw a copious amount of – on the culinary analogy of eggs – scrambled excrement. Evidently Sassy's pee had turned into a poo, perhaps – who knows? – she had forced one with a deliberate view in mind.

Afterwards, making an entirely spurious extrapolation, she had attempted to imitate her furtive father. Having only a partial view of my bog scouring, she had got the wrong end of the stick and as a consequence the wrong end of the brush. She had attempted to obliterate her excrement *before* rather than *after* the flush. She had tried to flog the obstinate shit into non-existence and *pari passu* the obstinate pink toilet paper as well. She had treated her poo as if it were a trifle or a jelly, and had given it a throughly good beating. Amazed, I stared around the room and saw, yes, there were little daubs and flecks of pink and brown at cardinal decorative points. What, I pondered, was that DIY ornamental technique called exactly? Stippling, marbling, stencilling, spray painting, what the hell, I asked myself fussily, did they call it on TV?

'Agh,' I cried demented. 'Sassy you're supposed to flush *then* brush. Not brush then flush! You pull the chain, then clean it, not the other idiotic way about!'

She looked at me stiffly. 'But if you flush it,' she sneered, 'it doesn't need to be cleaned.'

'Agh!' I repeated, because she was still busy hammering away at her papier-mached turds. 'It bloody well can sometimes! Think of diarrhoea. Flying in a dozen directions like Thunderbirds or Stingray or Fireball XL5. You have to clean up the stray bits of poo cos it's embarrassing, it's filthy bad manners if you don't. Which is not to say you do what you do, battering away at a bowful of shite and shitey paper! Because believe you me, it won't disappear, not even if you keep on flogging for a million blasted years!'

'Oh yes it will,' cried Sassy. And she returned with a selfless belligerence to belabouring those obstinate little sausages.

And apropos Sef, and Kelly the Prof, and problem child Tommy, Sassy was not after all trying to dodge her chores or drive her journalist father crazy. Rather, she was conscientiously attempting to clean the toilet and in passing defeat the very tedious laws of science. In doing which she was cheerfully attempting the impossible, and now, eighteen years later as a struggling fine artist down in Crouch End, she sometimes feels she is more or less doing the same.

## 234

Some sights are so extraordinary, so unintelligible at first blink, that the eyes cry out for immediate realignment. I do not believe what I am seeing, the left one hoarsely remarks, and the right one proffers an instant and independent confirmation of being flatly stumped. Then, like Flogger's Australians, we opt for the sensible empirical approach; finding our eyes to be of little use we balance upside down on the sofa and watch the TV with our backsides. Alternatively (like me, Roe Murphy, aged nine, on seeing a drunken middle-aged gargoyle with a damaged eye) we go into a state of uncomprehending shock.

Shock and fear are not what this extraordinary documentary is all about. A family of giggling South Indians, very poor ones, are down on their knees puffing smoke into the ground. The father is about thirty-five, very thin, with jet-black coconut-oiled hair, and with teeth either decayed, warped or absent. He has three very pretty little daughters, all with decorative marks on their foreheads, all as doe-eyed as they are in Sanskrit poetry, all hooting and gurgling with wild anticipation. They are in a farmer's field in Kerala and are as giddy as if engaged in impromptu carnival or a family picnic. Given that they are penniless outcaste Hindus, Dravidian tribesfolk called the Gojji, one wonders what the hell they find to laugh about. The ragged teeth are a give-away, for even the bonny little girls, who presumably don't see too many Cokes or Fantas, have warped and skew-eyed teeth. In their case the ugly dentition works on a contrary aesthetic principle and enhances their beauty with a protective aura of heartwarming pathos. Likewise their dog-eared Dad is not exactly beautified by his horrible choppers, but he has a gappy comic innocence that makes him look like a touchingly overgrown brother to these cackling little girls.

He has a burning, smouldering rag held above one of the ridges where the farmer plants his grain. He leans on his knees and blows at the rag so that dense smoke, mysteriously, is puffed into the earth. Many a simple Hindu sees the Earth as a benignant, fertile and life-providing deity; Bhu, Prthivi, Mahi and many another designation. In which case one wonders why this gappy chappy is impudently blowing a ton of acrid smoke into the deity's face. Meanwhile the three girls aged about eight, six and four are jumping on the spot at approximately five, ten and fifteen yards along the same ridge. Dressed in vivid but threadbare red and purple skirts they stand sentinels while their dad keeps grinning and puffing, puffing and grinning, as if he were Flogger Farrell aged ten trying his very first Craven A. The skinny little father beaming when he ought to have been spluttering and choking reminded me of the famous 1960 magazine advert. Craven A, it informed us, were strongly recommended by doctors on account of their unique cork tip, which filtered out the unpleasant tars without impairing the cigarette's exquisite flavour (and by cheerful implication made Craven A's as harmless not to say medicinally efficacious as Zubes or Hacks or Little Imps).

But look, those little girls are suddenly racing helter-skelter. Several bolts from hell have just bolted out of hell. The children are chasing after these darting demons chuckling crazily. The father stops his puffing and joins his daughters in their grabbing and their scooping. The camera shows us where the Gojji has used rags to block up certain give-away holes in the earth, so that only one burrow is left open a few yards down the ridge. The little demons have bolted so fast it takes three kids and one adult to grab them by their tails and fling them into a dirty old sack.

The Gojji is a Kerala rat-catcher. The Gojjis are a special-ist vermin-catching caste, masters of a subtle and highly prized art. They save the farmers incalculable amounts of grain and when they come to clear a field of rats with their sacks and their rags they certainly know what they are about. And look, they also laugh like buggery, they do their job with zest and pride and – let's not beat about the bush – with heartfelt unalloyed joy. Which goes to prove I'm not sure what uncategorically from my North Cumbrian armchair. That you can have terrible teeth, a job sparse in the glamour stakes, no money to speak of, and yet still have unalloyed joy.

Even in this day and age the caste system often works on a kind of formalised barter system. In Bengal it is called *jaj-mani* and the Kerala version in the old-fashioned south is not a lot different. I do this specialised service for you, and you do this service in return for me. In the case of Gappy and his bonny daughters, the *jajmani* is this. The Gojjis get rid of the farmer's rats, and the farmer gives them what sort of booty, do we imagine, in return? Money? Eh, come again, for these lot, these dirty, rotten-toothed gypsies, you must be joking surely? Farmer's produce, then, such as milk, ghee, panir, vegetables, coconuts, bananas? Those little girls possi-bly look like a bit of fresh fruit might do them a bit of good? No, no, wrong again, sahib. Grain, then, a fraction, however tiny, of the considerable amount they have saved the farmer?

You must be kidding. Instead old Farmer Appiyan gives them his priceless *rats* . . .

Their handsome wages are their handsome catch.

Farmer Appiyan gives them as many captured rats as they can cart away in their bulging sacks. He gives them as many first-class, grain-fed gourmet rats as they can eat.

As this stage you are permitted to snort with hysterical amusement or frayed and disconcerted nerves or a sense of enormous but entirely opaque revelation.

Night shot. A blazing fire in a Keralan field. In a discreet far corner the Gojji and his three girls are sat around a roaring camp fire. They have sharpened some stout twigs, which they are operating as highly efficient toasting forks. The twigs are employed as handily disposable eco-conscious barbecue skewers, and half a dozen expertly assembled kebabs are roasting odoriferously in the balmy winter air.

Behold six-rat souvlaki, their fat dripping musically into the fire. Does my gorge perhaps rise at this fascinating sight? You know, I believe that just possibly it does. Imaginatively gagging as I am, I am truly mesmerised and quite incapable of touching my satellite handset. The little lass aged eight, the handsomest of the three kids, as miraculously bonny as Sarasvati or Sita, grabs a skewer, pulls away the flesh and gnashes away with such lipsmacking rapture.

She eats her rat up, rump and stump. The middle sister stuffs hers in as if it were cream cakes or truffles. The gappy little pappy tears a lump of rat from his skewer and savours it as majestically as if he were a Viking, a Grecian hero, a swashbuckler, a man of parts and a man of enviable means.

So there you go then. This canny Kerala lad knows how to spoil his bairns outrageously on minimum outlay, and keep 'em as happy, nay delirious, as skylarks. Perhaps too bloody happy, dammit, for does anybody in the world in 2001 deserve this thing called joy? But this bugger, the rodent-roasting gourmet-guzzling Gojji, has bloody well got it cracked. I am severely frustrated that the film about Tommy and his desperate Mom is finished, that I can't switch back to it and press some unfortunately not-yet refined and patented gizmo, address anxious Kelly and let her know that I can probably help her where Sef the psychologist perhaps could not. I would give her it plain, no beating about the bush. You're not giving him enough to chew on Kelly, you're not giving your son enough *rodents*, you've pampered him so that he's lost the ability to drool over rat dripping! And consider, if you had errant Jeff at home nicely under your thumb (software tycoons are ten a penny, but master rat catchers are worth their weight in . . . rats) industriously catching vermin in Santa Monica fields and with boy apprentice Tommy in tow, keenly bonding and identifying with his penitent pop, no longer messing up his room, he your footsore, smoke-begrimed, extremely dossle rat-catcher husband, would have neither time nor energy to be humping in Bonn, Birmingham, Brussels or Bologna. Enough said.

*Gojji* (*speaking his best most decorous Malayalam – voice-over is in English*): Rats are assuredly delicious, sahib. More tasty than bhunaed chicken, sweeter altogether than kormaed rabbits, a deal more succulent than tandooried hare. Believe you me, sir, there is no finer thing in the world than a plump and lipsmackingly savoury rat (*suck, gnaw, salivate*). A well-turned rat is a blessing from heaven (*grinning very gappily, modest yet proud of his connoisseur's vehemence*). I can affirm in all sincerity, sir, that the world boasts no greater delicacy than a smartly spatchcocked ra–

## 356

(*voice-over*) . . . is a major British poet whose work is greatly admired because of its trenchance and abrasiveness, and it is partly for that reason that Selwyn Pinckney's verse, uniquely amongst English poets, sells abroad as well as at home, particularly in Spain and Italy where poetry and politics are often synonymous. Pinckney's bust is currently being sculpted by Margot Busse who was commissioned by the Arts Council to coincide with the Cambridge celebrity's imminent fiftieth birthday.

Focus on the sculptress interviewed in her studio which is decorated with handsome Tibetan and Nepalese wallhangings and batiked rugs. She is about thirty-five, thin, taut, very attractive and looks both brittle and pugnacious The rhythm of her speech is snortingly modulated by the mouldings of her clay as she sculpts Pinckney sat at a desk two yards off.

*Margot Busse*: Both my hafffather and my mother were

fine artists and both had a keen interest in comparative haff-religions and supernatural matters in general. I suppose if anything I'm a haffpagan in spiritual terms. I've always been fascinated by the Haffgreen Man legend which I see as something quintessentially English but an Englishness more I don't haffknow robust and virile though I don't like that word with all its machohaff connotations. Feistyhaff is that better, Selhaffwyn, you're a poet after all? No. Anyway I'm going to embarrass you Selwynhaff while you're on satellite telly. I know it might sound a bit fancihafffuI but I do see something of the atavistic greenness and the heroic manness of the Green Man in Haffselwynhaff. I see the Cambridge Professor of Poehafftry standing in front of me as quite a raw and primitive man underneath shall we say the haffdecorous and donnish exterior.

*Selwyn Pinckney* (*he has a cold, looks quite peaky, and sounds uncomfortably nasal*): I compose a poem I suppose every three weeks, and if I don't do so I feel ill, I feel, in quite a literal sense, severely indisposed. It's tantamount at times to a debilitating neurasthenic condition, a kind of chain, perhaps, around my neck, but you know how it is, I'm not seriously complaining. As for this Arts Council sculpture and my turning fifty, the Green Man thing that Margot mentions is certainly very interesting. Because by sheer chance, and it was only yesterday, I was in our garden playing an epic and demanding game of croquet with my wife, and there was at one point a teasingly epiphanic moment, the kind of thing that any poet would die for, where I happened to have my croquet mallet oddly, seemingly totemically, upraised. I stopped dead, froze, I suppose, and I felt just then in a Hertfordshire English summer the ripe vernality, the fecundity, the fertility, I don't know, sort of aboriginal nature, the festal aboriginality of . . . of the ripe and humming soil. There's that word in Lawrence Durrell whom you mentioned before Margot, he uses it in the *Alexan–*, you know, the heraldic, perhaps. The sense of, not the martial obviously, but herald in the sense of announcing, as the spring does, the return of growth and life and reproduction and burgeoning fecund promise, perhaps, I don't know. Anyway, right away, without prevarication, I dashed in the house at once, still absent-mindedly clutching my upraised mallet. As it happened rather dangerously, because I sent an expensive piece of slipware pottery flying as I ran. Still, I knocked off the bare bones, or rather I mean the frail integument, of a little poem I'm rather pleased with already ab–

## 636 *(Audio channel)*

Proverbs, Chapter 20

*Most men will proclaim every one his own goodness: but a faithful man who can find?*

*The just man walketh in his integrity: his children are blessed after him.*

*Who can say, I have made my heart clean, I am pure from my sin?*

*Even a child is known by his doings, whether his work be pure, and whether it be right.*

## 677 *(broadcast in Arabic)*

A weekly broadcast entitled *Points of View*. This week Tewfik el Hakim, Professor of Media and Communication Studies at Luxor Metropolitan University, is giving his point of view about events on and after the 11th of September 2001. Sat at a desk with an outsize cactus plant and a minute anglepoise lamp he addresses his audience for a half-hour lecture. Possibly the nearest analogy on British terrestrial television would be those idiosyncratic five-minute talks on Channel 4 that used to be broadcast every weekday evening.

*Tewfik el Hakim*: As I said earlier I have many friends who are Coptic Christians. I am not a Christian myself, I am a moderately orthodox Egyptian Muslim. But at present I am thinking very often of a certain verse in the New Testament which comes from Christ's remarkable Sermon on the Mount. The verse in question says *Judge not that ye be judged. For with that judgement*, it continues, *ye judge, it shall be meted unto ye.* The pot accusing the kettle of being black in other words. Rendered in a classical Arabic, a very beautiful poetry hasn't it, that gospel verse? Sacred scripture, in my view, from whatever great tradition, always has a beautiful poetry about it. Whereas the secular variety of 'scripture', I would argue, invariably and irremediably has not. I shall come to that rather confusing but important point later, when discussing the use of arms and especially all those terrible bombs which are currently raining all over Afghan towns and villages.

Sometimes in our schools older children are asked to compare and contrast various things in tabular form, often in science and history lessons for example. Acids versus bases, the salient and opposing properties of, and so forth. Last night on a piece of paper I found myself quite spontaneously jotting down a few of the salient characteristics of the opposing demagogues in this Afghan war. And I was struck – or rather, I was not struck at all, I was just, as it were, balefully confirmed in what I knew already – to see so many remarkable similarities amongst supposedly antithetical beliefs and ideologies.

The Taliban are widely regarded, both inside and outside Afghanistan, as brutal, often ignorant religious fundamentalists, fuelled by their mediaeval beliefs and a selective and manipulative reading of certain passages of the Quran. However on the left side of my little table of properties, I can truthfully write that the present American government, especially in the South and the Midwest states, has an identical characteristic. They, the Republican party, are likewise succoured and supported by vast numbers of Christian fundamentalists who interpret the Christian Bible in equally primitive ways. There are, for example, numerous elected political leaders in America who believe, or at any rate pretend to believe, that Darwin's Theory of Evolution is both wrong and sinful. Moreover they would wish, if it were within their power, to have it vigorously denounced inside the schools.

To anticipate their own rigid intellectual terms and their stated items of faith, it is apparently painfully inconceivable to them that their Almighty might be thus sidestepped and seen as superfluous to biological change. Myself I find this outraged literalism just a little astonishing. I find it strange indeed that it never strikes these worthies that the Almighty, God himself, might actually *wish* to use Evolution as one of his beautiful, economic and entirely appropriate mechanisms. That he, given that he is God and capable of doing anything he wishes, might lucidly have *elected* to design the process of Evolution just as he designed all other designs. Why, I ask myself, should God who created all things animate and inanimate, why should he be frightened of Natural Science?

There are no public floggings or Sharia amputations in the United States of course. They do however execute more people over there than the rest of the western world put together. Those who are executed are either injected, gassed or electrocuted. The first option is probably the most humane of the three, and the last one the least. The electric chair seemingly fries people alive, whereas the Taliban as a rule chop off heads, which though not pleasant is surely far preferable to frying. Apparently in some cases black smoke is seen to rise off the shaved scalp of the executed person and their eyeballs have been seen to melt on occasion. I believe even a hardened Taliban might be outraged by such an example of cruel and unusual punishment. And remember that those poor souls in Manhattan on the 11th of September were also fried alive, a very dreadful death for so many innocent people, some of them innocent Muslims into the bargain. Recently I had a rather strange and unpleasant thought, a highly uncomfortable fantasy that would not go away. I wondered how many of them in Manhattan in their last moments suddenly reflected that they were being put through a kind of impersonal, ironical and thoroughly terrifying high-elevation and mass-production, cruel and unusual electric-chair mechanism?

In the USA in a capital case the accused person, especially if he is not rich, is often given hopeless legal counsel. There have been cases of inept defence lawyers falling asleep and snoring loudly during the proceedings. As a result innocent people are frequently murdered by the due process of law. The present American leader's predecessor once signed the death warrant for a mentally retarded man when it was politically advantageous for him to do so. Subsequently that same leader was publicly accused of so many covert immoralities and adulteries going back over so many years, most of us both here and in his own country lost count. Worse still, those same Christian fundamentalists, those hellfire Islamhaters, also had amongst them people who with political connections all the way to the president were found guilty of colossal financial embezzlement and colossal sexual misdeeds. Certainly this kind of flagrant moral corruption, saying one thing and doing the opposite, is familiar enough in the Third World where money is in short supply and therefore honesty is so much more costly a quantity. And yet the Land of the Free would earnestly wish us to believe they are perennially incapable of such dual standards.

As for the vilification of the absolute bestiality of the enemy, that is as it were a matter of chronology and circumstances. You will remember that twenty years ago, during the Iran–Iraq war, Saddam Hussein was the favourite golden boy of the West, the secular quasi-socialist soldier with his admirably rough and ready methods for fighting the evil Iranian mullahs. Saddam since 1991 is no longer their blueeyed boy but the quintessence of insane tyrannical evil. You will remember likewise that the Afghan mojahedin, the current Taliban amongst them, were the plucky opponents (freedom fighters, not terrorists) who took on the monstrous Soviet expansionists after 1979. They were trained in their guerilla combat methods by no other than the American army and the CIA. The Taliban were indeed the much beloved of the Americans, but they are now having a great many American smart bombs rained upon them.

This bizarre linguistic usage is what I was alluding to earlier. This love that the West, and I include the rest of the Christian and secular West, including Britain, Germany, France and so on, have for the grotesquely oxymoronic. This term 'smart bombs', as a linguist, I find absolutely fascinating. Bombs as far as I know blow people to pieces, and this I would venture is a very painful business, especially if the death is not instantaneous. In fact I would argue that even when it is 'instantaneous' it is still a terrible experience. It might perhaps be a side issue but who knows how long a second or even half a second lasts in the case of a violent death? At any rate, a terrible thing is permitted to have a cheerful, altogether zestful adjective to describe it. And the remarkable thing is that the adjective not only speaks allusively and admiringly of the terrible thing, but it also basks admiringly and vicariously in that same admiration. What I mean is that he or she who talks about smart bombs is not only admiring such weapons for their smartness, but is also describing themselves as smart because they are on the side of those who smartly use smart strategies on those who are not smart, by implication on those who are profoundly stupid. I would therefore modestly propose that those who bandy and codify these chilling and wholly paradoxical twenty-first century neologisms should go the whole hog and expand their vocabulary in line with the smartness of their superior intelligences and imaginations.

What other couplets might they then beneficially employ? 'Smart mutilations', 'smart massacres', 'smart holocausts'?

Yes, but rather repetitive and redundantly unimaginative I feel. How about 'pretty mutilations', 'sumptuous massacres', 'hearty holocausts'? Or perhaps we need to go from vocable couplets to vocable triplets, if we really wish to extend our vocabulary, to refine our lexicon properly and thoroughly. 'Gorgeous little baby corpse', 'perfectly splattered toy horse', 'brilliantly incinerated teenager's blouse'. Am I speaking evilly when I speak thus, when I use my profoundly moronic oxymorons? Of course I am in my own ignorant terms but not in the superior terms of the smart. Smart people have smart bombs and smart words to imagine such smart coinings in the first place . . .

## 636 (Audio channel)

Isaiah, 26.2

*Open ye the gates, that the righteous nation which keepeth the truth may enter in.*

# 5

*Fingland, West Cumbria, 1966*

Sex was either everywhere or nowhere, seditiously rampant or entirely absent, and strange to say it was the television situation comedies which were overwhelmingly chaste. Baleful Eric Sykes, for example, lived in a semi with his spinster sister Hattie and did not bother with women, but instead enjoyed sarcastic banterings with the bespectacled bachelor snob next door. Eric sulked at obese and overflowing Hat and jousted with that fussy toff played by Richard Wattis. Likewise in *Hugh and I*, Terry Scott and Hugh Lloyd were pullovered middle-aged commuter-belt bachelors, the one irritable and impulsive, the other dolorous and dim. They were not – God help us – gay, because in 1966 it was still a crime to avow that strange infection. Harry Worth was not gay either, at least not in the categorical, though perhaps in the original, sense. He was a light-hearted, gormless, shoulder-shrugging, betrilbied bachelor, and like Bertie Wooster he was ruled or at any rate managed by his doughty elderly aunt.

Every Wednesday evening I watched the truly shocking *Wednesday Play* where sex was not only on the cards but was mesmerisingly flung in the face. It was all the more boggling given that until recently married couples were decorously portrayed as sleeping in adjacent single beds. One midweek evening I beheld Maurice Roeves (twenty years later appearing in *Tutti Frutti*, a lovelorn, hopeless Glaswegian rock musician, he got drunk as a duck and then literally immolated himself) – I watched M. Roeves in his underpants chasing a half-naked woman and bellowing at her with an upraised axe. I saw bare breasts by the score and uncovered female backsides by the gross. I was sixteen years old and found them all very interesting, even more than I did my O-Level edition of *Love and Mr Lewisham*. There was certainly sex of a kind in *Mr Lewisham* but it was of a different aura and era, it was tenderly and jocularly underexpressed, and was incongruously connected with the task of swotting very hard for exams. Much later I learnt that H.G. Wells was an insatiable bull of a man, and have ever since concluded that massive cerebral endeavours and massive feats of midnight cramming do irreversible things to the sacrococcygeal plexus . . . the seat of human fertility . . .

I meanwhile was struggling to find the non-televisual, the non-vicarious reality, and was finding it a great deal harder than my contemporary Flogger Farrell. Flogger at sixteen not only despised the vicarious, he even eschewed such risible constraints as simple privacy, and would copulate shamelessly in the open air or at rate in full view of whoever happened to be walking past him of a summer evening on Fingland shore. There was a slatted white fence next to the railway line that skirted the beach, and Flogger was regularly to be seen there standing, so to speak, erect, and humping away fully clothed with his back to the world. His girlfriend, who was always a different one, would have her chin over his shoulder and her skirt hitched up, and would be grimacing or pouting as they ground and groaned away. Once halfway through a copulation he seemed by acute telepathy to see that I, Roe Murphy, was walking demurely past, so he turned and roared a cordial hello, Roe!, and would probably have continued a discursive conversation had his partner not jerked him back pelvically to the business in hand. Five or six years later in New Delhi I was reminded of that heedless rear profile when I saw young men indolently turning their backs in public to do their urinations on the spot.

Flogger generally wore ice-blue jeans for his public acts of indecency and they were remarkably tight and clinging as if rolled onto his legs and arse by some sort of steam and transfer operation. One, by which I mean anyone, could see through those ice-blues that Flogger was burgeoningly well-hung or if not he had made a good job with the stuffed handkerchiefs and the cotton wool. We had both worn ice-blues in the last year at Fingland Junior School when sex was nowhere on our horizons, and it was simply that the gentle Mediterranean colour had appealed to our sombre West Cumbrian imaginations. Ice-blues were now Flogger's shagging pants and he also had some trusty screwing shoes in the form of a pair of razor-pointed winklepickers. It was a choice coincidence that Fingland shore was rich with covens and winkles and that Flogger's favourite Saturday morning hobby was winklepicking with his Dad. Flogger was no longer a feeble schoolboy, he was a wage-earning factory hand. The factory at Workington made cut-price chocolate bars and glutinous fruit sweets and those sand-cum-gravy-flavoured chocolate eggs generally set in a painted cup and purveyed in Woolworth's, and which no child, nor for that matter their dogs, would deign to eat. Flogger himself was a sweet and pudding omnivore and in his first week at Batty's (he christened his workplace Doolally's) ate so much rough chocolate he vomited it all back over the conveyor belt and almost got the sack. Abandoning the chocolate, a few days later he consumed such a quantity of fruit sweets from the hoppers that he suffered clinical dehydration and had to be taken to the hospital and put on a remedial drip.

Six months on he rejected this workplace vandalism and became a virtuoso on the conveyor belt, a star factory hand so electrically productive that he made more in bonuses than he did of a basic wage. When the sello packing machine jammed up it was Flogger who led the salvage operation. The conveyor process was not allowed to stop, so the marching sweet boxes, like so many goosestepping soldiers, had to be speedily removed from the belt and stored in wooden drawers. When there was a 'jam-on', Flogger used his hands in pincer-wedge style and removed a dozen cartons at a time. He could clear a jam-on single-handed and then put the cartons back with the same Edward Scissorhands technique. I mention all this ancillary detail because it made my friend Flogger a famous television star, and it was not just on bloody old, hellish old Border TV, but on the national ITV network, meaning twenty-five million admiring souls could gawk at charismatic Flogger if he was on the box during Wednesday night's *Coronation Street*.

No, he was not Elsie Tanner's enigmatic slow-on-the-uptake West Cumbrian nephew nor was he Albert Tatlock's recalcitrant (no bloody work in him, happen he should join the bloody army instead!) wrong-side-of-the-blanket grandson from Whitehaven called Cyril. Flogger Farrell was put on the Batty's telly advert that came out in late 1966, just as it was being taken over by a subsidiary of Cadbury's and the quality of its products was about to leap by a factor of ten thousand. The advert showed Batty's gorgeously revamped Cumbrian factory with a backdrop of the Lake District and some poignantly mewing lambs. The factory as I said was in Workington, so it needed an extremely brilliant bit of editing, where distant Skiddaw as seen behind ugly Siddick pit heap was made to appear in front of and occluding the industrial blot. Then cut to inside the state-of-the-art factory where a smirking teenage Flogger, wearing his white hygienic cap and his pretty industrial hairnet for even further cleanliness, was holding up a plastic shovel and scrupulously examining the appearance of his Batty's Magic Fruits. *Clean as Can Be Confectionery Made in the Countryside* was the calligraphic message on the screen, just as the mug of Flogger faded along with the seen-and-approved shovelful. Flogger, in the bar of the Workington Gunners' Club, soon invented an obscene variant on this jingle where the word 'country' was homophonised to repetitive effect and the 'fec' in 'confectionery' was also given due prominence.

'In the country!' snorted Flogger as we talked that Saturday morning by the scar where he picked his buckets of winkles. 'Pretending they're made in Kezzick or Hammelside when they're made in bloody Wukiton. If there's any damn lakes in Wukiton, Roe, they'll only be the lakes of puke come out of the Gunners' Club late tonight after I've been in for my Saturday night skinful.'

I nodded admiringly. He was two years underage but had put on so much sinew and muscle in the last few months he would have passed for nineteen or more.

'D'you drink?' he asked me, after accepting one of my Park Drives. 'Where do you go for your pint, Roe?'

I had once, just the once, drunk six pints of mild in Maryport, then been thrown off the Fingland bus for convulsing and decorating the conductor's knee with my half-digested fish and chips.

'The Black Lion in Maryport,' I lied glibly. 'Down by the docks. Most Friday nights I go down.'

'And are you courting these days?' he asked me in a faintly distracted voice. 'Are you getting plenty of egg, Roe?'

'Oh yes,' I stammered. 'Yes I am. A lass from Harrington. Sheila. Sheila Starr.'

'That's a lass from the Grammar School?'

I looked sheepish. I was painfully embarrassed to be an overgrown Grammar grub when he was a working man and a Fingland stud to boot. 'Yes,' then rather hurriedly, 'You know all these women that you fuck every night on the shore here, Flogger?'

'Mm?' he said, examining the inside of a dirty winkle, rather as if he was examining the phenomenon of women and the business of sexual attraction. 'Yes, Roe?'

'You must go through a hell of a lot of Durexes,' I sighed.

He glanced at me and guffawed. 'Like buggery. That's like

putting a bloody Weaver ter Wearra pacamac on if you want to have yersel a bath. I don't wear any bloody articles like yon.'

'In that case,' I said, 'you must have a hell of a lot of pulling away to do. At the critical moment I mean?'

Flogger snorted and said he did not go in for any idiotic jumping off. Elaborating his bath analogy, he said that it was like the plug being kicked out and instead of a comfy warm soak you had a freezing gust of air upon your naked body.

'So what stops them getting pregnant?' I asked him with a humble fascination. 'I mean you know how you do it so often, and with so many women? Statistically, you know it's –'

Flogger interrupted with a dry authority, 'Because we've never come together, Roe.'

I weighed these unusual words and could make no sense of them. I even thought he was saying that he and his women always approached the copulatory railway fence from different prearranged directions, from say North Fingland and South Fingland. It sounded like bizarre ritual sympathetic magic to me, as if the right kind of preliminary journey could avert an unwanted event.

'I don't understand.'

'It's easy,' said Flogger very seriously. 'She, the lass, any lass, can only get pregnant if you and her come together at the same time. But we've never ever come at the same time, me and any lass that I've bucked, Roe.'

'Eh?' I said stunned.

'I made damn sure of it! I generally try to stop them coming at all. If they have the cheek to come before me, they get a good sharp rattle across the lughole. If they look like they're coming after I've come, they get a good shaking to shake them out of it. There's no need for them to come at all as far as I can see, but now and again, despite getting clouted or shaken, they do still manage to come! But they've never come at the same time as me, and so they've never got pregnant, Roe.'

I began to regale him with my superior knowledge (I had just started doing A-Level Biology) but he wasn't really listening, and in any case his Dad Jimmie was impatient to move on towards Siddick where the winkles were even more abundant. Flogger Farrell continued his open-air Barrow-to-Carlisle railway-line love life for the next four years, until he was twenty, and despite his singular take on reproductive physiology never once got one of his lassies up the stick. In 1970 he settled down with a woman called Liz and they waited about five years before starting a family. Amazingly Flogger took Liz down by the same railway line for their sweetheart courting, but it was not of his stand-and-deliver teenage kind. They held hands and mooned and joked and lovebirded, and Liz, who was an Aspatria confectioner, looked the epitome of old-fashioned decency. By association, by benign contagion, Flogger himself seemed to become rather old-fashioned and decent as we swung into the early 1970s.

I had told Fingland's Casanova that I was going out with Sheila Starr, but that was all my artless eye, a flagrant bit of wishful thinking. I wanted to go out with her very much, but for some immovable reason could not pluck up the courage to ask. Instead I haunted her awkwardly and shyly in the school library where she was an appointed monitor for three out of five lunchtimes. Finally, one summer's day, just after our exams were out of the way, I blushed and walked up and asked her if she had anything about the life of Jonathan Swift. I had to write an essay on a famous writer for my General Studies, I explained, burning redder than the maroon history folder she was holding in her fine little, thin little hands. Sheila looked at me half-surprised, perhaps because of the blazing radiance from my earnest fizzog. She wandered off with sleekly moving hips and came back with a tattered copy of *A Tale of a Tub* and a 1948 fifty-page monograph on the great Irishman.

'*Tale of a Tub*?' she murmured, and grinned. To my surprise her vivid blue eyes seemed to turn faintly and curiously telly-shaped. I blinked away the hallucination but, as it transpired, she was actually thinking about children's television. 'It sounds like Hammy Hamster.'

I smiled very awkwardly. 'Tales of the Riverbank? Hamsters hurtling along in model jeeps? Rats wearing bosun's hats in little toy motorboats?'

'It sounds like you're an expert,' she challenged me, gently relishing her amusement.

At this point I dried up with sheer nerves. I had spoken only three sentences after hopelessly fancying her for the last twelve months. That evening, fretting obsessively about how I could take matters further, I watched yet another *Wednesday Play*. It was an adaptation of a Joe Orton stage play, *Entertaining Mr Sloane*, and the first of his singular oeuvre I had ever seen. It was very funny and very dark and very rude and oh so immaculately tasteless. It was such a riotous clout in the face to the ubiquitous stuffed shirts, to, for example, most of my Grammar School teachers and the more hidebound and unimaginative of my relatives. I decided there and then I wanted to be a playwright as impudent and hilarious as Joe Orton. Strangely enough, when a year later that playwright died a violent and horrible death at the hands of his lover, I knew nothing about it, or at any rate if anyone told me it failed to register entirely.

A week passed. Still agonising how I could invite her for an evening out, I sought some distraction with the notorious *Armchair Theatre* . . .

Whoever it was commissioned these outrageous TV plays obviously worked on the principle of the odder, the better, the madder, the richer, the more insolently plotless, the more artistically flawless. Tonight's immodestly absurdist extravaganza was no exception. In *Brains' Trust* epistemological terms (of categorical armchairs and categorical screens, that is) it was perfectly paradigmatic. It was about an extremely peculiar reclusive middle-aged bachelor who lived with his aged Mum in a minor northern industrial town. The bachelor, who was played by a youthful Freddie Jones, was too simple to hold down any ordinary job, but had a remarkable passion for all things to do with trains and railway paraphernalia. One assumed he was the oddball equivalent of an agoraphobic trainspotter, who, failing to have the exciting primary source to hand, had decided to bring it into his mother's cramped household. This is not to suggest anything as ordinary as he had provided himself with a gigantic train-set. No, because this was *Armchair Theatre* where the sky above was the imaginative limit, he had constructed a series of railway signals above the doors of all the rooms in his mother's house. So, for example, when Mum came through from the kitchen to the sitting room with the son's bedtime Horlicks and Kit-Kat, that put-upon old lady had to stop at the door before wide-eyed gormless Jones, dressed in a peaked British Rail signalman's hat, would raise his signal to allow her through.

So it madly teetered on, and the rest of the plot scarcely mattered. This impressively tensionless drama set me thinking about my approach to Sheila Starr. With regard to initiating a courtship, it was not the plot, the dogged linear sequence that mattered, it was the bold impulse, the lateral and liberating move that really counted. My conspicuous presenting problem was that I was far too pathetically inhibited with Sheila. I was too frightened to crack a wild joke or make an impulsive gesture as I stood there mutely gawping at her gentle glory. I stared at that lovely and blinding fair hair, and wanted to kiss it, taste it, eat it, and finally digest it. Instead of doing which I flushed and pretended that I wanted a treatise on Doctor bloody Swift. Whereas if I had been anything at all like outrageous Joe Orton or the author of this Freddie Jones play, I would have leant across her desk, touched her teasing chin, then planted a raw and massive kiss upon her startled but appreciative lips.

The following Friday I entered the library tense with the following all too tortuous strategy. This was what I intended to do. I would corner her at her monitor's desk and quickly ask her if she had watched that crazy little telly play about the witless railway fanatic. Then, whether or not she had, I would matter-of-fact inform her I was penning a TV play myself inspired by that same brand of charmed surrealist logic.

'You?' she would retort, in unconcealed amazement. I was after all a bumptious science student, scarcely a prime contender when it came to recondite part-time literary pursuits. My glamour index, my vicarious exoticism (he says he's 'putting together a script' for the bloody *television* . . .) would immediately rise to incalculable heights. 'You're writing a play for the *Armchair Theatre*?'

'Yes,' I'd reply to her in an affectless continental manner, like a pensive young Truffaut or an opaquely teasing Fellini. 'In fact, I've nearly finished it.'

My play, I would deftly explain, which was the regulation fifty minutes long, was set in a small town library, and was about an enigmatic young man, a young and altogether absolutely normal, yet tantalisingly enigmatic man, who was in love with a very captivating woman who worked in the library, but was far too shy to let her know it . . .

'Oh?' she would throw back in a strangely flaring voice, suddenly alive to that heartwarming impalpable frontierland where life and fiction lose their steely demarcations. Her eyes would appear both moistly glazed and tenderly expectant. 'Oh, are you?'

One day, I would continue, very weary of his painful inhibitions, and reflecting that she had never actually heard him speak a *single word* in her presence, only a meaningless grunt of shyness when she had stamped his books, he would walk up to her desk bearing the following remarkable message scrawled on a piece of card. I CANNOT SPEAK. THIS IS BECAUSE I AM PROFOUNDLY DUMB. PLEASE FOLLOW ME AROUND THESE

LIBRARY SHELVES. I WISH TO LAY BARE SOMETHING EXTREMELY IMPORTANT. Next, taking her shyly proffered and sympathetic arm, this bogus and reprehensible mute proceeds first to the science shelves, where, seizing a tome at random, he searches rapidly for a first-person pronoun. These items being rather thin on the ground in the *Intermediate Inorganic Chemistry* he'd impulsively grabbed, he could either point to the chemical symbol for iodine, or to the foreword where it would be absolutely inconceivable that the author, one P.C. Stitt, MA Oxon, former head of Chemistry at Shrewsbury Grammar School, would not finish his acknowledgements with the sentence. 'And finally I must thank the diligent and always good tempered labours of my wife Dilys whose typing and correction of this book not to mention endless provision of coffee and soothing reassurances at times of . . .' There was one indispensable single letter and personal pronoun buried in that lot, thank God.

Then to the cookery shelves, where again virtually any recipe book plucked at random would have in it, 'Some people hate black olives/capers/aubergines/anchovies/frogs' legs/goat's meat/strong spices/too many fresh green chilis, but I absolutely love the taste of them.' Having pointed to that last transitive and highly emphatic verb, the dumb bloke slyly continues to the biography shelves, where at least half the spines of those penned by film, radio and of course TV stars were titled something like *You Have to Laugh* or *You Must Be Joking!* or *You Orrible Little Blighter!* The restless mute chap would swiftly point to one of those strange and haunting second-person pronouns. In the biography titles it was always in the nominative case, but in the dumb man's eyes as he looked longingly at the glorious librarian, it was all too revealingly a fond and feverish accusative.

*I love you. I am very dumb, but I am dumb because I am dumb with the dumbness of love . . .*

Of course, neither of these little dramas had actually happened, neither the fictional one nor its strategic enactment.

It was all simply going on inside my head, on the circum-scribed green screen of my televisual fantasy. It had yet to take place, it was all at the intensive planning stage, yet I was determined to carry it through, even if it ludicrously failed and even if I was to die of public shame . . .

I had just got as far as approaching her desk, catching her eye and clearing my throat to say, 'Did you watch . . . ?' when the librarian himself came bustling down towards us.

'Miss Asterisk, Miss Asterisk,' he greeted her whimsically, and he cleared his forty-Senior-Service-a-day larynx.

There was no full-time librarian of course, it was a middle-aged English teacher called Sockett whose nicknames varied from Suck It to Soft Shit to . . . too tedious to recount the thousand obscene variations. He was a breezy, uneasily humorous man who perhaps because of his thousand hid-eous nicknames could turn sarcastic and even venomous for no apparent reason and at the drop of a hat. There was damn all chance I was going to tell his trusted monitor the fairytale plot of my fictive television play while he was lurking there.

'Rightio,' he gasped, and patted her kindly on her thin little shoulder.

Sockett pulled up a chair and commenced a ponderous monologue concerning library index cards. The head of English, Fanny Bigrigg, had recently complained about vast numbers of them either being illegible, out of alphabetical sequence, or without any accurate Dewey category. Previous monitors, not you, Miss Asterisk!, Soft Shit stressed, had been blasé to the point of library sabotage. Reaching blearily into his briefcase, he pulled out about a thousand of the dog-eared items, stacked in some twenty piles all secured by elastic bands. They were all laboriously handwritten and some of the ink looked definitely pre-war. He and Sheila sighed as they rolled up their sleeves and began putting them in painstaking alphabetical order. Suck It remarked that it would take them at least the next three lunchtimes to finish doing this dreary but imperative task.

'Bloody hell,' I groaned, as I buried myself behind the fiction shelves and stared uncomprehending at an ugly wartime copy of *Quo Vadis?*

Mad with frustration, that night I cauterised my aching heart by watching a repeat series of *Steptoe and Son*. At the risk of bathos and unflattering as it sounds, the TV served its remedial purpose. By some benign homeopathic principle, I found myself forgetting myself to the point of smiling and frowning in tandem. Lovelorn and self-obsessed as I was, I was eventually laughing my head off. My mother and father also cackled and wept with mirth, despite the strong swear words and the acidic and blasphemous dialogue. Here was a Sitcom, a Comedy of Situation, which aggressively broke every hidebound classical rule. It was vicious, mordant, tragic, full of gallows' humour, as dry and subversive as the grave itself. Like the pallid *Sykes* and the anaemic *Hugh and I*, it had its metropolitan bachelor, but this stark proletarian example wore no turtleneck pullover and lived in no hygienic semi. This one was a dirty, thirty-nine-year-old rag-and-bone man from the grubbiest bit of the East End. Steptoe Junior was also painfully sex-starved and forever desperately chasing after hard-nosed women, especially if they had foot-thick make-up, skirts halfway up their sprawling backsides, and a mouth as sharp as an asp's.

Unlike Sykes and Harry Worth, this bachelor had no truck with jovial one-liners, because his love life was authentically tragic rather than moderately sad. This was not Barbara Pym, nor Woody Allen, so much as East End Dostoiebloodyevsky. Not only did Harold Steptoe have a dismally demeaning job with a horse and cart, but he had a dependent widowed father who would not let him go. The father was a monstrously embarrassing septuagenarian who wore his battered black trilby in the bath, and once dined in the same bath on egg, chips and pickled onions. When he dropped his pickles in the dirty water, he speared them with his pickle fork and gobbled them regardless. The father was tender and vicious by turn, regularly mocking his son for his taste in women and jeering at his pathetic fascination with 'ugly birds'. The bachelor would try and overcome his copious humiliations by bamboozling these ugly birds with elevated cultural references (Picasso, Chablis, Renghwa etc) which made his ultimate and inevitable rejection all the more unbearable.

According to our boozy old French teacher, Stott, Gustave Flaubert claimed that Emma Bovary was simply Gustave Flaubert. By sympathetic analogy and with regard to Sheila Starr, TV's Harold Steptoe was just like me, sixteen-year-old Roe Murphy. True, I had no shameful family, no skeletal foul-mouthed dotard of a father, but I did have the overwhelming embarrassment of myself. Once this cathartic Beckettian 'comedy' had finished, I felt myself purged and relieved, but I was still no nearer jumping the abyss of my paralysing adolescent shyness. I therefore did what I always did and turned to the TV screen for some pragmatic prophetic assistance. I waited with great impatience for the next *Armchair Theatre*, hoping like some brainless adherent of the divinatory arts, that it would give me a hint of what to do next . . .

The next *A.T.* was certainly inspirational, although profoundly confusing in its subtlest implications, as no doubt any significant drama ought to be. Its message was clairvoyantly apposite to my own situation, albeit the remedy it proposed was so radical and so flagrant that it would probably have had me kicked out of school as well as polite West Cumbrian society for the next thirty years . . .

This drama, like the one last week, had an odd and, though the terminology did not exist in 1966, dysfunctional bachelor as its principal character. In this case he was a very quiet, virtually mute clerical worker in his colourless midfifties. The setting was a cramped insurance office in central London, and the clerk, *pace* Nikolai Gogol, spent his time sorting through tedious files and papers before passing on what he'd vetted to his superior. Whenever a sheaf of documents had been approved and returned by this pompous little office senior, our timid, colourless hero would take his rubber stamp and apply to it the message SEEN AND APPROVED.

Cut to the eyepopping new clerical assistant, a garrulous, arch and provocative young woman in her early twenties. She has a strong East London accent and she twitches her agile, teasing body as she slips between filing cabinets, the manager's office, and the cubby-hole where the tea is made. Her young male colleagues ogle her boldly, and make cheerfully brazen remarks, whereupon she flutters and snortingly giggles. Our hero also eyes her longingly, but very furtively and timidly, and of course completely hopelessly. The austere work atmosphere might be Dickensian or Gogolian, but the unbridled sexual obsession of these leering youths is more like H.G. Wells or Émile Zola. Suffice to say the dramatic situation is timeless and universal, but none the less painful for that. The situation of the lonely silent clerk even has complex sociological affinities with the tragedy of Harold Steptoe. One might be a rag-and-bone man and the other a besuited filing clerk, but both of them, unlike say ice-blue Flogger Farrell, are very desperate for their egg. Every day our lonely hero watches the flirtatious short-skirted beauty out of the corner of his eye, then averts his gaze and sadly broods. Every night in his unappetising Dollis Hill bedsit he goes so far as to tragically despair (that hopeless old *Armchair Theatre* filing clerk, one glassy teenage viewer from the distant provinces assents, *c'est peut-être moi*) . . .

One day, utterly overwhelmed by the crude electricity of this vibrant young tease, our hero can take no more. He has been watching her from his sly perspective for the last six months, and predictably enough she barely knows of his existence. He is fifty-five, grey, balding, bespectacled, entirely and unenviably anonymous. He is a solitary bachelor who like the fictional Uriah Heep, and countless flesh-and-blood equivalents, still has desires, passions, wills, ambitions, dreams. At the moment, the sinuous Swinging Sixties emblem is bent over a filing cabinet, moving her hips ever so restlessly for the delectation of a smirking junior clerk. Our solitary hero stares at those hallucinatorily twitching haunches and licks his very dry lips. Until with much loud ado ('Ooh, blimey, I don't seem to be able to find that flippin dockyment what I'm arfter, no matter where I goes and looks!'), the spry lass decides to stoop and rummage in the bottom-most draw of the filing cabinet. In doing so her skimpy skirt rides up, and her impossibly luscious and agonisingly succulent behind is thrust to the fore, rather like an ice lolly proffered to a man dying of thirst and inanition in the Gobi desert. Cut to the fish-faced junior clerk whose eyes are popping exophthalmically and whose lewd *sotto voce* endearments elicit a hearty titter from the bending girl. Meanwhile our maddened hero (who is in fact a hallucinating wanderer in his own profoundly waterless metaphysical desert) can simply no longer restrain himself.

He rises from his chair as he does perhaps a dozen times a day. He picks up his rubber stamp, the one that he has been wielding so remorselessly for the last thirty-five years. For the first time since he started here in 1931, he does not move across in a straight line to his superior, because today, uniquely, he is carrying neither files nor documents, nothing in fact but his trusty stamp. Instead he moves determinedly in the direction of the young giggler whose confrontational and preposterous bottom is still raised up like a ritual urn or a votive object. Our timid loner does not pause to pinch or spank it, but trancewise and reverently he raises up minutely the hem of her skirt. The sex-mad cod-faced junior clerk who has watched all these breathtaking preliminaries gasps out loud in horror. In a trice, before anyone can stop him, our alarming hero whisks up the pencil skirt to expose her drawers, and in another, applies his doughty rubber stamp across her snow-white and frilly backside.

The message he leaves in bold red ink is as plain as day and twice as blinding.

SEEN AND APPROVED, it declares . . .

The rest of the plot was strenuously beside the point, though it did include a canny act of blackmail by the girl's weaselly mother, as she demanded financial compensation for the assault on her daughter. Yet being the armchair component of the programme title, I felt there must be some telepathic message intended specifically for me, not least because library stamps and office stamps seemed to come out of the same imaginative mould. Was I really supposed to stamp *10th July 1966* on Sheila Starr's blameless school drawers as an act of communicatory mime, and if I did so, what exactly was it supposed to signify? That like some urgently requested volume, she had to be returned to the library by that specific date? But into whose care exactly? To mine? Or to Sockett's? Or was it just her newly franked underwear, a bawdily intimate love-token, had to be returned to me post-haste by the due date inst.? These engrossing daydream scenarios might have orchestrated a saucy private fantasy as conceived by two louche and adult lovers, but in the impossibly banal confines of a school library? I felt constrained and ridiculous enough myself, without embarrassing Sheila by this travesty of a Noh theatre dumb show.

This dumb motif persisted. On the few occasions I approached Sheila Starr I smiled but did not speak, and if I was rash enough to try, I found that my smile would subtly petrify and that in turn would freeze my lifeless voice box. I felt myself to be very anachronistic, very nineteenth century, and also very foreign. In some ways I behaved like a neurasthenic Stendhalian recluse or a blushing egotist out of Honoré de Balzac. But this was arch-mundane Workington, Cumberland, not Cività Vecchia, Italy, and it was 1966, and I had no right at all to be such an overwrought romantic. The following week Sheila was off school sick, and the week after that there was bustling, burbling Sockett doing much end of term to-ing and fro-ing. He was turfing out library stock so decrepit and dull that not even offering it free to any famished Workington autodidacts could find any willing takers. I poked around listessly in his cardboard box, wondering if it might elicit any friendly comment from Sheila sat close by. Fifty-page monographs on Pope and Richard Hooker, next to a faded copy of *Ecclesiastical Polity* by the latter. A mould-flecked *Yearbook of St Bees School, Cumberland 1938*. A virgin, absolutely untouched copy of *A History of the Cooperative Retail Trade in Barrow and Millom*, complete with pictures of the five bearded and scowling drapery managers at Askam-in-Furness Sub-Coop between 1912 and 1938.

I turned up at her desk in blushing desperation on the very last lunch hour of term. If I didn't spit it out today, there were six weeks' summer vacation and anything could happen during those. My brain raced overtime as I played with my jealous fantasies. She might holiday abroad and meet a handsome flamenco player in Madrid, the strumming and strutting Madrileno equivalent of Fingland Flogger. On the other hand if she stayed at home, she might meet another teacher's pampered offspring (her mother was a junior head) courtesy of the genteel West Cumbrian pedagogic network. Classic epicentres including the exclusive yachting club at Bass Lake, the dashing golf club at Workington and the vertiginous flying club at Carlisle Airport. My own Dad (shades of humiliating Albert Steptoe after all) made dog food in a Maryport factory, which explains why some of my nicknames were Chum, Chappie, Bonus and Bounce Murphy. I had no gleaming Lambretta like a spoiled teacher's son might have, nor could I expect a new Ford Cortina for my seventeenth birthday. All I had to boast of was the TV play I hadn't written and a huge collection of books and records, most of which I imagined Sheila Starr might well scowl at. Stan Getz and Hermann Hesse, Charles Lloyd and Colette, Claude Debussy and Fyodor Dostoievsky . . .

Inspired by that extraordinary SEEN AND APPROVED motif, I turned up in the library with my slyly concealed rubber stamp. I held it under my blazer as if I were nursing a weak heart or shielding a sick canary. Already at sixteen I was a fervent republican, not to say vehemently rigid Marxist, yet the stamp I held inside my school blazer was called a *John Bull* stamp. This was because it was out of a John Bull printing set, and I had located it with some difficulty in our attic where my mother must have shoved it somewhere around 1961. Once, that is, it was obvious I was unlikely ever to decorate my books again with *Roe Murphy, Solway House, Fingland, Cumberland, Britain, Europe, World, Mars, Space, Infinity, Cosmic Hole . . .*

Sheila Starr was sat at her lonely desk and it was a blazing July noon. The sunlight was streaming through the window onto her frowning hesitant eyes. It was also cascading across the fairness and softness of her long and flouncing hair. She was squinting, but it was a vulnerable and therefore a beautiful squint. She was busy glueing and mending the damaged cover of a William book, *Just William's Luck*, I could read inverted from where I stood and sweated.

'Just Murphy's Luck?' I mused soundlessly, then stopped dead.

'Hallo,' I gasped, turning as red as a jar of toxic strength chilli peppers.

She smiled at me through her blinking, pensive gaze and for once, and to my amazement, I broke all the rules and squinted back at her. It was a naively flirtatious imitation of her grimacing and gurning . . .

'You watch it,' she snorted sharply. 'You've a bloody nerve to imitate me pulling a face.'

I was still tongue-tied. But this time it was with neither inhibition nor anguish. I was silent, but for once it was a feeling of poise, of being there at the time and the moment, at the one and only victorious turning point. I might be completely dumb, but unless I was also completely blind, she was wrinkling her nose and pretending indignation to signify her own definite attraction. I therefore felt not even a trace of embarrassment as I whipped out my gleaming John Bull stamp, and prepared to slap it down regardless . . .

'Roe,' she murmured in a strangely scratchy voice, putting her hand over her eyes so she could see me uncensored, unedited, in the flesh, and in the raw.

'What?' I said, immediately anxious that the sudden absence of solar glare might cause her to reconsider.

'Roe?' she said again.

'What?' I sighed.

She blurted, 'Will you go out –?' She halted dramatically and seemed to be listening to some indecipherable echoes. 'I mean . . .'

'What?' I hissed at her. 'What was that?'

Then, as if it had a determined will of its own, my John Bull stamp went hurtling helplessly on in its elliptical trajectory. It had been specially double-primed with bright red ink to indicate the colour of my heart's blood. It whapped down like a singing, searing bullet on the scrappy bit of paper at the front of the scratched old desk. The streaked crimson message was not as pristine clear as I'd have liked, although visible enough to affect the naked eye.

*I'm completely mad, crazy, insane about you. Please come to the Oy-Kwan with me as soon as possible. Roe.*

The Oy bloody Kwan? She stared astonished at me and my lunatic stamping, at my non-librarian's blasé ignorance of job demarcations. She tried to see what it was this pathetic toy stamp had said. Unable to read the message upside down, she had to come shuffling round to inspect it. Her skirt backside touched my leg and I wanted to emit a loud cheer to toast the sheer electrostatic ecstasy. She picked up the flimsy bit of paper and I watched her bare arms in the sunlight. The fine downy hairs on her skin looked like a young infant's, even like a baby's. She scrutinised my unencrypted code, nodding matter-of-fact, and apparently uncritically. Finally she murmured, 'That's alright then. I ask you and you ask me, and with only a second's gap between us. Absolutely perfect timing. 'Swiftly face on, she examined me a shade too intently. 'But I notice you don't put a name on it?'

I blushed the finest John Bull puce. 'You what?'

'You've got your own name at the end, but not my name at the front. Do you use your red stamp for hundreds of women?'

I blinked. 'I –'

The double doors were flung open as if by a charging rhino, and Sockett's tarry tremolo came whinnying in our direction.

'Miss Asterisk! *Ola, buenas dias!* Miss Asterisk!'

The place was almost empty so that Sockett's shoes resounded with a museum attendant's clatter, as he made his way towards his favourite student. Meanwhile Sheila confided that although she was crazy about Chinese food she preferred the Lin-Fat next to the Hippodrome rather than the Oy-Kwan halfway down Finkle Street.

# 6

*High Mallstown, North Cumbria, 14th November 2001.*
*Lunchtime satellite viewing and listening.*

## 214

A skinny young man in his early twenties is sporting a brand-new and trim, though not particularly stylish, leather jacket. He has short, very neat hair, parted smoothly to the left in a way that would not have offended in the late Fifties or early Sixties. He also has an oddly amorphous and intriguingly elderly face. One imagines him looking older in significant ways than his own father, or rather that in the company of his father he might look like his father's father. He is sat on a leather chair in a do-it-yourself automated studio, rather as in one of those home-made videos as manufactured for community TV, and once, very briefly, the province of the franchised and socially-conscious BBC2. The young man all on his own here is apeing the debonair approach, but might just be stiffly self-conscious in this premium hotline satellite scenario. Self-evidently there are no affable, jesting cameramen or other paid technicians, much less helpful TV interviewers, in this niche-market, profit-conscious twenty-first-century digital studio.

   He is facing the invisible viewers as if being interviewed for a job, the job being that of showing us his remarkably candid humanity and incidentally asserting that we and he are of the same unspoken assumptions.

*Young Man* (*a strong Birmingham accent*): Mname's Kevin, my mates call me Kev, sometimes Kevo, and I'm twenty-two years old. I'm a manager in a Brummie shopping complex with four folk under me, but having said that I'm not stuck up at all. My hobbies are . . . sport, playing football and snooker, and going out clubbing and dossing at weekends, and usually five nights during the week. I think I'm really versatile and adaptable, because I like both going out and staying in. If I'm not somewhere outside the house, you'll usually find me inside it. I think, in fact I'm sure, I'm pretty good-looking. I get Costner thrown at me now and again cos I'm called Kev. I've been told by lots of people I'm as good looking as Costner, probably better looking. My favourite food's Chinese at weekends with chips not rice. But during the week mostly beef pie and chips not rice (you'd never have a dry thing like rice with a thing like steak pie when all's said and done). I love cheese, I'm fanatical about it, and my Mum sometimes makes me cheesy splosh like vegetable lausanne and Greek mussorgsky with the slimy purple things inside. I like that even though it's foreign, but I'm not strange or weird or anything. As a matter of fact I hate everywhere there is abroad apart from Higher Napper . . .

I'd like a very sexy and very attractive woman between eighteen and twenty-four who's (*Suddenly an improbably catastrophic thing happens to the fairly good-looking Brummie Costner man. The economy-standard studio sonics abruptly decide to snarl up and distort the rest of his speech, his public appeal for love, though luckily not entirely*) . . . midden height, fifootfo, fifootfi, fifootsex, or therebartz, fifootsefn at the arse-side, or there are bats, give or take an inch, pteet, tractif, nice figure, blonde, guff senza humore. I have a guff senza humore, so she needs to have one as well. She has to like partying, pups, gonads and staining during the week, and at the weekends. She must have a senseless human and like doing the things that I like to tuff (*fade as Kevin's dating hotline number at £2.50 per minute 0873–999999 appears in foot-high flashing numerals).*

## 555

A documentary round-up of a recent hotspot for a change alights on somnolent and hypercivilised England, rather than say Serbia, Macedonia or Kosovo. Even more surprisingly, it chooses the north of the country. This is, the commentator affirms, the first time ever Eurodoc has ever done anything about the north of Britain. Of course it is a tragedy – what else? – that has brought this obscure area to the attention of the rest of Europe. The recent tragedy which has made both it and the rest of the UK something of an extraordinary pariah when it comes to vital international exports.

In Cumbria and Northumbria they are still mopping up after the Foot and Mouth epidemic, the worst Europe has ever known. Aerial footage, July 2001, of the rows of massive disposal trenches at the disused Great Orton airfield, North Cumbria. The voice-over suggests that the sight of countless bovine corpses being flung in and limed over, seems incongruously reminiscent of the remnants being lifted and flung at Bergen-Belsen. This stark comparison does not strike me, a North Cumbrian, as glib or far-fetched. The inert and fast decaying cows, with their striking lack of muscular resistance, have that same poignant death-camp innocence, that same eloquent absence of culpability. As with the helpless camp victims, it is seemingly a contingent and evil process entirely beyond all possible evasion.

All the experts, the commentator explains, agree that Foot and Mouth has the same degree of toxic virulence as the ebola virus or lassa fever. For example one stray minute fleck of infected cow dung on any North Cumbrian farmer's wellington boot is reckoned enough to keep it all nightmarishly proliferating. Hence, even at this stage, the insistent

Cumbrian and Northumbrian emphasis on what the government organisation DEFRA (née MAFF) calls 'bio-security'.

Bio-security?, I repeated to myself, from my own remote place in the recent heartland of the plague. Most conspicuously there were those daunting checkpoint mats on our country highways, the giant absorbent rugs ramped and soaked with a careful cocktail of disinfectants. It was reckoned they were of little substantive effect but that they were very good for the county's morale, a highly significant placebo visual aid. Bio-security also meant all footpaths and bridlepaths were closed to stop the spread between farms and walkers, farms and riders, farms and carefree townies exercising their restless dogs. It included the path up to High Mallstown, a farmhouse which is not a working farm but is where I happen to live. At every farm gate there are still those troughs of disinfectant just as there are still those little bio-mats at every public venue: schools, colleges, village halls, churches, supermarkets, farm shops. All of our North Cumbrian footpaths are still closed nine months on, and will not be reopened, if at all, until 2002.

Interview with a wiry, grey-haired middle-aged man who is weeping uncontrollably at certain points in his lengthy reminiscence. It is a North Cumbrian smallholder from a few miles outside of Longtown. I certainly know him by sight but could not have told you his name. I am incidentally baffled to think of a Eurodoc satellite camera team turning up on those beautiful, extravagantly remote lanes towards Easton, Catlowdy and Penton. He is called Thomas Roe and his profitable day job is as a plasterer, his smallhold farming being a glorified hobby, nothing more. It barely pays for itself, much less supports him and his wife who is a mini-market manager down in Carlisle. Their tragedy happened during April 2001, around Eastertime, when the F and M outbreaks were at their height. The number of new cases was hurtling to an apex, assumed, using 1967 epidemic statistics, to be quite impossible. Thomas Roe's hobby was breeding

Pedigree Jerseys, and he had painstakingly accumulated a prize accredited herd, modestly nailing a plaque on his gable-end to announce as much. He had given all twenty-five of his Jerseys individual names, Florrie, Janet, Sadie etc. Roe loved T-bone steaks and shin beef as much as the next man, but he still called these pedigree cows 'his girls'. He always talked to them like so many pet dogs when he went in to do his milking.

The day F and M was suspected he was plastering at Burgh-by-Sands twenty miles away, and his wife, who had a day off, was required to ring up the vet's and notify MAFF. Over the next two days Roe had to sacrifice his plastering and get someone else to take the five-hundred-pound job. Once the symptoms were provisionally confirmed, and given that there were six infected farms in a two-mile radius, there was no scope for hanging fire. The day his wife rang him at Burgh, there were forty new cases nationally, almost all of them North Cumbrian. Hence MAFF could barely spare the lone vet who drove up the fifteen miles. She was a young woman of about twenty-two and she was perhaps five feet tall. She could hardly manage a labrador on her own much less a Jersey cow. Likewise MAFF could only afford to despatch a single slaughterer. Roe therefore had no choice in the matter. He had to be there to help butcher his young girls . . .

Thomas had to: a) chase and round up one or two of his more skittish girls, b) tether them all in their stalls, c) hold his prize lassies as you would a child terrified of the dentist while the slaughterman did his job. Sheep, not that Roe had any, were killed with a captive bolt fired by a contraption like a massive spud gun. Being gentle and biddable they were slaughtered front ways on. Very young lambs were given veterinary injections, rather like old dogs being put to sleep. Pigs, not that Roe possessed any pigs, had their squealing throats slit. Cattle being more powerful and dangerous animals were done in the back of the neck. They were also pithed through the head and the spinal cord, because the hazards of CJD, BSE and other patho-acronyms had additionally to be borne in mind . . .

Roe knew that the slaughterman and the vet were on their way and would be here in about half a hour. So what did he decide to do? First of all he got them all comfortably and tenderly settled in their stalls. Roe tethered them and murmured to them like a doting, gentle father. Then he gave them all a good feed, one last and lingering memorial meal. Roe gave them a loving feed and he bedded them comfortably down. He was a quietly perfect father to these harmless, very moon-eyed, very beautiful young cows of his.

When the slaughterman arrived it was as if it was for Thomas's personal execution. Tom felt the hellish dread and the apocalyptic gravity of it all. There was the scent of approaching damnation, though there was also the torturing inkling of grace and pity and some deliverance at the far end of something else. The freelance killer was from the West Country, from mid-Somerset he confided, he had come up where the money was to be made. He was about thirty and bog-eyed and bloodshot from the sheer number of hours spent slaughtering. But he knew they were Roe's pets and he was as decent as anyone could be in the heartless circumstances. He told him he would do it quickly and professionally, and that if Thomas Roe held them all while he did it, it would help them, him and Thomas Roe.

There is hell and there is a lower hell and there is a lower hell after that. There were in this case twenty-five infernal rungs down to the very lowest pit. To hold just one child while it's being petted and tricked and slain is sin enough. The bolt went through Roe's heart and it skewered him so that his mouth tore open and he felt his teeth fly up into his skull. The Somerset man didn't see that but he knew it in his bones. Then came the pithing of the skull and the spinal cord. To go through that once would kill any herdsman. To know it twice, three times, four times, five times . . . fifteen times . . . twenty-three and bawl, twenty-four and roar, twenty-five and howl. A terrible shrieking, a molten streaming of blood, one butchered animal's mighty convulsion. The twenty-fifth shriek, the twenty-five bloods, the twenty-five slidings like a folding baby's pushchair into those gore-spattered stalls. As with the business of giving birth, they never tell you how much blood is to be seen, the sheer and vivid amount of life's unreplaceable substance. Roe sobbed and convulsed each time, and with each murder he felt that there was simply no good anywhere at all in the world, past or present, there was only this evil wickedness. Only an infinite power of infinite wickedness would countenance the necessary murder of twenty-five moon-eyed and harmless young things.

That was all of seven months ago. Aside from the spectacle of the childrens' corpses lying piled up in the yard for a week, there was also that Old Testament ambience of pestilence and villainous stench. After that came the real aftermath, the one that wouldn't go away. He and his wife Jan had endless nightmares of the killings of their twenty-five doe-eyed bairns. Usually at dawn, between four and five a.m., they came upon them thick and fast. The Roe couple stuck it for a month until they could take those nightmares no more. The dreams of cows weeping like humans in grinning anguish, humans frozen like animals in a brute's terror, their Easton smallholding wired with explosives by a bolt-wielding madman, the old farmhouse being set on fire by a government body called MAD not MAFF, their cows and their calves being immolated live.

They stuck all this atrocious dreaming, until it occurred to them with lightning clarity that the best thing to do was *just to get out of bed*. From then on they rose every day at 3.45, like reclusive monks or the inhabitants of a Soviet Gulag. As Roe told the Eurodoc camera, if you aren't in your bed you can't have any nightmares. You can have the traumatic stress palaver, the sobbing, shaking and collapsing on the floor like a crumpled shirt. You can have all of that in double measure. But at least you are awake with it all, and nothing is worse, can ever be worse, than the unstoppable terror of a person who is trapped in his terrible dreams.


## 636 *(Audio channel)*

Psalm 145

*The eyes of all wait upon thee and thou givest them their meat in due season.*
  *The Lord is righteous in all his ways and holy in all his works.*


## 187

A countrified young Irishwoman is kneeling by a leaping coal fire. She is dressed in a fine shamrock green sweater and a shapely linen skirt, and has such an aura of wholesomeness and touching decency about her that one searches for some anthropological explanation. Why do so many Southern Irish women look quite so rock-solid damn decent? Is it to do with the famous national religiosity, the defiant antithesis of the Celtic tigerish verve, or is it that the old-fashioned Irish market towns are such ferocious emblems of smallness and unshakeable simplicity?

So to sum up, she informs us, and just to give you folks a convenient reprise, there is the smashing handcrafted bodhran made in Clifden, Connemara at only £49.95. Photographic still of the bodhran, and yes indeed it does look a very graceful, lovingly crafted blemishless Galway artefact. Her rapt English viewer, Roe Murphy, must be the only person, the last man in the western world, who does not possess a credit card, or he might well have done her bidding and bought one over the Hiberno-hotline and battered away tunelessly for the next twenty years. There is also, she continues with the most lustrous colleen-bawn smile and the loveliest flounce of her – I would guess – Munster brown locks, for only £25.95, this splendid little ceramic of the Custodian of the Blarney Stone. Isn't your man a little cute wee feller and all, I could sit him up on my knee, folks, and pet him like a wee baby no bother? I think now the fellers who made him down in the Dingle Peninsula in the pottery workshop, they did him straight from the heart, don't you? We're talking about true tender craftsmanship, not crude tourist tat, folks, aren't we? Lastly, as our pride-of-place finale item, and this is made down in County Carlow, this super scale-model music box of Murphy's Owld Pub with the motif *Powers Is Powerfully Good* inscribed there, I think I might go and buy that for my own Da as it's only £33.95 and you'd pay that for two bottles of Irish and it'd do him a whole lot more good I'm thinking . . .

There, she concludes, with another graceful smile, done and dusted, folks, and thanks for tuning in to Weekday Shamrock Shop Window. Bye bye for now, do take care, and mind you all keep the faith. More calxing of Roe Murphy's dopey, definitely menopausal heart. The fact that he has the same name as the scale-model pub makes him feel some ownership by sentimental proxy of that lovely person on the television. He bends forward a little in his armchair and actually touches the telly screen to see if he can somehow feel that lustrous young Munster lass's hair. There are of course a thousand ways of uttering the expression 'done and dusted', from the utterance of the Cockney cleaner to the Wiltshire farmer to the Cumbrian teacher to this beautiful thirty-year-old Gael, but there is only one mouth among them which expresses any poetry, and without a jot of brainless cliché. *Tha nighean bhreagha*, they would have muttered admiringly in an Outer Hebridean pub, the kind where he used to go on his summer holidays, and it ought to be something very close though with a different, harder pronunciation in the Munster Gaeltacht.

'How much does she cost?' I addressed the screen as the credits finished and with it the colleen bawn vanished for another whole week.

The television looked at me quizzically. You would assume, etymologically speaking, that a telly might be telepathic, but you'd be wrong.

'What the hell do you mean?' it said.

'Eimear O'Herlihy. What a name she has. It's like a pure little poem, like the finest verse. Such a beautiful assonance. What a pity I wasn't called Joseph Aloysius O'Herlihy. To borrow her expression, she was made by a craftsman straight from the heart. Eimear wants me to buy her Galway bodhran, her Murphy's music box, her Blarney Stone Custodian from Dingle Dell for £49.95, £33.95 and £25.95 respectively. But I don't want any of them. I just want to buy her. I want to buy Eimear O'Herlihy.'

## 212

An American woman in her fetching early forties, unarguably attractive, fair, limpid-eyed, tender-skinned, full of seeming poise, is plastering her face with a jar of cosmetic cream. She tells us that she is called Marsie Kantara and, more threateningly, and as if quoting an unassailable authority, that her skin is her life. The voice-over is evidently her voice, and the face cream it turns out is either made by her to a unique recipe in a backroom retort, or perhaps Ms Kantara owns a small factory where the exclusive and highly secret composition is concocted.

Nearly a million women worldwide, Marsie announces with a kind of stern Charlton Heston gravity, are in my No Cares Skin Club. As well as a very gentle but very deep cleansing agent, my No Cares Cream contains a UHV Catabolic Enzyme Complex, and in addition, and uniquely, a

Mild Exfoliating Depilatory Scrub. She rubs in more of her NCC with its UCEC and its MEDS, and explains that it fights the insidious and demoralising onset of crows' feet, fine lines, and premature wrinkles for ladies in their late thirties and beyond. It should properly be going at £150, but instead the Health Channel British viewers are being offered it at half-price for a strictly one month period. For £75 they are given a ninety-day bottom-of-the-jar guarantee. At which striking declaration I, the viewer, find myself furrowing my brow in perplexity. I, fifty-plus Murphy, who have copious and riotous crows' feet, wrinkles and coarse as well as standard as well as fine lines on my querulous face, I have no idea what the hell she can possibly mean by a bottom-of-the-jar guarantee.

Cut to a virtually identical replica of Ms Kantara who if not her sister must be her exfoliated clone. She tells us that she is called Boona (or is it Bhuna or Booner or Bewna or Burner?) P. Zimbalist. Now Zimbalist as far as I know is a Jewish name, so perhaps her Christian name is actually Beulah? This alluring Marsie-twin lady, dressed in strident motorcycle leathers of haunting tightness and voluptuous sleekness, has just lifted her sinuous slim backside off a beautiful 900cc Kawasaki. The bike appears to be parked in one of John Steinbeck's Californian orange groves and behind her is a splendid white and gleaming Monterey villa. The heat and the scent of the orange trees are palpable, and I can certainly smell citrus from where I am sitting in freezing bloody North Cumbria. That Kawasaki engine is so wide one would need to be a bow-legged old Bewcastle farmer to straddle it, so how on earth in those taut leathers has Beulah/Bhuna managed to spread her modest little thighs? Perhaps she is a Hatha Yoga adept, or perhaps those leathers are really made out of black tissue paper, Monterey being so perennially hot and sunny she is hardly likely to shiver.

Beulah pats her trusty Kawasaki which is a vivid crimson and as gleaming as a new pin.

'OK. I left my boyfriend's house here two weeks ago on the back of this Kawasaki. Since then I have spent the best part of that period riding all over Southern California. You can imagine the facial wind resistance and the potential for damaging dermal friction involved in that journey, I guess. But all I did, ladies, before I set off was put on my NCC, my No Cares Cream. I rubbed it on at the start of every day, and now *voilà*. Here I am, and I'm not boasting, but I reckon my skin looks fine for all to see. I call that the KERPOW, the Kawasaki Extraordinary Rite of Passage Ordeal Winner, as far as my precious skin is concerned. If anyone out there can think of a more rigrus and stringent test I promise that I will eat my –'

## 210

A married couple in their early fifties both with crows' feet, fine lines, wrinkles, epidermal friction and many other signs of wear and tear. They could only be English and (*pace* Eimear O'Herlihy and her ingrained Munster moral decency) their very innocuous ordinariness could only be English Home Counties. They tell us they are from Marlow in Bucks. He wears a tidy cream tee-shirt with radial brown stripings and works as a factory fitter, and she has a purple blouse and matching skirt and works as a dinner supervisor in a local junior school. They have only one child who is fourteen and he is called Kevin and he is dead . . .

Nobody, says James Brown the fitter, in an extremely sober and unwavering voice, no one who hasn't experienced it can understand the reality of the death of a child. The photograph of Kevin who was fourteen when he died six months ago sits above James's right shoulder, as if the exhausted father is somehow mysteriously supporting him or perhaps trying to elevate and reanimate his son. The photograph shows a bright-eyed good-looking lad with longish curly hair and a single silver ring in his left ear. Despite that glittering little earring, he looks like a wholesome and very ordinary schoolboy.

Nobody, agrees Katherine Brown the school supervisor, can really know what it's like. It's like an ugly, gaping hole down in the depths of your insides that can't be botched or filled. If a road has a hole in it, you can fill it with mortar or rubble, but there seems to be no bereavement equivalent of mortar. It's like a wound or a mutilation that can't be covered over with any dressing or bandage. At times, she says, quite calmly matter-of-fact, you can be bent double with it, like some excruciating pain, like severe arthritis. You can get gold injections for that, I believe, but no amount of gold or silver is any good for this kind of thing.

Kevin Brown died of Marlow backstreet solvent abuse. He died of sniffing butane which is the stuff of happy campers, sausage sizzles, church outings, Mike Leigh's comic outdoor play called *Nuts in May*. It is also of course cheap lighter fuel, plastic bags, drab corner shops, harassed or indifferent proprietors, and is as rampant in Workington or Woking as it is in Glasgow or Cardiff. The tissue destruction, the lung and bronchial damage, the laid-waste brain cells, the cheapest method of going mad or dicing with an early death if you are a reckless and a fearless young kid.

'We simply didn't know,' James Brown continues with a resonant emphasis. 'We had no idea. That turns the knife in the raw wound, of course. He'd been doing it for about a month, we learnt there at the coroner's inquest. It's the terrible speed of it all that confounds us. Just a year ago he was crazy about birdwatching with his uncle. Twelve months ago he could get dizzy and excited about seeing a heron in a pond or if he had watched a buzzard fighting with a crow. They went on a two-day trip, the pair of them, to the Scottish Borders to look for hawfinches, and then down to Kershope Forest in Cumbria just to see some crossbills. He could tell you a blinking serin from a siskin, where I can't tell a starling from a bloody thrush.

'A fortnight before he died, he told me he didn't really want to do anything but what he called "doss about" in the mall. His uncle was a bit hurt, but he shrugged it off and said, change, what can you do about it, change is always the thing at his age, isn't it? I didn't like that expression "doss about", it made me uneasy, but at fourteen years old I could hardly lay down the law. Now of course I wish I had, and to hell with it. I wish I'd grounded him and locked him up in his bedroom out of harm's way like a mental case. Because at least then he would still be alive, even if he hated my guts . . .'

As her husband breaks down, Katherine Brown looks at one of Kevin's pop posters and says, 'You simply can't go by appearances. You always have to allow for the worst.'


## 636 *(Audio channel)*

1 John, Chapter 5

*For whatsoever is born of God overcometh the world: and this is the victory that overcometh the world, even our faith.*

*This is he that came by water and blood, even Jesus Christ; not by water only, but by water and blood. And it is the Spirit that beareth witness, because the Spirit is truth.*


## 356

A programme provocatively entitled *How Far Should We Go?* It appears at first glance to be a loosely impressionistic discussion of travel and travel writing, of the exotic and the debatable nature of exoticism. Featured are two talking masculine heads, filmed at their separate homes, and with documentary footage of their travel specialisms. The younger man, though only in his twenties, is already in the super-league as a travel author. Tousled Etonian Brad Allman was born in 1976 and has been in print since 1996, with best-selling travelogues about shamans he has encountered all over the globe. He has written about his experiences with Haitian and Bahian voodoo priests, about his ecstatic, as he says brain-blowing, fly agaric feasts with the Samoyed spirit-handlers once proscribed by the Soviet government. It has long been mooted, Allman teasingly confides, that fly agaric is the *soma* that is mentioned in the Hindu Vedic hymns, and likewise the *haoma* that's referred to in the Zoroastrian scriptures. Brad has even been on and written about a weekend course in Stow-on-the-Wold for part-time English shamans, or rather open-minded New Age enquirers, who have briefly explored the techniques of fasting, trance, ecstatic dance and mystical sweating. In Brad's book these weekend shamans are nice enough weekend folk, but not perhaps in the same charismatic league as the genuine witch doctors, the real trance experts. Weary of their rather inexpressive reiki, bio-massage, crystals, diet detoxifications and so on, the Stow-on-the-Wold part-timers have opted for a little of the macho tribal and the vicariously savage, in the Old Etonian's engagingly laconic view.

1998 footage of Brad Allman in a hut in a remote Ecuadorian village being cured by an Indian witch doctor. Allman quickly confesses to the camera that there was nothing at all wrong with him as far as he knew. But the man with the bright bird feathers and face paint had touched and palpated him and examined his eyes, and decided Brad was sick with various demonic infestations and needed a kind of ceremonial purge. The shaman had told him he would have to exorcise these maleficent imps immediately. First of all he needed to purify the atmosphere around them by burning a brand covered in some sort of jungle herbal paste. The dense clouds of incense produced made Allman's eyes water, and he coughed and choked and assured the shaman in faux Cockney that he was cured already thanks very much. Turning to the camera, his eyes streaming like twin Ecuadorian waterfalls, he asked us cowardly telly addicts whether this cure was perhaps worse than the disease.

After the demons making Brad sick had been partially smoked out through his eyes, they had needed to be transferred elsewhere. The witch doctor opened up a small cage and lifted out one of his store of domestic guinea pigs. They were part of his staple diet, but they were also useful litmus tests of a patient's innermost well being. He began to roll the terrified little thing in the dust outside his hut. He turned it here and there a bit like a furious mop or scrubbing brush and now and again bizarrely like those gyroscopic musical tops small children delight in. The guinea pig must have been very dazed by the end of this tango twirling, but far worse unfortunately was to come for the small creature. Like many another spirit-handler this one had to perform a divination of the spiritual and invisible by examination of the physical. To do that he had to skin the guinea pig and peruse the state of the animal flesh within. For best results, and callow old Brad divulged the rest with no apparent grief or distress, the guinea pig had had to be skinned alive. This in order that Brad, who felt no sickness, should know infallibly that he was not really sick.

'Oh fuck,' I blasphemed, monumentally nauseated from my armchair. 'Oh hell alive.'

The feathered doctor skinned the squealing guinea pig as if it were an artichoke he were peeling for a quality *hors d'oeuvre*. His thumbs fiddled and prodded and pulled and the guinea pig of course, screaming its agony, could hardly fight back against the poker-faced priest. For a moment I thought of cosmetician Kantara assuring us that her precious skin was her precious life. The shaman threw the limp and sad little skin to one side and stared mournfully at the bloody flesh. Then he gazed at riotously blooming if smoke-blackened Allman, and assured him via the local translator that he was now in perfect tip-top health. The exorcism was a complete success, but for best results this process should be gone through at least twice a year . . .

'The guinea pig was right,' grinned Brad Allman who was so faultlessly good-looking he should have been on the Fashion First Channel at Number 215, 'because I've never had a day of sickness from that day to this.'

The question was, Allman opined with a sentient expression from his booklined study, what do we expect of our travel writers these days? Are they to go on horseback or muleback across impossible terrain, or should they go by four-wheel drive with a field kit of antibiotics and a laptop and mobile for handy copy and instant TV tie-in opinion? One thing is for sure, the tyro twenty-five-year-old drily assures us. The age of the rampaging explorer-writer is definitely dead. These days we don't want doughty officers fresh out of combat fatigues, derring-do travel writers with a gift for the gripping sentence. We just want plain as pie, matter of fact, Jack the Lad or Jane the Lass straight out of the *Rough Guide* travellers, but with an exceptional courage when it comes to taking risks. Or in my case, he adds, with likeable demureness, with a downright insane cheek and a penchant for reckless lunacy.

Cut to second talking head, again done as film, not as studio footage. This affable, tongue-in-cheek gent is Jack Lawless, the doyen of popular British travel writers, whose works are available in every newsagent and railway stall in at least thirty-five countries. Jack is fifty years old, hirsute and untidy, and is renowned for a lazy, inimitable wit as well as an easy and alluring idiosyncrasy. He is twice Allman's age but sells about twenty times as many books and has been doing so for the last twenty years.

'One thing I really need to stress,' muses Lawless scratching his luxuriant beard, and apropos his stressing there is not a trace of tension in his lazy voice, 'is that I don't invent things in my travel writing. I don't go and say I bumped into my old friend the Sultan of Zanzibar at the gaming tables in

Monaco if it didn't happen. If I say something extravagant like that, in my case it means that it's true, wild as it sounds. Some of my confrères, the more lushly exotic of our travel writers, have been accused on occasion of a little magical realism, meaning conflating real events and wishful thinking. The late Bruce Chatwin is a prime example according to some. Lisa St Aubin de Teran is another, so I'm told. Don't get me wrong, I'm not saying it's an ethical thing at all. Each to his own, and whatever makes for a good read. The proof of the pudding is in the eating and, after all, nobody wants to read a boring travel book. But I personally wish to put it on the record that I don't ever make things up.'

As for me, the provincial journalist with serious literary ambitions, I have two fledgling travel books in progress, both of a revolutionary thematic kind. The first less daring one is provisionally entitled *Remarkably Boring Towns In Great Britain*. Embellished with numerous impressively bleary-looking black and white photographs, it has lengthy and eloquent chapters on the non-attractions, suffocating anonymity and stifling deadly ambience of e.g. Amersham in Bucks, Daventry in Northants, Newcastle-under-Lyme in the Midlands, Walkerburn in Peebleshire, Gretna and Annan both in Dumfriesshire, Kidlington in Oxfordshire, and hundreds more. Colourless windblown town squares and bleak vistas of prosperous semi-detached housing estates on grey February afternoons are set beside bogus photographs of middle-aged women supposedly receiving librium, valium and mogadon prescriptions across the local chemist's counter. Being a naturally garrulous type and having chatted to some of these women in supermarkets and elsewhere on my journalist's travels, I can confirm that, obliged to dwell there courtesy of their husbands' jobs, not a few of them *do* in fact need these anti-depressants and sedatives simply to cope with the transcendent nullity of the places where they live.

My other prospective travel book, even more compellingly thematic, is tentatively called *The Very Best of British Grimacers*. The title itself is so curious that it ought to intrigue the weariest metropolitan publishers, and in it I have assembled all the surreptitious shots I have taken over many years of people *caught pulling faces*. I'm not, I hasten to add, referring to deliberate face-pullers, those competitive international gurners who assemble at Cumbria's Egremont Crab Fair, push their heads through a papered frame, and attempt, *pace* Rabelais' Panurge, to pull the wildest facial contortions. No, rather what I mean, is the startling range of bizarre grimaces one observes particularly on cold or windy days, when someone stopping to examine e.g. a distant church clock or an intriguing shop facade spontaneously and quite redundantly puckers their face up in an attempt to focus the thing in question.

The paragon of such unconscious grimacers I encountered in the early Seventies when I was a student at London University. I started off as a medical student but after a term confounded everyone, including myself, by switching to Arabic at the School of Oriental and African Studies. For my subsidiary subject I chose Turkish and my Ottoman Turkish lecturer was called William Griffe, a sombre, put-upon man in his early fifties, who would stand before his fifteen students and recount all he knew with the most mournful saturnine lugubriousness. Regaling us deadpan concerning e.g. the *Dede Korkut* in unbroken twenty-minute stints, Griffe punctuated these stints with two things. He would pause, sniff, stop dead, take off his glasses and rub away at his weary old scholar's eyes. As he rubbed those bloodshot eyeballs he pestled away rather like an onanistic maniac, his tongue poking out an inch or so with the vigour of the rubbing. Once his eyes had opened after this ferocious massage, he would retract his tongue and then begin his second engaging tic. Griffe, with glasses pushed back on his nose, would gaze to the back of the room at the wall clock. As he always lectured in meticulous twenty-minute blocks, and as he always took two minutes to do his ecstatic rubbing and tongue waggling, it could only be either 3.22 or 3.42, and yet every time he had to confirm as much by seeking out the clock.

Because it was a long way off, exhausted Griffe would grimace and peer at the distant object and his grimacing was of a maestro virtuoso style, eyes diminished to ant-size pupils, mouth puckered to a degree of contraction suggestive of having tasted his own urine or something worse, cheek lines and facial musculature tetanized as if he had been caught by an untoward Seventies English earthquake. Griffe ought to have been the kingpiece of my grimacers' collection, as its leading metropolitan example. But of course he had long retired from his post, and I could hardly trail him around outside his bungalow in Penge waiting for him to peer at his ormolu clock through the sitting-room window whilst pausing from mowing his lawn. For my prize shot, I have had to satisfy myself with a leering Humberside postman adjusting his specs and baring his teeth like a stallion while gazing into a betting shop in Goole. Next in line, a brightly rouged young woman in Barnoldswick, Yorks, raising her top lip like a supercilious beaver whilst incredulously scrutinising a two-for-the-price-of-one offer concerning sesame-seed burger buns from Barnoldswick Tesco back in 1979 . . .

And so on.

Both of these projected imaginative works with their highly original contents would emphatically assert that the apparently ordinary, the conspicuously banal, are far from being so. Incredible as it seems, every day, ordinary people like you and me are turning themselves into living, breathing gargoyles in Barnoldswick and Goole. And unless they were to spot themselves looking extremely grotesque in my photographic book and, it is to be hoped, laughing appreciatively at their comical exposure, they wouldn't even know as much. However, as for *really* bizarre and really outlandish travel itineraries *pace* Brad Allman and Jack Lawless, I have had at least one of these myself in the last thirty years. Though I would be the first to admit that it might not merit an entire book-length study, nevertheless it seems to me at least as riveting not to say devastating as young Allman and his exorcising shamans.

The vehicle in my case was not an amphibious four-wheel-drive being trailed by the Travel Channel cameraman, but a double-decker bus in West Cumbria which quite categorically was not being trailed by Border Television. The itinerary was not from Quito to a far-flung Ecuadorian jungle, but from the windy outskirts of an unusual small Cumbrian town called Cleator Moor, the destination being the historic industrial port of Whitehaven.

Cleator Moor, formerly an iron-ore town, was populated in the 1850s by the Irish and later by the Cornish, a second type of immigrant Celt. They came from the same few Mayo villages to work the mines, and so an inordinate number of Moor families are called Noone, Toon, Kelly and Salmon. I was living there in my mid-twenties in the mid-Seventies, single, a journalist, and though able to drive, I preferred to use public transport at every opportunity. I caught the bus as much as I could, mostly to nearby Whitehaven, but also to Workington, Cockermouth, Keswick, and in those days one could even get to lonely Ennerdale and Wasdale once a week by public transport.

One dark and windy evening close to Christmas, I was stood alone at the bus stop in a suburb of Cleator Moor called Bowthorn. I was waiting for the 7.15 to get me into Whitehaven for 7.30, so that at 7.45 I could go and see *Chinatown* at the Gaiety Cinema. I had seen this film once before with a very attractive woman called Nonnie, from whom I had painfully parted three months ago. Nonnie was now training to be an optician in Dundee, while I was doing sub-editing in Whitehaven on an advertising freebie. I was admittedly a little worried that seeing Jack Nicholson in

*Chinatown* again might stir up tender feelings best left unstirred. However at the other cinema, the Queen's, it was a boisterous TV spin-off, *Up Pompei*, starring an innuendoising ancient Roman called Frankie Howerd. There was no real choice when it came to innuendo versus sentiment . . .

The huge double-decker came flying down the hill, and though I didn't usually bother, for once I raised my hand. Bowthorn was technically a request stop though I had never known a bus not stop there. This one was hurtling at such a speed it looked as if it might just go on without me . . .

There were half a dozen middle-aged women sitting downstairs, and as at the time I chainsmoked miniature cigars I carried on up the stairs. There were no other passengers up there, only a surreal vista of empty shiny leather seats, which for some reason pleased me. I was looking forward to a solitary smoke and perhaps a tender and mildly masochistic reverie about the best times I had had with Nonnie Bright. It stayed pitch-dark outside on the long sweep after funny little Keekle as far as the straggling outskirts of Whitehaven. The empty countryside towards Weddicar and Moresby seemed exceptionally black, and as I was still completely alone upstairs with my half-smoked Tom Thumb, it began to feel just a little strange. For one thing, I suddenly realised that there was no conductor on this bus, or if there was he was hidden away downstairs in some unfathomable recess behind the six headscarved women. For a second thing, I could have sworn that our driver, instead of decelerating in anticipation of the junction and heading down into Whitehaven, was bloody well *accelerating* and turning right into the pitch-dark open countryside . . .

And so it was. Our deviant driver, conceivably a gleeful drunk or a reckless madman, had shot right past the school and was hurtling away towards the god-forsaken village of Moresby Parks . . .

'What the hell!' I gasped, as dazed as in a waking dream. 'What the bloody hell is the idiot up to?'

I need to emphatically underline that buses from Cleator Moor in the Whitehaven direction go only to Whitehaven, never anywhere else. There are none from the Moor to a non-destination such as quaint little Moresby Parks, much less urban Workington by the short-cut hill route over Swallow Hill. Cars might sometimes take that scenic itinerary, but never in the memory of man would a double-decker attempt such a folly. Such a quixotic public service did not even exist back in the Twenties or Thirties, when buses went absolutely everywhere and every hamlet had its little bus shelter. After all, the roads hereabouts were ridiculously narrow and winding, and if this Lodekka maniac came across a lorry or a nocturnal tractor just before the notorious Pica turn-off, that would be the end of him and us . . .

The enormous bus hurtled on at speed along the coal-black country roads. Any drunk and/or harmless pensioner walking his dog here would have been flattened and killed instantly, or possibly slowly. Down below could be seen the lights of two distant ships out on the dark vastness of the Solway Firth. The street lights of modest Lowca and meagre Parton, both drab former pit villages, were also visible. I imagined the amazement of those Lowca-ites as they observed an illuminated double-decker tearing along the crazy hilltop route. They would think they were hallucinating or that the Martians had at long last landed and had very sensibly chosen West Cumbria to surprise the world. Quaking, I looked ahead of me, and saw by the bus headlights that we had reached the turn-off for an extremely peculiar little township called Pica. One thing was for sure. We would be turning *left* downhill by Swallow Hill for Workington, because no one, not even an affiliated anarchist malcontent or a manic-depressive underpaid and overworked Lodekka conductor, could possibly turn right for bloody weird little . . .

The bus slowed to about forty-five, and I watched in horror as it ratched up and turned . . .

We were off to an unspeakably bizarre little Land Beyond Time. We were off to a place where every cosmic coordinate was more or less up in the air, and, so to speak, up for grabs . . .

Pica? Pica, one might echo with resonant wonder? Would that be a Latin word? Would that be a female first declension? And who the hell would that first declension, that Pica woman, be when she's at home? Talking of Latin and speaking of *ludibrio*, we have all heard of things called joke villages, no doubt. West Cumbria has hundreds of joke villages and joke towns, or rather there is a remarkable serial loftiness whereby Carlisle smirks at Whitehaven which in turn smirks at Workington which in turn smirks at Maryport which in turn smirks at Flimby which in turn smirks at Fothergill which in turn smirks at the nearby council rubbish dump which in turn smirks at . . . it has nothing left to smirk at unless possibly it be Pica.

Pica is two criss-crossing rows of sombre pit terraces stuck out in some severely blasted wilds. The approach there from Moresby Parks is grave, the windy road from Distington even bleaker, the route from Asby and Arlecdon so barren and terrible it is only recommended for those who have been in the services or on expeditions to the moon. Even the village pub sits a mile outside the village as if embarrassed by the association. Once upon a time it was a punishment village, the place where you were sent if you couldn't afford to pay your modest rent at say Distington or Harrington. These days it is sparsely gentrified or rather still as bleak and barren but populated by a few teachers and social workers as well as the tough and hardy villagers. Sad as it is, it remains impossible to say the name of the place without smirking. Though perhaps it needs underlining that I state all this without any smugness or unction. As I've said, the village of Fingland where I come from was also called Fartland, on account of its chemical works's malodorous expulsions of sulphuretted hydrogen . . .

We hypnotised wayfarers hied our way to a vision called Pica. Me, the journalist who only wanted to go to *Chinatown*, and the six headscarved women below who presumably wanted to go to their homes in Whitehaven. We had been crudely abducted and were off to visit Blennerbuggery, meaning somewhere rural, remote, buffoonish, downright odd. Those keen to comprehend the subtle relationship between language and location might just wish to consult the OED, which not many Picans have done recently as far as I know. There they would discover that 'pica' has two fifteenth-century significations and one of the present day. The modern one means a popular type of printer's font, but the older ones are: a) a magpie (the Pica terraces certainly are as black as that pilfering bird), and b) a perverted craving for substances unfit for food.

Need we elaborate on that last one for anyone's benefit?

The bus screeched to a halt at the village crossroads. There were lights on in all of the hundred terraces and yet the place seemed as grimly gothic as Wilkie Collins or Bram Stoker. There were fog and mist without, clawing insinuatingly against our bus window panes. There had certainly been no fog at Cleator Moor, nor any mist at Moresby, and those were both at a good elevation. Yet here in Pica there was a clammy spectral fog. The double-doors tore open with a groan, and a few middle-aged women shot like automatons onto the bus. I was hoping they were smokers and would come upstairs, where I could seek an explanation and hopefully share my consternation with them. Yet they had leapt on with what might have been a zestful alacrity. If so, they were making a serious and culpable mistake, they were playing with fire to leap so hopefully onto a hijacked bus. They must know better than anyone that there was no such fool's route as Cleator Moor to Workington via a desert oasis called Pica. Our driver deliriously enjoying himself below could only have had a nervous breakdown and decided to invent his own florid fairytale route as part of his unique derangement.

The new passengers all remained downstairs. Which was a considerable puzzle. There might only be six non-smokers in Cleator Moor, but it was inconceivable there were more than two abstainers in the whole of desolate Pica. There was nothing to do in this village but smoke like a chimney, to relieve the cruel isolation and the oddity. I listened to their chatter, to their gossiping away regardless. Smileless opportunists to a woman, they couldn't care less about the legality or otherwise of this pirated public transport. There was still no sign of our bus conductor, evidently a conscience-free absentee boosily insensate in some pub in Cleator Moor. Me the local journalist, I was still on my own up here on the top deck, like some postmodernist wraith, like a paranoid albeit provincial hero out of Kafka. Where the hell, I asked myself aghast, were we continuing now, at such suicidal speed, you demon-driven, remorseless Lodekka Desperado? To bloody old Asby across that terrifyingly empty Pica tundra? To bloody old Workington? To bloody old Prague? To bloody old Mars?

The lunatic seemed to hesitate, then began doing very complex if expert three-point turns. There was no particular haste as he manoeuvred his juggernaut in the middle of the road, as there was no other traffic for miles. He was turning the bus round on itself, and was apparently heading back to the fateful T-junction. In which case I assumed he was going to do an exact reverse itinerary, in order to pick up the conductor he'd left boozing back on the Moor. Though no, that was too crazy a notion even for a madman with no sense of time or duty or geographical direction. He was bound to fork right for Workington, and if I were lucky I could catch a train back to Whitehaven, see half of *Chinatown*, then take an unheard-of taxi back to Cleator Moor. My immaculate Luddite purity would then be a thing of the past. As of tomorrow I was going to start *driving my bloody car*, make no mistake. At least the damn thing went where I wanted it to go, it did not please itself like a stampeding West Cumbrian stallion. The cinema short must be over by now, and they would be rolling the title credits in The Gaiety. Jack Nicholson might even have had his nose slit already by Roman Polanski! He might even, I thought miserably, be sat there in his private eye's office with that colossal bandage on his wounded hooter.

Our driver was a very determined old soul, a real law unto himself. Clearly he apprehended rigid symmetry as the most comforting and least threatening of aesthetic forms. He saw nothing predictable or monotonous about reversing his senseless route and charging back to Moresby Parks. Indeed he bowled along gleefully as if he were headed for palmy Nice or balmy Cannes or the salubrious Azores. Perhaps he had heard the bush telegraph rumour that the Moresby Parks Working Men's served bitter at only *twenty pence* a pint, the cheapest in the whole of the county so it boasted. Perhaps he was already its star customer and had lost so many million brain cells on that five-pints-for-a-quid bonanza that he couldn't tell Whitehaven from Pica. Down below there in Lowca and Parton, they must be watching this brightly illuminated caterpillar doggedly returning along its insane axis. As we returned to Moresby Parks I decided to walk downstairs to make an anxious conference with my fellow travellers. The bus was hummocking at such a speed I staggered sideways as I made my way. Sealed safely inside his front cabin, the crafty driver seemed to guess of my treacherous intention. At once he took a vicious right turn, and plunged away down the hill in the direction of . . . ?

As he plunged, so I shot forward on the upper deck and collided with a vertical metal rail! I barked my right shin, my head battered against the bus roof, and I hallucinated a few brightly coloured and mesmerising stars. I swore and loudly moaned in my distress.

'Fuck!' I gasped. 'Fuck me stiff! Fuck. This is certainly not right.'

Which was a moral as well as a directional assertion. We would appear now to be heading in the direction of the

Solway Firth, by the elliptical idiot route. We were nearing of all places the pristine little country theatre at Low Moresby. Whitehaven itself has no proper theatre, but thanks to a beneficent local magnate, way out in the wilds was this purpose-built Rosehill, occasional home of Shakespeare, Rattigan and Beckett, not to speak of illustrious visiting string quartets, shopsoiled alternative comics, and sundry international mime artists. The driver decelerated, and blinking through my concussed trance, I spotted a billboard advertising Samuel Beckett's *Endgame*. Endgame, I muttered madly to myself? It did not seem even remotely fanciful to establish a connection between the message on that billboard and the lunatic in charge of this bus. An absurdist bus driver, turfed out of his English degree in 1962, retrained with Cumberland Motor Services in 1963, now after thirteen unstable and deadly tedious years has finally decided to get his dreadful revenge? He is obviously going to steer this lethal and apocalyptic double-decker through the entrance doors, via the dimmed auditorium, right onto the floodlit Rosehill stage . . and straight into Hamm's bloody *dustbin* . . .

He might have been absurd but he was no absurdist. The hijacker tore on down to the main West Cumbrian highway, the A595. He paused at the busy junction, his engine humming away. His wildly bubbling brain could be heard making descantwise accompaniment. Presumably he was going to rocket straight across to grubby Parton, then with a nod to Beckett and his solipsistic mania, without accepting or disgorging any passengers, would reverse all the way to Pica. Then no doubt gaily back to Parton, then perhaps sprily back to Pica, then . . . perhaps he would happily ricochet between the two ugly little Ps for the next twenty or thirty or three hundred years . . .

This was not to be. He thought better of assaulting Parton, and instead bore left in a suddenly docile fashion for the Copeland capital itself. He set off on the two-mile drive into Whitehaven, and immediately his engine seemed to quieten, even purr. I noted his quietened brain purring affably alongside. It was all as if orchestrated by invisible magic, or some outside hand. In a few minutes we were there inside the town station, and though I had never warmed to its melancholy interior before, no destination could have been more heartwarming. Still clutching my battered head, I stumbled in a daze down the stairs, the very last of the passengers to disembark.

Except, that is, for the 'conductor' . . .

To be a conductor, surely you have to do something on the lines of conduct? I jumped as this coy and brilliantined enigma stepped out from his cosy inglenook. Sixty-plus, bearded and close to retirement age, he had been lurking senilely in his comfy cubby-hole adjacent to the rear parcel shelf. Tucked away stealthily behind the chattering Moor and Pica ladies, he had remained throughout the journey completely invisible.

'Fares please,' he smirked aggressively. 'Thirty-five pee from Bowthorn.'

I did not grin back at him. I thought he was a most repulsive wraith. Though to be sure he did not look like a typical phantasm. He wore an incredible amount of Brylcreem and I doubt whether real phantasms use hair gel.

'Why,' I gasped, almost tearfully, 'did we go along that crazy bus route? Why the hell did we go the loony bloody way we went?'

'Uh?' he said vaguely as he pocketed my thirty-five pence. 'It's the same route that we always go, chief.'

I scoffed incensed. 'By Pica? By bloody Pica? I've been catching the bloody bus into Whitehaven for the last five and a half months, and we've never ever gone by bloody Pica!'

He wagged his sticky old head at me sagely. 'Don't worry,' he said. 'You'll be in plenty of time. Just look sharp and chase after that gang of ugly old women.'

I blinked, then hissed, 'I don't know what the hell you're

talking about! I wanted to go to the Gaiety picture house and I'm over forty minutes late! I'll have missed Jack Nicholson's nose bandage and –'

He yawned, wound up his spent yellow ticket roll, then pursed his lips judicially. 'It's your own fault you've missed Jack Nicholson. You should have got yourself on the 7.15.'

I clenched my fists at this crudely obstinate old joker, 'This *is* the bloody 7.15! What's more, by way of confirmation, it has the word "Whitehaven" written on the bloody front.'

His sunny indifference was dropped in an instant. At once he became remarkably grave. 'Wrong, boss. It says Whitehaven, OK. But this one is actually the *7.14.*'

I shuddered and gasped, 'Bollicks! There is no bloody 7.14.'

He furrowed his brow, flinched somewhat, but decided to forgive such surly outspokenness. Perhaps he had a son my own age, who was the same sort of unreasonable hot-faced egotist. He answered calmly, 'As of the last three months, there's one every Tuesday night.'

I glared at him. 'Rubbish man. Why the hell would there be two separate buses to Whitehaven only one minute apart? And why, more to the point, would one of them decide to go berserk, and go round by bloody Pica?'

He tutted at such laughable and 'pedestrian' ignorance. 'Boss, boss, boss, dear, dear, dear! We're not talking about any old common or garden service bus. We're talking here about a *Lodekka Customer Special.*'

A little pigeon hovered over us inside the bus station. I could hear myself making muted hiccupping sounds in my outrage. I growled, 'Oh yes? Don't tell me. We're talking in fact about the *Phantom Pica Special?*'

'Precisely,' he said in a mild, if serious tone. 'It is the Pica Special. This is the Pica Special. It's the Pica Special for the Bingo women of a Tuesday night.'

There followed a lengthy and resonant silence, as the

brylcreemed conductor surveyed this unorthodox twenty-five-year-old Bingo woman flagrantly sporting her far from alluring straggly beard.

'Bingo women?' I said with a hysterical cackle, victim of a sudden majestic dawning of I knew not what. 'For the Bingo? For the Housey-Housey? For the Lotto?'

'What else?'

'You mean to tell me I've missed nearly half of my very favourite film because of a bloody stupid *bingo bus*?'

The conductor scratched his doleful chin and gazed unseeing at the Peace Café opposite. 'Where there's a demand, boss, there's a bus. There aren't enough Bingo bodies on the Moor to justify a special bus, nor enough of them at daft little Pica. But put them both together and . . . bingo. Anyway, it's your own stupid fault, isn't it, for flagging me down as if it was a matter of life and death? I thought to myself, that hairy little feller doesn't look like a Bingo body to me. But then who am I to judge?'

# 7

*Fingland, West Cumbria, 1966*

In the BBC bachelor comedy *Hugh and I*, there was no sex or sexuality of any description, whether orthodox or gay, implied or assumed. However, nothing stands still, not even in a TV sitcom, and portly, fussy Terry Scott, who was the eponymous I, eventually branched out, took the plunge, bit the bullet, and married his ideal symbolic counterpart, the blonde and bustling June Whitfield. The quaint but vitiated *Hugh and I* was killed off in favour of the ebullient *Terry and June*. As an interesting parenthesis, long before his TV comedies, Terry Scott regularly performed a radio music-hall routine where he played a squeaky-voiced schoolboy, even more of a renunciation of the glandular and the driven. The overgrown cap-wearing pupil of *Workers' Playtime* in effect had behaved like a pupa, and metamorphosed twice over. In his third imago stage he became the blustering be-blazered bourgeois Terry in this comedy of suburban marital tiffs. The fictive characters Terry and June had of course the same names as the real-life actors, just as the real Eric Sykes in the fictional *Sykes* was also called Eric. This might be termed a powerful meta-reality, inasmuch as if Terry and June had been called Miles and Madge and Eric Sykes in *Sykes* had been called Arnold, there would not have been the same profoundly illuminating mystery of imaginative demarcations.

There is a point to this preamble, because this is a chapter of intimate confessionals. The year which saw me falling in love with the schoolgirl Sheila Starr also saw the first example of the British teleconfessional. By that, I mean what is now so commonplace, the UK chat show, it often seems as if it must have been with us from the beginning of time. However 1966 was a long time before Terry Wogan and *The Parkinson Show*, and several eternities before Oprah, Ricky, Montel and Jerry Springer. Still subject to Reithian strictures, the BBC had always disdained that vulgar transatlantic habit of broadcasting live disclosure by the famous, the infamous, the diuretic and the libellous. But the ITA, which had more to think about than pointless arcane strictures, chose to seduce and poach a BBC stalwart and then ordered him to *chat*. They took, unbelievably, an ex-boxer, a foreigner to boot, and they let this foreign pugilist fling affable verbal sallies at his interviewees. They took a Southern Irishman with his charm and his gift of the g, and let him and his guests regale, reminisce and *confess*. Nothing could possibly come amiss with a lynchpin like Eamonn Andrews and his revolutionary chat show. However, because of its radical and perhaps hyper-revelatory nature and because after all it was live before a studio audience, it was put on very late of a Sunday night.

The night after I had taken Sheila Starr to eat shredded beef at Lin-Fat's, Eamonn Andrews had two celebrity guests seated picturesquely side by side. Eamonn must have been a great fan of the rhetorical form *oxymoron*, as no one but he would have decided to seat guest A next to guest B. First of all, he had the metamorphosing blazer-clad comedian Terry Scott recounting his colourful showbiz memories; but then, as the comic was innocently enjoying his due ovation, Andrews slyly brought on another celebrity who had made his way through life virtually blazer-free. In this case the name of the game was R and B meets music-hall cancan, for the second chatty chap was none other than . . . Mr Mick Jagger.

Jagger seated himself next to a comic who had portrayed all three of life's biographical stages; the schoolboy, the bachelor, and the respectable married man. Mick just grinned of course, at Eamonn and at Terry and at the appreciative studio audience. He smiled or rather he smirked with a teasing moue of phlegmatic self-repose. Terry sat listening to Jagger's studiedly languid account of bohemian showbiz as he saw it, and I noted Scott's face showing something enigmatic yet possibly critical. It was just conceivable that something was worryingly on the boil in this man who had traversed all three biographical stages . . .

Before Eamonn could anticipate and safely defuse the situation, Terry Scott and his blazer began to blaze at the smirking rock star.

'The thing about you blinking pop fellers,' he blasted at Mick Jagger, 'is the awful blinking state of any blinking dressing room once you've been in it! The number of times I've gone into a TV or theatre dressing room after you and other blokes like you have been changing, the pigsty and the mess you would not believe. It really gets my blinking goat about pop blokes like you.'

Plenty of blinkings and blesseds, but thirty-five years ago no bloodys. This bewildering thing of imaginative demarcations. For a moment I genuinely thought I was watching *Hugh and I* or *Terry and June*, and that Mick Jagger was either Hugh or June being berated by Terry. Hugh Lloyd would inevitably have played his Stan Laurel part and looked basset-hound sheepish. June Whitfield would perhaps have bridled pugnaciously in return. Mick qua Hugh qua June (and bear in mind that Jagger might not have acted the three life stages but he had definitely mimed both life's genders in the Nicholas Roeg film *Performance*) simply grinned at Terry Scott. Far from being put out by this live TV excoriation, Jagger smirked at his stout accuser, vastly amused. This caused T. Scott to wax even more salivatingly testy and to repeat himself more or less verbatim, then to appeal to

Eamonn Andrews, the studio audience and the rest of the world to play the moral arbiters.

*Itaque nascitur,* as my Latin teacher Joe Pegg might have stated it. *Live British embarrassment,* the first ever example and courtesy of the ten-year-old Independent Television Authority. Captivating items are these things called definitions, especially if you are only sixteen and precociously cynical. As a *Daily Worker* reader I sneered at the 'independence' of the ITA, and even more so at the notion it was any sort of authority. Where was the authority, moral, custodial or idealistic, in game shows, *Crossroads,* and *Sunday Night at the London Palladium?* As for embarrassment, whatever next, we all wondered, who would be shamed next before millions of people? It was certainly very exciting to be confronted by a second tele-evisceration only a few weeks later. In this case the polarities were reversed, for this time it was counter-culture attacking orthodoxy, a Scott being attacked by a Jagger, so to speak. What's more, the person being attacked was an East European female, someone who had fled the Communists and defiantly embraced the tawdry capitalist idol. Before I saw her startling Sunday night humiliation, I had my Saturday night with Sheila Starr, of course. I can see now that my girlfriend's surname and my favourite day of the week were gently and touchingly alliterative. Both of her initials in fact seemed to chime very tenderly and poetically with the one and only day that a schoolboy can call truly free.

In the year that England won the World Cup, it was no trifling matter to bear a child out of wedlock. It was most definitely a huge embarrassment in the backward and let us say vicarious provinces like Cumberland. In the same year that the film *Alfie* showed the vicious hero brushing off a messed-up abortion as a tedious biographical detail briefly impeding his well-oiled rake's progress, a teenage Cumbrian pregnancy would have been a massive catastrophe. And though Sheila Starr had a considerable sexual hunger, was at least as appetitive as her boyfriend, she was also alive to reality. Her father was a joiner and her mother was a primary head, an odd combination for the period, and one which partly explained my girlfriend's oddities. One minute Sheila would be as dogged and bossy as a pedantic teacher, the next as irreverent and anarchic as a carefree working man. The sensible logical step would have been contraception, which in the Sixties for two northern teenagers could only mean rubber condoms. Sheila who had serious ambitions to be a dentist did not trust johnnies, not even if, as I obligingly volunteered to do, I wore a concentric pair. Let them, I said slyly, showing her an interesting sketch of two Cumberland sausages, be called J1 and J2. As a scientist like myself, Sheila doubted that such a thing could be done. I told her I could sneak into the sixth-form physics lab to do some tensile stretching on J2, but she pointed out that 'stretching a condom' was a wassacommee, just like Eamonn Andrews, it was an oxymoron, or, if not that, just plain moronic. Any condom, whether primary or auxiliary, needed every bit of its pristine tensile strength, it should not be buggered about with.

As a consequence of these thorny deliberations we enjoyed the same sort of sex life as the unmarried servant classes of the previous century. There was to be no *Alfie* or *Saturday Night, Sunday Morning* abortions in Sheila Starr's case. Instead we explored a hybrid variety of sex involving massive amounts of friction and tactile stimulation but nothing you could call a proper penetration. There are adepts of certain eastern religions – so I learnt, once I had switched from medicine to Arabic at SOAS – who do this kind of thing as a means of spiritual discipline. The literally endless and unspent sex of Tantric practice, or even the brahmacharya supposedly practised by Mahatma Gandhi. According to the waggish novelist George Moore, even the ancient Irish monks would deliberately sleep next to naked virgins as a means of testing their chastity. I knew nothing of this at sixteen, of course, nor I imagine did Sheila the future dentist. Besides, I was no Tantric adept, and my seed would not always stay put. Sheila Starr would likewise come to a noisy, if less palpable climax, though without the hazardous business of a full-blown, so to speak, penetration.

As for location, where did these friction marathons customarily take place? Neither of us had a car, nor did we rent a louche bijou apartment in Carlisle, nor even a chalet or caravan at bracing Silloth or blustery Allonby. All that we had was the darkness of the cinema or the darkness of back alleys or the darkness of the bandstand in the nearest park. The outside of Workington's town bandstand was partitioned with wooden slats, and bizarre as it sounds those partitions were regularly tenanted by local couples engaged in snogging, petting and I suppose occasionally the whole unbridled hog. In winter when it was pitch dark this touchingly communal congress could proceed unabated, a bit like a bowdlerised version of what Flogger had got up to on the Solway shore in broad daylight. In the summer months it was altogether more difficult, and the bandstand congress had to be saved until the dusk or darkness of ten or eleven o'clock. Anything that took place before that was either in the pictures or down a lonely alley, perhaps by the rear of a disused garage or the dismal gable end of a crumbled warehouse.

Her breasts were firm and full and succulent and sweet. Sheila had fine blond hair and her spirit seemed a far-reaching thing, wisping away to distant and unnameable waters, remote but poignantly alluring foreign lands. Down the back of some grimy Workington alley she raised her blouse and fed me with her beautiful ripe flesh, as if these were rich fruits or tender birds, two radiant and pristine swans perhaps. Brightness, dazzle, surpassing fairness, rare and hallucinatory Tir nan Og horizons down some dirty old West Cumbrian alley? For these two impatient provincial kids, it was the defiant trajectory of the hankering, struggling spirit. Sheila lowered her tights and pants and put my hands on her naked flanks, the sides of them like pillars of a fine if simple pavilion.

I held the concentration of her gentle small behind focused in a single tender hand. Meanwhile we were kissing and sucking, sucking and kissing, with our mouths buried for hours in each other's minutest depths.

This strange business went on for about two years, meaning at least a hundred Saturdays and a hundred alleys and a hundred bandstand partitions and a hundred innocuous climaxes. More than once we caressed each other in some extraordinary historical excavations, for example in the deepest mine-holes on Fingland shore. They were incendiary relics of the Second World War, and where mines had exploded in 1942, now we exploded almost as noisily in 1966. Once a large mouse scuttled past Sheila's naked buttocks and she shrieked, especially when it got entangled in her discarded tights and looked as if it had taken up house. Afterwards, up Fingland woods, close to the place where a lunatic had aimed a gun at Flogger and Murphy, we lingered to kiss by an infinitely weathered tree. It was a very old oak, gnarled and shattered looking, but it had a roughness and a venerability that were tenderly poetic. Perhaps it was dead rather than breathing. Dead or alive its decay was perfect and very beautiful. Examining Sheila as I kissed her, I saw that she was undecayed and very young and very beautiful, and that she and the tree standing side by side were a perfection of clean and natural opposites.

A surprise third party entered our woodland tableau. A beautiful white horse, snorting and restless, was chewing in the field behind the oak. This proud young beast had sidled up close to the two lovers, not out of nosiness, but because the grass was richer by the stark old tree. It looked at us briefly, shook its head and mane, then turned its lustrous backside on us. It was a burnished evening, with gold on the oak leaves and gold and glister on the riddled bark. Sheila and I were studiously melting into the furthest reaches of each other's guts. There was no one around us for miles. Even if there had been, we wouldn't have cared, we were at least as reckless as ice-blue Flogger tonight. We were as tender and willing to die to ourselves as two decaying oak leaves. Sheila murmured, 'Roe, Roe, I think I lo–'

I was about to say, Sheila, Sheila, I think I –

The white horse snorted and twitched its tail, then crowned our epiphany in its own modest way.

'PRUUUUUF!'

It had farted. The horse had guffed. It had a backside the size of a farmhouse sideboard, and it had farted loud enough to destroy what was left of the shattered old oak.

Sheila's eyes widened with amazement. She looked as if she'd been shot. I told her, by way of sharp analogy, about the mad gunman who had once aimed at me and Flogger, and said I'd now been potshotted *twice* in Fingland woods. The teacher's daughter erupted into dangerous hysterics. She turned to the horse and admonished it for eating too much starch and flatulent carbohydrate. It seemed both heedless and tender as it watched us. I pointed that out to her at rather too great length, those two incompatibles, and Sheila looked at me faintly discomfited. She might perhaps have sensed a premonitory account of how would things would ultimately develop for the pair of us . . .

Eamonn Andrews constituted another type of epiphany. Rather than flatulent he was generally costive, though his show at least was aiming to be pungent. From my point of view he functioned as a type of wrap-up man, as each week's thematic finale. He was live and confessional just as Sheila and I were as live and confessional as either of us could hope to be. His guests were not always provocative or shocking, but at least they always *confessed* something. Roy Hudd, the stringy radio comedian and expert on Victorian music hall, came on to agonise that he was far too thin, and that he would appreciate any viewers' remedial suggestions for his embarrassing emaciation. By contrast, far from skinny Raquel Welch appeared one Sunday night and immediately announced she was going to reveal something shocking to Eamonn. The world, not just windswept West Cumberland, stood still in lubricious expectation. Nevertheless a treacherous sense of anticlimax was palpable both at home and in the TV studio. What could Raquel Welch possibly confess to us that we couldn't already anticipate and imagine? Unmentionable sexual practices? Addiction to morphine or opium? Scarcely. She, Raquel, whose moist and mythological bosom would consecrate the Stone Age in *One Million Years B.C.* was the epitome of bursting lust and brazen lustre. Nothing she could announce to the whole world could possibly shock anyone except perhaps the Erse ex-boxer.

Raquel, it turned out, had been recently filming in Italy, and had had her very first encounter with Rome. She had travelled to the romantic European capital with certain well-defined cultural expectations. Why, it was such a cliché it was hardly worth saying it, but if in 1967 an unaccompanied woman strolled down a street in Rome, surely she could hope to be whistled at, and what's more, expect to be pinched.

'But Eamonn, nobody did. Not even any of the old guys, much less the young ones. *Nobody* wanted to pinch my behind! Shoo, was I so disappointed.'

Seemingly this brazen tele-candour was proving narrowly educative, and I might have given up my chat-show addiction altogether, had it not been for the assault on the East European. A few weeks after Raquel, another female film star was a welcome guest on the Irishman's capacious tele-couch. This cosmopolitan starlet really understood the subtle hidden meaning of the word 'chat'. No one could forget a name like Zsa Zsa Gabor, nor forget the woman herself, as she was frothy, effervescent, humorous, feather-brained, artlessly name-dropping, and a rasping Hungarian through and through. Some might have sneered that the feather brain was a gimmicky pose and that she plagiarised a successful formula exemplified by the American comedienne Lucille Ball. Whatever the case, Zsa Zsa thrived in her adopted land America, as did her sister Eva, and they both disavowed the disgusting Stalinist regime of their Magyar homeland. Zsa Zsa naturally chattered as well as chatted . . . and by way of pausing for breath, she sometimes chuttered and chittered, and if there had been any possibility she would also have chettered, chottered, chitted and chutted. She chatted and chattered at some length about her friends on both sides of the Atlantic, this darling man and that darling old chap, her tiresome diet, her sumptuous clothes, her necessary shopping sprees and more. The Hibernian pugilist loved it all of course, got heedlessly caught up in the spirit of the thing and egged her on for yet more revelations of feather-brained excess . . .

Unfortunately for Andrews and the feather brain, sat next to the latter was a guest who was a steely brain. This s.b. adjacent to the f.b. was a young satirical comedian with a most impressive CV. He had been to Cambridge University, he had debuted in the Footlights Review, he had ornamented *The Bernard Braden Show*, where as resident gaberdined eccentric E.L. Whisty he had perorated bathetically in a most amusing and scurrilous manner. Nonetheless this gentleman, Peter Cook, was in 1967 more youthful promise than mature fulfilment. Pete and Dud and the Dagenham Dialogues hadn't yet happened, so his satirical comedian's income was probably nothing remarkable as such. Perhaps Mr Cook had decided that to cause great offence on live TV would catapult his career exponentially, but it is just as likely that genuine disaffection with the garrulous Magyaress was enough to make him *confess* as much to the n-million guests at home.

'What do I think, Eamonn?' the dark and lanky satirist echoed, after Andrews had asked him to comment on one of Zsa Zsa's bubblier remarks. 'I think that you,' coldly addressing the smiling actress, 'are one of the shallowest, stupidest and most trivial individuals I have ever encountered in all my puff.'

Five or six million people watched this live and brutal tele-excoriation, and I for one was so disturbed in my Fingland

149

armchair that I spilled hot coffee on my lap and screamed.

As for Zsa Zsa, she choked and hiccupped, 'WHAT!'

'Gah!' gasped the dazed pugilist. 'Bu, bu . . . Peter!'

Zsa Zsa snarled and spat, 'Well! I have never heard the like. I can assure you I have never been so –'

Cook riposted, 'Nor, I can assure you, have I ever been obliged to listen to such brainless bloody tosh in all my born . . .'

There was this Irishman, this Englishman, and this Magyaress. One day the Irishman said to the Englishman apropos the Magyaress, '*Now then, now then, Peter! Please! There's no call at all for –*'

They didn't even cut the programme. Nor did Eamonn think to block Cook's mouth with some parcel tape. It was live and dangerous and indeed it stayed so, or at least it did in theory. A third guest enterprisingly changed the subject and cheerfully diverted the fire. Oil was poured. Waters were stilled. Peter Cook sat back and sulked. Or perhaps it was Zsa Zsa who sat back and sulked. I waited for further mean-spirited insults and for the Hungarian to fall upon and bite the neck of the Dagenham wag, but no it did not happen. I took mental stock of all the confessionals and recalled that so far there had been Roy Hudd's embarrassing emaciation, Raquel Welch's redundant behind, Mick Jagger's debatable tidiness, Zsa Zsa Gabor's debatable way with words. Where then, I asked myself, in this seminal and ultimately shocking revolutionary epoch of the mid-Sixties, was it all about to *lead* us?

That winter and for the first time ever, Sheila Starr and I had an empty house all to ourselves. It was Sheila's house not mine, although, strictly speaking, it was not a house at all. Purchased in the 1940s when such things could be had for a song, it was an improbably topiaried and turretted High Harrington mansion. It had been built by a spendthrift sea captain in the 1860s, and had attics and cellars, a vast larder and two pantries, as well as a boastful profusion of lounges and sitting rooms. There was a massive acreage of lawn plus a beck and spinney to the rear, and had it been sited in Surrey or Kent it could only have been the house of a Beatle, a Stones or a Pacemaker.

It was two weeks before Christmas 1967, and Mr and Mrs Starr were attending the headmistress's school pantomime, *Puss in Boots*. Their daughter and her longhaired argumentative boyfriend were to be left there unchaperoned from six o'clock until ten. As that was time enough to crack the Behistan cuneiform or to read the Kamasutra from cover to cover, it should, I thought, be long enough to demonstrate the merits of an unedited copulation. On the quiet I had brought along a very dogeared packet of Durex, together with a mail-order Japanese condom that supposedly had a fang attached.

I arrived for high tea on a cold Saturday evening and enthused politely about their beautiful old house. After friendly easy banter with her teasing father Dick, I attempted gingerly small talk with Mrs Starr the primary head.

'What kind of treatment are they giving it?' I asked her re the school pantomime.

'You what?' she said blinking several times in a row. 'I'm sorry, Roe, but I don't understand your question?'

Jessie Starr was a hurried, stiff, very determined woman, used to being promptly conceded to. She was in her early fifties, with a proud, razor-sharp figure and a barbed half-flirtatious manner. I knew from our three previous encounters that she did not admire or cherish me, though it was all tersely implied rather than blatant. I realised she didn't love my long hair, my back-combed centre parting, my beardless androgynous appearance. She had muttered to Sheila that with regard to London and medicine, I would make a damned queer-looking doctor, whereupon Sheila had snapped that I intended becoming a psychoanalyst not a boring bloody GP. This had briefly shut her up, but now I could see her worrying that I was observing her teatime behaviour and insolently 'analysing' her over the salmon sandwiches, potted meat and Eccles cake. Far from it. A perfunctory dissection of Mrs Starr's personality only suggested that there was nothing very startling to dissect. A generalised hunger for power, a weakly concealed disdain for most people, a driven, pugnacious self-seeking, an amnesic's disavowal of her poverty-stricken Twenties childhood. Against all the odds, she had made it to a headship and to a resplendent High Harrington mansion, not to speak of a good-looking daughter who was courting a brainy if deluded androgyne who hoped to become Fingland's answer to Sigmund Freud or C.G. Jung.

I mumbled blushing, 'I mean, how is *Puss in Boots* adapted? Is it just told straight? Or are there jokes and songs about contemporary events or . . . ?'

'Oh come on! Hardly. They're only-ten-year olds. I know you're deep into Communist politics but my little ones aren't quite at that stage.'

Sheila scowled at Jessie Starr, but Dick, who liked nothing better than a hot political argument, began an animated debate about 'radicalism'. Dick was tall and bald and clean-cut, yet still handsome in a careless, old-fashioned way. He told me good-humouredly that Khrushchev would force me to have a prison haircut, and would accuse my backcombed centre parting of manifesting bourgeois counter-revolution-ary tendencies. Once when he'd toiled for a Newcastle construction firm Dick had been a keen union man, but had been deeply disgusted by the two-facedness of some of his colleagues. Some on the sly sent their kids to posh private schools, and even to elocution lessons, whilst ostentatiously reading the *Daily Worker* and holidaying on Lake Balaton with other English Communists. Now he was his own boss Dick hadn't turned into a bloody old Tory, but he certainly knew what Communism stood for.

'Prisons, son, that's what the rock of their ideals is built on! Horrible Siberian jails and terrible bloody labour camps.

They jail any opposition that dares to raise its head. They send them into the bloody arctic tundra for ten, twenty, thirty, forty years, without a qualm or a second thought. Or they make out they're just crazy, and feed them with crippling drugs in the psychiatric hospitals.'

Before I could rally with a hot-faced glibness about free workers' holidays, free crèches and free health care in the matchless paradise that was East Germany, Mrs Starr butted in impatiently.

'Come on, you! You haven't the time to rant on with schoolboys. We have to pick up my mother and you know how long it takes to get her on her feet. And don't you have to shave and change? Sheila, do I need to alter my make-up? It doesn't quite seem to match this outfit.'

Her daughter scrutinised her bleakly. 'It's fine. It's perfect.'

'I really wish that you and your boyfriend would come with us. It's not right at all leaving the pair of you on your own.'

Sheila flushed and Dick looked at her benignly incredulous. 'You can't cosset them all their lives, can you? Khrushchev Murphy here will fend off any dangerous burglars or intruders. Won't you, Khrushchev?'

Stark premonitions of front-parlour fornication obviously hadn't entered Dick's twinkling bald head. Jessie Starr looked at me shrewdly, as if I were a Stalinist burglar and intruder rolled into one. Clearly Roe Murphy from Fingland was at least as devious as . . . Jessie herself had had to be in order to get all the way she had got. With those prescient pedagogue's eyes of hers, Jessie had no difficulty making out the moth-eaten Johnnies and the Tokyo fang stuffed away inside my jacket pocket.

They left just after six. Four unchaperoned hours was an undreamt-of eternity, twice as long as a night in the pictures, ten times as long as any clasp behind the bandstand. There wasn't the tiniest hint of demure prevarication as we wandered up to the bathroom. I needed to wash the plenteous scone crumbs from my mouth and Sheila had been told to put away some linen in the airing cupboard. With crumbless, pristine hands I turned and enveloped her accepting, sturdy shoulders. Sheila looked at me with a heavy load of melting tenderness which was altogether new. Self-reliant and always self-contained, yet she seemed hopelessly mooning and helplessly struck upon me. I felt so elated and uplifted with this unexpected access of sovereignty.

'It'll make a change,' she said in a resonant voice, 'to be able to spread ourselves. After those crazy acrobatics and contortions in the pictures. Or my ice-cold arse shoved against a roughcast wall in the freezing dark.'

I asked did she mean her bedroom, but she blanched and said Jessie the forensic specialist had a snout like a sleuthing wolfhound. Even the faintest rumpling of the bedclothes would be seized on and scrutinised for suspicious creases and evidence of lewd Marxist subversion. As for any lingering odours of body fluids or of hastily changed sheets, all that was . . .

'Let's stay here in the bathroom,' I decided with a military strategist's emphasis. 'We can lock ourselves in, for one thing. We're also convenient for running water, for washing and sluicing and tactical concealment. They aren't back till ten, but whatever time they land, we'll be safely barricaded in and absolutely impregnable. That white mat there will do as a love couch. It's soft and fluffy and it'll be as warm as a Turkish bath.'

Sheila frowned and temporised, and pointed to the gurgling, hiccupping bathroom tank. 'If it wasn't for that thing. It sounds like Siddick sewage works, if not worse. I can't make love with all that bloody grumbling and clanking. If I shut my eyes all I can think of is revolving liquid sewage. I would never claim to be hypersensitive, but it was bad enough with that farting horse in the woods and . . .'

I was impressed by her solid pragmatic sense. Though her

choice of words seemed even more to the point. 'Making love? Do you mean . . . ?'

She gave a sharp intake of breath and I stood there more or less shamefaced. In that instant she looked flagrantly vulnerable and naively wounded. 'No I don't. I don't mean the usual way of making love. I mean our own way of making love. Which is so beautiful! It's better than anything else I know. Nothing could be lovelier. And the way we do it is entirely safe.'

'I've got some condoms,' I said swiftly.

There was another stark pause and a second pained inhalation. She blushed and murmured in a bleak little voice, 'No . . .'

'No,' I echoed hastily. 'No of course.'

'No, Roe.'

'I brought them as a precaution. In case we got carried away. They were meant as an insurance policy. I'm not trying to put pressure on you.'

In my callow and unthinking way I meant it honestly enough. Sheila Starr glanced at my solemnity, and made an enticing liquid sound in her throat. 'I'd like you to put one type of pressure on me.'

I asked, 'Oh would you? Would you really?'

'I'd like the pressure of your hands upon my body.'

The delicate preliminary elaborations took place beside that gurgling overheated bathroom tank. The house was a hundred years old and it occurred to me that those hissings and fizzings might well have been ghostly presences, vicarious, polite observers of one thing that hadn't changed very much since the nineteenth century. Sheila lifted her thin black sweater but left the bra in place so that her big firm breasts were like a fertile gift for harvest time. She urged me to kiss what was exposed, to nibble it minutely, to mutter to her musically and repetitively. Sheila liked whispers, murmurs and sonorous gibberish, melting, viscid lovetalk and she spoke it expertly in return. My name became rohrohroh orohorohoroh in a fevered, hurried timbre I barely recognised as hers. She took off her skirt in one rough gesture and flung it on the floor. She ordered me to remove her tights, but only gradually, only slowly, only teasingly. We were stood opposite a full-length mirror, so her finely sloping, sweely tapering bottom was bit by bit, ever so slowly, revealed as its reversed image in all its fecund purity . . .

She gasped and choked. I gasped and choked. It was absurd, but this was the first time ever we had enjoyed a simple sexual privacy. She told me to unhook the bra and take that ripe harvest at the front of her. Gently she rubbed her stiff nipples against my teeth, then pretended to force them open. She petted and mock-suckled me. She took my hands and draped them like fans across the melting, yearning cleft of her behind, and asked me to squeeze and touch, touch and squeeze, orohorohorohorohorohoooooooooooooroh . . .

Sheila lay there naked and entirely revealed. She was here on proud display on that hallowed white rug. It was the first time ever I had seen her perfect wholeness. Before tonight we had laboured with each other in the darkness like two blind insects. Up to now in the cinema and back alleys, it had been this part bare, that bit covered, this bit exposed, that part hidden. She had been only a partial woman or rather a hallucinatory and unfinished self, a selective and strangely edited act of concealment.

'I lov–' she said, and she sounded drugged.

In a curious inversion of values and desires, I knew that the entirety of her nakedness, the ungraspable plenitude of Sheila's firm and perfect flesh, that my ability to feel it all at once and comprehensively, was altogether more probable through a thousand minute strokes and touchings. It was much more probable than it was through the vain and monotonous movements of a single reproductive organ. It came as pure revelation that really I would have wished to be a painter who painted Sheila naked all day and every day, that this struggle to capture her whole and inimitable self was a proper and very feasible life's work. And that this our quaint, anachronistic Victorian petting, our shy sexual dawdling, was actually a studied means of genuinely and patiently tasting the fullness rather than the part. Denied any banal reproductive objective, the end, the terminus, the quarry, the prize, it really forced the fingers to work, the eyes to really see, the mouth to really taste, slowly, temperately and unselfishly, and, most illuminatingly, radially and outwardly. There was not this spiritless linearity, this infantile thrashing and thrusting with a foregone goal in mind, a goal that had to be literally scored and netted like a battered old ball.

Sheila rose from the rug and ordered me to accompany her downstairs. She seemed half-mesmerised, but remembered to take her clothes with her and advised me to do the same. She led the way down that baronial creaky staircase, her blushing buttocks swinging in a quaint and decorous moue. A bit of white fluff adhered to them from the bathroom rug. Her shoulders rippled and swung like a young beast's, like an indolent young calf's. Her neck seemed fragile and infinitely sensitive. I saw that Sheila was a vivid very animal mystery or rather that anything as sensitive as that delicate woman's neck must be a true repository of mystery. Mystery, I decided as I watched her rippling naked hips, was nothing other than an impossible and lustrous excess of anything that was capable of a sensuous depth, meaning something of a supernatural and overpowering order . . .

We resumed downstairs on the sitting room carpet. Another hour must have passed and for half of that I was just stroking and touching her dancing navel. We lay naked and unhurried before the blazing coal fire, roasted to the colour of two mullets or two salmon. We were raised to a perfect mean of languid excitation. We had been naked for two hours which had felt like twenty years. The next two hours would obviously last a century, if not an aeon.

I was hazarding as much to Sheila Starr, when suddenly a car pulled up outside her mansion . . .

A car? A vehicle? Containing *people*? Which people-containing vehicle could that be?

My considered response was incredulity. I did not believe in that car. *The Brains' Trust* had shown me how to do this back in 1957, and I could still do as much ten years later. Sheila who had never ever watched *The Brains' Trust* had a different concept of knowledge. Her throat made an odd grating squeak and she whinnied in terror. She froze in farcical mid-step before scuttering bare-arse to the window. It was as if she'd been propelled bum-naked from a cannon. As for me, I was also frozen, but into a strangely serene imbecility. Car doors began to open and slam, faint voices were heard to offer advice, reproof, possibly conflict. Then through a gap in the sitting room curtains, the teacher's daughter observed the most instructive sight.

'Oh fuck, oh fuck, oh fuck!'

'Eh?'

'It's them, it's them, it's them. It's *them*.'

I said demurely, 'Who is them?' as if they might be Jehovah's Witnesses or pan salesmen or gypsies selling coathangers and brillo pads.

'My bloody mother! My bloody Dad! My loony crazy grandma! God in heaven I'm stark naked, and there's my bloody mad old grandma.'

'Oh,' I said. 'Oh it's them is it?'

I spoke in a ponderous, even complacent tone, drunk on the remnants of erotic euphoria, 'In that case, maybe we ought to put a spurt on.'

Sheila stared as she struggled with that ludicrous noun. 'Spurt?'

I frowned at her, 'Yes. Spurt on as in move on and shift on. Hurry up and get dressed.'

'Eh?' she bubbled tearfully. 'You what?'

I groaned at her helpless immobility. 'Look! Look at me! See how I'm getting dressed?'

'Eh?'

'I say we get our togs on faster than bloody lightning! I vote that you in particular, the daughter of this blameless household, should whip on your bra and tights and knickers and shoes and . . .'

Dazed and uncomprehending, she just dallied there and babbled, 'They're supposed to be at *Puss in* fucking *Boots*!'

'Yep,' I said gravely. 'That's what we were led to understand.'

'So what the bloody hell are they doing back here?'

'You said it,' I said.

'Look at my barmy old Grandma, scowling and tottering towards the front door! Agh! I don't believe it! We didn't even bother to lock it, did we? All she has to do is turn the bloody handle. Ugh! Agh! Oh! My Dad's got out of the car now. But I don't understand it, Roe. My mother isn't moving. She's absolutely motionless. She's just sat there staring like she's doped or drunk . . .'

I sighed, 'I'm really glad about that. If she's piss drunk, she won't mind at all about seeing you naked.'

'Arrrgh!' Sheila moaned like a tortured soul. 'But she hardly drinks and she never ever gets drunk. Never! And she'll *kill* me, Roe. She will! She'll destroy me! And you! She'll kill you too, she won't think twice about it. She'll put a stop to us, just like that. She'll grab hold of you and fling you out by your ear and she'll ring up your Mum and Dad and ask to have you gelded, and . . .'

So she went on with a remarkable discursiveness. She might well be out of her mind with panic, but she seemed to think she was watching a film rather than facing an imminent catastrophe. I told her harshly to get her bloody clothes on, as she was still stark bloody naked. But Sheila remained immobile as well as naked as she explained her senseless reasoning. Her mother, she moaned, always worked by obsessive pedagogic rote and the letter of the law. If she said she was going to be away until ten, so it had to be, no alternative was possible. Hence her being back home by eight must be some sort of hallucination, it couldn't be any proper version of reality. I lost all patience and insisted that she whistle on her bloody tights, knickers, bra, blouse and sweater. Meanwhile, like some smug *Jeux Sans Frontières, It's A Knockout* ace, I had whipped on my jeans, my shirt and slim-jim tie. My jacket lay folded on the sofa looking impressively blameless. As the door opened, I was not just respectably attired but seated where I could see both the invader and my gibbering naked girlfriend. By an impossible, quite incredible fluke, the final angle of the door had temporarily blocked the intruder's view of bare-arse Sheila. I knew now I had two seconds to enact the impossible and save the pair of us from a hellish fate.

As that stern, familiar figure entered the room, I rocketed across to the antique velvet sofa. I whisked off its garish crimson cover that had been put there to catch the hair from their moulting cat. I hissed at Sheila *sotto voce*, 'Kneel down! About six inches. No more and no less!'

'Eh?' she wept amazed. 'Eh?'

'Do it! Do it, or we'll never see each other again!'

Sheila sniffed and obediently stooped. I held up my screen in front of her. Meanwhile her heavily moustachioed old grandmother stopped by the door and gawped at me astounded. We had met just the once, and this hairy old beldame held even less cordial regard for me than her headmistress daughter. She was eighty-eight in 1967, which meant she must have been thirty-one when the First World War broke out, and six years old when D.H. Lawrence was born. I doubt if she had ever got round to reading *Lady Chatterley's Lover*, yet if she had only known it she was presently an unseeing witness of a West Cumbrian pastiche of that scandalous literary psycho-history.

'What the hell,' she growled, 'are you bloody well up to?'

Mamie Petch hailed from desolate Annie Pit, Workington's very roughest outer suburb. Though even by Annie Pit standards, moustachioed Mamie was not so much a rough diamond as a jagged shard of broken glass.

'I'm a toreador,' I told her, and I waggled my crimson sheet at her.

'You *what?*'

There had been a surprising note of confidence in that bilious and ludicrous announcement. I repeated, 'I'm a Spanish toreador,' and in fact my drape was of such a violent hue it did suggest fateful passion and a sanguinary Mediterranean melodrama.

'A corridor?' she echoed.

'I'm a bullfighter, Mrs Petch!'

'Bollocks!'

I twitched the red cloth at her again as if Mamie were an angry old bull as well as a rough diamond and a broken bottle. I said, 'I'm a pretend bullfighter! I am, honest to God. Sheila's mother isn't the only one who's involved in local dramatics. I'm auditioning next week for an amateur group. Seriously I am, I'm as keen as mustard. They're doing . . . that is, they're rehearsing, a dramatised version of, ah, *Blood and Sand* by Vicente Blasco Ibanez.'

Mamie croaked outraged. '*Who* bloody is? Who is? Which Amatass?'

'I –'

'Do you know bloody what? I think you're bloody light.'

'I –'

'Look at your terrible haircut for one thing! You look more like a woman than a man. Aren't you ashamed of parading around like a fluffy young nancy? Which bloody Amatass are doing a play about bulls?'

Hers was the proper raw slum pronunciation. Mamie Petch was one of the coarsest sociological exports you could hope to meet in a day's march. Though apropos blinding ironies, she mightn't like my womanish centre-parting, yet I had only to whisk back my toreador's crimson cape to show undeniable proof of a startling red-blooded machismo.

I babbled furiously, 'The Fingland Miners Welfare

Amateurs! It's a new group and it's a young group. We're a brand-new and a very radical new group. Mostly students on vacation, and a few sixth formers, and we've hired the Welfare Hall. Though it's barely official as yet, and you won't possibly have heard of it. Not a chance. You have heard of Blasco Ibanez though, haven't you? Rudolf Valentino was in the famous film of one of his stories about the First World War. You maybe saw it as soon as it came out in 1920. Do you recall *The Four Horseman of the Apocalypse*, Mrs Petch?'

Would she remember it? It all felt apocalyptic right enough. I listened petrified to what was going on underneath my bullfighter's cape. I could just make out some anaerobic gasps and groans which might or might not have been an incipient epileptic fit.

'Horsemen with puckered lips?' gasped Mamie.

'No, apocalyp–'

'I know nowt about that. Where's our bloody Sheila?'

I was amazed. This vicious Annie Pit termagant had *absolutely no idea* that her granddaughter was crouched bare-arse behind a makeshift doctor's screen! Was it credible, would anyone ever believe me when I related this story ten or twenty years from now? If it had been a TV sketch it would have impressed no one older than five. It was as farcical as Eamonn Andrews' *Crackerjack* or Richard Hearne's *Mr Pastry* or the clown Charlie Carroli in *Billy Smart's Christmas Special*. Modestly if quietly I applauded myself for being such a natural and impromptu amateur Feydeau, for being Fingland's reply to Whitehall farce and pants-dropping Brian Rix.

'She's busy up in the bathroom, Mrs Petch.'

'Well she can get her bloody self out of it! Her Mam's gone and collapsed during *Puss and Boots*.'

'What!' gasped a naked ghost, and I drowned its cry with my own exclamation.

'What!' I bawled by way of hysterical descant.

I tautened my cape as Sheila groaned and whimpered. I

was quaking and shuddering myself, of course. Unless I gagged and bound Sheila she was sure to race off to see Jessie, no matter the final cost.

Mamie fiddled with her moustache and leered at me contemptuously. 'What the bloody hell d'you think you're doing? Put that bloody cloth down will you? Why the bloody hell are you making that peculiar noise?'

I shimmied my cloth again as if I'd been doing a magic trick. Simultaneously I hummed and snorted random snatches of Iberian sounding gibberish: '*Hasta la batata!* I'm tussling with the bull! *Hasta, hasta.* When a toreador does this, Mrs Petch, he always sings and grunts a bit. There's a Spanish technical term for it but I've forgotten it. *Aye aye aye aye. Ole bambino, putana e manana.*' I paused and shoved Sheila firmly down by the top of her skull. 'Collapsed did you say? Mrs Starr's collapsed? Is she al–?'

Mamie tugged her whiskers and voiced a stony derision. Doubtless she had done the same during Jessie's Annie Pit childhood at anything not lethal nor involving a prospective amputation.

'Of course she's alright! She just got overbloodyheated. It was boiling in that bloody old school hall. I told her to pull down her corsets and shove her head between her knees as far as she could stuff it, but she hissed at me and ordered me to shut my gob. It's probably her stupid, blasted nerves for all I know. She worries and frets like the fool she is. She worries about stupid Dick and worries about stupid Sheila and no bloody wonder when her chap's a capering nancy flossie who thinks he's a dago bullfighter.' She paused to hawk her throat and then, finding no suitable spittoon, decided to swallow it. 'At any rate, she was sick all over her lap, and we came back right away because of the stink. Dick's taking her up to the bathroom, so Sheila had better stop her titivating and get her bloody self out of it. I'd best wander up and see how Jessie's doing, I suppose. As for you and your Amatass, just you cut it all out before they come down here! The last thing Jessie wants is to see you prancing around like a music-hall fanny with a bloody great crimson duster. Though it might stir daft Dick to give you your marching orders. The sooner the better as far as I'm concern–'

She snorted and cussed and staggered out of the room. I blinked at the slammed door. On the spot I offered up stunned thanks that secular miracles were still possible in High Harrington as late as 1967. I turned to Sheila who was still hysterical beneath her abracadabra screen. Instead of chivvying her out of her paralysis, I began to dress her as you would a child. We had about half a minute's grace, if we were lucky. I made her sit down like a little girl. I pulled her knickers over her feet and dragged them up over her thighs. I rolled on her crumpled new tights as if I was doing textile screen printing for A-Level Art. While she mumbled and fretted, I buttoned her blouse, and as she asked her senseless questions I pulled her black sweater down over her head. It popped out like a child's, and she blinked and smiled, but I did not offer to kiss her as she wanted.

# 8

*High Mallstown, North Cumbria, 16th November 2001.*
*Lunchtime satellite viewing and listening.*

## 240

Today's listings.
    1.00 Genghis Khan
    2.00 Benny Hill
    3.00 William Thackeray
    4.00 Simon Dee
    5.00 Kiki Dee
    6.00 Pol Pot
    7.00 Slim Pickens
    8.00 Marcel Proust
    9.00 Tom Mix
  10.00 Vlad The Impaler
  11.00 The Great Train Robbers
  12.00 Dave Dee

## 156 *(keyed in in error)*

Bordered caption with programme details for Cwmri Digidol.
*Tyddynw* followed by *Wedi 6* followed by *Planed* followed by
*P'nawn Da*.
    *Tyddynw. Mae Sioe y Tyddynwyr yn ddigwyddiad blynyddol*

*a bydd tim Gwynnio'n ymweld a'r sioe ar gyfer rhifyn arbennig o'r gyfres arobryn* [Gwynnio visits the Smallholders' Show].

I didn't linger too long over Gwynnio chatting about pot leeks to those sombre old chaps in flat caps. The Welsh channel, sad to say, was not one of my favourites, it was just my hamfisted keying in of the handset numbers. That said, I mean it sincerely when I use the adjective 'sad'. It troubles me considerably, just possibly crankily, that I can understand Arabic but know almost nothing of the three Celtic languages of the British Isles. So although I can follow Akbar TV and its regular bulletins about the Afghan War, I can't even follow the plot of *Postman Pat* when it's dubbed into Hebridean Gaelic. Just possibly this sounds like the whimsical complaint of a blustering Great Britisher, but it's more a case of acknowledging some pathetic and inappropriate limitations. After all, I'd have to travel thousands of miles to make use of my Arabic, but only two hundred miles to Stornoway or Port Madog or Donegal to make use of Gaelic, Welsh or Ulster Irish. Even though I know that Cwmri and Cumbria are philologically cognate, and even though in most respects that matter my county is an outcast quasi-Celtic province, as a middle-aged middle-class North Englishman I feel very ashamed of my arrogant linguistic hegemony.

Of course in 2001 there is no such thing as a monoglot Welsh-speaker, or a West Corkman without the English, or a Raasay weaver who only has the Gaelic. No doubt such innocents had vanished by say 1901, for it's hard to imagine a British soldier plucked from remotest Uist in 1914 making it through Flanders or Ypres without knowing a few handy English words like 'mud', 'bullet', 'gangrene', 'shit', 'fuck' or 'hell'. These days anyone who refers to 'a fish' as '*an t'iasg*' in Lochmaddy has also to call it 'a fish', whether they like it or not. It is certainly a fine and very admirable thing for anyone to be bilingual, but it is invidious that for our British Celts it is obligatory, and that no reciprocal demand is made on a visiting Sassanach. Compulsory Welsh for prospective Cardiff civil servants aside, a B and B owner in Barmouth or Scarinish would indubitably and violently shit a brick if a cove from Taunton or Tunbridge whipped out his phrase book at the breakfast table and in the Hebridean case said, *Ciamar a tha sibh an-diugh? Tha mi ag'iarraidh* Cornflakes *agus* Maxwell House decaf, *tapadh leibh!* (How are you today? I'd like cornflakes and brand-name decaf, thanks!)

All this is highly pertinent to a bizarre and incredible encounter I had twenty-five years ago with a man on the run from the police . . .

Appearances are sometimes misleading hallucinations of course, and the truth was altogether more complex. The individual in question was not in fact a criminal, or at least not a criminal in the context in which he was sought. However, for a man in a panic and on the run, and just possibly because he had drunk a considerable volume of Jura whisky in an attempt to control his terror, he was also unbelievably prolix. Once he'd finished his frenetic and protracted account, his strange old friend sat opposite went one better and regaled me (or do I mean 're-gaeled' me?) with a tortuous and fantastic species of living Celtic myth or, perhaps more accurately, a didactic Celtic fable?

I met this 'criminal' on a small Gaelic-speaking Hebridean island which might have been Coll, might have been Tiree, might have been Raasay, might have been Berneray, might have been Eriskay, might have been Scalpay, but I refuse to identify it on principle. As a journalist I know everything there is to know about confidentiality and protecting my sources. In any case, for all I know this strange man is still on the run twenty years on, so I do not wish to give the island policeman, who by now must be in his early sixties, any excuse for rousing himself from his colour TV and the latest cliffhanging episode of *Brookside* (broadcast needless to say in Liverpudlian *Beurla* not in *Gaidhlig*) . . . and pouncing like Hugo's Javert upon this island fugitive who so convincingly professed his innocence.

But to sketch in the appropriate background detail. In 1975 the BBC decided to broadcast nationwide every Sunday morning a Gaelic for beginners series called *Ceart Ma Tha*, roughly translatable as *Right You Are Then!* It had been shown originally only inside Scotland, and it was a puzzle though a delight to me that someone like myself living in Moreton-in-the Marsh in the English Cotswolds was able to enjoy the entire six-month series. The programme was contemporary, amusing and irreverent, and among other things had a devious gift-shop owner in Portree selling tartan claptrap to gullible Canadian tourists anxious to practise their stumbling ancestral Gaelic. I bought the accompanying book and cassettes, watched all twenty-five programmes, and by the end of it had enough Gaelic to ask for a bar of chocolate, a double Jura without ice, or a Campari and soda (*campari agus soda*) the next time I took a trip up to the beautiful Hebrides.

Not that I needed too much Gaelic in Moreton-in-the-Marsh. I was only twenty-four but was freshly divorced (I have been married and divorced four times in all) and was living in a comfortable but isolated caravan on the outskirts of that quaint old tourist town. Moreton-in-the-Marsh, or let us call it Moreton or M-in-M for short, with its famous midweek market and its proximity to Broadway, Chipping Camden, Burford and Banbury, was a pleasant enough place to spend a year on *The Cotswold Advertiser* whilst gathering my post-marital bearings. Unfortunately there was a yawning paucity of Scottish Gaelic-speakers in M-in-M, nor for that matter did I ever hear any Welsh, Cornish, Manx or Breton uttered in any of its busy pubs, not even on its cosmopolitan market day. In fact the only language other than English, Bengali or Urdu I ever heard uttered in Moreton was of all things Malaysian. An affable if sinister looking posse of Malaysian army officers was being shown around the vast market by their British army hosts, and I noticed one of these military foreigners looking at a pair of toy handcuffs on a stall and muttering something comically sardonic to his colleague in his own tongue.

Sometimes I would sit in a Moreton pub with my *Ceart Ma Tha* book, and industriously chant the Gaelic sentences. *A bheil thu ag'iarraidh tea cosy tartain agus egg cosy tartain?*, I would chunter (Would you like a tartan tea cosy and a tartan egg cosy?), and the two pub waitresses would titter because they could see at one glance I must be divorced and hence in emotional disarray, and instead of saving stamps or learning to play the trumpet had decided to teach myself a useless and comical language. I didn't particularly care what they thought, although I definitely fancied both of those young women. I loved this beautiful language because of its sibillant seashore sound and because like all decent languages it is byzantinely perverse in the things it does. For example the verb 'fag' meaning 'to leave' as in 'to leave one's wife', and pronounced as per Embassy Regal, aspirates when it becomes the past tense meaning 'left'. 'Fag' becomes 'fhag', but unfortunately the 'fh' is mute, and hence the new word, if it actually existed, would sound like 'ag'. Clearly this cannot be allowed, for it would seem too much like a meaningless throat clearing or a public-house hiccup, and especially in the context of anyone being halfway through a bottle of Jura and saying in lugubrious Gaelic, e.g., 'I was a twenty-four-year-old journalist when I left my first wife'. It is therefore given a second special aspirate, a 'dh', and thus becomes the mindboggling formation, 'dh'fhag'. The anomalous 'dh' is sounded like a swallowed throat yodel, and as a result the final form is pronounced 'gark'. 'Fag' becomes 'gark', is what I am telling you, as the present tense turns very mordantly into the past, and that seems to me at least as miraculous as an ugly little caterpillar turning into a beautiful butterfly . . .

\*

*Dh'fhag mi mo nighean Mhairead ann Di-haoine.* (Gark me mo niyan Vaireet awn Ji-hoona.)

*I left my woman Mary on a Friday . . .*

I left my caravan in Moreton-in-the-Marsh on a Saturday in June 1975, and drove up to, shall we say, either Oban, Uig or Ullapool. I left my battered saloon in a special lock-up garage and took the ferry on a blazing lunchtime to the remote little island. It was so small it could be covered on foot in a day, or in an hour or two on the bicycle which I hired from the port. I was camping near the only pub, in a small green sloping one-man tent. Of course there was no such thing as a bona fide campsite, I just pitched my tent where I felt like it and nobody objected. The island had just one tiny village, its port, with about a hundred souls in it, half of them in a new council estate and the rest in handsomely modernised crofts. The only tumbledown spectacle was the Free Presbyterian vicarage which, I saw through the window, still used old gas mantles to cope with the ubiquitous butane. Outside the port there were reckoned to be about a dozen crofting townships, which in most cases turned out to be a single farm. I spoke as much Gaelic as I could, which unfortunately wasn't very much. Paradoxically my pronunciation was a long way ahead of my understanding, and it sounded as if I knew a great deal more than I did. Once they realised in the sleepy public house or the little shop that all I knew was stumbling child's sentences, they replied to me indulgently in polite and discursive English.

Then on the Wednesday night I bumped into Criminal Domhnall, or I suppose we might also call him Criminal Donald . . .

Domhnall was a short dark-shaven man in his middle thirties, and was already extremely oiled when I entered the public bar. He wore an ill-fitting pork-pie hat and immediately put me in mind of a travelling gypsy or a fairground worker. He was visibly nervous, a literal bag of nerves, and was chainsmoking Very Low Tar Benson and Hedges, which was possibly the only concession he would ever make to caution and sensible discretion. He was sat at the bar where he was imbibing continuous replenishments of double Juras. The barman who was in his late fifties and wore denims with foot-high turn-ups, looked at him both tolerantly and scornfully. Domhnall was spending his wages like water, which was good for trade but definitely bad for anyone's dignified estimation of one's fellow man. Now and again Donald would turn to a very old chap by the door who wore a type of peaked bosun's helmet. The old man had high cheekbones and an exceptionally pink face, and would frequently whistle, pause, then murmur away to himself in his native tongue. At one stage his young collie leapt onto his knees to beg a prawn cocktail crisp, at which point the old sea salt raised his knobbly palm and admonished him, *Cha bhi!* (Don't!)

I sat on the stool adjacent to Domhnall and ordered a Sweetheart Stout and a Bunabbhain. The beer ought properly to have been the ancillary chaser whereas it was in fact the other way about. I downed the stout in one go, then bolted the Bunabhainn in order to encourage a feeling of vaporous dilution. I swiftly consumed another three of these odd combinations, though I was scarcely matching the lightning pace of my neighbour in the fairground hat.

'You are camping?' enquired Domhnall in that ponderous Teuchter English which Glasgow comedians parody so remorselessly in their Para Handy take-offs.

'It is a good healthy lifestyle when you are young,' remarked his old shipmate, the custodian of the door, who, it occurred to me through my malt and stout, might feasibly be the prototype of the original Handy. 'Provided that you do not go and get yourself pished upon by horrendous downpours.'

True enough, I replied to them, emphatically and respectfully. The conversation promptly diverged onto such interesting matters as did I the holidaymaker have a good job, a girlfriend, a wife, any children? The old man, whose Gaelic name was Sim, helpfully suggested that a young English divorcee like me should take a crack at the junior-school headmistress Shona freshly arrived from Perth. She had good money, a fine big backside, a new Vauxhall saloon, even though there was nowhere to drive it here and the sea salt soon ruined its bodywork. Domhnall, listening distractedly to the old man's candour, grimaced and glanced very anxiously at the door. Eventually I asked him gingerly and discreetly if he was just possibly suffering some sort of short-term notionally urgent private difficulty, or, alternatively, undergoing a protracted personal crisis. It was the cue for Domhnall to release his pent-up anger and vengefulness, the majestic inversion of that chainsmoking terror. He stubbed out his Very Low Tar and informed me he was sitting here waiting to be arrested by the police at any minute . . .

'Oh,' I said very gravely. 'Oh I see.'

'For a bloody crime that isn't even mine! Can you believe it, what I'm saying? How can I put it, what is the best comparison? It is exactly like that unhappy Fugitive man Richard on the ITV who didn't kill his much-loved wife but spent his whole life trying to prove he was actually on the toilet at the time . . .'

I must have looked alarmed, because the barman assured me, 'Don't worry, mister. Daft Domhnall here didn't kill any hypothetical wife. No half-sane woman would ever marry a silly drunken bugger like this, so that particular contingency would never arise.'

Domhnall looked surly, not at this standard bluff calumny of his personal integrity, but at those strange English polysyllables. He had the barman translate them for him and grunted sourly at the reply, though for the life of me I can no longer recall what the Gaelic is for 'hypothetical contingency'. In any event, I asked Domhnall what his crime had been, or rather what it was he was wrongly accused of. Rather than horrific wife-slaying, it turned out to be dangerous drunken driving, though of an interestingly tangled and fictive nature. Domhnall's job, he disclosed, was as a builder-cum-plasterer, at which point Sim the bosun made a punning jest about drunkenness and his friend's slippery trade. Domhnall scowled at the stupid interruption, downed his fifteenth Jura, and added that two weeks ago he had taken on a casual helper, against his better judgement, a man from Mull, a joiner from Mishnish called Oxie Munro . . .

Sim snorted and scratched the apex of his cap as if he had itchy dandruff beneath it. 'Never trust any bugger who hails from Mull, son. They are all extremely wily, no-good bastards.'

Donald did not demur at this gratuitous inter-island slur. He went on hoarsely, 'We were driving in my pick-up to the job down at Caolas, a bungalow conversion for Fat Robsie, together with an Acapulco patio incorporating a cocktail bar conservatory annexe. It was the end of our dinner hour, and I was altogether far too happy. I was full of drink consumed in that chair behind you, as Tormod behind the bar can testify, because he was the same bugger that served it me. Oxie Munro did not drink, he was as sober as a Mishnish seal. Because I was well over every limit, I played the white man and gave him the keys to my pick-up, and said, you drive Munro, otherwise there might be a nasty fatality between here and Caolas. Munro said very well, OK, if I have to, though he looked at me queerly and critically, maybe because he is a stiff little to-teetal Wee Free and always ties his budgie's swing up every Sunday morning.' The plastered island plasterer suddenly stopped and stabbed his finger at me, as if I were some sceptical judge at the Oban assizes. 'But it was he was doing the actual driving, son! It was Oxie who was doing the bloody driving, not me! This barman with those beautiful turn-ups on his denims saw me give him the keys, didn't you, Tormod?'

Tormod looked terminally bored. 'So you say,' he sighed, then complained that he had heard all this rigmarole twenty times a night for a week, and so its hundred-and-forty-first narration had him less than gripped.

Domhnall fingered his pork-pie hat and hissed, 'Bastard! You bastard! You saw me damn well chuck him them! You bloody well did! After that undeniable action of mine, we set off from here with him sat in the driver's seat and with me the bloody passenger. But as we walked outside, I saw Oxie looking a gey bit sly, or I would say downright wicked at something busy turning around inside his little to-teetal head. Definitely wicked-seeming, even if he is reckoned to be a good old Mishnish elder who won't let his kids play Beggar My Neighbour on the Sabbath, and never enjoys any decent bloody binge. Between here and Caolas it was an open road, nothing around but ourselves, and Oxie seemed to be smirking away in a funny sort of way. But then, bugger me, he slyly pushes it up to sixty. And then, bugger me, to seventy, and then, bugger me, to seventy-five . . . and of course because I'd had plenty inside me I didn't mind what the bloody hell he did.

'I did mind soon enough. Going about fifty-five on that bad bend near Traigh Bhaigh, we had a very terrible catastrophe! MacLennan, the other island builder, has his pick-up parked in a senseless place on the wrong side of the road, just cos the fat and brainless bastard can't be bothered to walk the five yards to the croft he's roofing. Oxie Munro screams and shouts and swerves as sharp as hell, but all the same sheers straight into the fucker on the off side, then winging narrowly past pulls off its reinforced bumper six inches from the bodywork, scrapes its lovely brand new paintwork, and by way of a show-off encore busts the front headlamp with its imported German halogen fitting . . .'

I gulped. 'Bloody hell! Weren't you badly hurt? Neither of you? Not at all? And what did this man MacLennan say?'

The plasterer was leerily disdainful. 'Fuck knows. We weren't going to stay around to ask the obese, bad-tempered cunt. He's a big man and a very ugly type of bugger. But only an idiot would have parked the pick-up where he did, and so serve him bloody well right. We did the proper thing and kept on driving straight to Caolas. Even Oxie the old Muilleach Presbyterian was very anxious to keep on going. In fact it was he took the initiative, he didn't ask me should we keep on driving, Domhnall, or should we stop and say sorry to old MacLennan, he just keeps his bloody big foot down. I am very decent about our dramatic mishap, and I tell him right away that I won't tell anyone he had crashed my pick-up next to Speckle-Haired Hector's croft conversion. My own pick-up wasn't even marked you see, so I had nothing to get in any large stew about. But Oxie Munro stays very quiet, extremely silent all afternoon while he's working at Caolas. Then at the end of the day, after I've given him his day's money, he just vanishes on the evening boat to Tobermory. He says nothing about scarpering to me, he just disappears like the wind. But I have his bloody phone number written down back at home, and the next night I ring him and ask, what's up you bloody sly and sneaky Muilleach get, why did you just fuck off like that when the bloody job there isn't even finished? I can hear him gasping and wincing and asking me to stop all my ugly blaspheming, and then he says he simply does not ever wish to be associated with that awful crash. Not him with his church elder position at Mishnish, stone-cold sober as he always is, quite out of line with his blameless character. The embarrassing gossip, if it ever got back to Mull, why it would completely ruin his spotless reputation. He says to me that he's been up praying and pondering the moral pros and cons of our misadventure all the night long, and has decided that if ever it catches up with him and he's contacted by the Mull or Oban police about the crash, *he'll tell them that it was me Drunk Domhnall was actually driving the guilty pick-up!*'

At his woeful and poisoned expression I felt obliged to expostulate, 'What a bloody hellish rotten bastard!'

'Oxie says to me that because I was very drunk when the collision took place, that makes me definitely guilty "by proxy" and "by association". He also says that it was my immoderate drinking and nothing else that pushed him into a situation that should never have happened. Firstly, because it forced him to do the driving at a very unlucky time, when some careless fool had parked his vehicle on a very dangerous bend. Secondly, because the alcoholic fumes off me sat next to him and my blasphemous babble, as he calls it, distracted him from driving in his normal sober manner. I might have only been the passenger, but he says I have no reliable witnesses to prove that I wasn't doing the driving of my own vehicle. No one was there at the scene of the crash, he says, and when I exploded and called him a terrible wicked lying bastard, and mentioned my infallible witness Tormod, he said come on now, no one would believe Tormod's unbiased word about the car keys, given that I spend ninety per cent of my wages in his sinful pub . . .'

He paused and slurped so hard at his Jura, his lip seemed to be glued to it by liquid magnetism. Heedlessly yanking the glass away, he addressed me in a solemn, beseeching tone. 'What's more, Oxie calmly informs me, I am such a byword for dangerous driving that it's an unbelievable fluke I wasn't actually drunk in charge of my own pick-up. In a nutshell, no one would believe it wasn't me who crashed it, not even my own mother. He says that in any case I have absolutely nothing to lose when it comes to a moral reputation, and a spell in Inverness jail might actually do me the world of good. Whereas he, Mr Oxie Munro, has his numerous vital Free Church responsibilities to attend to, and it would be a criminal loss to the pious wee flock at Mishnish if he was ever to be publicly done for any misdemeanour or scandal . . .'

There was a lengthy pause as the four of us contemplated these interesting moral syllogisms that had propelled Oxie Munro to this flight from secular justice. So deeply affected was old Sim that at length he deafeningly broke wind, as if speech alone, even sonorous Gaelic speech, was inadequate as a moral commentary.

'The lesser of Oxie's two evils,' the old man commented as he gave his collie his last prawn cocktail crisp. 'You should never trust any sly little sod from *Muile*, son, because he'll only stab you in the backside and then ask you for the price of the bandage.'

Domhnall's existential predicament was like that of someone suffering a horrible anxiety neurosis. He was on terrified tenterhooks because every minute he was expecting to be rumbled by the island policeman who had been making intimidatory if fruitless investigations ever since the crash. PC MacLeod had come down not once but three times to the drunkard's workshop, to inspect his Hyundai which had barely been scraped by the impact. Those few risible scuffs on the paintwork made no satisfactory forensic correspondence with the hideous mess that was MacLennan's pick-up, which was also a Hyundai. Even though it was the fat man's pride and joy, even with that luxurious German halogen fitting, the stingy overweight bastard hadn't insured it fully comprehensive, so was having to fork out a fortune to have it mended. Once he'd discovered the accident outside Speckle-Haired Hector's, he had rung the police house sobbing and ordered MacLeod to go and breathalyse the three prime suspects, but with Dipso Domhnall at the top of the list. MacLeod, who hated the plasterer at least as much as MacLennan, had mysteriously delayed the investigation for a full six hours, by which time of course Oxie Munro had decamped, and DD had achieved a unique and grotesque sobriety. PC MacLeod had told MacLennan the six-hour delay was because of a hush-hush top-secret suspected but thankfully negative sheep Foot and Mouth case on the little islet below Caolas. That islet was uninhabited apart from the twenty sheep, and their shepherd, a former hippy from Weston-super-Mare, commuted by boat from a sister islet twenty miles to the west. Convinced his excuse was baloney and that MacLeod must have bribed the English shepherd with unlimited after-hours boosing whenever he came to Caolas for the auctions . . . MacLennan followed his suspicions and consulted the previous week's *Radio Times*.

There it was in black and white, just as all the tellies on this island were still jumping and crackling away in Hebridean black and white. On the day of the crash, BBC2, which had nothing better to offer of a midweek summer afternoon, had broadcast a *six-hour* marathon of vintage *Startrek* to celebrate the fact that the show had been going ten years. And PC MacLeod, as everyone well knew, was a bloody sci-fi fanatic and an overgrown kid who liked to play with his Hornby Dublo and Scalextric sets when he thought no one was peeping through his bungalow window.

'Maybe,' builder MacLennan had ranted furiously to a furtive and blushing MacLeod, 'maybe it was *Dr bloody Spock*, Leonard bastard Nimmo, who went and crashed into my Hyundai next to Speckle-Haired Hector's! Maybe it was a pointy-scoped alien who trashed my lovely van and then disabloodyppeared off the face of our island machair.'

There was no solid proof of Domhnall's involvement but there was every chance that Oxie would send in an anonymous letter of denunciation. Tormented by the extremely mixed messages from his hypocritical and highly-strung conscience, he would likely decide that to rat on a sinner and see him jailed for his sixth drink-driving offence was better than to have the sinner strike first. Domhnall had already thought of subpoenaing Tormod to incriminate Oxie Munro, but the barman had flatly refused to testify as a witness. Dipso Donald was completely innocent, amazing as that was, but a barman by definition spent his time abetting his patrons by lying about X, Y and Z to wives, husbands and employers. To that extent, Tormod was like a kind of confessional priest who ought to maintain his professional confidentiality at all costs, otherwise his sinful, lying and all too human customers would feel obliged to shift to the pub at the other end of the bay . . .

Sim and the fugitive between them filled me in on these puzzling ramifications. Sim likened the worrying indeterminacy of the thing, viz. whether Oxie would rat and perjure himself and sacrifice a sinner like Donald, or whether indeed he would do nothing at all, to the baffling paradoxes encountered in Uilleam Shakespeare. It was just like those extraordinarily pithy dramas, *The Merry Wives of Hamlet* and *Much Ado About Shylock*, where people got tied up in tragic knots of love and hate and even murderous violence, from which to be sure there was no possible escape . . .

Domhnall listened glumly to this fatalistic commentary. He turned on this geriatric mariner toper who also doubled as his personal spiritual adviser, and told him to stop making him even more miserable.

'Miserable?' scoffed Sim, before opening up a third packet of prawn cocktail crisps. 'You, and young fools like you, don't know what a decent bloody fit of misery is! *Real* misery, the proper thing, is a noble element fit only for great heroes like in Uilleam Checkspur. Or,' he added with an infinite gravity, 'as they used to know it in the prehistoric old days on this island . . .'

'Meaning when you were just a boy?' sneered Domhnall, who was growing ever more surly in his cups.

'Not at all,' admonished Sim coolly. 'All that is just in the brooding blink of a contemplative cormorant's eye. I am not even talking, you ignoramus, about the splendid fighting clan days of the MacNeills and the MacLeods. Nor for that matter am I hearking back all the way to the eighth century, when the Norsemen invaded and likely dallied somewhere like we are dallying now, drinking and spitting and calculating their notional historical significance. Nor am I thinking of three hundred years later when Ronald, which in English is also called Reginald, was king of this island as well as being simultaneously Burly King Reggie of the Isle of Man. Neither am I relishing the wondrously heroic memory of the life of Rugged John (Iain Garbh) who fought hard and bloodily at the Gully of Despoliation (*Sloc na Dunaich*).' Suddenly he poked me amiably in the stomach. 'I'm sorry, I'll stop teasing your bursting curiosity, young divorcee from *Sasunn*, and without more ado tell you I'm referring to the days of *The Silent Ones!*'

There followed an epic public house pause and I stared at him mesmerised. The reason being not so much my dizziness at this severely condensed island history, but because that expression 'The Silent Ones' made me think immediately of nothing more wondrously heroic than the banal semantics of . . . contemporary British television! *The Persuaders, The Avengers, The Man From U.N.C.L.E, The Men From Room 17*. And now, more unhingingly, in the guise of fictionalised Hebridean history, following on from Roger Moore in Scott's *Ivanhoe*, we had a forty-part STV series with Sean Connery in *The Silent Ones . . .*

'*Na Samhaichean,*' glossed the old bosun through a mouthful of stout-moistened crisps. 'Which is to say, The Silent Ones.'

Domhnall leered at him balefully. 'The only Silent One I wish to hear about is Oxie bloody Munro. I want the greasy old bastard to keep his trap nice and shut, apart from maybe his Wee Free sermons on the Isle of Mull. So I don't give a herring's little bollicks, Sim, for your ancient bloody Silent Ones . . .'

Sim shook his head despairingly. At length he felt obliged to turn his attention to the Englishman who, as an empty mainland vessel when it came to island lore, might prove a more responsive ear. '*Na Samhaichean,*' he explained, 'were a very ancient class of people who would have been an object lesson to a mad gobby drunk like Domhnall, had the two parties ever met up across the unfordable gulf of history. Those Silent Ones, young *Sasunnach*, correspond to the very earliest inhabitants of this island, the ones who were already existent here when the invader Celts arrived. Those conquerous Celts of course spoke an early kind of Gaelic, but we have no record at all of what The Silent Ones spoke, and we assume from various second-hand historical reports that they mostly talked in *silence . . .*'

There was a predictably cracked guffaw from the hysterical fugitive. Scoffing rudely at Sim's fatuous paradox, Donald held out the money for a whole bottle of Jura, so as to save, he informed baleful Tormod, the rotational wear and tear on the barman's wrists.

'The only real records,' Sim continued staunchly, 'that we have of these *Na Samhaichean* are from the earliest folk tales of the victorious Celts. You see, son, these primitive island aborigines, these humble, autochthonous peoples . . .'

I gaped at this queer old salt amazed. 'How on earth –?' I began, and then blushed.

Sim beamed his ready forgiveness. 'You are wondering perhaps how I know the word "autochthonous"? Well it's not because I am primed in whatsit, Aunty Polly Jane, that they teach down in Aberdeen University, but because it was a Christmas tongue-twister out of the 1972 *People's Friend Annual*, and they very kindly explained what it meant in a footnote. No, you see, *Na Samhaichean*, like all examples of routed aboriginals, they retreated into the inhospitable wilderness, so that the dominating race, the pugnacious Celts, could do their necessary domination. In this case, they retreated into the numerous empty caves about the island, and so were also known as The Cave Skulkers. They slunk off, *Na Samhaichean*, and hid themselves away, and meekly huddled in those cold and rainy caves, where according to the old accounts they subsisted almost exclusively on limpets and wrack . . .'

That last word eluded me and Sim had to clarify that it was a common podded bladderwrack which was invariably eaten raw. Likewise the salty limpets were also eaten uncooked, as The Silent Ones, in their desperate troglodytic subjection, soon retreated into a permanent state of twilit melancholy and could not find the energy much less the means to cook their spartan repasts.

'Inadequately attired against the unpitying elements, these vanquished aboriginals languished in their dark and freezing caves, sucking away at their saline limpets and gnashing away understandably listlessly at that far too fibrous bladderwrack. What they ought to have been doing, I suppose, is loudly bemoaning their unkind fate, like old Domhnall here is bemoaning his at the hands of MacLeod and MacLennan if ever he is charged with the Caolas car crash. But the truly awful thing that happened to those poor aborigines was that over only a single generation *they completely lost the will to speak*! Or rather, their day-to-day vocabulary, understandably enough, became reduced to a handful of essential nouns like 'limpet', 'wrack', 'cave', 'mind' and 'sorrow'. That plus a few grudging verbs like 'don't', 'can't', 'won't' and 'shan't'. They also used a very few monotonous reference points like 'far too near' and 'far too far', and a few unhappy comparative terms like 'cold, colder, coldest' and 'wet, wetter, wettest' . . .'

Listening to the old man's bleak and sodden narrative I became overcast with a dank sort of Hebridean gloom. This harrowing picture of those desperate Silent Ones, subjected and expelled into cave bantustans by the hegemonising Celts (just as centuries later the Celts themselves would be subdued, expelled and 'cleared' by the barbarous English), it all but made me want to weep into the froth of my Sweetheart Stout. I hinted some of this to tale-spinning Sim, but he stopped me brusquely in mid-sentence, determined more than anything to impress me with the unbelievable extent of the *Na Samhaicheans'* misery.

'Not only, young Cotswolds chap, did they lose the ready will to speak! They also developed a most agonising sensitivity to even a smither of utterance among the ones sat next to them in those pissing caves . . .'

He stopped to dip a crisp in his glass of stout, then fed this pungent pap to his panting collie. Frowning mournfully, he raised his index finger to indicate the introduction of a salutary didactic motif.

'There is the notorious and infinitely illuminating tale concerning three long-gone *Na Samhaichean*, all of them bachelor males and all of them without a billowy female spouse. They were sat together one frosty evening shivering away uncontrollably in their dismal domiciles . . .'

I found myself leaning towards the old man with a studious attentiveness. Even the woebegone plasterer looked moderately alert at the prospect of some useful, practical maxim on how to cope with life's overwhelming troubles. Sim's collie meanwhile was dripping a copious saliva and he looked like a peculiar little lop-eared schoolboy as he anxiously followed his master's riveting tale.

'The first one, plunged deep inside a melancholy mist of torpid lethargy, suddenly cleared his throat for want of anything better to do . . .'

Sim paused to scrutinise his listeners. Were we sharp enough, his dim old eyes seemed to ask, to realise we had already embarked on such deep, oh such infinitely bottomless philosophical waters?

'Whereupon the one seated next to him leapt out of his ice-cold skin! With the unbearable premonition that this insensitive fellow was about to mutter something of a terrifyingly *conversational* kind, to articulate perhaps a full sentence!'

Sim's collie, hardly able to formulate any kind of sentence, stood up on his hind legs and barked at us in canine Gaelic. It was Domhnall this time, not Sim, who bellowed at him, '*Cha bhi!*'

'Much aghast,' the storyteller went on gravely, 'the second chap whimpered his terrified response, a silent or at any rate barely audible plea, not to alarm him again with any of this exhausting inter-social communication . . .'

By this stage even Tormod of the Splendid Turn-Ups (his time-honoured Gaelic nickname) was hooked by the uncanny narrative tension. His fag had gone dead after he had forgotten to smoke it, and his counter was mottled with copious ash.

'The third chap, having heard both throat-clearing and whimper from his so-called "friends", was seized by an excess of rage at having his quiet so cruelly interrupted! He rounded on the pair of them in the unpleasant pitch dark, and addressing their spectral outlines, he bawled at the top of his voice: *"What the pissing bollocks are you two gobby bastards chattering about? How the deuce am I supposed to maintain my fragile equilibrium, if you two so-called 'Silent Ones' can only indulge in deafening and unbridled gossip like a pair of Celtic bloody fishwives?"'*

There followed about ten seconds of silence, and it would have been fair enough to describe Sim's audience as four anachronistic *Na Samhaichean*. Tormod emitted a shrill little cackle, but it might have been at some private joke rather than at the fate of The Silent Ones. I for one felt altogether less confident about the generally accepted demarcations of tragedy and comedy. Listening to this riveting not to say deeply confounding Hebridean folklore, I didn't know whether to laugh or to cry. I was not a philosophical pessimist, yet I felt that mordant and ubiquitous misery was somehow the natural human baseline. Or certainly it seemed to be the case throughout the ferocious history of these remote and forgotten Scottish islands. The drunken plasterer was definitely less impressed and altogether less reverent. He slammed down his whisky glass and went into sarcastic hysterics at what he suddenly decided was an absolutely idiotic fable. He told Sim that what he Domhnall needed from him was a story with a happy ending, and the ending had to be one that helped him with his fugitive's predicament. The last thing he wanted was a lot of depressing and meaningless drivel about streaming caves and grunting bloody darkies. The old man watched him stalking off to the Gents and shrugged his shoulders wearily. He glanced at me and indicated that if the island's best known drunk was not interested in a valuable object lesson then the young English journalist would have to do instead.

'There is a word for Domhnall and his type of mind,' he sighed, 'and I believe you also have it in *Sasunn* and in *Beurla*. Have you ever heard the very useful expression "piss-wise"? The so-called wisdom being that of the excretory, urinary and disposable type?'

Then came the crux of the storyteller's homily. Set beside The Silent Ones' agonising sensitivity to human speech, not to mention their appalling ethnic and sociological subjection, Daft Domhnall's personal crisis was wholly piffling. For argument's sake, just consider the worst outcome for the feckless plasterer. Let us suppose Oxie Munro was to shop him to MacLeod and MacLennan, and he was to be sentenced to six months in Inverness jail. Far from being a tragedy, it might actually prove the making of the human shipwreck that was Domhnall. For one thing it would give him a decent chance to dry out from his lethal drinking. For another he would get some proper prison meals full of high fat carbohydrate vitamins, not to speak of a balanced diet of healthy frozen vegetables. Last but not least, it would tide him nicely over the winter when all building work in gale-force Hebridean winds was at a virtual bloody standstill anyway.

I said to Sim dubiously, 'Oh come on. That seems a very drastic rem–'

He interrupted me curtly, with an old man's stony finality. There was absolutely no comparison, he insisted, between Domhnall's very contemporary and The Silent Ones' very classical troubles. The changeless and hideous fate of *Na Samhaichean*, meaning vitamin-free limpets, leathery seaweed, brutal exposure to the elements, influenza, headcolds, rheumatism, constipation, traumatised muteness . . . that was what Sim MacDhonnachaidh, one-time cook and cleaner on an Ardrossan puffer, would call a *genuine* expert connoisseur's experience of the awesome depths of human misery . . .

## 636 *(Audio channel)*

Isaiah, Chapter 2

*Enter into the rock and hide thee in the dust, for fear of the Lord, and for the glory of his majesty.*

*The lofty looks of man shall be humbled, and the haughtiness of men shall be bowed down, and the Lord alone shall be exalted in that day.*

# 9

*Ladbroke Grove, London, 1970–1974*

I endured it as a London medical student for all of three
terms. I won't name and shame the particular university
school, although I'm sorely tempted to publicly excoriate
anywhere that could overload its pressure-cooked students in
such a cynical and calculating manner. Like many a prestige
medical institution of thirty years ago, it was run on the
enlightened Malthusian principle that they took in three
times as many students as could comfortably be accommodated in the second year. Two thirds were necessarily booted
out at the end of the first, whereupon some hurriedly
retrained in accountancy or business studies, a few became
worryingly suicidal, the rest became God knows what, I
wonder? Perhaps they hitch-hiked to Kathmandu to obtain
some spiritual tranquillity, or alternatively they panicked and
got jobs as trainee producers, presenters and script writers on
the BBC radio and *television* . . . ?

For no reason that anyone could fathom they obliged us
new medics to do enormous amounts of physical chemistry,
including four-hour practicals in colorimetry and elec-
trophoresis. We also had to learn biological mathematics and
statistical method in the form of chi-squareds and mean devi-
ations. By the end of an hour on chi-squareds, I felt so mean
and so deviant I would have liked to truss and daub the droning old lecturer with tar and feathers, or alternatively impale

him with formalin and anatomical stuffing. Somewhere around the start of May, in a physiology practical, I was ordered to excise the muscle of a recently killed frog and subject it to an electric shock. A week before that, there had been a lecture on the autonomic functions controlling human blood flow, and by way of demonstration they had brought in a sedated cat and opened it up to show how the baroreceptors controlled vasodilation, and why one's blood rushed to one's head when one stood up too quickly. The demonstration specimen was of course killed and disposed of afterwards and I still think about that little cat even thirty years later . . .

That day we were studying muscular contraction, I rose too quickly from my laboratory stool, the blood rushed to my head, and I knocked over my dissected frog. I was partnered with a snub-nosed and querulous student called Wethers, the son of a Rotherham maths teacher. My Yorkshire colleague looked at me sternly and bent down to pick up our specimen. Wethers studied for eight hours a day seven days a week, birthdays and Christmas Day included. His sole relaxation was the study of vintage public transport, and he took photographs of old London trams and buses, and stuck them in a sumptuous album donated for his recent nineteenth birthday. When he saw me putting all my books and files in my rucksack he asked me where the bloody hell I thought I was going.

'I don't know,' I said. 'Probably to a pub. It's come to me like prophetic illumination that I wasn't meant to be giving electric shocks to frogs in London in 1970. It wasn't the reason why I was born. However I don't know what it is I *should* be doing, and I probably need a stiff drink to help me to decide.'

What I opted to do, after only a couple of drinks in a noisy bar, was a revolutionary about-turn. I decided I was going to apply to transfer to the London University School of Oriental and African Studies. I already knew of one or two people who had belatedly done the same thing, and in bold practical terms it wasn't quite as preposterous as it sounded. After all, hardly anyone starting a first degree at that particular institution had A-Level Turkish, Chinese, Armenian or Sanskrit under their belt. I had specialised in sixth-form science but a friend of my girlfriend Mona was studying Classical Chinese at SOAS, and her A-Levels were in Music, Art, and that indispensable linguistic standby, PE.

I rang and made polite enquiries, and it all proved a great deal easier than expected. Linguistically speaking all I had was O-Level French and Latin, but the middle-aged Professor of Arabic, who chainsmoked the same little cigars that I did, accepted me after a half-hour interview. He told me that I sounded very keen and that I looked and sounded very intelligent, and that keenness and intelligence were the only things that really mattered in his view. To my surprise he knew West Cumbria very well, and had even been through Fingland on the train from Whitehaven to Carlisle. Carried away by his own enthusiasm he even claimed that he could picture legendary Fingland Welfare Hall where apoplectic Horlick had screened *Cockleshell Heroes* for us deafening urchins back in 1957. Professor William Garner, sixty cigarillos a day, had been a student at St Bees public school back in the Thirties, and had been drawn to Arabic as his best friend there in pre-war Cumberland was the son of a sheikh called Aziz.

So in 1970 R. Murphy from Fingland, sporting flares and a Rod Stewart fly-cut, was studying Arabic and Turkish and living in a modest little room in Ladbroke Grove. And while this Northerner was busy studying the East in the South, the North itself was also busy conquering the impressionable South in metropolitan media terms. Such tendentious hyperbole needs to be both clarified and qualified. The North, despite what they tell you, is not a cheerfully homogeneous mass, and it was only a customised part of it that suddenly found a special London patronage. By the time I did my Arabic finals in 1974, it was quite impossible to switch on the TV without hearing a plaintive singsong North-East away-the-lads *Geordie* accent. Original half-hour and hour-and-a-half dramas were still a staple of all three channels (Channel 4, it should be noted, did not arrive until 1982). Fads being what they are, it was decided that impoverished but doughty Thirties Tyneside was the most apposite motif for the pampered but feckless Nineteen Seventies. It all started with that smash hit *When The Boat Comes In* by Alex Glasgow, and thereafter it never bloody stopped. Without being set to music like a cheerful musical, the legendary *WTBCI* sounded as if it really was set to music like a cheerful musical. It was the ridiculously sentimental fault of the Geordies after all. They intoned as metrical poetry their heartfelt monologues about this desperate Thirties poverty, these soft-spoken Geordies . . . and whenever they opened their gentle mouths to speak, why it was sheer euphonious music itself.

*Noo then, oor lad, where yer gannin the day? Doon the assistance bwoard, the owny place ter gan these days? In my day, yer knaw, there wasen even that. Back afoor the Fuss Wuld Waar, yer had to raffle the coal bank fer slack and gan in the bluidy woods ter pick mushrums or starve, forbye. A weel, yah simly hod ter, yer knah, there wus neah holtunatiff in them times. In ooer day there juss wasen the money comin in at aw, hinny.* There just wasen the money. *There was nowt forbye.*

Thirties poverty in the North-East was certainly terrible, and yet its set-in-sepia Seventies teledepiction made it altogether something else. And not just the telly but the theatre itself was eager to take some truly virtuoso shortcuts. My new girlfriend Mona Roche, a paid-up member of the Finchley International Socialists, took me one night to an agitprop play in West Hampstead put on by a touring company from Camden. They were all close friends of Mona's, these gifted London actors, and all sported impressively flawless Tyneside accents in their play about the Jarrow marchers.

As for their northern characters, they were all courageous and comradely and overflowing with human warmth, and all somewhat less credible as three-dimensional Geordies than the mouthpiece cut-outs of old-fashioned temperance tracts.

Afterwards we met them in the pub next to the theatre. Prised loose from their dramatis personae, Mona Roche's old college friends were extremely likeable and perceptive people. But as we left the pub and waved goodbye, I said to Mona that a night in the bar with them would surely have been preferable to such pathetic and disgraceful theatrical whitewash. She stopped to glare at me moderately dumbfounded, then grunted something angry and inaudible. I sighed and kicked an old fag packet and said by way of stony justification: 'It's to do with simple cause and effect. Or maybe I mean just ends and means. Well-meaning speeches in well-intentioned mouths aren't going to make for powerful drama, are they? I just didn't believe in any of that Jarrow family. I was supposed to be deeply moved by them, but I ended up bloody well hating them. Were they anything better than mouthpieces?'

'Eh?' she gaped distractedly, hurrying along at her usual Billy Whizz pace. 'No, no, true enough. But the point is it wasn't meant to be toweringly high art for the intellectual élite. It happened to be a play with an important social message, and it was written by a writer with something urgent to say. If as you say Joe Torless was preaching, then he was preaching what damn well needs to be preached. Torless was banging his drum for ordinary working peoples' solidarity against heartless neocapitalist exploitation.'

I grunted. After which I snorted. So many ironies abounded, I didn't know where to start. The theatre audience had been choking with teachers, social workers, community workers and the like, and if there were any bricklayers or check-out assistants present they were doing a brilliant job of disguising themselves as gleeless liberal professionals. Meanwhile Mona Roche, the daughter of a Harley Street heart specialist, was a card-carrying I.S. Trotskyist. I on the other hand was a bourgeois liberal nonconformist whose father was an underpaid West Cumbrian factory worker. That said, Mona was twenty-six while I was only twenty, and she often viewed me, intelligibly enough, as an immature and hedonistic youth.

'Messages?' I sneered. 'Messages are ten a penny, Mona. But really good plays are rarer than gold. I should know, I've tried writing the bloody things myself. It's a monumental bloody sweat, it's not a game for pious kiddywinks. It might sound rather simple-minded, but they need – good plays – to have convincing 3D characters that you can care about.'

Mona looked as if she thought someone had put me up to ruffling her, and paid me handsomely for doing so. 'You don't say?'

'No one in their right mind cares about ideas divorced from human emotions. They can only really care about flesh and blood individuals. Real characters don't need preordained speeches stuffed into their gaping mouths. The right place for trenchant polemic is journalism and essays and books . . . not . . . not in bloody . . . imaginative art.'

Mona didn't bother replying but instead stopped at a kiosk to purchase the last copy of the *Morning Star*. Five years ago, as a starry-eyed Stalinist, I had bought its austere predecessor *The Daily Worker*. We walked back in combative silence to her flat in Shepherd's Bush where we sat side by side on her dusty velvet sofa. While she slogged her way through *Marxism Today* and the *Morning Star*, I sat and watched a BBC serialisation of Jean-Paul Sartre. Sartre, of course, was an ideological Maoist in 1974, but this *Roads To Freedom* trilogy had been penned just after the War. That wispy little genius Michael Bryant played the listless existentialist Mathieu, and even that oddly faded eye of his put me in mind of the revered creator of Mathieu. On his road to freedom Bryant/Mathieu could not commit to monogamous relationships with various troubled women, but could only commit to the authenticity of his genuine needs. His wavering eyes and his piquant look of shrugging diffidence were wholly riveting, as if Bryant had recreated and canonised the wartime existentialist and given him a hidden perspective that had not been there in the books. The books, I thought, were remarkable, but Bryant too was remarkable in this under-the-skin role he had assumed. In fact, by an irony that the Frenchman would have relished, he was more like J-P Sartre than Mathieu was like J-P Sartre, or even J-P Sartre was like J-P Sartre.

I commented as much to Mona who answered less irritably than anticipated. Nevertheless, she wasn't really interested in Mathieu's rejection of the monogamous pair-bond, not even in its glamorous televisual representation. This was because Mona herself was a real-life practitioner of that revolutionary polygamous ideology. Mona Roche believed in what others might naively term 'promiscuity' as a radical political tool. And apropos 'tools', I knew of at least three I.S. campaigners-cum-newspaper vendors who had graced her Shepherd's Bush sheets in the last six weeks. They were called respectively Jim, Sid and Dick, and those terse and spartan monosyllables said something significant about the men themselves. They were all in their mid-twenties, all curt, committed activists, two of them community workers, and the third, Dick Wren, a detached youth worker.

I never understood the signification of that term 'detached' but vaguely comprehended Dick as being something like a detached retina or a detached bungalow. Aptly enough, Wren was deeply estranged and unsure of himself, and was certainly considerably shaken by the behaviour of Mona Roche. His estrangement he would have preferred to term 'alienation', a.k.a. that Hegelian conceit *Entfremdung*. When it came to his unreformed heartstrings, Dick simply couldn't bear Mona sharing him with Sid or Jim. Certainly not in that comical dip-dip-dip way she practised after an I.S. branch meeting, as if she was in a children's gang picking teams for tig. On common ideological grounds, he couldn't openly berate her faithlessness, so instead subjected her to massive and protracted sulks, thereby reducing his possible share of her versatile dip-dip-dipping.

'But you, Roe,' Wren informed me affably, when she was busy down the street at the laundromat, 'I'm not worried about you. I don't mind you, because you're only twenty and just a sleepy little student. You're her loveable young toy-boy who lets her imagine she's still a blushing teenager. On the other hand, I really do mind Sid and Jim, my loyal ideological 'comrades'. You should see the way they smirk and preen themselves whenever she gives them the nod towards her bedroom door. Of course it's the right thing to be free and independent in any relationship, and dirty old jealousy isn't kosher. But I tell Mona, whenever she ticks me off for it, that it isn't stinking sexual jealousy in my case. Definitely bloody not! It's just good old-fashioned anger, that's all it is. I don't like my so-called comrades leering like bourgeois bastards of brothel owners. In fact I'd like nothing better than to punch their fucking lights out when I'm worked up about it.' He tailed off barely audibly. 'If good old-fashioned lights-punching wasn't so macho, so retro and so stupidly reactionary . . .'

I have omitted his phonetic East End accent, tempting as it is for sarcasm purposes. Sid the son of a doctor and Jim the son of a judge both spoke manufactured Cockney but in his case it was genuine. Dick's Dad was a Communist docker from Poplar whose son had worked very hard to read politics and philosophy at Essex University. At this point I was tempted to inform Wren of something else that might make him very angry rather than weakly jealous. But it was not the best moment and I decided to bide my time . . .

It was 1974, well after the Swinging Sixties. Yet a dated if esoteric phenomenon was just about to repeat itself in numerous metropolitan squats and communal city houses. To expand my Seventies canvas, it even outdid some recent musical chairs orchestration involving Mona Roche and her doting, lusting menfriends. Last weekend Mona, Sid Warriss, Jim Suggs and Dick Wren had travelled across for a two-day I.S. convention in rural Sussex, to a baronial Trotskyist mansion out in the sticks near Hassocks. Mona had been nominally booked in as the partner of Dick, but had peremptorily decided to sleep with Sid Warriss in an adjacent bedroom. Sid however had been booked in to share quarters with Jim Suggs, so Jim had had to vacate the room and take Mona's empty bed next to deserted Dick. Wren now explained to me how he and Suggs had been obliged to listen transfixed to the deafening and feverish moans from the pair-bond-smashing lovers next door. And how, though adamantly not unreconstructedly jealous, which was puerilely negative not to say feebly reactionary, he was bloody well incandescently blazing, man, and had wanted to batter Sid Warriss's lights out! Lights-punching, he had eventually decided that night, as he'd listened to the agonising rupture of the pair bond, was after all an expression of simple human anger, therefore potentially a positive and revolutionary force.

'Wouldn't Mona, Jim and Sid think it counter-revolutionary?' I asked him solemnly, though sympathetically.

He looked very worried. 'You think so? Well I didn't even scowl at Sid Warriss, much less flatten him or lay him out. I would only have gone and butted the bastard if I'd been boozing and lost all control.'

Three days after the Hassocks imbroglio, Mona found a solution to Wren's bourgeois sexual jealousy. For the present, feeling sentimentally loyal to Sid Warriss, even pleasantly and harmlessly infatuated by his laconic sniff, his smart cod-Cockney vowels, his hard and muscly torso, she had hit upon a very elegant third way. Having consulted with Sid who had given his cheery anything's-worth-trying approval, she had suggested that the two men share her not on alternate nights or on alternate weeks, but *simultaneously.*

'Eh?' I said, as Wren outlined this alluring equilateral triangle with a poisoned face. 'I don't understand.'

'Both of us together, Roe. Both with her both together, and both at once.'

I said, a little stunned, 'Troilism?'

He looked suspicious. 'You what?'

'You mean three in a bed?'

'I thought you said "Trotsky". I thought it was some kind of sarcasm.'

I coughed and asked wonderingly, 'Did you go for it?'

'Sort of. Kind of. But first I blew up right in her pretty face, and told her she was just a nasty little game-player, a heartless Marlene Dietrich torturer. You just like playing men off against each other, and driving them completely nuts! I shouted. I don't feel like this is any revolutionary and liberating situation, Mona. To me it feels more like what we had to study for Russian A-Level in 1965 at Poplar Comprehensive. The Karamazov brothers and that terrible woman who drove one of them crackers, sent him flying off his whanger. Of course she stormed out of the room while I was ranting, and I felt my willpower buckling right away, just like Ivan Whatsit's did. I drove off, waited a few hours, and then rang her up and apologised. I said I'd changed my mind about her idea and I was game for giving it a try. I said I'd just been reading David Cooper on *The Politics of Liberation*, and yes, fair enough, anything to subvert the pair-bond, the nuclear family, the rancid imperialist package. She listened and said nothing for ages, and then told me to meet her and Sid at his Crouch End flat, Wednesday evening sharp at ten. After our next monthly policy meeting, that is. When I laughed and said dressed or half-dressed or totally nude?, she didn't chuckle at all but said take it or leave it, Dick, it's my final offer and you don't deserve it.'

I was very attentive to his story. As conspicuous odd man out in Mona's love life, I knew almost nothing of these advanced algebraic approaches to the simple arithmetic of sexual jealousy.

'Did you turn up at the appointed time?'

Certainly he did, Wren answered in a curiously abstracted tone, as if he were relating some sort of ill-resolved ghost story. He had driven round there to Sid's flat in his old Ford van, at first queasily excited about the lurid prospect of a three-pronged erotic orgy. True, he would have preferred himself and two old-fashioned carnal females in this troilist cameo, but as long as Cadre Warriss stayed on his own side of the bed and didn't dare lay his hands on Wren for whatever playful, perverse or inadvertent purpose . . .

By the time he got to the flat, the excitement had become unadulterated queasiness, or rather incipient nausea. On a bare practical level he couldn't imagine performing anything in this physical state. He apprehended that his unreformed neocapitalist penis was in a state of independent bourgeois trembling impotence. Satisfied that there was no one anywhere near his van, and spreading the I.S. newsheet as ample camouflage over his lap, Dick Wren unzipped his flies and sought out his petrified manhood. He had to look for a very long time before he found an impossibly tiny carbuncle down there that might or might not once have been a pair of genitals.

'It had shrunk to absolutely nothing, Roe! It was a microscopic bloody pimple. I was so pitifully nervous I couldn't even have used it to take a piss, never mind use it on a woman.'

I told myself how glad I was to be spared all of this. Mona nagged me often enough for not being a political activist, but at least whenever we had a date there was no third party present for my sexual education. She had never suggested that we do anything 'together' with her comrades, not even a night out much less any erotogymnastics. I could not have endured any of the bilious sexual anguish that Wren had been put to. I certainly couldn't have stood being alone in a bedroom while she humped next door with a mutual friend, even if he were the wisest dialectical materialist since Hegel. In any event, I didn't entertain the puerile notion that sexual troilism was politically, socially or spiritually liberating. I thought that it was pagan and debauched and obscene and extremely inane . . .

I conveyed some of this to Wren and he squinted dubiously at my fossilised vocabulary. He told me once again that I was Mona Roche's little safety valve, I was her one vicarious romantic outlet. I had no avowed ideology, so with me she needed none either. And as icing on her unreformed cake, I was her six-years-younger toy-boy who somehow took the lines out of her forehead and flattered her old-fashioned, unideological side.

'I wasn't aware she had any unideological side,' I said. 'Though I suppose when we're giggling together at Battersea Fun Fair, she lets her hair down as unselfconsciously as anyone. Mona screams and whoops like anybody else, not just like a screaming Trotskyist. Do they have things like funfairs in socialist Cuba, by the way? Are they allowed there?'

Wren was staring at his tightened knuckles and wasn't listening. As for me, the feckless and unaligned toy-boy, I was sitting on a bombshell if only he had known. Was it a moral obligation to tell him, given that he flattered me as a confidant and that neither Sid nor Dick was likely to put him in the picture? I hesitated, then deciding it was better he knew the worst all in one go, I said: 'Have you met that old schoolfriend of hers called Maggie?'

He showed few signs of alertness or anxiety. 'Maggie Lessing? The posh one who gasps and hisses like Margaret Rutherford? Her whose Dad is another Harley Street bozo. Once or twice I've exchanged words with her, yes.'

I stroked my chin and looked at him protectively. 'You remember how they bumped into each other in Holborn tube station after a ten or was it a twelve-year gap? How incredibly excited they were, absolutely rapturous after losing touch for all that time? And how gradually, slowly but surely, they've been spending more and more of their evenings together since that chance reunion? Has it struck you precisely how much they monopolise each other's time these days? First of all it was an occasional weekend climbing together in Wales, plus an Indian thali once a month in Dalston where Maggie lives. These days they're spending almost every Tuesday, Thursday and Sunday evening together. Those are the ones when Mona has no meetings, so you could say it's virtually every free evening of her life. Mona's eating so much thali she smells like a walking cardamom pod or a giant garlic bulb. I don't know about you but I've been told to keep away from her flat during those sacrosanct hours. She and I meet up during the day, but hardly ever in the evenings these days.'

He was already looking as white as a Dalston garlic bulb, and I hesitated yet again. Eventually I told him how one day last week, despite her injunction, I'd gone back to retrieve a bag I'd forgotten. It had all my painstaking essay notes on Al-Razi, and as the essay had to be handed in at SOAS the next day, I had no option but to enter Mona's flat. I had knocked extremely gingerly, then hearing two distant-sounding voices, had opted to snitch in and out in an instant. I pushed the door open anxiously. I saw my bag was sitting where I'd left it on the sofa. I grabbed it and was about to run. Suddenly I heard a spitting, gasping, incredibly passionate exclamation from Mona's bedroom. I heard someone tell her at the top of their voice that they loved her to absolute desperation. Maggie Lessing's Rutherford staccato was like no other, and Mona's reply, a resonant avowal of mutual love, was remarkably melting and tender. Of course, I ought to have buggered off immediately, but instead, appallingly, I lingered to overhear what happened next.

'What did happen?' blurted Wren, looking as if he had tertiary amoebic dysentery or perhaps been robbed in a supermarket by a very beguiling-looking crook.

The talking was soon over, I said, and then it was all

action, or did I mean all fevered activity? Mona and Maggie started to make love, very fast and very furiously. At that Wren gasped and made a soprano hiccup sound. It was the first time I'd ever heard women make love, I assured him candidly, and it was a real education, a really sentimental education, it was not at all as I'd expected. I'd imagined, *pace* Radclyffe Hall, it would be all quiet and embarrassed and tender and inaudible and restrained. But they gasped and panted and moaned like any unbridled heterosexual couple, and though I saw nothing of what went on, it seemed very much like one was the leader and one was the follower, one was the active and one was the relatively passive partner.

'Oh really?' snorted Wren, as if that were some fatuous anthropological detail.

So where did we go from here. Or rather where did Wren go from there? Two or three years later it was a commonplace for feminist women who had been scarred in ugly ways by selfish men to turn towards their own sex as a safety measure. But Wren was pondering this strange arithmetic in antediluvian 1974, and he could not reduce his simultaneous equations in any easy manner. In 1973 Maggie Lessing had doted on a beautiful married man, a symphony oboist called Frank, who had turned very grey and very strange when she'd told him she was pregnant. She had had the baby aborted at his panicky insistence, but afterwards he'd deserted her anyway. Then she was both manless and childless and she'd wished with such grief and such guilt that she had had her child instead of doing away with it. As for her old schoolfriend Mona Roche, things were no better in her case really. Her I.S. lovers, Dick, Sid and Jim, all in the last analysis made her very impatient. They were all confounded by the unbridgeable gulf between their idealistic beliefs and their unidealistic feelings. If they were not swaggering they were sulking, if they were not sulking they were grovelling, and if Dick Wren wasn't sulking or grovelling he was alarmingly capable of becoming completely emotionally disabled.

Mona said, as she showed me the door for good at the end of that summer, that of all them I was the best of the bunch. I was the one she'd kept apart as her innocuous teenage romance, the one she kept hidden away for an old-fashioned – what was the idiotic word? – 'courtship'. But now Mona had found both romantic love and her purest erotic instincts focused together upon another woman. It didn't seem to matter that the woman in question was entirely unpolitical. Maggie Lessing like Roe was just a milk-and-water liberal, and like him she symbolised an old-fashioned courtship. They had their long and drawn-out luxurious breakfasts in bed. They had their ten-ton bourgeois Sunday newspapers, complete with glossy supplements. They had their pungent red wine cosily imbibed between the sheets after a gentle Renoir movie at the Everyman. All that corny old rollcall was of the unreformed but remarkably unproblematic heart. Mona's ideological head, long immune to all sentimental change, was safely left to its own devices.

I took my notice to quit and walked back desolately to Ladbroke Grove. I was not quite crushed beyond repair, but I felt that kind of disconnection and hollowness that comes with any broken love affair. Mona had been the second romance of my life after Sheila the schoolgirl, and now she said she had no desire to see me ever again. There would be no more confidings of an ideological backslider over strong French coffee. No more serendipity trips for us to see any old stupid film as long as it was on a screen and there was ample popcorn and ice cream to offset the tedium. I calculated that there would be a finite or possibly infinite amount of bleary stagnation to get through between now and finding some-one else. The best antidote would obviously be academic work, meaning arduous evening study as opposed to arduous evening pleasure. I looked wearily at the row of Arabic texts on my bookshelf, all of them crying out to be read, digested and expounded on. The infinite subtleties, the allusive nuances, the decorous Persianised geniuses of Ibn al-Muqaffa and Abd-al-Hamid al-Katib? Or no, perhaps I should profitably start with the courtly mediaeval *maqamahs* of al-Hariri and al-Hamadhani? I stared at the stern and glittering tomes and at my foot-thick Classical Arabic dictionary and decided yes, yes, I would bury myself in learning instead of burying myself in the stony granite of a reformed and reconstituted Lesbian Marxist! Brickwalls be damned, I quietly cried aloud! Life was hard enough in your early twenties in the early Seventies, without saddling yourself with such a millstone. Better to work diligently at getting yourself a really good degree and . . .

Though first perhaps I would . . . watch a little . . . ever such a little . . . ever such a negligible bit of *telly* . . .

Purely as a restorative and an emotional calmative, perhaps even as a helpful carminative. But truthfully, it needs to be reiterated that mine was the very first generation to grow up with the television, a.k.a. the *Fernsehschirm*, meaning literally if gracelessly *The Distant-See-Screen*. I grasped the little black knob and twisted it hopefully. My 1974 telly was a twelve-inch portable black and white, and its inside aerial was a twisted metal coat-hanger. To switch channels you trundled a rotating circular scanner just above the screen. By this homely if antiquated means you soon apprehended as if by neural reflex that dignified, intelligent BBC2 lived to the right of vulgar, unprincipled ITV, which in turn dwelt and exerted its influence to the right of the almost as undemanding BBC1.

I tuned as always to BBC2, and to my amazement who should be staring me in the face but my guardian angel *Mathieu* . . .

It was Mathieu himself! It was the brave and legendary existentialist who could not commit himself to an expression of bad faith, meaning needy women who had the colossal impertinence to demand his soul and his heart as well as his time and his money. It was Sartre's charismatic alter ego

Mathieu, who might have met his match if not his defeat in the shape of Shepherd's Bush Mona and Dalston Maggie. But where exactly would these two strange women have fitted in the great philosopher's schemata? As philosophical aberrations? As rogue equations entirely off the scale? As bastard phenomena, if not bastard epiphenomena (as in a gardener's bastard-trenching or those bastard sizes referred to in old-fashioned printshops)? Weren't, after all, Sartre's/ Mathieu's coordinates of emotional autonomy based on the supposition that it was only put-upon *males* who needed such autonomy?

I sighed with great disappointment as I saw that no, it wasn't J-P Sartre's Mathieu after all. It was rather meta-Mathieu, Virtual Mathieu, Mathieu's Ghost, whichever convenience title you prefer. It was in fact the brilliant actor Michael Bryant, who was, as I've said, much more like Mathieu than Sartre's Mathieu was ever like Mathieu. It was M. Bryant in a half-hour one-off original drama. Of course anyone born after 1970 will have no idea what I mean by this, as those costly risk-taking, quixotic entertainments are somewhat less conceivable now in 2001 than say a three-hour Lutoslawski recital would be upon BBC Radio 1. In 2011, when I will be a surly old sexagenarian, perhaps I shall tell my assembled grandchildren about those preposterous preCambrian days when they had *one-off plays on the telly* ('days when they had "one-off plays", grandad, on the television, old man? Nah, go on, you're pulling our legs you one-off mendacious old bugger, you!'). In any event I licked my lips in keen anticipation as surely Michael Bryant was the finest TV actor of his day . . .

I watched in torment as the play unfolded. It was a remarkably hopeless conception, a real prizewinning failure, as only an ill-thought-out TV playlet could hope to be. It would have been a lie to call it a drama, inasmuch as it was in no conceivable sense dramatic. Structurally speaking, it was a bare two-hander with an eminent TV comic cast in a serious role. The comic Ted Ray, usually a master of dry one-liners and false starts on his trademark violin, was acting as Bryant's father. Bryant tonight was portraying an all-purpose artistic type, a celebrity writer of sorts, come to monied fame, but wrestling with his past in the shape of his tyrannical working-class Dad. Ray did his very best with the brutal old father's lines, but sadly impressed not even my landlady's cat Willy who was gazing with a stunned expression through the sitting-room window. The tyrant had actually died a decade earlier, but Bryant had repeated fantasy conversations with his ghost, including traumatic childhood confrontations where the grown man aped the troubled schoolboy. This was a *de rigeur* convention from some recent Dennis Potter plays, but in Potter's case expensive film rather than parsimonious studio sets was employed to convey the fantasy. This pallid bayko-set design certainly didn't give tonight's offering that imaginative thrust up the backside it so direly needed.

Talking of backsides, at one point short-trousered Bryant, now the deracinated literary man of 1974, was being disciplined circa 1940 by his father Ray for some deed of appalling wilfulness. Bryant the man was forced to touch his toes while the dead father caned him harshly for an intractable spirit of rebellion. The chastised adult thereafter addressed the camera with a glum, inconsequential rhetoric, and the flagellant tyrant made a fitfully ruminative speech to the same object. Despite the hieratic ritual of the flogging, there was no real pain perceptible on the visage of either son or father. There was no real pain and therefore no dramatic gain, though inevitably there was plenty of talk, talk, talk, of an incontinent and peevish and – why not underline it? – supremely *decadent* kind.

This play was a perfect oxymoron, as it was entirely without any drama. Why then did I sit and watch it to the end, rather than confronting the genius of Ibn al-Muqaffa?

# 10

*High Mallstown, North Cumbria, 18th November 2001.*
*Lunchtime satellite viewing and listening.*

**240**

Today's listings
    1.00 Tutankhamun
    2.00 Norman Wisdom
    3.00 Marie Corelli
    4.00 Marie Stopes
    5.00 Marie Lloyd
    6.00 Semprini
    7.00 Mae West
    8.00 Emmanuel Swedenborg
    9.00 Chubby Checker
  10.00 Horatio Bottomley
  11.00 Maurice Maeterlinck
  12.00 Mrs Mills

**212**

A health-magazine programme called *Good For You*, one
where the title puns, regularly signifying, bravo, well done!
especially in those cases where viewers are following spartan
weight-loss regimes or trying to improve their unhappy sex

lives through taxing types of foreplay . . . and giving selfless and unsparing televised confessional to that effect. Today the final news report on *Good For You* is of a very different nature, a cross between tragedy and apparent farce. It takes the form of an extraordinary bulletin from Spalding in Lincolnshire, where the commonest crimes are shop burglaries or occasionally organised sabotage of fruit crops at the nearby nurseries. A haggard-looking fifty-year-old called Willy Willis, a Spalding gents' hairdresser, has finally been arrested and convicted for assault or rather for his twenty-seventh assault on various innocent members of the public.

'And once I'm out of Lincoln jail,' Willis defiantly informs the *G for Y* cameras, 'I shall do the same kind of thing again. I know what's the right thing to do and what's not, and I'm prepared to pay for my deeds.'

Willy's first twenty-six victims, with the identical consideration in mind, had declined to prosecute the barber. Though to be sure plenty of them had remonstrated or screamed at him when the bizarre ambushes had occurred. One heavily tattooed butcher in his mid-twenties called Alvis had raised his bulging fist and threatened to lay Willy out if ever he did that again, no matter his excuses. Likewise a woman in her early forties had said that the barber should be sectioned in a mental hospital if he thought it was proper to commit these assaults in the name of necessity and personal conviction.

This woman was called Sadie Withers and she had been walking home from her job at the Spalding specs factory, preoccupied with her copious day-to-day worries as she explained now to the Health and Family Channel presenter. Sadie was forty-two in 2001 and had been amazed to conceive for the first time aged forty, a very elderly *prima gravida* in Spalding terms. Her 1999 boyfriend Barrie, the miracle baby's father, had taken up long-term employment in Saudi Arabia once he'd digested the joyous news, so as well as being an elderly *p.g.* she was now an elderly single mother. This partly justified why the e.s.m. was doing what she was doing when she came face to face with Willy Willis who after about two seconds' hesitation committed his attack. Sadie was flabbergasted. She thought he was aiming a deranged blow at her person and shrieked in demented terror. At this Willis solemnly explained why he had assailed her, a speech which encouraged Sadie to burst into a torrent of pent-up misery. She told him she was a geriatric single mother, meaning ninety per cent of the time at the end of her tether, one whom everyone sneered at, especially the bloody Labour government who thought she'd gone in for senile conception to get family credit and sponge off the socialist state when in fact she worked at a bloody boring slave-wages specs factory, all too par for the course in an exploitative industrial backwater liker rural Lincs.

'Oh?' said Willy Willis moderately attentively, and he dallied to listen to the rest of her outburst.

At first he seemed to show a glimmer of something akin to human sympathy. Then he shrugged his skinny shoulders and advised her that made no difference to his future policy. A week later, having secretly watched her wary exit from the factory for the previous five nights and seen what she was up to every time, he had confronted her at the same corner, and this time with a handy weapon of sorts. He had flung it willy-nilly in her face, covered her from head to toe, and told her that next time, if there was a next time, it would be a bigger version of the same.

There then followed amateur video footage of the barber and his wild behaviour on a recent market day, the 4th October 2001. Willy Willis was to be seen boldly pushing through the crowds, circling round the clothes and cosmetics stalls, carefully scrutinising everyone as he went. At roughly every third or fourth person his fist would reach out to grasp or buffet the hapless citizen. Alternatively, as if just for the fun of it, he might give them a duellist's to and fro slap about the chops. On another occasion he seized a pint glass of Guinness from a startled stallholder and flung its contents at someone he'd already buffeted but who hadn't heeded his sinister warning.

'Next time, mark my words, it'll be far worse!'

'Eh?' from the drenched innocent who was regurgitating the unsolicited alcohol. Gasping. Snarling. 'I've had enough of this! Bugger off you bloody madman! I'm going to get the police on you this time.'

'See if I care! What do I care? Why the hell should I, after what I've been through?'

'Yes, we know all about that! But it's not our problem, it's nothing to do with any of us, not at this point in time. You've got no right to keep on doing what you're doing.'

'If you refuse to care about it, then I will! I'm going to do your caring for you.'

The twenty-seventh victim, the one pressing charges, was a corner-shop proprietor. Forty-five, completely bald and humorously surly, his name was Dexter Pinckney, and he also knew all about Willy Willis. What Pinckney was frightened of was the logical extension of the barber's limited logic . . . viz. to attack the hated thing at source, and more than likely Pinckney's premises, whose antiquated nameplate, first put up there by his Dad Clarence back in 1967, gave the game away rather too conclusively.

Dexter's shop bore the cheerful insignia *Sweets–Pinckney– Smokes*, and you've doubtless already guessed our postmodern twenty-first century rural Lincolnshire riddle: Willy Willis was a small town *fag vigilante* . . .

Whereas government health-warning signs on gorgeous advertising billboards variously assure the public that smoking Silk Cut or Embassy Regal can damage a pregnant woman's foetus, seriously wreck the health of any smoker whether pregnant or not, cause heart disease, cancers of the lung and mouth etc. . . . and while that same freedom-espousing government tolerantly refuses to proscribe the seemingly lethal, possibly abortifacient activity, the Spalding barber matches their golden words with his bold as brass deeds.

*

When the fit takes him, and Willis on one of his walkabouts sees some citizen flagrantly puffing away, inhaling tars that as every schoolboy knows turn a white hankie shit brown, swallowing nicotine that is superaddictive, carcinogens that more often than not are not carcinogents etc., Willis storms across and knocks the burning gasper out of that puffer's kisser. Once the fag has hit the deck, Willis stamps and screws his heel on it for good measure. Then he emits a victorious hooting noise. Of course he is committing a serious criminal assault, but on the other hand he is probably lengthening the life of someone's mother or father or brother or sister. You'll be relieved to know that W. Willis never attacks anyone even remotely like a teenager, lest it be misconstrued as some sort of interfering sexual assault. Instead he simply hands the chimney-aping young un a photographic poster of his wife Cecily in her final stages of lung cancer, taken on the very last day of her life, in a leafy Spalding hospice called The Bower.

The photograph never fails to shock even a hardened ten-year-old Spalding chainsmoker. Cecily, a community dynamo and founder of many a campaigning group for better playgrounds, better youth clubs, better nursery-school provision, better everything worth having, had fought her cancer right to the very end. The last stages of lung cancer when she was eaten to emaciation by secondaries and it had spread out to her delicate bones (in her teens she had been a very promising young ballerina) and she was in such terrible pain that her morphine level was off the scale . . . she weighed three-and-a-half stones and looked an unadorned and unapologetic skeleton. Normally that word is intended as a hyperbolic simile, but for once it was a true and absolute comparison, she was a fleshless and terrifying corpse, a hideous rattle of bones that croaked and weirdly spoke.

What she said to sobbing Willy was, 'Now mind.'

'Ugh? Yes? Ugh?'

'I've only got two words to say.'

'Oh? Ugh?'

'NO FUSS. That's all. Those are the two words. I'm glad to go. I've had enough. Don't cry for me Willy, just be glad that I'm leaving all this pain behind me.'

'Ugh, ugh, ugh!'

Willis also flashed his skeleton picture at those adults who were set to pulverise him once he'd ground their B and Hs and Dunhills into the dust. In 24 point bold it bore the message, *This is my wife who smoked forty cigarettes a day for twenty-five years*, and in 12 point bold underlined italic below that, *Can you believe that once she was a beautiful amateur ballerina?*

On the reverse of his A4 poster Willis had penned a kind of angry polemic, preceded by a detailed and stomach-churning account of the progress of Cecily's lung cancer. She had had to have an arm amputation and then a leg amputation as part of her terminal treatment. Willy now had regular nightmares, sometimes set in Saudi Arabia, sometimes set in Spalding, where he himself was forcibly obliged to have an arm removed, a limb removed, and once – he nearly choked with terror in his thrashing sleep – his head removed with a scimitar for vital medical purposes. Cecily was inside a green hospice blanket on the poster, so her double-amputee status wasn't visible graphically speaking. Depicting the horror of seeing a handsome ballerina wife with first only one arm, then with only one leg, Willy went on to argue along the following lines:

'Why do these licensed murderers, the cigarette firms, give themselves such hallowed names? Embassy Regal? Aren't things like embassies meant to be the last word in official responsibility, places that represent the country and can't afford to have a blot on their reputation, a stain on the national honour? Why not 20 Slaughterhouse Regal or 20 Charnel House Regal? And what about that second little word? "Regal" meaning as splendid as a king or queen? Cecily Willis used to look like a queen when she was a young woman, but then when she was a lopsided double amputee in a hospice and weighing three stones she looked more like a horrible circus freak. So maybe it should be 20 Slaughter-house Scums or 20 Charnel House Vermins on the fag packet, should it?

'As for that other beauty, Silk Cut? Silk meaning something delicate and beautiful? It might be more accurate to call it Bleeding Rag Cut or Soiled Clout Cut or 20 Surgeon's Cut or 20 Butcher's Hacksaw Amputations. Likewise Dunhills should maybe be called Dunghills, or 20 Low Tar Shitheaps or 20 Stinking Cesspits, if you please! Not 20 Senior Service, please, but 20 Rank and Verminous Dregs, please, 20 Absolute Vermin Extra Mild, please. As for Woodbines, they are supposed to be just blameless wild flowers aren't they? So perhaps they should be renamed 20 Deadly Nightshade or 20 Wills' Stinkwort or 20 High Tar Viper's Bugloss and a little box of matches, please.'


## 233 (keyed in in error)

I had just stubbed out my lunchtime miniature cigar, a Café Crème (q.v. lip cancer, mouth cancer, throat cancer, teeth cancer, gum cancer, fillings cancer. Memo, write to the man-ufacturer recommending they be immediately renamed Cancer Crème?). Then I turned by accident to the Science Channel at 233. I had intended the adjacent Hobbies Channel, hoping I would come across that wispy-eyed Wisconsin landscape painter who had urged me to relax, enjoy myself and disdain any pedantic virtuoso brushwork. But instead of a soft-burred Midwest cowpoke encouraging me to relax, hang loose, boy, and to live life to the full, I heard a rather different transtlantic voice-over in arresting mid-sentence.

'One of these guys here is an arthropod. He's so new on the scene he still doesn't have a name . . .'

I sat for a minute agape in my credulous provincial's

armchair. At the revelation of this pristine and above all identity-free animal. In fact this nameless thing was a little fossil, and its graphic representation by 3D computerised colour imagery would have taken the stoniest cynic's breath away. I coughed and applauded with a hoarse and noisy admiration and the lingering fumes of Café Crème only added to the appreciative spluttering. *An animal without a name?* How then could anything in biological science, first and most fastidious of the classificatory disciplines, be without a bloody name? Bearing in mind that even a certain obscure astronomical asteroid, no less, was named after the Forties comedian Will Hay (in his spare time an avid amateur star-gazer), how could there be a soft-bodied zoological specimen without any denomination? How was it generally referred to taxonomically? As Thingumee, Wotsit, Yer Man, The Strange Little Thing Without a Handle?

Scarcely. The caption on the screen said it was called 82756sil-wr-900-01. Ah yes. Fair enough. We could all relax just as long as we could manage that prison-code formulation. The earnest Disney-sounding voice-over reminded us that Silurian fossils of any variety, nameless or not, were only available in three places in the world. One of these locations was in the Welsh hills, and was top secret, trespassers being arrested on sight. We are talking, warned the stern voice-over solemnly, about a time span of approximately five million years. The orthodox extraction process is much too crude for these soft-bodied fossils, so instead we have to make minute sectional scrapings of this little feller without a little name, and take detailed digital photos at every stage. Jurassic Park style animation is then used to provide us with the stunning 3D image we have displayed before us.

Of what? Of a cosmological and biological scandal? Of a creature Five Million Years Old Which Lacks A Linnaean Classification?

I tried for a few minutes to imagine myself as the freelance journalist who plied his vocation without a byline/name, so that everyone who knew him would have to resort to laborious and ridiculous circumlocution. They would all do their best with their their makeshift descriptions and their struggling, inadequate vocabularies, but as long as I had no name they would never be able to lay anything definite and incriminating at my journalistic door. I pondered all the tedious and restrictive professional taboos, the petty privacy laws and pointless little nitpicking, hairsplitting conventions I could ignore, then all the criminal, outrageous mischief I could get up to, given plenty of time and planning and cash. I grew so mindlessly excited at this infinitely childish prospect that without even thinking about it I lit up a second lethal Café Crème . . .

## 121

Logo in bottom right corner indicates we are in the LA studios of the *Kelly Windsor Show*, and a caption rolling intermittently above it asks the viewers, *Can This Really Tell Us How We Tick?* There is a little flashing graphic next to this rolling interrogation, which I take with some puzzlement to be the mysterious 'this'. I assume the drawing is a feeble representation of a ripe tomato or a red pepper and I wonder if at long last divination through the shape of fruit and veg (haruspication vegetarian-style?) has caught hold of the talk-show imagination. Kelly aged about thirty-five, with jet black hair and a frank, teasingly good-humoured manner, is halfway through an introduction.

'. . . various indications of our personalities. It's a commonplace, even a cliché now in business institutions and industry, to talk about body language, and to analyse a person by the way they stand, lean, sit, fold their arms, cross or uncross their legs. My guest Professor David Mankovic of the Applied Psychology department of Los Angeles Metropolitan University is a leading authority on this subject, and has written over a hundred (that's right, in excess of a hundred) bestselling books on the subject. His latest work is set to be his most controversial to date, because David has recently abandoned a number of his earlier ideas in favour of what might just strike some of you as a leetle wacky.

'In the past David has argued that the subtle analysis of the human smile can tell us almost all we need to know about a person, if only because the smile, says David, quoting numerous classical poets and philosophers, is "the perfect mirror" of the soul. In more down to earth terms, he has also said that the way a guy hangs up his jacket tells you a colossal amount about his inner man, his job preferences, his hobbies, tastes in women, whether he prefers eggs over-easy or sunny side up. Furthermore David has also devised a unique mathematical synthesis based on computerised images of smiles, winks, nods, shoulder clasps and other basic greeting patterns. He is the inventor of a Mankovic Behavioural Index derived from a CCTV analysis of the way a person enters and leaves a room, hangs up their coat and shuts the door behind them. This type of give-away psychological profiling expressed as a complex algebraic coefficient has been used as supplementary material for job interviews including academic appointments in Professor Mankovic's own university.

'With this fearsome international reputation behind him, David Mankovic has all of a sudden decided to step out on a highly controversial limb. He now says that his complicated mathematical understanding of all these grins, backslaps, door slams and so on, has been assimilated and superceded by a far simpler body language universal. Only one part of the human body, David Mankovic claims, and a surprise part of it at that, is worth our attention if we wish to understand its owner's hidden depths. Or perhaps we should say their absolute fundamentals. I shall say no more but let you see the cover of his new book whose title says it all . . .'

The title of Professor Mankovic's hundred and eighth book was *Take A Look Behind You*, subtitled, *It's All In The Butt*.

I noted that the rosy tomato/capsicum animation was still flashing hell for leather on the screen, and at last it dawned on me it was meant to be a blushing naked backside . . .

As for the contentious professor, he was not exactly blushing, more alert and humorously vibrant with the understandable excitement of explaining his revolutionary theoretical position. Dressed in a sober tweed sports jacket, Mankovic was somewhere around forty-five years old, moustachioed, intent, smilingly assertive and with a brisk and finely rehearsed delivery. He moved fluently between the academic and the colloquial, and clearly saw no categorical gulf between them, the one being as apt as the other for practical scientific purposes. In answer to Kelly's first question, how on earth he came to this radical theoretical focus on the humble rear end, Mankovic gently tolerated the studio laughter before peremptorily raising his lecturer's hand to still all misconceptions.

'OK, Kelly. About a year ago I was very intrigued by TV reports of a middle-aged blind guy over in the Czech Republic who claimed to have a remarkable new way of assessing and describing the human personality. This blind man was no prof scientist, but he was recognised to have some kind of extraordinary faculty of "insight" which could help anyone hoping to "see" themselves better. Until recently he had fingered and touched his clients' hands, and been able to give them uncannily accurate tactile indicators apropos their positive and negative drives, meaning their potential for work advancement, or their tendencies to subvert and sometimes damage themselves in their professional relationships. Then one morning at the end of a standard hand session, thinking he was about to shake bye-bye to his lady client, he accidentally put his hand on this woman's skirt, on his client's butt that is. She had stood up rather more abruptly than he anticipated, turning round to lift her briefcase, and the blind man had made an understandable *faux pas*. At which point he couldn't help but exclaim, "Gee!

That's so much better!"'

At those hectic musical guffaws from the audience Mankovic raised an indulgent pedagogic hand. 'Not, this Czech guy categorically asserted, because it was a pleasanter place to put one's hand! Rather it was because that female client's particular personality aura was clearly focused most concentatedly at this – what shall we say? – this lush rear embonpoint. This blind guy Menzel from Prague has since developed an entire therapeutic treatment called Posterior Rolfing and some arguably cultish New Age formulations of Binary Buttock Auras and Gluteal Hemispherics. But intriguingly the two of us, myself and the Czech, have come to extraordinarily similar conclusions even though my own approach is inevitably rooted in empirical science.

'By trial and error Mr Menzel soon discovered that he could find out infinitely more about a client when the butt in question was naked and uncovered. OK, OK, laugh if you must, guys. Get it out of your systems, you giggling folks at the back, and then we'll talk more science. Sure, you find it funny, but if you think by analogy of the blind man's original hand analysis, it would have been worse than useless for him to try and help someone if they were wearing three pairs of gloves. Vaclav Menzel has likewise been derided in certain quarters because he has given up working with his male clients and now restricts himself entirely to females over the age of eighteen. OK, OK, fellers. Have a party on the back row there if you must. But, if you'll allow me to continue. His reasoning is that his wife Alena, who also happens to be blind and whom Menzel has trained up as a "feeler", has a far stronger "touch" with the naked male behind. Hence these two blind analysts have sensibly decided to specialise, as Vaclav Menzel, for no reason that he can explain, has a stronger prescience with the information to be gleaned from the exposed female butt . . .'

At which point Kelly blinked away her incorrigible merriment and posed an obvious question. How exactly had

Professor Mankovic moved from being intellectually intrigued by the Czech's 'hands-on' discovery towards making his own independent researches? Did the Prof also use Menzel's intimate palpation technique, or did he rather focus on the strictly visual and interpretative aspects? And, added Kelly, with a baffled gulp, how on earth –?

Mankovic interrupted with a scholarly terseness. 'I don't actually need to *feel* anyone's buttocks, Kelly! I'm not blind, for one, and for two, as an academic I would clearly be open to all sorts of terrible accusations. But let me backtrack here a little, and fill out some pertinent details. I decided to start my researches close to home, in fact very close to home. With the aid of two large mirrors in my family bathroom I set to work immediately. I took down my pants and examined my own butt minutely, the same way, you comedians at the back, the old European physiognomists would stare at their own craniums! For good measure I then got my wife Cindy to take a magnified digital photo of it. I stared at this butt photograph and scrutinised it intently, and I also got Cindy to take certain relevant measurements with a tape measure. Next, I plotted ratios of the separate buttock-cheek widths versus their lengths/heights, employing a special dietician's calibratory device to measure the curvature of each cheek base, cheek side and cheek apex.'

The camera focused briefly on Kelly Windsor whose lips were moving in a fibrillating moue of hysteria. She placed her hand on her mobile mouth as if stifling an overpowering cough.

'Nonetheless, even at this early stage there was something much more glaringly apparent than all these mensuration factors. It hit me immediately as I stared at my own fanny in the bathroom that there was a simple *intuitive* connection between the singular shape and construction of my ass and the "shape" of my personality as I know and have studied it for the past twenty years! Just using my two eyes and what I would call my intellectual commonsense, I could see that my ass was me, Kelly, it really was me to the nth! It was my ineffable template, the most cursory glance told me it said almost everything about me that was worth knowing. Conversely I, Dave Mankovic, was at bottom no more than my own ass, its subtle thrust simply duplicated my subtle thrust, its gestalt mimicked my gestalt, its thusness was my thusness, its being was my being . . .'

Reaching delicately into a plastic folder, the professor retrieved his supportive evidence. To the accompaniment of braying hoots and piercing wolf whistles, he held aloft Cindy Mankovic's magnified digital photography.

'Just simmer down you pranksters there, and let me carefully explain. By analogy with a far inferior personality indicator, namely graphology, I am going to talk some elementary posteriology. My pictorial butt here, as you can clearly observe at fourfold magnification, is an unambiguously confident butt, a definite no-nonsense type posterior. It looks you democratically in the eye, so to speak, it doesn't sag and droop and try to efface itself. But now take a closer look at this lower section of the digital picture. Uhuh, and do restrain those deafening cheers. I am of course extremely flattered that you like my ass so much, but . . .

'You see here how my left buttcheek has a humorous lower pucker line? While over here my right buttock lower curve expresses itself rather more tersely, less indulgently, less patiently? The MCC (Mankovic Curvature Coefficient) on the left cheek is 0.3, but on the right buttock is a meagre 0.25, the perkier more smiling cheek boasting the higher arithmetical ratio. To which highly revelatory statistic, I would add QED and *voilà*, folks! This decimal ratio, you see, perfectly expresses the two antithetical halves of my personality, which anyone of my acquaintance will immediately confirm. You see, I can laugh and indulge people for so long, Kelly Windsor, but when my patience is over-exploited I can get pretty damn sharp! Furthermore I would also argue that the decimal difference of 0.05 is an *exact* indication of how in the end my indulgence wins out over my impatience. In the end, as anyone who knows me can assure you, I am more of a soft touch than a hard touch, more of a patient tolerant OK guy than an intolerant, unjovial and un-OK feller.

'So. Once I'd substantiated my intuitive hunch, that a subtle lexicon of the human personality could be constructed by establishing a subtle lexicon of the human behind, there was no time to be lost! I guess I felt the same kinda excitement as the nineteenth-century phrenologists who examined the bumps on folks' heads and immediately sensed they were making profound discoveries about the character via the bumps. But of course instead of feeling bumps, I was simply looking intently albeit objectively at butts. The next stage saw me taking down every art and photographic book from our domestic bookshelves, and spending an entire weekend studying every derrière I could find from classical Greece to Renoir to Cartier-Bresson. I even sent Cindy out to purchase some soft-porn magazines displaying a good many naked men as well as naked women. All in all, I studied a total of four hundred and twenty-five butts, some of them being almost two thousand years old. Many of them obviously enough were "secondary" butts rather than primary butts, meaning they were filtered through the eyes of a painter rather than an objective camera lens. Though also, and this is rather a subtle point admittedly, I would say that not even a photographed butt is the same as *das Sitzfleisch an sich*, the backside itself, it is actually a meta-butt which includes the distortive input of the editorial eye of the photographer.'

Kelly Windsor suddenly wriggled like a restless schoolgirl in her interviewer's chair as if to confirm that her own butt was a primary, not a secondary, sensation.

'In any event, the sum of my conclusions from my four hundred specimens . . . was both simple and devastating. Once again I only needed to use my two eyes to see that, hey, this demi-monde Parisian woman here has a markedly sly and insinuating ass, and hence this Cartier-Bresson original was a sly and insinuating dame of the streets. Similarly I looked at the butt of a young man in a Michelangelo drawing where the cheeks seemed to me a good bit lopsided and more than a little depressed and altogether with a guilt-ridden, loaded, heavy look about them. I took a hunch that maybe, just maybe, this young guy had had a recent bereavement, and was also sexually confused in the light of the particular MCC gap I noticed between the left buttcheek and right butt-cheek. I promise you, Kelly and the folks out there, I know virtually nothing about the history of fine art, and had no inkling at all of what eventually I would discover. But when I went away to the university library and read up on the life of Michelangelo – bingo! – I discovered that the original of that butt drawing was indeed a young Florentine courtier, who had killed his male lover in a duel held the year before, in 1533 that is. As you can imagine, I was flabbergasted to see myself apparently turning into some sort of scientific clairvoyant courtesy of my diagnostic MCCs! In the event, over the space of that weekend, as I pored over those four hundred behinds, I noticed the glaring posteriological signs of infidelity, of inferiority complexes, of obsessive neurosis, of financial greed, of duplicity, of dangerous violence and more. That said, as well as all those negative traits, the rearside of the backside, that is, I was gratified also to notice the thoroughly positive posteriology of folk whose asses declared them to be hardworking, conscientious, spiritual, tender, generous, and so on and so forth.

'But as I've already said, even before I got my wife to measure the dimensions of my own ass, I had intuited the same conclusions. Clearly the next empirical stage was to find another real and living *in vivo* butt. It would ideally be one that I knew very well, and it would hopefully permit me to compare my intuitive knowledge of its broad, shall we say, anecdotal appearance with its objectively verifiable MCCs. What I needed was a living, breathing primary source which I could study minutely and without resorting to mirrors. Of course it didn't need great deliberation over whom to employ as a primary posteriological paradigm. With her complete and disinterested consent needless to add, I took countless digital photographs of my wife Cindy's derrière, one that I have naturally been highly conversant with on a regular and bona fide intimate marital basis for the last fifteen years.

'Cindy's butt, I have to confess, over the last five years has changed its subtle geometry, its cheek curvature indices, considerably. For the first ten years of our marriage, her right buttock, I would argue with hindsight, had a 0.3 perkiness similar to her husband's corresponding buttock. In Cindy's case it was a symmetrical perkiness at that, because ten years back her opposing cheek was almost certainly an identical twin of 0.3. My eyes and my eager marital hands assured me of that delightful physical reality during our lively nuptial period starting from 1986 through to 1996. For that decade timespan Cindy Mankovic was objectively viewable as a paradigm stable unconflicted individual, equable, contented and always ready to accommodate to any intelligent ideas and suggestions. For example, she always agreed with me over most of the major life issues such as not having any kids, just having our two substitute kids, our pedigree Schnauzers Sigmund and Melanie, a whole lot more fun, liberating and infinitely less hassle day or night in my view. Plus, not in the end purchasing that cutesy little hideaway holiday condo on Monterey beach, but buying our big four-berth tourer instead, a berth for each of the Schnauzers of course, or it would have been unbearable for both them and us.

'Sadly however, over these last five years, as well as fighting very aggressively and vindictively with me over every damn issue, and becoming altogether less affable and teamspirited as a person, less of a conscientious, personable faculty wife, more of an all-night bourbon drinker and more of a junk TV watcher, Cindy Mankovic's fanny has also lost a major part of its erstwhile mega-MCC allure! OK, OK, do stop that hostile and immature catcalling at the back there, we are currently halfway through the divorce, and while she gets the fu–, scuse me, the tourer she claims she despises, I am dumped with both of the Schnauzers, a colossal responsibility for any hardworking senior prof, however pet-loving! Nevertheless, Cindy Mankovic has agreed before our respective lawyers that none of our posteriological research is *sub judice* or is her exclusive copyright – she's traded me that on condition she gets the classy beach house and both of the digital cameras. At any rate, as I just was about to point out, Cindy's behind these days is altogether very flat and featureless, very dumpy and sluggishly amorphous, a very unattractive proposition indeed. Why, can you believe this, when I measured her cheek curvatures last month they were down to an abysmal 0.1 and a truly catastrophic 0.05, a profoundly distressing asymmetry all too clearly indicating a seismic conflict in Cindy's mind between loyalty to me her husband and . . .'

Suddenly there came a comically hoarse cry from a sixty-year-old black woman right at the back of the audience. Encouraged by the mischievous Windsor, she commenced a terse impromptu analysis of the professor's spurious conflation of science and sentiment.

'Loyalty to you and *what else*, Prof Mankerfish? Loyalty to them damn ugly Schnauzers, baby! You consider, boy, them Schnauzers don't particularly care what your wife's ass looks like, do they now? Well I reckon you oughtn't to too! Fyou buy her that pretty little Monterey conaminium shack place, and mos' important give her a lil baby to take care on, or adopt one maybe fyou can't have one, you watch her poor lil squashed behind grow back curvy and luscious like a couple of big, ripe Florida peaches and . . .'


## 240

*Playful female English voice-over:* Believe it or not, which of the following celebrities *was once notorious for throwing stones at the poor old ladies in a nearby retirement home?* Study this picture of him as a naughty little schoolboy and see if you can guess.

*The Archbishop of Canterbury?*
*Silvio Berlusconi?*
*Pierre Boulez?*
*Frankie Laine?*
*Aldous Huxley?*
*Kenneth Wolstenholme?*

Find out at 3 o'clock exclusively on The Lifestory Channel . . .

# 11

## *London and North Cumbria, 1974–1999*

1974–1999? I must be joking, mustn't I? That is all of twenty-five years, a totemic quarter century, a third of the average lifespan. And in my own case it takes in the crude allure of the furious metropolis as well as the deceitful innocence of the remotest countryside. Neither of which, God help us, corresponds to any cosy silver wedding interregnum. As for the quite appalling parallels in the televisual media over that period, I will postpone my résumé until I have a free century or so to put it all down in glaring TV black and white . . .

But back to silver weddings. Instead of being married the once and manfully thriving on it, I have been wedded and divorced four times in all. Some people will regard this as a considerable if not hilarious achievement. Let them think what they like. I am definitely no glutton for psychological punishment, much less inflicting it, but it wouldn't astonish me if I marry again in my late fifties, or come to that my late sixties, late seventies or latter eighties. Sometimes it occurs to me that if I'd had children to more than one wife, it might have tempered this uxoriousness. As it is, there is daughter Sassy by moody old Fran, and the other three either could not or did not want to be mothers . . .

I have a theory which might strike some as insane but which makes perfect sense to me. I believe that I couldn't sustain any of my four marriages between 1974 and 1999 because throughout that period *I had no access whatever to satellite television*. Yes, yes, I told you my hypothesis was crazy, but there is a solid core of sanity in that nuttiness. Just before you toss away this media-bound, seen-at-a-distance confession of mine in contemptuous disbelief, let me offer two small items of confirmatory evidence. The more anecdotal of the two is this. Given that whether toiling as a freelance in Shepherd's Bush, Moreton-in-the Marsh or rural Cumbria I was always on the move, sniffing for leads, scoops, intrigues, moderately embarrassing scandals and so on, isn't it inevitable that I was bound to be a very restless and volatile individual? How else could I be, when, in addition, my income came in in the most staggered and uncertain fashion? I should have been a chainsmoking alcoholic with all that instability and stress, instead of which I generally smoked only fifteen cigarillos a day and drank no more than a bottle or so of cheap Valpolicella. Now, two years on, in 2001, I have something else, a shield, a foil, a tool, an infallible device, which stops me going down the pan or up the Sewanee or out of my tree or off my freelance rocker. In these unarguably catastrophic not to say apocalyptic times, I have at the end of my hand a gleaming sword in the shape of my beautiful digital handset . . .

At the fag end of 2001, thanks to this gleaming rapier of mine, I can battle myself around the globe geographically, politically, comprehensively. With a second puissant swish, I can also traverse it intellectually, culturally and sentimentally. I can discharge any functional restlessness through these twitching fingertips, superficially rather like those stunted imbeciles who spend all day playing video and computer games. I will go one step further and put that last word in italics: *games*. Thirty years ago they loved to make a cultural fetish of that word 'ludic', and a man called Huizinga even made a passable living out of it. Three decades on I like to play and fool about more than most, and you have it from me that there are games and there are 'games'. To manoeuvre a black electronic blip through an electronic maze and score fifty, fifty thousand or even fifty million points is, I suppose, a form of play, but without any time-bound or timeless significance. Because sadly, no one apart from the pop-eyed player concerned would ever wish to videotape and play back the progress of any individual game. Unlike chess, bridge, backgammon or even tiddlywinks, it has no depictable dramatic – or do I mean narrative? – shape. Nor, God help us, does it ever suggest any filmable anticipatory tension . . .

As I manoeuvre around this digital handset, I might be 'playing' but I am also giving myself an uncompromising education. As well as coming to terms with the universal post 9/11/01 restlessness, I am learning a great many things. I see, for example, what it is to be a war-hating intellectual from Cairo, and I hear it in choice Cairo Arabic, and I realise that I have left my own provincial backyard, and that it is indeed a salutary and educative thing to have to have left one's own backyard. Ditto even for the Hobbies Channel where the curly-haired Harpo Marx American tells me that my painting a snowstorm, however badly executed, should not be a cause for neurotic self-castigation. Even the ugly Brummie lad on the cut-price Date Me Channel, who stoutly assures me that he is 'fairly' good-looking, is assuring me of more than his frail and oh so human wishful-thinking. He is telling me ever so eloquently that both he and I are stuck in our pampered and bomb-free English backyards, and that though to be perennially bomb-free is certainly very pleasant, it is perhaps not, politically, morally and structurally speaking, outstandingly just.

In those dim pre-satellite days before The Year of the Total Eclipse, I had no matchless toy that could both divert and educate. Of course digital TV was already available by the late Eighties, but my only experience of it had been widescreen football-goggling in various rancid, smoke-filled pubs, channel-flicked on occasion to the most unbelievably moronic adventure cartoons. Sheer ignorance of its real possibilities, especially of those optional subscription channels devoted to the arts and film, kept me an unnecessary decade in terrestrial darkness. Meanwhile my incontinent workaholic habits led me to excessive boozing, brief and extended romantic affairs, small, big and enormous lies, absurdities, close shaves, embarrassments of every kind. A related consideration was that, as a hampered terrestrial, non-satellite man, somewhere around the end of 1990, it hit me with a terrible jolt that, day by day, month by month, year by year and channel by terrestrial channel, *there was absolutely nothing worth watching* on the bloody television. By that date they were crudely and ruthlessly obliterating the idea of original one-off dramas, even on the august BBC2 and the once courageous Channel 4. On the former, there were suddenly starrily effulgent costume versions of the classics, of, shall we say, the more Bridesheadian of nineteenth- and twentieth-century fictions. Moreover they were obliged to recoup their outlay on these costly cabaret slots, and had to sell them on to New Zealand, South Africa, America and Canada. Simultaneously, as if by divine or imperial diktat, everything under the sun had to pay its individual way. Meanwhile on Channel 4 in lieu of proper plays, there were stuttering fifteen-minute impressionistic 'films', affably cobbled together by pharmacologically euphoric and metropolitan art students. They were all broadcast between one and three a.m., and cost anything up to twenty-five pounds to make, though not even their doughty creators got round to watching them, much less any film- or drama-hungry autodidact from the provinces.

As a terrestrial man born in 1950, I was victim of what some might regard as mesmeric hallucinations, which were in fact worryingly genuine televisual memories. It was for example profoundly disturbing that I could relive a 1971 BBC adaptation of Aldous Huxley's *Eyeless in Gaza*. The original novel, you may remember, took on all the major sociological dilemmas of the whole world past and present, or certainly of those most pressing in the early twentieth century. Ian Richardson was Aldous's doppelganger mouthpiece Anthony Beavis, and indeed he bore a striking resemblance to the great sage, satirist, acid head and public conscience. On that same channel in that same decade I had even conjured up an adaptation of *Esther Waters*, a scandalous work about wet-nurses and horse racing by the Bohemian Irish novelist George Moore. A bilious and outrageous Gallic apparition called Émile Zola eerily materialised on BBC2 in 1972 (*Germinal*) and once again in 1980 (*Thérèse Raquin*). I could even with a trembling disorientation bring to mind Harold Pinter on *commercial ITV*, with J. Gielgud and R. Richardson giving H. Pinter hell for leather. Worst of all, and this really sent out the alarm bells for my menopausal sanity, I could still project the fearful simulacrum of *Guy de Maupassant* on the *Sixties black and white ITV* where William Mervyn, Isla Blair and Nyree Dawn Porter disported in an entertainment called *The Liars* . . .

*The Liars* was a weekly portmanteau drama with four little tales divided up by three lots of commercials. This, by the way, makes a comparable analogy with my own fourfold nuptial history, which instead of lasting sixty minutes lasted a quarter of a century. Guy de Maupassant, you may recall, as well as being a priapic literary genius died of syphilis and insanity. He paid for his libido with his life and his mind, whereas I have only been knocked about a bit by mine. My four wives were Mary (1974–1975), Fran (1975–1979), Jane (1979–1989), and Lulu (1989–1999). As for those Christian names, I like all their friendly and unassuming sounds, and for that matter most of the time I liked if not loved all four of them to the bone . . .

In summary, Mary was fair, quiet and shy; Franny was impulsive, insecure and blonde; Jane was defined by her jet black hair and by lips that were intensely crimson; Lulu was dun-haired, fine-featured and the only one of my wives who assertively enjoyed her own considerable depths. As for their specific television preferences, there seemed to be no or very little correlation between what they enjoyed on the box and what they were as individuals. For example, I was married to Lulu twice as long as I was married to Fran, even though Lulu liked telly which I considered outright rubbish, whereas Fran, after her own lights, was a selective connoisseur. Typically Francesca would writhe with highly dangerous hysterics on the sofa as she watched *Fawlty Towers* in their 1976 repeats. They were shown on beautiful August evenings when the temperature was in the low eighties and had been so for two remarkable months. She should have been sweltering on Allonby beach with her month-old baby Sassy, but instead she sweltered and chortled in front of ranting John Cleese.

Lulu gulped up highbrow novels like others gulp up pasta, yet she found the perennially repeated comic classic curiously demeaning and even racist in the matter of the idiotic Spanish waiter Manuel (*Che, che? Meester Folty, Meester Folty!*). Instead she enjoyed listless soap operas like *Coronation Street* and *Brookside*, and whilst chastising herself and considering them a weak indulgence, still clocked up four or five hours a week of these pearly if eternally fraught dramas. In 1996, without any cognitive disjunction, Lulu would turn from watching Fred the blustering sausage-maker on *Corrie* to reading her Rosamond Lehmann, Djuna Barnes or Virginia Woolf. Conversely, Fran, who rarely read anything and was indifferent to any sort of abstract theory, pursued some perversely taxing interests. In 1976 twenty-four-year-old Fran was a social worker with an enormous caseload on some of the meanest Carlisle estates. Utterly exhausted every evening, by rights she should have been ogling brainless TV soaps, but instead attended twice-weekly night classes in, of all the most recherché vocational fields, *Latin*.

'Latin?' I said amazed, when she warned me of her remarkable new field of interest. At the time she was five months pregnant with Sassy, and I thought perhaps this belated yen for the classics was on the lines of a yearning to guzzle coal dust or ice cream or kippers.

'Yes,' she answered stoutly. (She was stout, of course, being heavily pregnant but also fair-haired, handsome, unconfident, yet combative.)

'What the hell for?' I asked her. 'What are you going to do with Latin? Read up on the Punic Wars? Or the Georgics that Mr Quelch used to force on the Fat Owl of the Remove?'

'I don't know,' she said calmly, as she rubbed at her pregnant belly. 'I have no idea what I'll read with it. I don't even think I want to read anything in Latin.'

I was a graduate of Arabic and Turkish but had never used either since finishing my degree. Perhaps a lingering guilt explained why I sniffed at such pointless decadence.

'You can't actually communicate with people in Latin, you know! It's no good going abroad and shouting, *ave, vale, salve!* to anyone and expecting a heartfelt response. It wouldn't mean very much, not even to the most Latin-looking ice-cream vendor on the fish quay at Brindisi.'

'So what,' she protested, 'if I have no practical motive for doing it? For whatever futile reason I fancy learning a classical language. I was forced to do geography instead of Latin at school, and I always felt one down at not being allowed to study an ancient tongue. I know every town on the American Fall Line: Baltimore, Raleigh, the whole stupid lot . . . but I don't know a single Latin tag.'

I snorted. 'Well I was forced to imbibe an inordinate amount of the ancient tongue. I like to feel one up as much as the next, but there is no known way of feeling it with schoolboy Latin.'

Fran counter-snorted, 'But you don't feel one *down*. Isn't that the whole point? If only because you have it under your belt, you don't feel its absence. If you didn't know any Latin at all, like me, you would feel one down.'

'Are you sure?' I scoffed. 'That sounds like upside down snobbery to me.'

'Oh don't be such a patronising bastard! Damnit, you know what *ad* bloody *hoc* means, don't you? You can drop it neatly into a conversation just like that, and have everyone nodding at your effortless cleverness. I, on the other hand, can only think of a bottle of hock, and by fatuous association Germans, Bavaria and the Nazis. Admit it, Roe, you also know what nem. con, op. cit. and decree nisi and –'

I broke in, 'I knew that last one with Mary, yes! A fat lot of good it did me. A decree *unless*. A decree unless a marital miracle would happen with me and Mary Murphy . . .'

'Stop feeling sorry for yourself! You got me instead of her so you should be grateful to the decree bloody nice eye. And admit that you even know what *mutatis mutandis* means.'

I protested with excessive vehemence, 'No I don't! I wish I bloody did, but I don't! Whenever I see it written down I rack my brains, but I never know what the bloody thing means. *Having been changed with changings*? It sounds like Flann O'Brien sending up Brian Boru or Queen Mab. What the hell can it possibly –?'

'You see! You have some sort of inkling of what it means. You have a fair idea because you understand that bloody *mut*-whatever-it-is means "change".'

'But,' I growled, 'not enough of an idea for it to be any damn use! I'd be better off not knowing any Latin at all, wouldn't I? Then I wouldn't be pointlessly flogging myself with my unchanging incomprehension? What's the bloody grammar of it, anyway? Past participle with a gerundive? Or an ablative bloody absolute?'

Fran looked righteously sorrowful. 'I haven't a clue about any of that. You could be talking nuclear physics for all I know. But I would give my eye teeth to know what a past gerundive is! In the meantime I'm going to learn some elementary Latin, so that I can have the optional luxury of later discarding it.'

I shook my head disparagingly. 'You are bloody crackers, the illogical connections you make. Why don't you do a night class on syllogisms instead, the stuff they used to chew over on *The Brains' Trust* twenty years ago?'

'Silo what?'

'Let me give you a Latin induction, Fran. Here's your first beginner's lesson, and I won't charge you a penny, I mean a denarius. Part one, the verb and its conjugations. You and I are a conjugal pair, so that's very apt. *Me toe, me tiss, me tit.* Part two, feminine declension, and no snide pun intended in your case. *Wipe her eye, wipe her ham, wipe her eye, wipe her eye, wipe her arse.* Part three, idiomatic sentences. *Marcus adsum jam for tea, Julius aderat.* Now you have a go, Fran. It'll make 'em laugh like hell on the Raffles estate where that pit bull shit in your handbag.'

'Eh?' she snorted with a reluctant smile. 'Do that rigmarole again! Go on, it's bloody funny. Write it down first though, and tell me what it means.'

'Nah I won't. It'll only turn your head. Here's some deathless Virgil for you instead. Courtesy of the Joint Matriculation Board of the Northern Universities of Manchester, Leeds, Sheffield etc, O-Level Latin, circa June 1967.

'*Fit via vi. Nec claustra neque ipsi custodes sufferre valent. Labat ariete crebro janua et emoti postes procumbunt.* The terrifying siege of Troy, can you picture that, here in tranquil if tedious North Cumberland? The serried ranks of the hoary combatants, the cowering Trojans, the searing temperature because Troy was somewhere in Aegean Turkey, and it never snowed and rarely rained. *Labat ariete . . .* "The gate totters with frequent ramming." It sounds quite obscene, eh, like you and me battering away and gasping of a Friday night. Then we have *procumbunt.* "Procumbunt", I ask you! What does that word make you think of? *Pro-cum-bunt.* It sounds like a cross between Billy Bunter and a giant haemmorrhoid up the backside. "The gate posts fall down." It doesn't add up though, does it, categorically speaking? "Fall" and "down" happen to be two nice simple poetic English words. But what sort of lyrical effect is there in "procumbunt"? What sort of poetry is there in piles? It's really not worth the candle, Francesca, struggling with Caesar and Virgil. Why don't you tackle a decent language and learn an oriental one? Why not learn Japanese or Chinese or Arabic instead?'

Jane, who followed Fran and to whom I was married for a decade, really used to enjoy watching *Jeux Sans Frontières* or *It's A Knockout!* This frontierless knockout was a team effort which pitted nation against nation in farcical competitive games. The Finnish team for example, genially egged on by the be-blazered gentlemen referees, might be trying to beat the Belgian team at wading through a treacle-like substance in a gaily coloured paddle boat. The Spanish team, all handsome young men and women with hair as jet black as Jane's, might be trying to go backwards up a vibrating factory chute in a purpose-built little truck while racing to do it faster than their fraternal Portuguese colleagues. Aside from the incidental irony that the Portuguese have always understood themselves as exploited inferior cousins in any Luso-Iberian relationship, there was inevitably the unconscious metaphorical element to these so-called 'games'. Paddling in a garish vehicle through a farcical but ultimately obstructive medium was an apt enough allegory of the prosperous, neo-capitalist, consumerist, vitiated, bourgeois western European way of life, it seemed to me as a sceptical young freelance. Though, true enough, I never heard the British referee, a cheery rugby-league commentator called Eddie Waring, comment discursively to that effect. And when I voiced the same theory to Jane one evening as she was glued to her favourite show, she shushed me aggressively before flinging her *Next* catalogue and accidentally giving me a nose bleed.

Looking back at my ten years with Jane, I can see how her combative temperament was some sort of game-without-boundaries, and true enough she also went in for merciless knockouts rather than modest concessions or provisional capitulations. Jane was a fabric designer of great originality, and as well as executing lucrative commissions at home, she also taught the subject in a college forty miles off on the Scots side. It was the intensity of her jet-coloured hair and the vividly crimson lips that impressed everyone about Jane. She was a dry woman too, with a sardonic, attractively weary sense of humour. Her other mode, more in line with *It's A Knockout!*, was an occasional clownish adoption of an exaggerated Wiganish voice together with dilated saucer eyes and a ponderous halfwit delivery. This was very funny and an attractive foil to her sometimes unpleasant pugnacity. In any event, she was not from eeh-bah-gum Wigan but from the Home Counties, from sedate old Reigate. Her parents were of the minuscule Reigate working class and her father was a great deal older than her mother, which perhaps explains a certain protective distancing and a certain steely toughness about her. She was twenty-seven when we married and thirty-seven when we divorced, but neither then nor now aged forty-nine has she ever expressed any regrets about not having children. She is an exceptional playmate with other peoples' kids, of course. She can distract the noisiest, most obnoxious infant with her crazy grimaces, and Jane and her adult step-daughter Sassy are still close pals, more like snorting, chuckling sisters than otherwise. The fact they are both creative artists helps, no doubt, and now that Jane is living in London she sees much more of Sassy than I do . . .

Jane and I began to come irreversibly apart after about seven or eight years of upness and downness, somewhere around the middle of 1987. That year we took a camping holiday in Ireland, heading north via Stranraer to Larne, working our way across North Ulster and then down through Sligo and Galway and Clare to end up in the Dingle Peninsula. It was late June and it being temperate Ireland we campers should have been washed out ten times over. Instead we hit a freak heat wave and even discovered the remote Blasket Islands to be sub-tropical in 1987. In fact it was when we were walking through the deserted village past Tomas O'Crohan's house on that sweltering afternoon in that beautiful but achingly sad little hamlet that I suddenly knew I had lost her good and proper . . .

To backtrack a fraction, I had been having what I would regard as a totally inconsequential little fling with a trainee local radio reporter called Tanya Busse. It had all been done in scrupulous secret, not a whisper to Jane, slyly assigning ourselves simultaneous protracted projects at the far end of the county. Tanya had been recording numerous historical archive interviews with surly stone-deaf octogenarians in Millom, a.k.a. Cumbria's Tierra del Fuego. I meanwhile had been doing an endless series of mile-long features on the state of further education and vocational training in the adjacent Furness area. I had rented a spectacularly ugly caravan near Barrow-in-Furness, a.k.a. East Berlin, in which the two of us had stashed our tape recorders, notebooks and essential clothes, not to speak of cigarillos, gin, contraceptives and other ancillary resources. And there in 1987 was a challenge for anyone, greater than the most daunting mythological task conceivable, harder than anything Eddie Waring had ever forced those smirking lads from Wuppertal or those sprightly *ragazze* from Rimini to attempt for the delectation of *Knockout* addicts like my wife, Jane Murphy.

If you think you are up to anything short of kidnapping or experimenting with heroin, then try committing adultery *in Barrow-in-Furness*. I would not recommend it to my very worst enemy. The caravan, which sat in a coastal dip halfway between Barrow and Dalton, was not only remarkably cheap, it was remarkably cold. The paraffin heater purred away like nobody's business, and though it stank up the atmosphere with its sultry fumes, it did not seem to cast out any heat unless you actually sat on it. We did once try coupling naked on this portable artefact but not only did we get puce blisters on the arse and thighs, the damn thing began to roll on its castors as we reached our percussive crescendo. Hence the repetitive need for warming substances like gin and whisky, and our sometimes being obliged to have it away fully clothed, coat, gloves, hats, mittens, wellies and mufflers included.

Jane did not rumble Tanya specifically, she had simply scented an invisible presence. It wasn't the first time she had sensed an adulterous phantom but in previous cases I had broken it off at once after guessing as much. On this particular occasion I was not being blasé or careless. Sighting the danger signals, I had killed it off promptly and more or less painlessly with Tanya, who was in any case moving to a far better job in palmy Wolverhampton. But in the meantime Jane had adopted a counter-strategy and had embarked not on a fling but a major infatuation with a smirking gent called Bix, who was Head of Sculpture at her college. I discovered as much right at the end of our Irish holiday when it all came out in the lounge bar of a pub in County Wicklow. Everything turned out to be more complicated and more damning than I could ever have imagined. Jane's 'relationship' with Will Bix (whom I genially referred to as Weetabix), Dumfries and Galloway's retort to Henry Moore, was the real McCoy. Nevertheless she emphasised she would stay by me, stay married to me, and try to keep the two men in her life content. She loved both me and Bix, how could she possibly not love me after eight whole years as man and wife? She loved Will Bix because he was funny and entertaining and brainy, and because they were both addicted to galleries, previews, exhibitions, everything to do with art and sculpture. Of course you, Roe Murphy, are also amusing and intelligent and entertaining, but you can hardly claim that trudging round municipal art galleries is your favourite means of passing the time.

'That's all true isn't it?' she said calmly with those fiery crimson lips of hers in this smoky noisy Wicklow pub.

I did not dispute it. I was still reeling from the revelation that Start The Day With Weetabix wasn't the first person at the Dalry College of Fine and Applied Arts who had been to bed with my wife. As we compared notes and chronologies, it became obvious that Jane Murphy had had her own short flings, in response to presumed but unconfessed flings of mine. There was an impressive if depressing symmetry about it. I had had eight flings in eight years, and Jane had had eight counter-flings in the same eight years. But whereas she had guessed every single one of my flings from the start, I had had not a ghost of an inkling about her counter-flings.

All of which was prefigured in the loaded look of her shoulders as she climbed up from An Gob through the Blasket village. Jane seemed to be bearing some heavy, invisible burden, and I assumed it was her guessing about Tanya who by now was happily working on Radio Wolverhampton. I looked tenderly at the thin shoulders and was tempted to say, no need to be sad, it's all over now. I had no clue whatever it was my own downfall was at stake. We paused at the top of the village where there was a summer-season café in the form of a rickety shed with two tables outside. It was managed by a pair of twenty-five-year-old hippies who looked painlessly happy together. He had a goatee beard and a kaftan, and she had braids and a Victorian grandmother skirt. They had a goat tethered outside their shed who looked slightly more prescient and worldlywise than its owners.

A misconception if ever there was. I might have felt kindly inclined towards these Munster bohemians if their prices had been fifty per cent less extortionate. The tea was one punt fifty a cup and the cheesecake three punts a slice. We were sitting ducks, of course, given that we had brought no picnic and it was boiling, and the boat would not return from Dunquin for another two hours. I scowled and forked out an Erse tenner for this repast and advised Jane it cost the equivalent of two days camping back in Ballyferriter. That too was expensive, but at least we had hot showers and an immaculately mowed bungalow lawn for our site. The proprietor, rich on our camp fees, only consumed the best French wine as he strolled round his site, though he talked in nothing but Munster Irish to his family and employees. I definitely preferred him to this goat-rearing summer-season sybarite idly tooting his penny whistle as he flicked through, I observed, the hypnotic pages of Carlos Castaneda . . .

We left the shack and walked the length of Great Blasket, all the way to Ceann Dubh. Halfway along we sat on a gentle mound above An Cro and gazed at the sister isle of Inis Tuisceart. It was so beautiful, that simmering turquoise sea in the dazzling heat haze, and yet both of us were blindly self-absorbed. We were at the most westerly exposed point of the British Isles and the next dry land was the USA. All around us were noisy swooping choughs, the first I had ever seen. They did their show-off tumbling acrobatics and those piercing kee-ow calls, as if to amuse the two forlorn young foreigners. I watched one padding the clifftop, pecking at ants with its bright crimson beak, and wondered if I dare ask my wife what exactly was on her mind, or rather on her shoulders. The pecking chough had a vivid crimson beak, and my raven-haired wife had her fierce crimson lips. I hadn't the courage to ask her anything, of course. I stood up and suggested we carry on to Ceann Dubh, which is to say 'Black Head'.

Jane, who was avidly reading *The Islandman* every night in our tent, suddenly broke her silence. 'It looks like the Garden of Eden, doesn't it? But they had such terrible times on the Blaskets. Tomas O'Crohan lost two little kids with measles and whooping cough.'

I frowned distractedly. 'I can believe that alright.'

'Somewhere around 1890 that was. It happened a couple of years after losing his eldest son over a cliff. He was hunting for young gulls for the family to eat, but he slipped to his death.'

She turned to me moderatety accusingly and I flinched. 'After the little ones died, Tomas wrote, *It was imprinted on my mind that there was no cure for these things, but to meet them with endurance as best I could . . .'*

I cleared my throat and said, 'They had bloody hard lives in the old days. We don't know we're born, do we?'

Jane dealt me a strange old-fashioned look and her black and crimson intensity stirred me with both passion and fear. She said, 'Oh, I think I know that *I'm* born, alright!'

I had no idea what the hell that meant. The next day at her suggestion we abandoned camping and went to stay with a friend of hers in Dublin. Eilis, as she was called, was a musician, in fact a serious composer, and her partner Sid was likewise. Eilis and Sid had recently produced their own CD of contemporary atonal Irish cello music and they played it for us during lunch. It was both admirably defiant and unmitigatedly hellish, a bit like the fortitude my wife and I were attempting in the face of something increasingly dreadful. Eilis who was beautiful and Sid who was bony and ferretish had always had a rocky, atonal relationship and saw nothing amiss in our poignant silence. However they also had their frank and human sides, and as if to prove it, played highly melodic fiddle and mandolin in a folk band. That night we accompanied them to a public-house gig in County Wicklow. The town was called Blessington and the pub, unbelievably, The Poulaphouca.

'Poolafucker?' snorted Jane, staring saucer-eyed at Eilis. 'Are you sure of that?'

On the way down, the weather broke dramatically. Half-way to Blessington the rain began to lash, monsooning on Sid's car like it does in Madras. Sat there in the front with fer-rety Sid, I suddenly began to feel soaked around my legs and wondered if I had become incontinent with marital anxiety. I looked down to see a four-inch hole in the floor through which pools of rain were cascading across my shoes and pants.

'Ha,' I informed the emaciated cellist. 'There's a bloody big hole down there in your car.'

'Right,' he sniffed, squinting through the blinding torrents of rain. 'Right enough. So it is.'

'How,' I asked him, temporarily distracted, 'did this car of yours get through its MOT? With that huge bloody hole in its bodywork?'

'Em oh what?'

I explained at length about MOTs, and he said, 'I dontink we have em in Dublin. I've never had one at any rate. I never really wanted one to be honest.'

Arrived at the Poulaphouca, Sid jumped on the stage to tune his fiddle, while Eilis collogued with her fellow musicians. Jane and I were left emphatically to ourselves for the best part of an endless night. Perhaps it was the strange and comical setting with the incomparable name, but it all came out in angry hushes and whispers, in jagged fits and starts, our punitively embarrassing confessions.

Or rather it would have hurtled out with the fluency of accusation, counter-accusation, recrimination and so on, if it hadn't been for the bloody *television* . . .

It might seem odd that the telly was blaring on while the band was playing its excellent, extremely tonal Irish music. Yet surely it is the modern custom in pubs across the globe that The Box is never knocked off, no matter what, and on pain of death to anyone who touches it. It is certainly never off in the pubs of Portugal, Spain or Florida, and it is even now compulsory at deafening volume on the Calmac ferry which took me once to meet the falsely accused plasterer Domhnall. The volume on this Irish TV was loud, and as we were sat next to it, we could hardly fail to be distracted. The programme on Telefis Eireann was in any case bizarrely mesmerising, as it was an English children's programme approximately thirty years old. It was in crackly jumping black and white, and I had last seen it on a fourteen-incher in 1961 when I was ten. Don't ask me why those capricious Dublin schedulers were showing *Billy Bunter* on Erse TV at half past seven of a Friday night, as I have no idea. Maybe Irish children are catered for up until an eight o'clock watershed, or maybe the Irish don't have a watershed, or maybe the English public-school comedy was deemed sophisticated enough for intelligent grown-ups. Alternatively its datedness and amateurish stage sets were possibly meant as a bracing assurance to modern Irish citizens that they had never, not even in the gormless Fifties, been guilty of enjoying such televisual pap as this English monstrosity . . .

But before I proceed, I need to check my reference points. Given that many individuals born after 1970 know less than nothing of the Old Testament, it is conceivable that they might know even less about Bunter of Greyfriars. His reclusive bachelor creator Frank Richards, a twenty-thousand-words-a-day man, wrote scores of stories and novels about his obese, bespectacled, ridiculous schoolboy. Born changelessly somewhere between about 1915 and 1945, Bunter was a hopeless scholar, a prodigious guzzler, a liar, a cake-thief, a coward and a first-class buffoon. He was mocked good-naturedly if remorselessly by the Chums of the Remove: Bob Cherry, Frank Nugent, Harry Wharton, Johnny Bull and Hurree Jamset Ram Singh, the 'dusky nabob' of Bhanipur. In class meanwhile, he was tyrannised by a rigid and mortar-boarded beak called Samuel Quelch who routinely referred to sweets as 'sweetmeats' and anything else surreptitiously edible by the incorrigible Fat Owl as 'comestibles'. Bunter was also –

'I've given Tanya up, Jane,' I whispered irritably, not least because I was seriously hampered by this farcical programme. 'In any case she's moved away down to Radio Wolverhampton. It meant nothing whatever, not a thing, in the long run. But I think you and Weetabix are engaged in something very different. It really sounds like you think you are in love, and honestly I've never been even remotely in love with any of mine. I've met Weetabix once or twice at your college functions, and to be frank I simply wouldn't trust the way he –'

*Bunter (pausing in front of a tree in Greyfriars quadrangle where the Chums of the Remove are gathered):* I say you fellows.

Quelch has given me an impot for some beastly Latin I couldn't constew . . .

*Bob Cherry*: I think you mean 'construe', old fat man. It might just have been cos you translated 'Caesar adsum' as 'Caesar had some' . . .

*Chums of the Remove*: Ha, ha, ha!

*Bunter*: Oh really Cherry, you beast! I mean, jolly funny old fellow, ha ha! I say Cherry, could you do this beastly impot for me?

*Johnny Bull*: You priceless ass, Bunter!

*Hurree Jamset Ram Singh*: The preposterous assfulness of the esteemed and priceless Bunter is indeed terrific.

*Bunter*: Oh really, Inky!

Looking stonier than I had ever seen her, Jane said, 'Stop calling him Weetabix or I'll throw this pint of lager in your face. And grow up and acknowledge that it had to happen sooner or later. Eight flings apiece, once a year like Bonfire Night. But in my case, on my eighth, I was properly hooked, and unfortunately it was no longer a fling.'

*Nugent*: You frabjous fat ass!

I protested, 'But I didn't know about your flings! I hadn't the faintest clue. I reckon that must have taken some doing on your part, there must have been a good bit of planning went into the hoodwinking. You guessed all of mine without any effort, so you say. At the end of the day maybe I feel that I've been unfairly tricked somehow.'

'You what!' she snorted, outraged. 'Why, you appalling bloody –'

*Bunter*: That frightful old ass Quelch! I'm blessed if I'll ever ask my pater to invite him up to Bunter Towers for the Christmas hols. Even if he begs me to come and hobnob with all my titled relatives.

*Cherry*: Bunter Towers? Draw it mild, old fat man! I'm sure your pater's a ripping ol' guv'nor, but I can't believe that you're drowning in titled relatives.

Jane hissed, 'I see you suddenly and clearly in a strange

242

new light. You would appear to be the clichéd epitome of masculine hypocrisy. Or do I mean plain masculine deceitfulness?'

I glowered and hissed back, 'No I'm not!' (though I nearly said to her, *draw it mild!*).

*Bunter*: I bet you fellows that Quelch would love to meet all my titled relatives. At Bunter Towers there are always scores of dukes and Right Honourables and courtyards –'

*Cherry*: Court who?

*Bunter*: No, I mean whatsit, courtiers –

*Chums of the Remove*: Ha ha ha!

My wife said witheringly, 'Maybe your not guessing about my adventures wasn't a function of my deviousness but of your own selective blindness.'

*Bunter*: I don't mind telling you fellows that if that ass Quelch was standing in front of me now, I would tell him *exactly* what I thought of him.

Fiddling morosely with her empty glass. 'Anyway, let's drop the accusations. What exactly is it you want from me at this point?'

I groaned. 'God knows. I don't know. Yes I do. That you stop feeling so much for Weeta . . . for this bloody bastard Bix!'

'Hah! Some request, some sensible petition that is! What an adult demand I must say. How does one resolve to feel less for someone than one does? I would love to know.'

*Bunter*: You know, it wouldn't surprise me if that beast Quelch was born of two really common sort of parents. Lowly ruffians of racecourse touts, maybe, Wharton, what do you say?

*Wharton*: Quelch's old mater was a racecourse tout, old fat man?

*Chums of the Remove*: Ha ha ha!

*Bunter*: Blessed if I see anything to cackle at! Let's just say they were two common criminals then, two ugly, beastly old jailbirds.

*Quelch* (*suddenly appearing from behind a second tree in the quadrangle, he roars*): Bunter! You deplorable, quite incorrigible boy!

'Roe . . .' Jane sighed, but with no trace of remorseful softening.

*Bunter*: Ooh! Ooh crikey! Ooh! Woogh! Oogh! Sir, that wasn't me you overheard! It was these awful fellows who said all that, it wasn't me. I didn't call you a beastly silly old ass, sir, and I didn't say your pater was a bookie and a crook.

*Quelch*: Bunter!

'Jane . . .' I pleaded.

*Quelch*: Bunter, I have inadvertently eavesdropped on your egregious impertinence! Your monstrous and villainous impudence, your disgraceful, absurd and utterly outrageous calumnies!

*Bunter*: Sir, I didn't! Honestly I didn't say any colonies, or any igreech–

*Quelch*: Silence!


And there was a considerable silence between the sad English couple for the rest of the evening, or at any rate until Eilis and Sid had finished their performance. That night we slept on the floor on a shake-me-down, a pampered luxury after our camping, but as far apart as we could make it. Jane was miserable but sleepy while I was as wakeful and fretful as anyone could wish. As Jane snored away, my head began to fill with crazy crackling monochrome images of Billy Bunter, which by association led to Quelch and Latin, which in turn led to my second wife Fran. Fran, that is, who attended Latin night classes in Seventies Cumbria, so that she could improve her wavering self-esteem. Flattened by this dismal impasse with Jane, I felt myself growing ever more nostalgic about those colourful years with Francesca, who was, after all, my only child's mother. In the pitch darkness of the Dublin flat, I lay there picturing my second marriage in every minute detail. The geographical prelude to this present misery with

Jane was an abandoned Irish-speaking island off County Kerry. Aptly enough Fran and I had enjoyed some entrancing summer holidays on several Gaelic Hebrides. Those bad times with Fran the Carlisle social worker had been poignantly awful, but the good times, those tender early days, had been as beautiful as Coll or Iona or Tiree . . .

One of the really flattering things, if we are to ponder this painful business of self-esteem, was that she was the one to seek me out, not the other way about. Out of the blue Francesca Toner turned up one lunchtime at my door, blinking, tense and unsure of any welcome. Silent for a second or so at my wondering scrutiny, she informed me she had just 'dropped by' to see me. I had only a vague recollection, but she and I had both been at the same jazz night in a Longtown pub a couple of weeks ago. Blushing to the roots of her hair, she reminded me how the two of us had nodded and swapped smiles from opposite ends of the bar. One of her social-work colleagues whom I'd assumed to be her boyfriend had subsequently advised her who I was. He was called James Stone and I had picked his considerable brains once for a feature about juvenile crime, and I liked him very much. As if to clear the horizon at once, Fran insisted gravely that Jim and she were just good friends, and that Stone had more or less encouraged her to get to know me . . .

I nodded with a thudding, expectant heart. I could scarcely believe my luck. Not only was Stone's friend extremely good-looking but she was heading straight for the bull's eye without preamble or deceit. She smiled at me openly and tenderly, and showed me something she had purchased en route. It was a Joni Mitchell album entitled *Hissing on Summer Lawns*. It was a broiling July noon, which made the choice all the more timely. She asked me if she could put it on, so I took it and sniffed its fine vinyl newness and admired the artwork on the cover. I listened enthusiastically to the virtuoso jazz influence of the bassist Maxwell Bennett. The title track starts with a riveting earthquake percussion which is a mixture of passion, defiance and ominous war-dance solemnity. Joni Mitchell started to sing and Fran bristled and said this was her very favourite musician. Then she looked at me and smiled a smile of gentle anticipation. I stared at my surprise guest and also smiled. It all happened like beautiful clockwork after that. Our arms and lips were upon each other in feverish seconds. I desired at once her tautness, her tension, I was even stirred by her perpetual restlessness in those first few weeks. We tore upstairs while *Summer Lawns* was booming, and stayed there the entire afternoon. We were in the bed, out of it, across it, and remarkably at one stage, underneath with all the dust and fluff and long lost coins and paperbacks. Had there been a pisspot, we would have knocked ourselves unconscious with our heedless rampance. Back downstairs again, we did two things. Firstly, ravenous after so much exercise, we acquired a Chinese carry-out from a place two miles up the road. Fran drove to get it, and I carried a flower jug to the nearest pub and filled it with a pint of draught sherry. Fran, I can recall very clearly, had sweet and sour prawns, and I had chicken in lemon sauce. That first dish was heavy with Chinese sherry so she had twice any sensible alcohol quota. The jug was rapidly emptied, which meant we were very drunk, but we were in any event intoxicated with each other and with Joni Mitchell. Fran hiccupped and burped her sherrified prawns, then snorted and apologised. Suddenly she stared at the clock and said, God help us, she'd almost forgotten, it was time to watch *Fawlty Towers*! There was such mad urgency in her voice I even felt envious of the unknown quantity. Incredibly I had never watched a single episode and knew nothing of its astringent flavour, its byzantine plots, its bilious characters, its vertiginous ranking in the scheme of television comedy.

I could not credit just how funny it was. True excellence, despite what they say, is extremely rare, and is arguably proportionate to: a) the originality of the work's inspiration, and

b) the amount of labour expended on its creation. Any fool could see how much delirious slog had gone into John Cleese and Connie Booth's scripts about the pretentious Torquay hotel. Years later we learnt that they appended pages and pages of elaborate graphs and chart-flow diagrams, so that every bit of timing and comic juxtaposition was determined to the very last dot. Tonight's episode was that where Cleese/Basil's car refuses to start at a crucial and marriage-threatening point. If the monumentally testy hotelier cannot get where he wants to be in order to avert his latest catastrophic folly, Sybil his harridan wife will destroy him. As the little car resists all efforts to start it, Basil is so incensed that he decides, incredibly, to subject it to ferocious corporal punishment. Ranting and slavering, he breaks off a branch from a nearby tree and flogs his wilful vehicle across its naughty bonnet. At this point Francesca Toner, whom I had known for less than eight hours, was dementedly hysterical, emitting countless helpless sweet and sour burpings. I meanwhile was weeping with euphoric mirth both at Basil and my hiccupping young lover.

Lying next to Jane on that lumpy Dublin mattress, I clung to my TV memories with an obstinate and immature fixity. Jane and I would possibly stagger on another year or so, and then it would end just as it had ended with Fran. But how impossibly easy the going had been right at the start with her, with the young mother of my only child. I blinked in the cavernous Dublin darkness and conjured up ever more vivid and tender pictures of myself and Fran, some of them so striking it was as if they must be my maudlin and obsessive inventions . . .

Once, long before we had Sassy, we were hiking through a remote part of the Pennines. In the tourist brochures the North Pennines were advertised as England's Last Wilderness, and true enough, although we had been out half the day, we hadn't encountered a single soul. We were both sweating like pigs and greedily swigging our water bottles. At last we came to a lonely tarn, brilliant and ink blue, on a vast and empty plateau. The water was so dark I couldn't see how deep it was, and when I put my hand in, it was icy cold. There was no chance of swimming or even paddling, but we decided to fill up our bottles. Fran complained she was roasting alive, that it was like being in the Moroccan desert, and I felt biliously sweltered. I suggested that we strip off and gingerly flick ourselves with small quantities of tarn water. Francesca frowned as she peered about and said someone might arrive to disturb us. I took a confident survey and said there was nothing but buzzards and rock pipits between us and Weardale. The nearest human being was likely to be the grinning check-out assistant at the Middleton-in-Teesdale Spar twenty miles off.

'OK,' she conceded. 'But if anyone turns up, you stand guard in front of me and insist you're the only naked hermit for miles.'

'No one will turn up,' I said stoutly. 'And even if they do they can hardly call the police.'

This being in those pearly days before the fellside mobile phone of course. Before long I was ballock-naked and she, by analogy, was womb-naked. Fran stood there with a quivering little belly, blinking, self-conscious and scanning the horizon for County Durham voyeurs or possibly voyeuses. We both made brave attempts to paddle in the tarn but came out screaming at the arctic cold. The physics made no sense to either of us. It was eighty-five outside the tarn and minus eighty-five inside it. Fran's arms and legs were lobster pink but her taut little backside was as a white as a virgin tea towel. That colour contrast I found profoundly aphrodisiac, and despite the temperature and our beetroot faces I suggested that we fall upon each other without delay.

Fran smirked and said she also felt stirred, perhaps because this was her first experience of so-called naturism. It was true what they said, wasn't it? There was something so freeing about parading as naked as a baby, and especially in these weirdly tropical conditions. But she couldn't resist a three-hundred-and-sixty-degree survey, and I watched her ripe breasts swing through that same carousel circle. Eventually she snorted and shook her head, and shouted to a soaring skylark, ach, what the bloody hell! We searched effortfully for somewhere to disport ourselves. The sand beside the tarn was hot enough to fry an egg. After a long five minutes we settled in some parched and tufted grass which offered a nat-ural if prickly mattress. Fran lay down on her belly and invited me to rest upon the gentle cushion of her perspiring rump, a flagrantly selfish move on her part as my own was rapidly roasted while hers was nicely shielded by my stomach.

Suddenly I noticed a curlew stepping pensively about a hundred yards off. At first it was quite oblivious of these tasteless orgiasts hammering away in its favourite nesting ground. I was holding with reverence my wife's tender haunches as we approached an impassioned and overheated summit. As I stroked and petted her, we quietly declared our love for each other, and as an afterthought (I nearly wrote, as a rider) I said to Fran that there was a curlew watching us mating.

'A what?' she gasped.

She was almost at orgasm but was characteristically patient.

'A curlew,' I repeated.

'I love you too, Roe!'

'No, no, Fran! I said *a curlew*.'

'You too! I really love you too, Roe.'

'No, no, Fran . . .'

'Ayiugharughaiuuuuughhh.'

That was not the curlew's mating call, it was the field social worker at her extravagant vocal summit. I hadn't yet reached my own, and this obsessive birdwatching, or perhaps I mean twitching, was unlikely to help matters.

*

Land of my heart, land of the barley. *Tir mo chroidhe, tir na eorna.* We were on holiday in Tiree, a tiny Inner Hebridee which is flat and entirely treeless but with the tenderest, most delicate beaches outside of the Aegean. In the red-hot weather it was just like Greece, and we spent a fortnight dreaming like two ruminant calves or other moon-eyed beasts. We were both just twenty-five, so we didn't mind a poky tent and a budget restricting us to packet soup, instant coffee, and two drinks a night in the Scarinish Hotel. True to precedent, one morning we had some feverish bare-arse congress in the open air, tucked away by the remote Kenovara cliffs. We got there by bicycles hired from a tumbled cottage for all of forty-five pence. Even in 1975 this was far too reasonable, and it might have been because neither bike had functioning brakes. To stop them, we leapt off at full speed and stampeded to a sparks-flying halt, just like two cowpokes steadying a pair of crazy bucking steers.

One evening we found ourselves outside Tiree's only other hotel, only yards from the sand and machair of Gott Bay. Its Arabian Nights' glory is of such miragic beauty that even Sir Billy Butlin was affected by the sight and wanted to build a Tiree holiday camp. Sadly the generous old philanthropist wasn't allowed on Gott Bay, which is perhaps why Fran and I could sit so entranced on its machair as if before the tender belly of the Living God. It was at Gott Bay we talked about having a child, and where we held hands and hoped our life together would never ever end. We were calmly drugged in our young love like two fawns or larks or kittens or kids.

After an hour or more I roused myself and turned to stare at the Gott hotel. At once I nearly shot out of my skin.

'Look!' I snorted. 'Look!'

She was startled by the strangeness in my voice. She even thought I'd seen something like a ghost or a violent crime. Either conjuration on a blazing August evening on the Isle of Tiree being monumentally im–

'It's him,' I squeaked. (Like everyone else I was buggered if I was going to exclaim, 'it is he'. The only person who had ever said, 'it is he', was Billy Bunter's teacher Quelch, and I had long since parted company with him, whether in print or TV guise.)

'Who?' she said, craning her slim little neck. As soon as she saw him, the one who was drinking coffee and scribbling in a notebook, she was in even less doubt than her husband. Because of course no one on the whole planet looks even remotely like him. Rubbing her fine blue eyes in wonderment, Fran exclaimed coarsely, 'Bugger me stiff. Well I'll go to sea and fuckaduck!'

Why keep anyone in suspense? Though here is a teasing clue. The treacherous television had caught up with us yet again. Even though, obviously enough, there was no outsize telly blaring away in a Tiree pub garden in the summer of 1975. Nevertheless the smirking universal leveller was reaching out and molesting us with its adhesive tentacles. And there's yet another cryptic clue, that mention of tentacles. Think of animals . . . zoology . . . biology. Now think again. Think of someone more animal than plant, and who could not be mistaken for anyone else. No, not the dauntless zoologist and one time BBC2 controller, David Attenborough. Nor for that matter the bald and brainy Oxford don, Dr Desmond Morris, with his first-class buttocks-equals-misplaced-breasts theory propounded so attractively in *The Human Zoo*. Nor was it the bass-voiced Belgian Armand Denis, and certainly not his mezzo-soprano Walloon wife Michaela. Nor was it either nuptial half of submarine/benthos/bottom-hugging Hans and Lotte Hass. Neither was it the animal-defending antipodean cartoonist-artist Mr Rolf Harris, though very close indeed with that one.

Yes indeed. It was he. I mean, it was *him*.

I mean it was . . . *David Bellamy* . . .

One per cent of the British population does not possess a telly, so perhaps they need to be told. He is of that genus which looks like a beaver and talks like a walrus, or equally talks like a beaver and looks like a walrus. He is the TV botanist who is bearded, vivacious, playful, barmy, and above all, impassioned. He does not stand motionless like a plant, but leaps and prances like a rabbit or a wallaby in front of the camera lens. He also booms, salivates and chortles like a gorilla. He is regularly associated with two other histrionic and 'loony' TV scientists, viz. the astronomer Patrick Moore who talks five hundred words to the minute and has total autonomic control over his eyebrows, and the physicist Magnus Pyke who flings his arms and capers like a mandril. Why the combination of popular science and the visual media should encourage such eccentric showmanship is a debatable area. But leave it at that, at that notorious, irrepressible, indefatigable trio of 'mad' and, of course, unabashedly masculine TV scientists.

A botanist who slaveringly expounds on his beloved monocots and dicots, Bellamy the booming walrus also knows a phenomenal amount about ecology, zoology, biochemistry and biophysics. And certainly to see a charismatic TV celebrity like Bellamy in the flesh, unaccompanied, virgin as a redwood forest, and alone as a hybrid fungus, was to feel incongruously as if one was in the pages of Jean-Paul Sartre's existential opus, *Being and Nothingness*. What we are talking about is the phenomenon of 'the observer observed', this walrus who was not in fact a walrus, but was that fictive apparition called *a man*, and who was there, or at least appearing to our senses to be there, in his perplexing existential nudity. It was certainly too much for my hesitant wife Fran who whispered to me: 'Let's go and talk to him. Should we? I think we should. Do you think we should?'

'Eh? What? Bugger off! Not on your life!'

'Eh? But what an opportunity! He looks such an approachable, intriguing sort of chap. Look at him scribbling away so furiously with his biro and his jotter. Look at him again! He's stopped to have a helpful little chew at his pen. What's he pondering about, d'you reckon?'

'Should he choose chips or a baked potato with his Gott Hotel lasagne?'

'Eh? Oh I think he looks much more like a bake . . . oh shut up and don't talk such rubbish!'

'Or the virgin ecology of uninhabited Gunna. This morning he paddled across from Tiree through the lethal currents, bawling at any sharks or whales who got in his way. He's busy penning his impressions before they evaporate.'

'I'd love to have his autograph! My mother down in Dagenham would really love to have his autograph. My brother and my nice old Dad would so love to –'

'We're not prancing over there to ruin his peace! It would look so pathetic and we'd be such a pair of intrusive idiots.'

'No we wouldn't!'

'Wouldn't we? We could hardly say, we wonder if you are the extremely famous David Bellamy? It's not like identifying an elusive TV species. Why would he want to meet a Cumbrian journalist (yawn) and a Cumbrian social worker (yawn), when he's got half an hour's peace away from the camera?'

She sighed and contented herself with staring at the great man as he absently gazed in her direction. He looked with indulgence at this attractive and spellbound young woman and smiled back kindly. Fran hesitated then waved her fingers at the media star, grinned outlandishly, and had the incredible audacity to blow him a kiss! Bellamy guffawed and snorted, and I yanked my wife away before she could shout, Coo-ee, Davie, would you like some Mellow Birds with Marvel and a nice and sticky frosted cream in our smelly little tent . . . ?

Bellamy, the Denises, the Hasses, Cousteau, Attenborough and Morris are all custodians and conduits of the living, breathing, fecund natural world. And the fecund living world in all its ungovernable power would not leave us alone that

night. The Tiree twilight seemed eternal, the air was suffo-
catingly close. We decided to make the most of our last day
on Tiree and take a long walk around Gott Bay. So we abandoned our bikes and tramped across the lush and fragrant
machair, hoping we might glimpse a corncrake or an otter.
We clambered over a fence and set off through a massive
field, vast enough to host an airplane runway or a thousand-
metre race. A long way off we could see two white horses,
chewing at the machair and tossing their powerful manes. It
was a scented island twilight where the aromatic clover, the
sea air, the mordant laments of the gulls, all powered an
intense epiphany. Furthermore it was an epiphany which was
meant to honour us, a passionate young English couple, and
our special relationship with this beautiful place. Even a TV
superstar had opted to be here, as if to pay us an elliptical
media homage. I was leisurely explaining some of this to
Fran, who was still much annoyed at being forbidden to
fraternise with David Bellamy. Suddenly she cut me short.

'What the bloody hell are they doing?'

Her voice was very anxious. I looked where she was looking. She was referring to the white horses who were still a
long way off, but were no longer prancing, much less capering, on the spot. Nor were they peacefully chewing their
machair cuds. Even in the shadowy pungent twilight it was
clear enough that they were rapidly on the move. How to
state this filmic scenario with maximum clarity and documentary vividness? They were *running*, those two white
juggernauts, or rather, to use the apter equine verb, they
were galloping. Had we been able to rehearse various *Match
of the Day* replays, those two milk-white steeds might have
galloped in at least three or four different directions. Towards
the far gate, for example, and in the direction of an easily
recognisable animal-lover called David Bellamy. Alternatively
to a smaller gate on Bellamy's left, beyond which was a
rusted tractor and a tumbled, long deserted croft. Otherwise,
overwhelmed by their freedom of choice, they might have

chosen to stampede to the right or left of us, with a hundred-yard berth either side. Instead, rejecting all those predictable and 'pedestrian' options, they were pounding furiously in a straight and snorting line towards an immobilised young professional couple from the far north-west of England (a.k.a. *Sasunn*).

I cleared my throat and said, 'They probably mean no harm.'

Fran's vocal chords were frozen, yet she managed, 'If they don't slow down and don't stop, they might –'

I frowned. 'Kill us, I should say. Or certainly cripple us both seriously. But perhaps they'll change direction at the last minute. Let's hope so, eh? I think on balance I'd sooner be ki–'

Once Francesca had tolerated me discoursing about curlews while she was close to a North Pennines climax. Now when two Tiree stallions were just about to flatten her, she was in no mood to 'dilate' about her preferred mode of death.

She shouted, 'Oh shut up, will you! Just stop babbling and run like fuck!'

Thus the experienced young social worker who could tell a melodramatic fake from a genuine psychopath, a bona fide GBH from a drunken punch . . .

We turned and raced towards the nearest bit of fence. Not only was it a long way off, it was a very high one and a barbed one. Those extremely photogenic stallions looked exactly like those on the Galaxy advert as they kept up their insane pursuit. It might well be that they liked and admired us, but it seemed more as if they wished to flatten two noxious *Sasunnach* trespassers. They were at least twice as far as we were from the fence, but as they could move three times faster, it 'behooved' us to defy the laws of arithmetic by any possible means . . .

It occurred to me that like an old TV repeat I'd been through all this before with Flogger and the Fingland gunman. Back in 1959 on the same day as *Highway Patrol*, I had been forced to run for my life in idyllic surroundings. Today, instead of being reassured by the fact I'd survived a childhood sniper, I felt all the more dread, not to say *déjà vu* terror. I gabbled to my breathless wife: 'You go to the right a bit. I'll go to the left a bit! If we split up, it'll maybe fool them. At worst only one of us'll be killed. It'll be rather like the philosopher's ass and the two bails of –'

We were back to philosophy as discussed on *The Brains' Trust*, but my wife didn't ask for elucidation. Instead she did as she was bid. We raced like terrified hares and I knew myself aged twelve again, competing for this do-or-die, all-or-nothing hundred yards . . .

Not only in athletics, but also in the professional and personal spheres, I was good at short sharp bursts but bad at protracted endurance. As for Fran she was bad at both, yet she was first to reach the fence. As she explained later, she more or less waltzed over it as if it were a step ladder. Meanwhile her husband vaulted his section of fence with a miraculous high-jump scissors, which ought by rights to have messily castrated him . . . instead of which he seemed to take wing and fly like Puck or Ariel.

We were as safe as houses, but it took some time to register. We knelt there panting and gasping, and in my case viciously cursing.

'Bastards!' I screamed, and I even shook my fist at two suddenly indifferent horses. I could scarcely believe their flagrant hypocrisy. They were standing there by the gate like two phlegmatic sentinels. They even had the nerve to look mournfully hungry in the gathering dusk, as if expecting us to hand them grass across the fence and let bygones be bygones.

Fran was less phlegmatic as she gasped, 'It's no good screaming at them like that. And as a matter of fact, if it's anyone's fault it's yours!'

I hearkened to her dumbstruck. Eh, I babbled indignantly? What the bloody hell did she mean? OK, OK, it might have been my stupid idea to go for the dangerous walk, but she had happily agreed to it! After all, she'd also spotted these ugly Tiree Pegasuses, so she could have advised against entering the same bloody killing field . . .

Every inch the future litigant, Fran flounced her hair dismissively. 'I don't mean that at all! I'm talking about you listening to me for once. Instead of me always listening and bowing to you! If we'd done what I wanted and walked across to David Bellamy, we'd still be there chatting about Tiree machair and drinking Sweetheart fucking Stout!'

'But –'

'We'd not have had to run for our bloody lives and dice with fucking death! Would we? There'd be no need for you to be ranting and screaming at two innocent bloody horses . . .'

# 12

*High Mallstown, North Cumbria, 20th November 2001.*
*Lunchtime satellite viewing and listening.*

## *237 (keyed in in error)*

I knew within seconds that I should not linger over this
programme, even though it was broad daylight, even though
the film was in crackly, jerky black and white, even though I
was a hardened and unflappable journalist who was old
enough to be a flinty, fearless grandad. I had been hoping to
check the Lifestory Channel schedules, just to see if they
intended doing my cinematic hero Jack Nicholson, but had
punched in two wrong digits. Nevertheless, faced with what
was before me, I could hardly fail to be numbly fascinated.
This was the FSF (Fantasy and Science Fiction) channel, an
entertainment option to which I normally give a massive
berth. In a world full of insidious and mindboggling actuali-
ties, the first to come topically to mind being the thousand
flaming pyres in plague-ridden North Cumbria and the cre-
mated New York towers in terror-stricken North America,
why anyone should need to be imaginatively diverted by
fantasy utopias, nightmarish dystopias, antennaed Martians,
parallel galaxies and the like is wholly beyond me. An appropriate response to the partisan SF enthusiast might express
itself variously and vauntingly as coals to Newcastle hinny,
livestock lorries to Longtown, Cumbria, marra, unbelievable

abyssal grief to Manhattan, buddy!

It was just at the start of an ancient *Twilight Zone* episode. Faint stirrings in the crepuscular zones of R. Murphy's tele-memory suggested he had seen this one or one very similar some forty years ago, on a newborn babe called Border Tele-vision. In those early days, of course, ITV was notorious for showing limitless amounts of unReithian US imports whose unembarrassed aim was to titillate in lieu of educate. In 1961 aged ten I had had every right to be frightened out of my wits by a programme as eerie as this, which made it all the more shameful that I felt twice as scared in 2001. *The Twilight Zone*, like its sister series *One Step Beyond*, presented very creepy, imaginatively convincing tales designed to raise the hairs on the back of your stricken neck. Each thirty-minute programme offered a crude twentieth-century variation on that doyen of literary horror, Edgar Allan Poe. As with EAP the terror in *TZ* tended to be subtly suggested rather than B-movie blatant. Much might be frighteningly implied by the camera focusing on a dark forgotten corner of a large and empty room, and with suitably grim, not to say hauntingly monochromal, music.

Today's hero had an extremely specialised, in fact laudably Poeish skill at his disposal. He was a highly renowned transat-lantic waxwork sculptor, and he provided the nearby version of Tussaud's with their admirably lifelike figures. The rogues' gallery at the waxwork museum was presently being refur-bished, so to kill two birds with one stone, so to speak, the notorious murderers and murderesses had been conveyed to our artist's studio where he could execute (!) some necessary renovation work. His ground-floor studio was in a non-descript suburban, semi-rustic setting, but for no objective reason it seemed subtly suggestive of a gloomy basement. Lined up there in gaunt and goggle-eyed black and white were some eminent American murderers and a motley assort-ment of headline-thumping felons. As well as Caryl Chessman, only recently gassed, and the notorious pair whom Truman

Capote had watched hang in a Kansas penitentiary, there were those who had died by electrical frying. That poignant pair at the end seemed to be accomplished likenesses of Sacco and Vanzetti, the immigrant Italian, highly unAmerican anarchists framed and frittered and buried as fast as anyone could wish. Was *TZ*, I wondered, presenting these two innocents ironically and subversively, or did it reflect a mainstream US conviction that odious anarchists should be durn well turned into home fries whether or not they were strictly culpable?

Our sculptor has a goatee beard and a harmlessly bohemian look, and as he potters about his ill-lit studio, his glaze-eyed likenesses seem to pierce the small of his back somehow. Their cadaverous waxishness is an eloquent statement that they are painfully irreversible corpses, most of them judicially executed. Their waxen mimicry, the grim template aspect, has all the suggestive power of masks, puppets, ritual, animism, and somewhere, I suppose, right at the limit of all that suggestion, perhaps the notion of a blind alley named . . . evil. They are, after all, all wicked souls. The sculptor meanwhile is the acceptable opposite of all that, if only because his unconventional lifestyle is an innocuous sort of deviance. He is a bustling blameless cipher of a man; a caricatural beard, a Montmartre beret, an obsessional workaholic. One cannot imagine him existing outside of this film, and one certainly can't imagine him doing anything but making waxworks. Ditto, it occurred to me forcefully, with regard to all those ancient Hammer horror heroes, who never ever seemed to sit and puff a B and H, or slurp an innocent cup of Typhoo tea, or goggle at the ten o'clock news, or stump along to the electric board to pay their quarterly bill, or do anything else faintly if banally indicative of the rest of the non-horror world . . .

Nevertheless our bohemian sculptor has a wife. We know this as he has just grumbled to himself that he must drive into town to buy an important sculptural fixative which his wife (such a typical female!) has foolishly forgotten to get for him. Single-minded eccentric artist that he is, he doesn't bother to tell her where he's going, he just bashes out through his French window and we hear the Buick or the Dodge revving up off-stage. Immediately after which we hear his wife's tender voice calling from the garden. It is lunchtime and she is asking the waxworker whether he wants it upstairs, dear, with her, or, as is his incorrigible preference, on a tray down here while he toils away at his beloved mannikins.

The bob-haired spouse in her optimistic forties steps into the deserted studio. At once we find ourselves fretting obscurely about her long-term health and happiness, if only because the music reaches a peak of forlorn monotonal intensity. It might be lunchtime according to cheery Mrs Sculptor, but this *TZ* film is cast in those sullen twilight shades familiar from *Naked City* or *87th Precinct* or sundry other noirish US cop shows, where for some reason, even at the height of summer and at ten in the morning, it is always as gloomy as the most funebral aspects of mankind. There she goes, passing briskly along the frozen line of gawking, waxen rogues, shouting, Geoffrey, Geoffrey where are you, dear? Are you perhaps out there in the back somewhere, my dear?

At which point one is tempted to reach out and pat her innocent filmic shoulder and cry, no, no, he isn't, dear, no alas, is your esteemed bohemian husband fuck! No, my dear missus, he's gone to purchase some vital waxwork adhesive in town, all your shameful fault apparently, because you forgot to buy it after your ten o'clock Daughters of America bash, and meanwhile, if I were you, I should seriously consider buggering off out of this infernal basement as fast as your carca–

Too late! That waxwork figure in the middle, one I can't strictly identify but who is either an evil serial killer or an unrepentant unAmerican Trotskyist union agitator, but in any event an extremely ugly, depraved, ferocious-looking bastard, this waxen mannikin suddenly reaches out his massive wrestler's arm and clasps poor Mrs Sculptor around her neck!

'Agh!' shrieks Mrs S. 'Ooh. Oh! Oh no. Oh no. Ooh! *Geoffrey!*'

She carols for her workaholic husband with his London, England MA in restorative waxing and marbling, but of course the useless bohemian bastard is not there! Nor do we hear his car revving to a timely halt, nor see him arriving at the last minute to smack his playful creation across the lug, and say Hey Buck, Bub, Duke, hey feller!, how many times have I told you *not* to come to life like that, just because I was chump enough to make you look so *lifelike*? No, Geoffrey has not arrived as *deus ex machina*, and meanwhile his bob-haired helpmeet is being horribly strangled to death by the automaton's extremely expert armlock.

My 2001 replay of that archive narrative is couched in jovial tongue-in-cheek. But in reality my tongue was in my horripilating ears, and my ears were up my petrified arse, and my moon-cold arse was on the white and frozen moon. Evil outsize puppets coming hideously to life and strangling a body? A dummy becoming an animate thing, and the animate thing being powered by a senseless bloodlust so that it kills whatever is nearest and handiest? What after all were we talking about? Edgar Allen Poe and M.R. James? Or in suitably gothic and melodramatic terms, the gory history of the horrible twentieth century, where the puppets were our black and murderous collective impulses only waiting for a chance to stir themselves and delight in a homicidal totalitarian evil . . . ?

In the five minutes before I changed channel and aborted *The Twilight Zone*, I relived a second tale of terror also forty years old. The setting was crude enough, and it was certainly not in an American waxworks. It was Fingland, Cumberland 1961, and it was the evening of the village carnival. This of course was the ideal night to experience fright, because carnival, even in an austere little northern pit village, meant it was the the time for dressing up, tearing about regardless, and breaking a few hidebound taboos. Fingland mightn't have been New Orleans or Rio, the voodoo and hoodoo might have been in abeyance, and yet it had its nasty moments. The fancy dress on display would either be gaberdined scowling ten-year-olds pretending they were the Great Train Robbers, or younger ones flaunting lipstick and Woodbines *pace* Elsie Tanner and Len Fairclough in *Coronation Street*. But there were also drunken thirty-year-old colliers in war paint and grass skirts roaring and wielding spears and terrifying little children. Five years earlier in 1956, they had certainly terrified me, whereas now aged ten I was more or less frightened of nothing . . .

Or so I assumed. On the eve of the carnival of 1961 I was sat prosaically watching the television. My mother was visiting a sick neighbour, my father was working his allotments, and so unusually I was entirely on my own. It was a rare and a very liberating occasion, for apart from anything else it gave me unfettered access to our seventeen-incher. I could have vulgar, brainless ITV on if I wanted, which was not always what my parents wanted. Ten is an idiosyncratic age and for some reason I was much less discriminating then than I was at nine, eight, seven or even six. At ten I loved any vulgar, mindless entertainment, the mindlesser and vulgarer the better. Brainless quiz shows, brainless cop shows, greymatterless cartoons, vulgar variety, common comedy, decerebrated crooners, coarse buffoons, witless impressionists, shitless balladeers, vulgar, oh so vulgar female glamour . . .

Michael Miles's *Take Your Pick*. Hughie Green's *Double Your Money*. Clark Kent's *Superman*. The glamorous Yana. Tug Boat Annie. The glamorous Kathy Kirby. Ronnie Carroll. The glamorous Alma Cogan. Ronnie Hilton. The glamorous Sheila Buxton. *Mark Sabre, Dragnet, Lassie, Torchy, Sugarfoot/ Tenderfoot, Bronco Laine, Hawaiian Eye*. The unglamorous *Billy Bunter. Hi Hazel*. The glamorous Jill Day. *Candid Camera. 77 Sunset Strip. Bonehead*. The glamorous Anne

263

Shelton. *Gary Halliday.* The dolorous in fact suicidal Tony Hancock. *Mr Pastry*, Charlie Chester, *Charlie Chan.* The glamorous Canadienne Barbara Braden. *Cannonball.* Alfred Marks and his glamorous comic foil called Marion Ryan. The caddish Cardew The Cad. *Border News and Lookaround* (a.k.a. *Border Crack an Deekaboot*) . . .

Doleful Ted Ray, not to mention his lipsmacking protégé Benny Hill, *No Hiding Place*, not to mention its racy off-shoot *Echo Four-Two*, the glamorous Shirley Abicair, *I'm Dickens, He's Fenster*, Cardew the Cad's *Children's Caravan* oppo Jeremy Carrad, *Border Crack and Deekaboot*'s one and only protégé, the Cockney chef Stopani, *Hiram Holliday*, *Criss Cross Quiz*, *Laramie*, *Tales of Rubovia* (with its Chinese-accented Hindu puppet), *Cool for Cats* fronted by a hoarse-voiced Canadian wrestling buff Kent Walton, *Playbox* fronted by an unpugnacious Irish boxing buff called Eamonn Andrews, sniff-sniff, grimace, squint, squint, anthropomor-phism-is-my-middle-name Johnny Morris, Larry the Lamb's *Toytown*, *Four Feather Falls* (with its theme tune sung by a sad inexplicable suicide called Michael Holliday), *The* [break-ing-all-previous-viewing-figures, stopping-the-nation-dead-every-Friday-night] *Army Game* starring blistering Bill Fraser as choleric Sergeant Snudge, not to speak of its bastard off-shoot *Bootsie and Snudge*, *The Edmund Hockridge Show*, *Six-Five Special*, *Pick of the Pops*, Jack Jackson, endless golf and leucotomised conversational two-handers in *The Dickie Henderson Show*, *The One O'Clock Gang Show* from vaudevil-lian Glasgow, *Top of the For* . . .

It was nine o'clock of a Saturday night some forty years ago. I wanted to watch vulgar and mindless *Candid Camera* on Border ITV, but instead it was tuned to the marginally less v-and-m BBC. There were only two channels to watch in 1961, hence to change them could only mean a left or a right twiddle, there was nothing in the way of imaginative psycho-geometrical associations. In the event, I stared in amazement at what was being broadcast on the BBC. Or should I say 'in amaze', and thereby convey something of the antiquated and Shakespearean sense of being shaken and convulsed to one's infinitely fragile roots and timbers?

At what exactly? At who exactly? At whom exactly? Well might we ask. Would we acknowledge a sense of farce or of ludicrous anticlimax if we said it was at *Charles Laughton*? At the end of the day all it was was a dead Frenchman called Victor Hugo, he who once announced that all he ever needed apart from a pen and paper was 'soup and whores'. All it was was an old-fashioned Gallic/garlicky yarn. All it was was a lipstick-on-the-men-as-well-as-on-the women technicolor US costume version of The *Hunchback of Notre Dame*. All it was was a ten-year-old who had never ever heard of Victor and knew nothing about his soup and whores, and was wholly unprepared for this grotesquely deformed spire-leaping, woman-molesting, terrifying bellringer called Quasimodo.

Oh what a visage! Oh such a mug! What else? Do we recall the one horrible eye on C. Laughton that was lower than the other horrible eye on Charles Laughton? Whoever did Quassy's make-up must have graduated alongside Geoffrey the *TZ* waxworker and picked up a London, England MA in Historical Make-Up and Marbling. It was the desperate misalignment of the eyes that did for me. My blood turned to freezing cryogenic nitrogen. I was confronted by the most terrifying face I had ever seen. I was all on my own in that Fingland house, all alone in the world, alone in the limitless universe without a comforting voice to tell me Roe, *all it is is a man made-up in a made-up film. It isn't real. He's talking Burl Ives American after all, not proper, dignified and classical French. On top of which it's not even a proper film in a proper picture house. It's a pretend little miniature picture, a piddling swindle of a feeble seventeen-incher. All it is is the telly that rhymes with belly, jelly, welly and smelly! It's a child trying to pretend it's an adult and at the end of the day it's a pathetic little joke . . .*

What I needed to do was get off my arse and switch channels. But I was comprehensively paralysed, and by far too many things. Firstly, by a massive incredulity that anything could look as ugly as that skew-eyed gargoyle. I just could not believe my unskewed eyes. And because this phantom was wholly unimaginable, then something, some cruel, demented agency or weirdly malignant party had chosen bizarrely to thrust it upon the world and on my world in particular. Secondly, any bodily movement on my part, because it was a premonition of physical change, would surely elicit changes in the fearful object. If I were to budge, however slightly, the disfigured monster would also budge. If I were to twitch, he would also twitch his way out of the TV and –

The grotesque thing might slobber and molest me in unimaginable ways. Look at how insanely terrified that young gypsy girl was. Maybe when a woman is being crudely raped she feels the same, if on a grander scale. That if she makes even the tiniest move, it will be misconstrued, and oblige her assailant to murder or disfigure her . . .

I stayed put, and by staying put I quaked. I wanted my Dad to come home, but I was afraid it would be lop-eyed Quassy who would saunter through our door. I stayed in suspended petrifaction for ten or fifteen minutes. Each minute was at least a century. If the camera left Quassy I felt relief, but as it rarely left him for long my panic moved to a graphical constant. At last I could bear it no longer. I walked like a man facing death to that infernal seventeen-inch screen. It was my first great love, but it was now my cruel enemy. The television no longer liked me because it was torturing me. I did not really want to cry. I simply felt harried and persecuted. I stumbled towards the Ekco and put my hand on the channel selector. In 1961 they were comical doorknob affairs set immediately below the screen. This one looked remarkably like the television's left eye, though nothing at all like Quasimodo's left eye. You turned it with a rotational twist but it was always stiff and needed a strong exertion. A four-year-old child for example could not have switched channels on a forty-year-old Ekco.

As I rotated the left eye, a second one loomed up before me . . .

Quasimodo had jumped over a wall! The camera went full close-up on his face. As I approached him he leapt up at me and leered his unaligned eye. I shrieked. The fevered knob went tearing round in my sodden paw skittering past half a dozen unreceivable channels (Tyne Tees, Granada, Ulster, Scottish BBC and ITV . . .). It went round and round like a demented thing three times through the full carousel while I closed my eyes and surrendered to Death.

And I kept them tight shut. I was damned if I was going to let him torture my blood by watching him watching me.

At last I hit a proper channel. And I knew such chasmic relief as I recognised that voice.

It was the finest voice in the universe. It was the voice of Bob Monkhouse. It was that of the discursive comic, the amateur philosopher of comedy. Forty years on, his stanchless fluency and tireless unction are still a legend. But for a stricken child in 1961 his voice was like a gentle father's. I opened my eyes and saw that it was *Candid Camera*. I looked at radiant Monkhouse and his saturnine hoaxster Jonathan Routh. To my amazement all four of their eyes were perfectly *aligned*. I smiled at Monkhouse. Monkhouse smiled at me. Pointing very warmly, though omitting my name, he announced: 'Smile! You're on *Candid Camera*!'

## 240

Today's listings
    1.00 Billy Cotton
    2.00 Mrs Blavatsky
    3.00 Baruch Spinoza
    4.00 Eliot Ness

5.00 T.S. Eliot
6.00 The Loch Ness Monster
7.00 Tessie O'Shea
8.00 Chick Murray
9.00 Chick Corea
10.00 Lenny The Lion
11.00 Plato
12.00 Lord Longford


## 625 *(Audio channel)*

The dying strains of some rarefied church organ music make me think of some dusty, mote-filled loft in two very different locations, both of them imaginary. One is a far-flung cathedral and the other a humble little chapel. Specifically I can picture them as: a) a scene in an eerie Hermann Hesse novel I read as a wide-eyed student, possibly *Demian*, where the hero overhears some organ music composed by someone I'd never heard of called Buxtehude, and b) on an altogether more elevated scale, the gentle old puppet organist in the Children's BBC's *Tales of Rubovia*. Just as the eccentric, tender old chapel organist was worked by strings, so his pedals were worked by his obliging little puppet cat.

A speech-handicapped Radio 3 music expert, whom I picture as looking the exact twin of the *Rubovia* organist, then lisped his way deftly through a lightning commentary.

'. . . definitely one of the gweatest of Bawoque organists and also one of the finest of German composers of all time. He was cited as one of the three gweat S's of his pewiod, the others of course being Schütz and Schein. For twenty-one years he was employed by the Margwave of Bwandenburg of Halle.'

The *Composer of the Week* presenter jovially interrupted. 'For the minuscule proportion of our erudite Radio 3 listeners who've never heard of it, a Margrave being a . . . ?'

'A Teutonic Ward of the Marches. A *Markgwaf.* A German title of nobility. Unfortunately however he fell into a major altercation with his august patwon concerning his wesponsibilities for the city choir schools. Notwithstanding, more pwofoundly cwucial in his musical development was a year he spent under Sweelinck in Amsterdam. Sweelinck's own innovation was his keyboard vawiation technique which the Dutch genius had adapted from his wole models of the English virginalists. The German organist inevitably adapted some of this from his gweat Dutch mentor. Though our German also had another important cweative source in the shape of the Flemish–German contwapuntal motet.'

'So,' the presenter challenged the expert, 'are we to regard our composer of the week as an exceptional innovator or as an exceptional traditionalist?'

'A bit or wather a heck of a lot of both I should say, Wichard! At the end of his life he wote to a musical colleague, "I have wemained twue to the old style of composition and the strict wules of counterpoint." Although I would say his major contwibution to the genwe must finally be assessed as what he did for the chorale vawiation, not to speak of the phenomenal owiginality of his harpsichord toccatas and fantasias. He also wote music for voices and instwuments, for example his *Cantiones Sacwae* of 1620.'

'It's perhaps a little beside the point, Simon, but he was also quite a striking man to look at wasn't he, our composer of the week? Bearded, bushy-haired, definitely a very imposing seventeenth-century gentleman in his middle years?'

'Indeed Wichard. To my mind he always looks "a dead winger" – is that the appwopwiate epithet? – for the eminent television actor, the late Leo McKern. Take a look at this funewal engraving of him with the Latin inscwiption below.'

'Indeed he certainly is. I wonder if Mr McKern was ever aware of the fact. A remarkable verisimilitude. The effortless all-rounder that was the Baroque organist Samuel Scheidt. Alas, I'm afraid that's all we've got time for today. But don't worry, tomorrow Simon and I will be playing as well as talking a great deal more Scheidt.'

'I –'

'And thanks once again to our resident Scheidt expert, Simon Dympney, organist of Milton College, Oxford.'

'My pleasure, Wichard.'

'A lot more Scheidt tomorrow then. Goodbye for now. Though before we go it's time to remind you that next week's *Composer of the Week* is that extraordinarily prolific gentleman called Fux. And after that, in two weeks time, we will be getting to grips with that rather elusive Mexican, Ponce.'


# 555

The European channel is just finishing a survey of the momentous EEC currency changes destined to come into force at the start of 2002. The last shot is of a conscientious grey-haired Portuguese priest visiting some of his remoter parishioners near Ourique in the Alentejo. They are a long way from any handy bank, so the overweight old padre with his government-provided information pack is in the tumble-down tin-sheeting village hall showing them how to use the mysterious 5, 10 and 20 Euro notes. In lieu, that is, of the always-hard-to-come-by, and especially in the impoverished rural Alentejo, Portuguese escudos. A grizzly old farmer in his black pork-pie hat, watched by his just as grizzly old wife, looks as if he has bizarrely taken leave of his wits and suddenly decided to play a kids' game of shops with his seventy-year-old contemporary, the priest.

The next programme whisks us from Ourique to somewhere just as remote and considerably more stricken. Once again I am struck by the fact that EuroTV is actually covering England, which, although it might by some be hallucinatorily regarded as Europe, remains in every significant aspect steadfastly not. One glaring index of its stalwart insularity being that there will be no priests visiting the remoter farms around this lonely bit between Haltwhistle and Gilsland to tell them how to use 'euros' in lieu of 'punds an pence'. There is no great mystery why EuroNews is filming in the Cumbrian–Northumbrian borderlands in 2001. It is because we are back again, we lunchtime satellite viewers, in the heartland of the sheep and cattle plague. By contrast the citizens of Holland, as well as matter-of-fact ditching the guilder and embracing the euro, have also inoculated their cattle and swiftly put paid to their own Foot and Mouth. But we 'sterling' Brits, as well as spurning those flimsy little euro-notes, are clinging to our homegrown murrain with every last atom of bulldog ardour. We won't inject our cows in case we can't export our beef to that hallucination called Europe we do not hanker to be part of. And as John Bull is, par excellence, all beef and sinew and nothing by way of brains, we have with this the makings of a perfect Euro(euro)solipsism . . .

The Cumbrian plague is a European issue on two accounts. It has avalanched to such an improbable extent that we are obliged to have some foreigners imported in a professional capacity. F and M is so extensive, especially in Cumbria and Northumbria, that the Brits have finally run out of vets. The camera pans on a bare and lonely Gilsland hillside, where three male examples, all in their mid-thirties, are stood outside a Northumbrian byre engaged in something of a cosmopolitan dispute. The squabbling Eurovets comprise a German from Stuttgart, a Czech from Prague, and a Spaniard from Huelva. They are called Ruprecht Richter, Bohumil Pavlov and Manuel Ayala. As the only tongue they have in common is English, we have little trouble following the gist of the tele-altercation. Richter in particular has a flawless, not to say frightening English at his command.

The farm they have been called to is a big one with a great many dairy cattle, hence the need for three of them to make a foolproof survey. They have left the terrified sixty-year-old farmer inside the byre while they share their suspicions outside. Joe Tyson had that morning spotted apparent blisters on the tongues of four of his beasts, and also on the udders and teats of four others. According to no-nonsense Pavlov, these eight English animals were all at the primary vesicle stage. Hence between twenty-four and forty-eight hours from now the virus would enter their blood streams to cause the fever proper. During which infinitely contagious phase, the F and M virus would be excreted via their milks, salivas, urines and dungs.

*Ayala* (*shaking his head dourly*): No, they is already at once smocking their leeps, this sick cow. So I fing we are at the popper-fiver stage, not at pre-fiver stage.

*Pavlov* (*dolorously counter-shaking*): Not at all, not at all. They are *not* at all smoking the lips. They just muff their moth, like any stoopid cow will muff its moth. It is therefore now at primer vehicle stage.

*Richter* (*in an unmatchable parody of brusque Teutonic impatience*): In my own view it is at neither of these highly dramatic stages, gentlemen. As I presume you are both aware, Foot and Mouth disease, also known as epizootic aphtha, eczema epizootica or aphthous fever, has a great affinity for the epithelial tissue of the mucous membranes of the gastrointestinal tract. Hence this so-called lipsmacking that my Spanish colleague is referrring to would necessarily be the harbinger of the dreaded secondary vesicles. These would customarily rupture within another twenty-four hours to leave unpleasantly raw and painful lesions. But any intelligent and above all valid diagnosis of F and M has to allow for the other two vesicular contagions of vesicular stomatitis and vesicular exanthema . . .

*Ayala*: *Que?* But –

*Richter*: Allow me to continue, if you please. We need therefore to discriminate between the three conditions by means of appropriate veterinary tests. The horse, as you know, is not susceptible to F and M. Likewise the cow and the pig are not prone to the exanthema. Hence if a fever plus vesicles develops in pigs, cows and guinea pigs but not in horses, clearly it can be justified as F and M. However should all four of our trial animals develop vesicles, then we are instead talking about stomatitis. If, however, we see lesions in 'porkers' but not in cows or guinea pigs, and only to a moderate degree or not at all in horses, then swine exanthema is obviously the name of the game, esteemed colleagues. Like Herr Pavlov here, I see no clear manifestation of lipsmacking, but contrarily, and unlike my Spanish colleague, nor do I see any unambiguous indications of a pre-fever stage.

*Pavlov* (*baffled but sardonic*): *Gar nichts, Herr Doktor?*

*Richter*: I see nothing as yet.

*Pavlov* (*throwing up his arms dismissively*): Oh rilly? So what do we do in accord wif you, Meester Rubneck?

*Richter*: It's very simple. We just wait. We defer diagnosis and we wait.

*Ayala*: *Que?* Accuse me, but you are complete cressy! When they develop full futt and mutt, and we have to take out ship on every farm near here in filch is called Guizlana, and the whole Guizlana ship farmers is want to kill us, what you bloody say then!

*Richter* (*folding his arms, quite unassailable*): I say we exercise discretion and we wait. And that we tell Herr Tyson the farmer to wait too.

*Pavlov* (*shrewdly*): Meester Rubneck, which agence bringed you over here?

*Richter* (*suspicious*): A German agency, of course. One that is based in Stuttgart and which liaises with a partner agency in London.

*Ayala*: Ow mush they pay you for bein Inglesh vet, Senor Roop–?

*Richter*: It's absolutely none of your business, Herr Ayala. But suffice to say it is the same as my remuneration would be were I doing the same veterinary work in Stuttgart.

*Pavlov*: A pig fat dollar wedge, *nicht wahr*, Rubneck? How mush are you get, Manhole?

*Ayala*: Fivety pro zent more than in España. Mebbe one fiveth of what the Alemaner get. My haze-on-sea also is in London, but they have no bruiser haze-on-sea in España. I get one hunnert-fivety pound for wick. The London haze-on-sea muss get two hunnerts cowmission from MAFF wif me. My haze-on-sea is called Agroknow. What is yours, Bummel?

*Pavlov*: Is called Aggro, poor and simple. I get hunnert seven fife pounds in a week. I am blurry fockfockin angered, Manhole, that the fat Deutscher here get five time what I get! It is plenty obvious he does not know five time what I am know.

*Ayala*: An he does not focky know five time what I know.

*Richter* (*arms folded, smiling ironically*): As you say, gentlemen. Just as you say . . .


## 103

It is a blunt and callous admission of disloyalty to my native county, but this is not one of my favourite channels. Most, let us say the rump, of Border's programming is just standard network ITV, but it also has its own regional input, which has a certain ineffably reductive flavour. To call it industriously amateurish is only approximately accurate. It has the frank amiability, the sunny affability, of a homely regional channel warmly buttonholing its friendly regional viewers. Like all the local papers, it is all about inclusivity rather than editorial stringency. A hound trail or a Fellside League darts match or a Carlisle fashion show is as structurally important as a radioactive leak at Sellafield or an employment scare at Maryport. This does not bespeak complacency so much as a surprisingly oriental (and bear in mind Cumbria is actually in the west) mindset. Hallowed tradition invariably overrides any novelty, and there is, right enough, nothing at all new under the Cumbrian sun. Above all, whenever conducting a

TV interview, rather than seek the considered opinion of one interesting voice, it is a whole lot more valuable to ask the opinion of five hundred people plucked at random on the street, whether they be interesting or not.

I turned to Border because I knew it was the lunchtime regional magazine. I was suddenly wondering if they were covering the Foot and Mouth on the Cumbrian news in that same revelatory fly-on-the-wall manner as EuroTV. As it happened I did catch the end of an interview with the unhappy villagers of Great Orton, site of the huge disposal trenches for the animal culls. Some of them were complaining about the noise from all those flying carcase lorries, not to speak of the churned-up mud and the disturbance. Not to mention the incredibly ugly and demeaning image ('the killing fields') that it had left the unfortunate little community. But then, just as I was warming to the editorial integrity that had commissioned these candid interviews, the whole thing, as it were, stopped dead. Without pausing for breath, we galloped onto a considerably less fretful feature, namely the development of Reiver-themed tourism as a means of attracting visitors back to the devastated county.

So what exactly is a Reiver? Some people have a starred A-Level in History, but they still haven't a clue. Were you to do a typical Border interview and ask a thousand people in the streets only a handful would be able to give you an intelligent definition . . .

Film of perhaps a hundred outstandingly English-looking ladies and gents, mostly late middle-aged, all of them smartly dressed in decorous designer-label outfits or smooth and sombre grey suits. They are to be observed with nodding scopes and beaming mugs on three luxurious Cumbrian charabancs making a comprehensive tour of the reiver locations. Reivers, to put you in the picture, were the sixteenth-century cattle thieves who plagued the Debatable Lands on either side of the present-day border. They ransacked and pillaged, burned and robbed, molested, tortured and hacked to pieces, and thus have that fetching homicidal Sunday supp glamour associated with Vikings, Indo-Europeans, Mongols, Tartars and the like. Interesting that these innocuous bus travellers in their best brushed suits and half-moon glasses, all of whom would be roundly horrified by the sight of a Chetnik, Ustasha, Interhamwe etc, should be so romantically stirred by all that unfettered historical rape and sanguinary pillage. Interesting also that everyone in Cumbria and South Scotland called say Kennedy and Nixon (perhaps even the eponymous US presidents were no different on this point) love genially to refer to their ferocious reiver lineage, hence their own hereditary bloodthirsty propensities!

Carlisle Heritage Services, the voice-over informs us, has invited these hundred tourist supremos drawn from every British county for a buckshee three-day charabanc ride. They will be conducted around all the important reiver sites, all the forts and bastles, the peles and the towers, the Hoddoms and the Hexhams and the Bewcastles, as well as being put up in a very nice comfy Carlisle hotel with Reiver Tourist-friendly satellite TV, bidets, homemade Cumbrian oatcakes (just as the reivers ate them), and tea and coffee making facilities (just as they would have loved to have had in those frugal old reiver days, all else being equal). On the final night of their educative junket they will be feted with a reiver-themed banquet in Carlisle's illustrious Tullie House museum. This will comprise authentic fermented reiver potations (aqua vitae by the liquid yard), samples of oaty and farinaceous reiver grub, mellifluous and heart-stirring reiver poetry about death and destruction and mutilation and vengeance, and of course raucous reiver music . . . the last in the shape of a long-haired, legless, incoherent, unintelligible, bekilted minstrel-raconteur from the Scots side.

Interview with a Carlisle Heritage supremo, a neatly beard-ed young gentleman in a flawless blue suit. He is expatiating deftly on all the dazzling entrepreneurial possibilities. As he explains, both local and national IT merchandisers are already queueing up to provide reiver CD-rom packs for knowledge-hungry schoolkids. IT interactivity, pedagogic packaging is definitely the name of the heritage-in-education game by the year 2001. This is not so much the year of a space odyssey as of a virtual space odyssey. For example a twelve-year-old schoolboy in Wigton or Annan, or Bexhill-on-Sea for that matter, while idly shifting his bubble gum to the other side of his mouth, will simultaneously be enabled to click a computer toggle and set a virtual bastle on fire! With the convincing adornment of his US commander's chewing gum, he can pretend to be an unprincipled incendiary twelve-year-old reiver, what? There would also be plenty of scope for virtual pillaging and virtual cattle rustling and –

But would there, I was dying to prompt the Border interviewer, be scope for *virtual rape* and *virtual torture*?

The implications of this mimetic interactivity were then chewed to the bone by three local headmasters (from the toupeed Carlisle one, 'exciting', from the bearded Moffat one, 'varra exciting', from the balding Hexham one, 'extremely exciting'). Border TV, who could no more resist a soundbite or a trawl around the Carlisle streets than they could resist the urge to imitate London Weekend in the manner of souped-up graphics and jazzy jingles, now decided to go democratically public. This morning, they revealed, they had sent out interviewers round the streets of the county's capital to regale the Great Border City inhabitants with the following highly pertinent and heritage-friendly query.

*What does The Border mean to you* exactly?

*Cadaverous-looking old man who is effortfully cupping his ear somewhere down Botchergate*: You what?

*Interviewer*: The Border between England and Scotland, sir? What is its significance for you? Does it make you think of reivers or –

*Old man*: Eh? What do I think about beav–? Stop talking rubbish! Go away!

*Headscarved woman with a large mole, also down Botcher-*

*gate*: The Border? (*lengthy pondering until a sudden startled enlightenment*) You just mean *you lot*, don't you? You just mean 'Border TV'. You're 'The Border' aren't you? You're the only border we know around here.

*Three young workmen covered in white paint and hurtling down Lowther Street*: We've just finisht oor bait and we wanner gerr in yon pub. (*sotto voce but inadequately edited out*) *Deek at the tits on yon!* In a nutshell, nowt, nowt and nowt. We don have a clue why you're askin us, marra. Who bleep cares? Who bleep cares? Who bleep cares? *And look, deek at the tits on that udder!*

*Interviewer*: But don't you count the Border as part of your heritage?

*Same headscarved woman down Botchergate*: You'd need to ask me husband. He's big in the Masons and he sometimes reads a book. I don't understand things like that. I don't know nowt. I really don't know nowt . . .


## 636 *(Audio channel)*

Jeremiah, 10.14

*Every man is brutish in his knowledge: every founder is confounded by the graven image . . .*

# 13

To be married and divorced by the risible age of twenty-four is quite an achievement. That said, I still have frequent, troubling dreams about my first wife twenty-five years later. In any case, I am hardly alone in the late adolescent marriage stakes. I have a college friend, a graduate of Persian and Hittite called Peel, who was married at nineteen and divorced at twenty-two. They were living in Hounslow for those three short years, and his wife got into a Seventies spiritual cult and changed her name to an Indian one which meant Full of Unconditional Bliss. She might well have been full of unqualified ecstasy, but Peel wasn't even mildly enraptured that he could no longer address her as Katie, nor was he bursting with joy to wake every morning in an overpriced and featureless West London semi which Katie eventually deserted in favour of a Shepherd's Bush ashram . . .

The dream I have about Mary is always the same. She is living on the other side of a very steep fellside (though in fact she came from Cumbria's western seaboard) and either I am obliged to make the arduous and endless hike over to her new home, or she is compelled to make the same trip over to me. It feels imperative, exhausting, yet pointless if I go over the hill to her, and if she makes the trip it seems dully poignant and sometimes harrowing. Perhaps the mountains aren't Cumbrian fells after all, but are displaced Cuillins of the subconscious? Mary Shona MacLean's parents moved down to West Cumbria from Skye just after the War, and she was born, their only child, six years later. They were kindly, peaceable, hardworking, serious-minded, and very old-fashioned Free Kirkers. There was no Free Kirk anywhere in West Cumbria, of course, so they went for the nearest substitute which was good old Primitive Methodism collier-style. John MacLean was a fitter at a Whitehaven pit, and Eileen MacLean was a catering supervisor for the county's schools. They didn't swear, they didn't drink, they didn't do anything on Sundays apart from go to chapel and maybe tune to the Home Service on the wireless as long as the listening was wholesome. Unamused, in fact deeply dismayed, by the mainland fascination for saucy double entendres, they certainly would never have listened to *Round the Horne* or Tony Hancock or *Much Binding in the Marsh* on the unbridled and spluttering Sunday Light Programme.

I met Mary down in London where she was busy qualifying as a secondary teacher. Her main subjects were P.E. and Scripture, a curious but quite standard combination. At my own school I never knew a PE teacher who didn't teach RE though I did know at least one RE woman who never taught press-ups or handball. Wholesomeness and fitness interchangeable with holiness and fitness? Hard physical exercise driving off idle lusts and capricious 1970s fancies? Mary was as fit as a stable lass, and went running round the streets of Islington long before anyone used the verb 'jog' or had heard of endorphins or anaerobics. After her BEd she stayed on and taught in a Richmond comprehensive, even though her parents would have preferred to have her safely back in Cumbria. They feared nameless and faceless metropolitan influences, when all they need to have feared was one young male Cumbrian abroad in the pagan city. They needn't have worried themselves on most accounts. Mary and I were scarcely debauched sybarites, because even at twenty she would glance behind her shoulder when watching TV that her father would had disapproved of. This included all soap operas such as *Coronation Street*, *The Newcomers* and *Crossroads*, all variety shows and comedy half hours, and especially the blasphemous Steptoe type full of those ugly TV expletives git, bleeder, tart and ponce.

Once aged sixteen back in Whitehaven, Mary Shona had been caught *in flagrante delicto*. With the telly that is, not with a hot-faced and unrepentant Whitehaven boy. One Sunday afternoon when she was menstrual and full of cold, she was allowed to miss chapel and encouraged to lie on the couch with her mother's current copy of *People's Friend*. Five years later Mary could recall that it had a pen and ink drawing of Annan's cheerless town centre on its cover, complete with 1968 Hillman Imp, a Scottie dog on a leash, and a lugubrious woman with a pre-war hat about to enter Muriel's hairdresser to have her biannual perm. Tiring of all those coley and kedgeree recipes, bootee-knitting patterns and true-romance stories so chaste and sinewless they seemed to have been written by a literary committee manned by Primitive Methodists, my future wife rose from her sofa and switched on the forbidden telly. She deliberately switched on Border ITV, on the grounds that if there was to be any forbidden fruit it would more likely be there of a Sunday than it would on the BBC. On the mother of all channels, it would likely be Harry Corbett and Sooty, or *Going For A Song*, a polite little antiques show that always began with an antique trilling cage bird. The tedium of West Cumbrian Sundays and the tedium of Sunday's BBC viewing seemed all of a deadly muchness to an attractive and spirited teenage girl with as much interest in the body and the physical instincts as the next.

This was in 1968, the year of *Revolution* by the Beatles and the year of revolution on the bloody streets of Paris. Mary knew very little about either of those, but she was dimly aware that sexual mores these days were irreversibly different from what they had been a decade earlier. At five o'clock of a Sunday there was scheduled a phenomenon that would have been inconceivable even two years ago. It was a frenetic sort of interview-cum-sketch-cum-special-guest show, fronted by the Liverpudlian DJ, Kenny Everett. On his BBC Radio 1 slot he was notorious for the insanity of his surreal patter and his suggestive language, and on this ITV debut he would essay to be likewise. The programme was called with open-faced artlessness *Nice Time*, and to help Everett and all his viewers enjoy just that, he had a simmeringly beautiful and outrageous young female assistant. As far as Mary could recall, this woman did not utter a single word, but her frizzy, astonishing Zulu hair and her transatlantic if not cosmopolitan aura more than made up for that. What was retrospectively momentous from the point of view of modern cultural history was that this young unknown Australian also happened to be called *Germaine Greer* . . .

It was just two years before she would publish that incendiary bombshell *The Female Eunuch*. Likewise it was only for a year, since 1967, that the homosexual Everett had been able to exercise a legal sexual preference. Perhaps that explains the buffoonish nature of the item that Mary watched next, given that the 'glamorous' assistant was a brilliant proto-feminist and the presenter himself had no vicarious interest in women's bodies. Mary MacLean watched astonished and guiltily entertained as Everett pushed Germaine Greer around the studio on a kind of outsize tea trolley. Sumptuous and splendid Germaine was flat on her stomach with her legs hanging over the side, and she was clutching a nautical telescope up to her squinting face. In front of this weird equipage was a line of young women assembled like so many specimens in a small-town beauty competition. Though with the intriguing variation that they had their backs to the jabbering DJ, and to Capn Germaine and her scrutinising lens. In fact they were displaying their skirted backsides to the ogling Antipodean and Everett was conducting a *Nice Time* competitive buttock contest. There followed many subtly apposite puns in which the words rear, behind and posterior effervesced on Kenny's lips as he leapt and fizzed about his studio set. The line of young women giggled wholeheartedly, and the one with the finest rear embonpoint, according to Germaine's discerning telescope, hooted the loudest of all.

Mary was chuckling and bristling at this anarchic bacchanalian fun, which as far as she knew had no uproarious ceilidh counterpart up in Skye, Lewis, Harris or Scalpay of a Sabbath teatime, when a human throat was hoarsely cleared behind her . . .

It was a grotesquely embarrassed throat-clearing. It was the larynx of her father, John MacLean, whose father, also called John, had been a Portree Kirk Elder for thirty years. As Mary learnt later, her Dad had come down with the same sweating headachey flu as his daughter, and he'd had to stagger home halfway through the service. He had come in by the back as he always did, the door from the kitchen to the sitting room was wide open, and she was so engrossed with Germaine and her buttock judging she had no idea she was being observed. In fact she was watched in her idolatrous deceitfulness for a full five minutes. Her father was a fair man as well as a strict man, and he just wanted to check this wasn't a new variation on, say, the harmless buffoonery of Leslie Crowther's *Crackerjack*. The Skye man sought in vain for schoolboys in blazers manfully clutching booby-prize cabbages, but instead all he saw was bizarre and bearded Everett and a frizzed and painted woman whom anyone over the age of forty, Free Kirker or not, would immediately have discerned to be a wilful Jezebel. His blood froze at this horrifying and blasphemous carnival. Old Testament verses about deliberate sinning came to mind, and Mary MacLean knew this because that same evening, despite his flu, he quoted them to her for the good of her troubled soul. No, this wasn't a gimmicky Sunday version of Crowther and Glaze, nor was it remotely intelligible as anything but a provocative and offensive besmirching of the hallowed spirit of the Lord's Day.

Mary turned red, then purple, then very white. Her father looked at her diagnostically as if to see whether there were some ineffable pagan signs on her face or person he hadn't previously noted. He strode across to the sinful television and amazed her by kicking it. Not hard enough to damage it, but perhaps to indicate he would have liked to kick his teenage daughter instead. He was not one for violence, and she had never had any sort of proper hiding from him. John was so upset he turned the volume knob the wrong way so that Everett's demented blather filled the same room where they held their family prayers. He shuddered, lunged at the thing and banged it off. Then as if to make doubly certain he went to the socket and unplugged it. He had to stoop to do so and his wholly virtuous masculine backside was presented not for any judging but with an absolute and touching Hebridean innocence. He walked back slowly to his daughter and loomed over her.

'Have you some kind of explanation?'

Mary MacLean was already crying and shaking. 'It was the first thing that came on. So I just left it on. I hadn't even looked at the *Radio Times*. I didn't mean t–'

He regaled her in the same way he might have orated a Gaelic Psalm, 'I saw you ogling it for a full five minutes! You were laughing and tittering and were obviously enjoying it very much.'

The hideousness of that, the ubiquity and power of the Evil One, the Liar, the Father of all Liars, the tireless vigilance required, the perennially being on one's spiritual guard for oneself and one's vulnerable family. He raised his mighty hand incensed and brought it down in an arc which would have connected with Mary's cheek had she not shrieked and started, and had he not changed its trajectory and brought it down on the sofa arm.

Dust came billowing out and the sofa seemed to shriek as well.

'Go to bed,' he barked at her. 'Go at once, for your own sake. Go upstairs before I chastise you. If you weren't ill with flu and I wasn't ill with flu I would beat you with the dog strap. For you to be ogling at that demented wicked filth of a Sunday of all days. I felt very sick in the chapel, but now I feel much sicker.' He raised his trembling hand to his burning forehead. 'I think, after all, I will have to give it away.'

He was referring of course to the television which currently had a vividly leering and vaunting expression on its nineteen-inch face. That was what John apprehended all too clearly because he picked up the tablecloth and carefully draped it over that feckless conduit of all things profane, unloving, uncaring, unsober, insane . . .

It ought not to be the case but absolute fidelity and absolute uncompromising decency do not always excite a young husband's heart. I don't mean that I wished Mary had had affairs or had shown signs of having them so that I might have found her more exciting. Far from it. I had just left the maelstrom of Mona Roche and her Marxist polygamy, not to speak of her new-found love for her own sex. Aside from that last touching volte-face, it had all felt like advanced algebra or a kind of abstract physics of the emotions which put principles before people and ideals before instincts. I was ready for a tranquil monogamous convalescence through the rest of my twenties, and also ready to offer Mary MacLean an equally tranquil berth. Two young northerners abroad in the massive metropolis, we often spent our Saturdays searching in vain for some non-existent countryside. Being so central, Hampstead Heath had its obvious limitations, and in the end it was Richmond and Kew Gardens that gave us the deepest, simplest pleasure. In the summer there was a special delicacy to the light and the leaves of the limes and plane trees and sycamores. Even the sleepy shady avenues of Richmond with their handsome, prosperous terraces seemed to be more of the country than the town. Had we been stinking rich we might have bought a house there and settled down to the consummate life of Riley. But in 1974 a young reporter and a young teacher were both paid in buttons and so we lived in an extortionate one-bedroom flat which consumed more than half our income.

And in the end and shamefully I became enormously bored. Mary's hereditary virtue in the end lost its ineffaceable lustre. John MacLean had done his job well and he had taught his daughter goodness, kindness, fairness, gentleness . . . not to speak of patience, modestly anticipated horizons . . . and an innocence of mind that was not so much irritating as seemingly set in stone. Of course we were only married a year, but at that age a month can feel like a century, and a bleak weekend can feel like an eternity. Sometimes it felt as if we were stuck inside the anteroom annexe of some spiritless piece of modern civic architecture. Mary worked in a brand new comprehensive and I worked in a modern highrise office and in most respects their designs, meaning their imaginative worlds, were indistinguishable. Linearity, rectangularity, glass, concrete, filing cabinets, brown and odorous varnish, formica chairs, a rigidly geometrical and economical disposition of doors and endless corridors. It might be a crass observation but a truly beautiful building has ornament and embellishment for its own sake and practicality is never the first consideration. Likewise our Nineteen Seventies marriage needed some ornamentation, some superfluous and stimulating non-necessities. I don't mean any of the luxuries that money can buy, but those that are the fruit of inspiration, risk, serendipity and chance. Let me try to put it as accurately and appositely as I can. Just as here in my tranquil native county, even in the resplendent county seat of Carlisle, one is never taken authentically by any real surprise, if only because one knows exactly how things will always be, so in our brief and dim little marriage I could never anticipate any fruitful possibilities of change. Mary's lineaments and dimensions, her hopes and expectations, her expressions of desire, her expressions of surprise, her facial expressions, her bodily expressions, her subtlest contours and coordinates, both visible and invisible, were without any hope of surprise.

*

Writing this down seems callowly cruel and I am tempted to write no more. If Mary MacLean were here now in front of me I would take all the blame for our separation. I would say that it was my fault for being weak, not her fault for being strong. I wouldn't accuse her of having been a dull partner, I'd accuse myself for having wanted the sky as well as the earth. I wouldn't dare tell her that even her breasts at one point seemed far too placid and her tender smile at another seemed some unwelcome sign of self-protective stagnancy. Apropos satellite channel 121 and the *Kelly Windsor Show*, Professor David Mankovic was perhaps not quite as mad as he seemed at first sight. His bestseller *Look Behind You (It's All In The Butt)* wasn't available in 1974, but if I'd chanced across it then I might have found my own suspicions confirmed. Once, in the bedroom about three months into our marriage, I watched Mary turn in her comfortable but shapeless pink nightie and thought two uncharitable things. Firstly that by an inexplicable consequence of our marriage, as in some Grimm or Andersen fairytale, she had mysteriously doubled in age, that she was not a chronological twenty-three but an actual and emphatic forty-six. The second was that her placid wifely backside which was dimly visible through the rayon nightie was a virtuous and a zestless old specimen. It was a backside that like its owner did not dream or wonder or set itself any imaginative tasks. I shuddered at what felt like an hallucination and blinked to try and make my wife, her menopausal nightie, and her cosy matronly behind an emblem of possible surprise.

Mary Shona turned and said: 'I didn't prepare too thoroughly for 9AD tomorrow. I know that I did for 9PS, and I could get by improvising for 9AD, but . . .'

To conceal my unpalatable hallucinations, I pretended to be intrigued by the initials. 'Why are they called AD and PS?'

'What?' she said putting her comfy sweater over her comfy nightie as she prepared to review her notes in the sitting room. 'They're the names of the form teachers. AD is Al Denby who teaches physics and PS is Pam Stowe who teaches needlework. I look after 7MM of course.' She smiled far too forgivingly. 'I thought I'd told you all that.'

I snorted to myself soundlessly. Why did so many school-teachers have to be called Pam instead of Pamela, and why were so many of their male colleagues called the charismatic Al to hide the fact they were christened the moribund Alfred or Albert? I would have preferred her to be irritated with me for having no idea why 7MM was called 7MM. They were her married initials of course, Mary Murphy née MacLean, and she had talked to me frequently and uneditedly about 7MM for the last three months, yet never once had it registered that it was her own special acronym.

She went off to write some notes on the healing miracles in the Synoptic Gospels. As she did so it occurred to me that our three-month-old marriage needed a healing miracle without delay. Instead it was a brutal indicator of how things were going that I felt no sexual frustration. Once, say just a month ago, the sight of her pink thighs dancing under any old nightie would have stirred me to a reflex desire. An hour passed as I sat in bed pretending to read a novel while pondering the unmysterious mystery of my schoolteacher wife. It turned one o'clock as she walked in, took off her unalluring sweater and climbed in beside me. She yawned enormously and engulfingly and remarked at my reading so late. She had decided to get up very early to finish her preparation so she gave me a sisterly kiss and a conclusive night-night. It was a tortuous and unflattering irony that although I didn't desire her I still felt annoyed by her unavailability. How could she be sure that I wasn't bursting to have her, and why for that matter should physical tiredness be such an all-purpose, automatic excuse? Wasn't I, all else being equal, always available for love even if terminally bog-eyed, even if laid-up with backache or toothache or flu?

I extricated myself from a lacklustre marriage by extricating myself from a lacklustre metropolis. Prior to which the way had been paved by a feverish embroilment with a teenage office temp called Connie Bray. I took a badly paid job on a Cumbrian freebie and rented myself a tidy little house just a few miles from my Primitive Methodist in-laws. I imagined after our split Mary might also move back north, but she had enough sense to stay put and let the storm blow about her. She tended to her marital wounds, which were gaping, in the pitiless, contourless capital, and a few years later found happiness with a teacher called . . . Al Bickley. Al was short for Alfred, and Bickley also taught PE and Scripture, and I have learnt they are now both grandparents and have a smart bungalow in a leafy part of Bromley. The Bickleys of Bromley were and are more or less blissful, whereas the Murphys of N16 would have made a hideous and irredeemable Darby and Joan. Mary Shona was tempted to move back home in my wake of course, but she knew that her parents would grieve at both her broken marriage and her efforts to pursue the one who'd left her. At which point Fran entered the Cumbrian picture and simultaneously John and Eileen followed their instincts and moved back to Broadford in Skye. In summer this has one of the highest concentrations of midges in the universe, but my in-laws doubtless welcomed this tormenting plague as a sign of a world where the morals at last made a punitive sense. Fran of course had her eyes opened to my limitations on the Isle of Tiree, another Protestant and Gaelic island, though with far fewer midges and none of that Wee Free austerity. I had ordered Fran about and prevented her chatting to David Bellamy and consequently we'd almost been killed by two stampeding white horses. Later still came my third wife Jane, who passed judgement on me and my furtive philandering on another Celtic island. Jane let me know, in the shape of her sad but angry shoulders as we walked the Great Blasket, that she had had enough of my puerile deceitfulness. No less than Billy Bunter, that blithering bandersnatch on the black and white set in the Poulaphouca, finally put the lid on it. Twelve years ago, in 1989, I then made vows to brainy, handsome Lulu, and her reciprocal vows, wholehearted as they were, carried things forward another decade.

Of course I am regularly mocked by my colleagues (no learning curve in that stupid bastard's case) even though two of my marriages have lasted ten years. Those who mock the loudest have been through a single divorce, then refused to risk themselves again for the rest of their lives. Once bitten, twice shy, I suppose, but in my case I always live in hope, not to say hunger, not to say passion, not to say tender expectancy.

I was thirty-eight years old when I became the second husband of forty-year-old Lulu. Her previous one, Ben Graham, had been an artist, an extremely talented, arrogant and successful painter who'd held an honorary sinecure at a Durham art college. Turned fifty in 1987, Ben had taken up with a talented and wealthy young student called Lacey who was barely half his age. Lacey was an American, and when she went back to Chicago Ben went with her, having surreptitiously arranged a paid sabbatical and a year-long junket as a visiting prof in an art institute close to Lacey's sumptuous downtown duplex.

Lulu loved and hated Ben in equal measure. She admired his prodigious talent and was particularly impressed that he could make a decent income from his heaven-sent gift. The juvenile adventuress Lacey didn't need his money of course, nor did she need to be so bovine facile when it came to reproductive fertility. Lulu had established five years ago that she was unable to conceive children, and though she'd been keen to try the latest fertility treatments, Ben had been adamantly against them. It demanded careful prior planning, diary organisation, setting entire days aside, not to speak of the unmentionable business of reading pornography in a hospital annexe and ejaculating into a bottle. Ben, like a caricature mad-artist, refused to operate by using a diary, and for most of his

Durham lectures he turned up fifty minutes late and offered his students only ten terse minutes of his scatter-gun genius.

Lulu had met Ben at the RCA in the early Seventies. It was part of his genius that he'd encouraged her to be a mundane art teacher so that, should his own reputation ever falter, he had always something to fall back on. Lulu was Head of Art in a massive Northumbrian comprehensive, a job so frenetic that she found no time at all to express her own talent. Instead, her principal means of relaxation were highbrow novels and low-brow soaps . . . together with an inordinate fondness for ancient TV sitcoms. *Man About The House*, *On The Buses* and *George and Mildred* were her three favourite Seventies repeats. About three years ago, determined to give me a short intensive course in classic comedy, she had made me watch the feature-length version of the last. As with all sitcom spin-offs, a half-hour format will not stand a three-fold stretching and it was, to put it kindly, execrable. Brian Murphy as George, that curmudgeonly emblem of all selfish and sexless middle-aged males, effortfully did his best of course. Bill Maynard played a seedy restaurant assistant up to his eyes in greasy catering trays and filthy crockery. The plot was sheer idiocy but Lulu guffawed and roared in that Haltwhistle cinema as if she had been watching vintage Buñuel or Fellini or Jacques Tati on his postman's bicycle.

It is character we are talking about after all. It is character and nothing else we have been talking about since the first line of this seen-at-a-distance chronicle. George and Mildred had first appeared in an earlier comedy called *Man About The House*, and were deemed to be such towering characters that they were given their own eponymous spin-off. In the original show George was the shifty Cockney landlord always out to make a sly bob while never spending a penny on his clamorous, youthful tenants. Devious and skulking to the last, he was forever eavesdropping at their doors, telling outrageous barefaced lies both to them and his raddled, fractious and long-suffering wife. Instead of chauffering Mildred a.k.a.

Yootha Joyce in a car, he parked her roughly on the back of his farting scooter. Instead of a dashing Seventies helmet, he proffered her a hideous bucket skidlid made in 1956. Instead of frittering good cash on a romantic candlelit meal, he would cart home greasy fish and chips on his putting Vespa. He wore a shapeless, antique cardigan, was balding, had a draggly, dandruffy tash, and a severe absence of bedtime libido. A set piece was for Mildred to attempt to nag him into carnal intimacy, and for George to hurriedly gasp, 'Well, night-night then, Mildred!', then dive into darkness and immediate snoring slumber.

So there we were, there was the explanation. Or at least it was Lulu's explanation. Take away the cheap London accent and the put-put Vespa and there was no great difference between *George and Mildred* and *Lulu and Ben*, the notional and not very amusing C4 sitcom. Slobbish and selfish males free of any leavening of self-knowledge prevailed in both these hectic comedies. Ben had Lulu slaving as the bread-winner while he devoted himself to his painting and basked in his Sunday supp ubiquity with such shameless self-satisfaction. Ben was certainly not undersexed like George, but he was, shall we say, selectively sexed. He liked to have Lulu when he wanted her, but if fagged from his all-night painting he pushed her away with an ill-concealed disdain. When she wasn't in the mood for love and he was, Ben was little short of brutal. He would turn it all into a hoarse thespian monologue, a wounded and venomous tirade against her flaccidity and frigidity. Instead of being like a delectably frisky dame out of Chaucer, Lulu was more like a weary old dyke out of Radclyffe Hall. There was no limit to his nonsense or his nastiness when his penis was hurting him. Born in 1937 he was just old enough to have missed out on the elementary lessons of feminism and to call Lulu now and again by the unappealing soubriquet 'wench'. Once, out of spite, he told her she was getting way too fat around the hips, and as this coincided with her final diagnosis of infertility, it left her as flat and sad as a blade of windblown grass.

She explained to me in the interval of one of these ancient sitcoms, 'When you get snooty about my TV habits you miss the point. Take that brilliant idiot George in *Man About The House*. George represents the unrepentant rock-bottom worm's-eye view, the horrible little Andy Capp they still print every day in the *Daily Mirror*. He is without any principles or ideals at all, his grubbiness is unconcealed. Or at any rate it's so feebly concealed that anyone but a child could see what he's up to. He's just a plain, unthinking city landlord who doesn't have an eloquent polysyllabic tongue like Ben the painter had. You see people with big brains and big vocabularies can bamboozle sadistically with words, it's their most precious asset. But unfortunately,' she finished drily, 'we shall know them by their ugly deeds and not by their silken words.'

I looked at her dubiously. 'Meaning Brian Murphy, Reg Varney and Andy Capp cartoons offer you some sort of homeopathic relief?'

'Of course they do! Because, isn't it obvious, really blatant rogues are always funny? Blatancy is always comic by definition. Your boyhood hero Billy Bunter caught in mid-cake-snatching is a perfect example. What was it he used to say to Quelch? "It isn't me, sir, hiding under this table with this cake that I didn't steal from those beasts of the Remove!" Ben Graham on the other hand was a rogue whose roguishness wasn't remotely funny. It was manipulative, arrogant, self-aggrandising, chauvinist and completely selfish. But then like many another rogue he was also charming and funny and extremely talented, so everyone forgave him everything in the end. All of which helped him to forgive himself on every possible score.'

I poured the last of our bottle of wine. We were halfway through a 1972 *On The Buses* repeat, but the commercials were all for the latest mobile phones. 'So it's an emotional catharsis which happens to be addictive. You can't stop yourself watching these painlessly comic versions of Ben?'

'Possibly. If I really wanted to understand Ben Graham in every subtle psychological nuance, I might read an expert dissection of male shiftiness by Edith Wharton or Rebecca West. In the meantime I like to laugh my head off at sneaky, artless sitcom buffoons who aren't *clever* enough to pretend they're something else!'

So far so good. And in any event, at his best, weaselly George was an impressive 3D creation. Not so Reg Varney in the London transport comedy *On The Buses*, a programme whose staple gags were obsessively smutty innuendo and a cloacal fixation that seemed the opposite of anything aphrodisiac. But then Lulu also loved the *Carry On* films which by now had a TV series in the form of edited clips from the complete ribald oeuvre. How long, I asked myself more than once, could anyone, even a thrice-sedated geriatric, continue to cackle at Kenneth Williams's seminal (literally) 'bunking up' pun in *Carry On Camping*? Lulu Murphy must have chortled at least a dozen times at that same five-minute clip. Likewise she snorted uproariously at wafer-thin creations called Mrs Prodworthy, Sidney Fiddler, Harold Hump, Cecil Gaybody, Mrs Dangle, Arthur Upmore, Private Widdle and the 'Khasi' of Kalabar. She also laughed herself to near incontinence at Kenneth Williams's Julius Caesar with his immortal lines, 'Infamy, infamy, *they've all got it in for me!*' . . .

To adopt the addictive *Carry On* lexicon, I certainly proved to be a Big Dick in my fourth attempt at marital give and take. I am not talking about genital dimensions of course, I am talking about plain wooden-headed idiocy. The demon drink, in the shape of off-license wine, was also to blame in large part. Lulu and I both worked far too hard and therefore our nightly imbibings worked as Pavlovian rewards to help us wind down and start again tomorrow. Lulu liked expensive reds and I liked cheap rough ones, so we regularly compromised by buying moderately priced whites and in particular Hungarian rieslings. Lulu also did some hatha-yoga on a daily basis, but I hadn't the patience for oriental relaxation. In fact doing it made me tense, and I found myself halfway through some asana thinking wishing I was reading a book or watching a foreign film instead of fooling about with this. Once, halfway through a complex stork posture, instead of thinking about storks, I started thinking about fish and chips, and simply couldn't get them out of my head. At once I resumed my unreformed journalist boozer's slouch and tore off up the road in my car, and came back with three haddock and two quids worth of chips. Lulu who had just finished her faultless bhujangasana, having polished off the same three-course dinner as me, gaped at me in amazement before deciding to ape my gargantuan greed . . .

It was the drink that did for us because it brought out our subtle differences. These differences were so subtle they seemed laughably ephemeral, of apparently no consequence when the two of us were sober. In a nutshell they were about Lulu Murphy's tastes in telly versus Roe Murphy's tastes in telly. If that sounds utterly fatuous I would refer you again to that emblematic entity known as fish and chips. Given that the statistically proven commonest cause of marital rowing is where one half of a couple *steals chips* from the other half's plate (vide the identical press release in the *Guardian*, *Telegraph* and *Times* of 12.9.99), is it that surprising that their TV differences can lead them to the existential brink? In my case as I argued my corner, I got rhetorical and impassioned and at certain points plain bloody nasty. In our ten-year marriage we only had three major rows, and it was the last one finished Lulu because I wounded her more than anyone deserved to be wounded. Prior to all three arguments we had broken open a second or possibly a third bottle of Magyar riesling, and were not just oiled but swimming belly-flap through a haze of hang-it-all euphoria . . .

Until the euphoria flagged, that is, and vile cussedness and lack of elementary inhibition got the better of us.

That vicious argument in the spring of 1999 started over

*Coronation Street*, or *Corrie* as its cheerful addicts call it. It then spread like measles or AIDS or chlamydia to *EastEnders*, *Emmerdale* and *Brookside*. Lulu followed the Manchester and Liverpudlian sagas religiously, and the London and rural Yorkshire soaps, the two E's, on an intermittent basis. If she had urgent schoolwork to prepare she switched the latter off with moderate difficulty, but on a good night she could sit through a solid hour and a half of *Emmie*, *Corrie* and *Brookie*, or alternatively *Eastie*, *Corrie* and *Brookie*. (Aside from bona fide *Corrie* those are my own insulting diminutives, but it gives some indication of how much I scorn these nightly soaps, drunk or not.)

Here is a brief but considered excursus on the siting of your television set. I am not by the way mincing delicately about the arcane Feng Hsui geometry of your twelve-inch 1974 black and white portable, or the scrupulous siting of your pristine new digibox. If you are stupid enough, as most couples in the world seem to be, to put your TV in the principal sitting room, you will encounter immediate and serious difficulties. If she loves soaps and hates subtitled movies, and he likes subtitled movies and hates soaps, then a heaped pyre of incendiary faggots is already being prepared underneath their innocent TV armchairs. While she enjoys her favourite soap, he either writhes in torment or stomps into another room to do something else. But to talk some prim realities, supposing it is winter and all the other rooms are cold and cheerless, and that in any case his work-induced exhaustion is such that he cannot get off his lethargic and selfish arse. Everyone by now has heard of that decadent medical condition, unknown before 1961, known as 'TV backside'. There might have been some analogous vicarious condition known to the Picts, Scots, Angles, Jutes, and Celts (possibly with too much gawping at their enemies being slowly tortured, their gluteal tissue began to turn flabby) but there are no references to it in surviving documents. The modern condition of TV backside is a dangerous and unlovely steatopygia, which in severe cases can lead to a lethal obesity, variously preceded by cardiac arrest, chronic diabetes, and even dementia praecox, hallucinations and other types of florid insanity. In my case I never quite succumbed to TV backside in my fifth decade, as my fourth wife Lulu drove me so relentlessly from my favourite armchair.

I avoided most of these torturing scenarios by taking a bath when *Corrie* was on the TV. I always took a magazine and my radio upstairs to the bathroom, and in a variation on Albert Steptoe fishing for suppertime pickles in his bathwater, I digested contemporary events via the *New Statesman* and classical concerts via Radio 3. However adaptable as I was, by 1999 I was obliged to take at least four time-prescribed baths a week (Sunday, Monday, Wednesday and Friday) whereas had I been ten years older and married to a *Corrie*-nut called Lulu in 1961, I would only have needed to bathe the Monday and the Wednesday. Sometimes, especially if there was some breathless cliffhanger (murder, rape, incest, a sex change, swindling, bankruptcy), *Corrie* was broadcast twice in a single night at staggered intervals and with a half-hour break. My difficult choice then was either to bathe from 7.30 to 8, when *Corrie* the first was on, then lurch out of the bath to which I must drunkenly return like a severely obsessional neurotic from 8.30 to 9 when *Corrie* the second, the cliffhanger within a cliffhanger, was shown. Alternatively of course I could stay in the bath continuously from 7.30 until 9, and thus become a malcontented prune. If the immersion heater hadn't been on long enough, I would be obliged to linger in a warm, then tepid, then cold, then freezing bath, which not even the finest novel or classical concert could mitigate. As nightmare scenario I foresaw the inevitable day when to satisfy its insatiable addicts *Corrie* would be broadcast at three, four or five split shifts of a night, whereupon I would be yo-yoing in and out of a hot, then cold, then icy tub like a grinning *Jeux Sans Frontière* nutter from the TV archives of 1976 . . .

Sometimes I stayed in our sitting room and vainly attempted to read while *Coronation Street* was blaring. It was then that I noticed in this soap the disturbing prevalence of some serious and gifted actors reduced to talking in lugubrious Mancunian rent-a-line. They were brought down to it because of the lucrative money of course, but did they really need the cash so badly? Here bizarrely was an ageing and portly Roy Hudd (refer above, the comic's public confession of embarrassing emaciation on the *Eamonn Andrews Show* of 1966). Hudd had recently played an accomplished and dignified part in a provocative Dennis Potter drama about covert wartime operations. Now here he was blandly mouthing software-generated soap lines. Here he was in the pub babbling away in battered clichés about a personal relationship crisis, when his soap-smeared crisis was not a crisis but a soapy trope, a Corrian trope or paradigm, a precalibrated unit of recyclable anxiety that came and went like the snow until a fresh fall or flurry came hurtling along.

And what of Fred the *Corrie* butcher with his ponderous 'I say, I say' vehemence that invariably preceded some deathless truism? Lulu thought Fred was very funny but this wobble-jowled butcher wasn't at all funny. I advised her in my Hungarian riesling sagacity that that rare commodity 'funniness' demanded vividness, invention, surprise, shock, paradox, deviation and umpteen other imaginative possibilities. The butcher was played by a gifted actor called John Savident who in decades past had graced many a fine adaptation of the classics, foreign as well as English. Savident was a magnetic character actor who as a soap butcher was a pitiful wraith, a numbly one-dimensional butcher, not like any real, much less convincingly invented butcher, no Zola or Herbert Jenkins or H.E. Bates or E.F. Benson butcher, not even as sentient as a straw-hatted Twenties variant as depicted in a *Just William* book.

Lulu downed a combative slug of the Olasz (pronounced oddly enough exactly like the Cumbrian 'old lass') and snorted, 'You are wrong, dear husband, on every score. If soaps really are the rubbish you make out, how come literally hundreds of Oxford dons write in to Radio 4 about the latest plot development in *The Archers*?'

At this, I turned as acerbic as, say, Gilbert Harding in *What's My Line?* This radio saga about everyday country folk, *The Archers*, was the classical template or rather the audio-prototype of the TV *Emmerdale*. It was agri-audio drama rather than agri-visual drama, and it happened to be set in the cider and rosehip West Country rather than tight-lipped if warm-hearted rural Yorkshire. But those fragile correlates aside, and even acknowledging the fact that *Emmerdale* was currently racier and hotter than any other television soap (so that its parent prototype *The Archers* was now obliged to feature AIDS, child abuse and beef-induced BSE), both of them were still confections of rent-a-line melodrama.

'Oxford dons applauding Walter Gabriel's hayseed psychology? It's striking a pose, pure and simple. It's the brainy eggheads slumming it and making out they are oh-so-touchingly human after all. They feel warmer in themselves in their cloistered SCRs if they think they can enjoy ordinary uncerebral things. It's their frail umbilical connection to the terrifying outside world. If they're being honest they prefer to relax in the bath with Thucydides, but when they're on the bog or in the SCR and they're halfway through their third bottle of Madeira, they like to divert themselves with brainless rustic melodrama.'

Resentfully filling my glass, Lulu swiftly rebutted that last judgement: 'Melodrama by definition is about sentimental and unreal issues, not about urgent contemporary ones. The current dramatic focus in *Coronation Street* is about a bloody schoolgirl pregnancy! Sarah Lou is thirteen and she's pregnant, and to heighten the family's agony her parents Martin and Gail are already in turmoil because Martin's been having an affair, and Gail has just found out.'

I swirled my riesling and sneered as I examined its meniscus.

Before I could tear back at her, she added, 'Even more on the edge, there is Roy who runs the caff who has fallen in love with his assistant Hayley. But now it transpires Hayley has had a sex change, and originally she was called Harold.'

I stared at her, then burst out cackling like a waterfall. In fact, I didn't know whether to laugh or cry.

'Serve him right!' I said brutally. 'From what I've glimpsed of Roy, he's a lachrymose, not to say one-dimensional halfwit. He's like Uriah Heep shuffling about in his bloody cardigan, but not imbued, needless to say, with Dickens's imaginative energy or agile wit. Roy and his egg and chip café and his bacon fucking butties! Even the way he says "butty" like it's some sacred and exquisite northern cultural gem makes me bloody well spit . . .'

Lulu glared at me incredulous and half in shock. 'You mean you've actually watched it and *followed* it when it's on?'

I snorted majestically. 'I try my best not to follow it, I can assure you. That's why I have so many half-past-seven baths and am so spotlessly clean, haven't you noticed? The truly insidious thing is that if you are in the same room as *Corrie*, it crawls under your skin and enters your brain like a parasite. I can't prevent the odd stray line lodging there hard as I fight it. But hang on, let's just backtrack. You've got your definitions all wrong, I'm afraid. Melodrama versus drama is not about cosiness versus absence of cosiness. Melodrama is about crude, literally discoloured drama, meaning bad drama plain and simple. It is drama that is not actually drama but is ersatz drama. True drama, whether it is Dennis Potter circa 1968 or Ibsen circa 1888, is very easily defined. It is drama that is imaginatively rooted in *true passions which are truly felt*. The trouble is, you see, that Roy and Hayley, God bless them – and I must have watched their antics three or four times to date – they do not truly feel the shock and pathos of their cooked-up paradox. Meaning Harold–Hayley's life-shattering sex-change, and Roy's gentle loving tolerant accommodation thereto when he discovers he has fallen in love with a Hayley who is actually a Harold.'

Lulu blushed at my vaunting pugnacity. There I was with all guns humourlessly blazing as I tried to pulverise this thing she loved. She said, 'Surely there couldn't be a more harrowing issue, could there? Why be such a heartless, sneering bastard? Why not allow credit where it's due instead of these bombastic blanket judgements? After all *Corrie* and *Emmerdale* and *Brookside* are nothing like the old *Archers* where half the dialogue was, "Do you want one sugar, or two sugars in your cuppa?" *Corrie* is no longer about how many sugars, but –'

Undeterred by that crack in her voice, I said, 'You're right, it isn't about sugar. It's about how many genders instead. One gender, or two genders, Roy?'

'Oh you bloody –!'

'Point A,' I battered on regardless. 'If Hayley formerly Harold is such a convincing, rounded and sympathetic character who has been through so much by way of radical surgery and cataclysmic psychological change, how come she loves such a spiritless skulking bacon-bap shuffler as *Roy*? Surely people who have been through gigantic upheavals need a partner who has some appreciation of life's uneven shades and chromatic tints. But whoever writes Roy's lines allows him to perceive only in flat and deadly monochrome, not in rich and varied colours. Point B, why when it comes to both their gender-crisis and Gail and Martin's double crisis with their marriage and child Sara Lou's pregnancy, why is it all resolved or rather fruitfully dragged out and unresolved through a kind of continuous high level *whining*?'

'Eh?' said Lulu, and oddly enough there was a ghost of a soap whine in her own voice.

'They all whine, don't they? Literally and metaphorically, week in week out it's all they ever do. They either whine or they do an inverted whine, which is to say they bluster in a tedious one-dimensional way like butcher Fred or Mike Baldwin the thuggish factory owner. There are no in betweens, no subtle chromatic shades, no? Roy whines as he slices his baps; young Sara Lou whines at having no social life now she's pregnant; Sara Lou's doubly traumatised and envious brother whines; even vintage 1961 *Corrie* graduate, the eternal spinster Emily Nugent, even she bloody well whines. And par excellence, Martin's injured wife Gail is a cosmic whiner to beat all whiners and reminds me of every self-pitying, repulsive, half-baked, insincere imbecile I've ever bloody met!'

Lulu hissed, 'You fu–!'

'Pouting pettish, hamming, dim-witted . . .'

'You sneering bloody bas–'

'And it's nothing to do with the brilliance of her acting. She's no overwhelming *femme fatale* who *really* makes our skins crawl in a satisfying and authentic manner. She only fractionally makes our skins crawl, does our bleating monotonal Gail, because: a) she cannot act, she has never learnt the mysterious skill, and b) even if she could, she doesn't have a writer who can provide her with any decent bloody lines.'

'You arrogant drunken bastard!'

'You know, some of those folk who write the soap scripts take themselves oh so seriously. They wouldn't dare to describe themselves in their true colours as jobbing pimps, so instead they declare themselves to be writer-protagonists for the working class, the literary arbiters for the working man and woman! Twenty years ago it used to be agitprop playwrights giving us Everyman morality plays in village halls packed with middle-class socialist teachers. These days it's these deluded fantasists who think they are the new Shakespeares, because they command unbelievably enormous tele-audiences up to four times a week! Did you know half of these telly writers are actually failed novelists who have given up the fight and turned to where the money is? They go on a Granada TV writing course and learn how to write a soap and also how to make a packet. This package is called a "soap packet" and once you go for this whiter than white Omo or

Daz there is no going back. Between twelve and twenty million people, between a fifth and a third of the country watch these addictive melodramas n times a week! These druggy melodramas are written by all these failed writers who have decided that their failed drama is real drama written by real writers instead of by real failures. Their TV audience doesn't want really real drama, they quickly realise, they don't want really real truth, they just want truly soapy drama and truly soapy truth –'

'Shut your fu–!'

'Has it occurred to you, Lulu, that this is more than just a question of value judgement and snobbish aesthetics? Has it occurred to you in this apocalyptic year of 1999, that it also relates to the *end of the world*?'

Moderately ashen at this point, she said, 'You what, you ranting bloody madman? You bloody *what*?'

'Because it is melodrama, Lulu, that has infected the whole world, not just our bloody TV sets! Did the telly create it, or did it create the telly? Whence comes this addiction to phony trivial drama, be it terrestrial or be it satellite? What for example do you think the current US president and his entourage amount to in TV terms? Was he raised on grown-up TV, or on junior TV, this ageless grinning junior? Is he a real feeling human being, or is he a hammy character conceived out of a melodramatic soap? And ditto for our glassy British premier who seems to have been plucked from a squeaky-clean schoolboy saga circa 1964? Do either of them in anyone's view ever express any true feeling truly felt, any authentic emotion authentically felt? Aren't perhaps the pair of them cheerfully leading us to the abyss with their addiction to the soap scripts they call their political briefings? Isn't a political soundbite or an item of spin just another kind of two-line melodrama? What's the difference, Lulu, for crying out loud?'

With tears in her eyes she snarled, 'Will you stop your arrogant bloody hectoring? Right now. At once! Just stop it.'

'If that doesn't impress you, here are some unarguable

mathematics. You've been glued to *Corrie* since 1982, you tell me, when you were thirty-three-years-old. It's on for a minimum of two hours a week, and assuming you live to be eighty-five and keep on watching it until 2034, you will have watched it over a fifty-two-year period. Let's say fifty years for ease of calculation . . .'

The tears were stanchless now, and for some reason so was my mouth. Lulu cried, 'Shut up, will you? For God's sake shut up. Please!'

'That's 50 times 50 weeks a year, times 2 hours, which is 2500 times 1/12th of a day, meaning approximately 208 days. Which is roughly seven whole months, day and night, forget about any sleep, Lulu, of non-stop *Corrie*-goggling! Seven whole months out of your life, Lulu! What do you think of that remarkable fact?'

I never found out what she thought, because instead of replying she threw the empty bottle of Olasz at my head . . .

I ducked, of course, and it missed. But it still did plenty of significant damage. It went full tilt into guess which totemic household deity?

Into our television screen, no less! It hit our twenty-four-incher smack across its beaming face, and shattered it to buggery . . .

And it was, all too painfully, the final nemesis of that innocent electronic conduit . . .

And it was, all too obviously, the beginning of the end of marriage number four . . .

# 14

*High Mallstown, North Cumbria, 23rd November 2001.*
*Lunchtime satellite viewing and listening.*

## 356

An outstanding new production of Mozart's tangled and byzantine love opera *Così Fan Tutte (They All Carry On Like That)*. It is sung, to my initial disappointment, in English with an original translation by a young New Zealander called Clara Badel. This hour-long film contains excerpts from a recent sell-out performance in Sydney, interspersed with certain reflections on the opera by the leading singers (all in their twenties, and all, male and female, remarkably handsome). These eloquent meditations are sometimes filmed straight from the participants' mouths, but more often are given as unattributed voice-over. The overall effect is of an intelligent and incisive collage of the music, and its considered if unorthodox interpretation by some leading contemporary interpreters. The libretto extracts (which I have copied from a video tape) are rendered by standard dramatic conventions, and the commentary as straightforward text within quotes.

'The voices you hear in *Così* are actually Wolfgang Mozart speaking about the private anguish of Wolfgang Mozart. *Così* is about two men in love with two sisters testing their fidelity by pretending to go off as soldiers, but sneaking back cunningly disguised as 'two flamboyant Albanians'. They then do their damnedest to make the faithful sisters Dorabella and Fiordiligi unfaithful. And perversely, with all that painful and misguided effort, they partially succeed. It's like Shakespeare, all that plot convolution and deception and disguises business. But it's also very poignant and pertinent that Mozart was himself at the time involved with two sisters. He ended up marrying one of them, but was actually in love with the other. So all this heartache and confusion and turmoil in the opera is all real in origin, all rooted in powerful autobiographical feeling. It's not some jolly kind of soap-type opera. It's not a soap, *Così Fan Tutte*, definitely it's not.'

*Ferrando: To Dorabella, absolutely no one can compare. As true as she is handsome, as faithful as she's fair.*

*Guglielmo: Not trust Fiordiligi? Why, you're out of your mind! Why, she's the perfection of goodness and beauty combined!*

*Don Alfonso: I may well be bald and grey but –*

'True enough, Act One might be seen to be a kind of light and amusing ensemble piece. But then in Act Two we dive straightaway into some very grave and deadly earnest arias. The players more or less expose their raw insides and examine them out there on the stage. If that's not too gory an image, in genteel high-art operatic terms. It makes Dorabella for me an extraordinarily powerful piece to sing. To be honest, I can't think of a more powerful piece in the whole repertoire.'

*Fiordiligi: Oh my darling! Be kind and please forgive me. Forgive a sinful lover. Dark shadow, hide forever, conceal my awful secret in the depths of the night!*

'But things turn very nasty in Act Two. The music is by turns tender, furious and passionate. And these people clearly mean what they say, indelibly so. I quote, *There is a volcano in my heart.* That's not vacuous, colourless hyperbole, it happens to be a personal truth. The opera's set in Naples in the eighteenth century, but it is far from being a macaronic comedy of manners. There is for example in *Così* the famous never-ending kiss between the two reconciled lovers. Mozart meant it to appear infinitely passionate, eternal and never-ending, and to do it properly you have to maintain a lengthy silence on the stage. In my view Mozart deliberately planned it so as to make the audience extremely uncomfortable. All that remorseless eternity of passion, all that deafening silence really disturbs people. After all, audiences hate silence in an opera. They think that something's gone wrong, that one of the singers has had a stroke or had the impudence to go and die on stage. And again to mention some more unforgettable lines. *Change is a necessity of the heart.* You can say that rhythmic sentence a thousand times, and it never loses its sting and it never sounds a cardboard cliché. And in the original Italian that we sang last year in Dresden there is also *Bella calma trovera.* Let me say it with the appropriate stress. *Be-lla ca-lma tro-ver-a.* That's really something isn't it? Isn't that heartbreakingly beautiful? Don't you think? Isn't it?'


## 626 *(Audio channel)*

The breathless tail end of a midday news magazine:

*Presenter (with that staccato joviality touchingly peculiar to BBC Radio 4):* Our long-established Reithian educative role here at the Beeb – is it as cast-iron as we like to think it is? That much respected watchdog, the Coventry University Media Group, is about to publish an extremely critical analysis of the BBC's reportage on the Middle East. With regard to the way we cover the conflict between the Israelis and the Palestinians, it appears we inadequate Beeb journalists give grossly defective accounts of any of the historical background. Indeed, the trenchant Media Group asserts, any sort of meaningful context seems to be ignored, including the arguments and points of view of either side. Seemingly our reports on the conflict convey the impression that these dreadful things – the bombings, the bulldozings, the suicide attacks – are just randomly and unintelligibly happening. It is almost, Coventry Univ adds, as if we are presenting a rather meaningless and highly unpleasant and badly scripted soap opera. When their researchers conducted a recent question-naire, they found that an astonishing number of viewers and listeners didn't even know whether it was the Palestinians or the Israelis were the settlers or the refugees . . .

### 625 *(Audio channel)*

The gentle clearing of a BBC Radio 3 larynx which is like the decorous vacuuming of no other.

'Now let us tiptoe on to some sadly neglected masterpieces of the Minor Baroque. Later I shall be talking about the splendid Bohemia-born Samuel Capricornus, but how many of you listeners, I wonder, have heard of the oddly named Plà Brothers? *Die Gebrüder Plà*, a.k.a. the Plà Bros, worked as oboists in the Herzog Carl Eugen's Hofkapelle. Alas, we know neither their dates of birth, nor when they died, nor even what their Christian names were. However the learned commentator Schubart certainly knew of them, as he men-tions the enigmatic duo in his seminal commentary *Aesthetik der Tonkunst*. He says of the Plàs, "If Castor and Pollux had blown the oboe, they could scarcely have blown better than this pair! They were two Spaniards, who had uprooted and transplanted themselves to Germany. There they developed their musical bent under Niccolo Jommelli (music master at the same Hofkapelle between 1752 and 1768) and attained an unparalleled virtuosity with their instruments."

'Before long I shall be playing you their Trio Sonata in D Minor for flute, oboe and *Generalbass*. But just before I do I need to pull into the picture a Frenchman resident in Germany a little earlier. Yet another doyen of the Minor Baroque, Jean Daniel Hardt was Stuttgart Kapellmeister from 1725 to 1755. His sonata for viola da gamba, which I shall be spoiling you with after the Plàs, certainly shows a resoundingly French influence (as indeed was the contemporary ecclesiastical architecture in Germany). By the way, as an unabashedly partisan aside on my part, this terminology "Minor Baroque" is one to which I at any rate take considerable exception. You may have noticed me using it in somewhat ironical quote marks throughout my talk. This notionally "minor" music which I have played and am about to play is surely truly stunning stuff in the main. Is it not quite disgraceful that geniuses like, say, Ritter and J.C.F. Bach and Fux and Pachelbel should be routinely regarded as very small fry compared with the unarguably divine Johann Sebastian? Is it not also appalling that vast numbers of serious music lovers haven't even heard of Jommelli or J.D. Hardt, much less discovered their remarkable music? What are the mainstream record companies doing, for heaven's sake, when there is not even one representative anthology at time of talking, much less any recordings of the individual composers? The departed spirits one assumes of these Minor Baroque composers must surely be feeling their neglect very painfully. The Plà Bros must be roundly turning in their graves in November 2001 . . .'

## 121

'. . . was he fond of brightly coloured ties, your Uncle Billy? Yes, yes, and did he go overboard with the salt, he could never have enough salt on his potatoes? And he preferred chips to mashed ones, am I right? No, the other way about, mash to chips, fair enough, you're right, I had it the wrong way round, they didn't bother very much with chips in Bristol in the early 1900s. OK, OK love, you've caught me out on a straight historical fact. You have to bear in mind that when you're dealing with the spirit world like I do, and especially when you do it on TV, it can be quite exhausting. Also if they were fond of fooling about here when on earth, their departed spirits can be prone to exaggeration or plain teasing. In the world beyond this one they're not afraid of a good laugh, and your Uncle Billy was always a bit of a compulsive joker, am I right? Yes love, I thought so, I thought so. That's cos he was a sailor if I'm correct? I'm picking up the maritime influence, and the love of salt on everything about me definitely. I know we're in Bristol, the sailor's favourite city, and I think he was a sea captain, wasn't he? No, I've exaggerated, he was in the merchant navy but just as an ordinary deckhand? No, wrong again, so what was he, love? Ah he was a cook you say, or more exactly a cook's assistant. Right, and that's why I pick up that he really liked playing tricks on his boss the cook. But you know they were never nasty tricks, they were always good-hearted and really innocent tricks, and Billy's boss the cook never got too upset about them! And of course a cook's assistant is handling salt all the time, no wonder I felt the salt vibrations ever so strongly. The cook's name was Ben, I believe? Oh you don't know, your uncle never actually told you? Well it was Ben definitely. It was Ben Wetherby for definite. Anyway, my duck, we have to move the show along a bit cos it's getting near the commercial break and we don't want to irritate the sponsors. What your Uncle Billy is telling you now from the spirit side is first of all he's very very *happy* there. And secondly Sadie, Sailor Billy's niece here in the Talk Channel studio, secondly he's very very *proud* of you Sadie. He's really very proud of you his all-time favourite niece! When was it he last saw you, my precious? It was 1938, the year he died, when you were only eight? Well his heart is fairly bursting with a loving uncle's pride, he says, I have to tell you here in the studio. Now then love, no need to cry, no need to get so upset, lend her a hanky someone for pity's sake! There there. Let me give you a hug from your Uncle Billy. Your Uncle Billy says if he was here beside you now in his physical and earthly body, he'd give you a huge and loving hug and tell you to your lovely face how proud he is of you, my darling! Look here, folks, at her crying her eyes out, bless her! And just cos she's heard that her Uncle Billy the sea captain and the eternal prankster still loves her from the beyond . . .'

## 240

'. . . among pirates of the time. Blackbeard's favourite method of ordeal was to light sulphur underneath his protégés, to see who could stand it the longest. Sulphur being redolent of the very devil himself of course, a title which Blackbeard earned often enough for his exploits. Once, for example, Blackbeard had the audacity to blockade Charleston, Virginia, a town which had grown fat on the slave trade and was therefore worth any pirate's serious attention. He employed six ships for the blockade, and among the hostages he took there was a leading Charleston merchant and the merchant's four-year-old son. They were held hostage for eleven days – one can only imagine how terrifying it was for the father and his little child – until Blackbeard got what he wanted. His impudence, the sheer brazen effrontery of his demands became the stuff of hoary legend. On a similar hostage-taking escapade insolent Blackbeard even succeeded in acquiring a contract of indemnity and an official pardon from the governor of South Carolina. This most notorious example of the Maritime Mafia only met his downfall when he was duped or, better to say, frankly conned by the actions of a treacherous British ship.'

## 216 *(keyed in in error)*

'Feel your breathing accelerating, boys? Sandy's mouthwatering cellulite-free booty in close-focus display is so superbly, delectably appetising because Sandy says she eats nothing but yoghurt for lunch and does endless anaerobics in the gym every spare minute she gets. Now that she's turning round to the camera and is offering an uninhibited full frontal exhibition, you fellers can appreciate how those low fat hazelnuts and forest fruits which are her fave flaves have found a way into her equally scrumptious boobies. Sandy informs me that her idea of a perfect night in involves a romantic candlelit dinner just for herself and her dream feller, a splendid collation which she herself will prepare in something very light to the point of being frankly diaphanous, while her ideal Adonis looks on appraisingly in his stylish silk kimono. A vigorous, a very vigorous stir fry in a wok perhaps? And with a little incendiary ginseng seed added for some rare eastern promise? This will be followed by a lazy, a sinfully lazy wallow on the mat next to her exquisite imitation coalfire. Sandy is also very keen on soft and pliable cuddly toys, which she admits might be used for a revolutionary dual purpose, especially if the feller in question has a trace of imagination. Ideally too she would bring out for you – whoops! I mean for her favourite love partner, and who's to say you wouldn't prove to be just that? – a luxury massage oil. This oil, Sandy promises, she would rub slowly and lingeringly into whichever bits of you – whoops again! I mean of her dream Apollo – needed the voluptuous and lascivious tee-ell-see. OK, I admit I've swallowed the dictionary today, but after she had you, I mean him, gasping in an assured paroxysm of insane ecstasy, it would be your, I mean his, turn to do the same to Sandy's legendary booty-bootissimo and . . .

# 212

'. . . see the practice of meditation as a common or garden and basic stressbuster. In my clinic I emphasise to my patients who are often people with heavy responsibilities at work, and who need to keep on functioning come what may, that the Taoist Cosmocentric Breathing technique is a useful way of busting stress. People tell me I'm an attractive, very young looking healer and ask me how the hell a gal like me has managed to build up a successful business here in LA when I'm not even thirty. When I tell them I'm actually forty-eight and have three children in their twenties, they can only faint at the confession! I tell them that looking twenty years younger is all down to controlling my ins and outs, meaning my breath, it's as simple as that. The ancient eastern disciplines have understood this from time immemorial, but it takes the average westerner a long time to take on board the basic principle. In classic pranayama it's a case of learning to develop a natural breathing pattern. A natural breath goes all the way down into the stomach, right? You can see as much in babies and animals, that deep, deep breathing from, excuse me, the guts. Whereas your average stressed-out westerner breathes in and out shallowly and far too quickly. And not to put too fine a point on it often ends up a shallow and neurotic and highly dissatisfied person skimming along far too quickly on the surface of –

## 356

*Despina (to Dorabella and Fiordiligi): Men are all birds of a feather. Always in motion, fluttering like April leaves, just like waves on the ocean. Even the weather is less changeable than a man. Faithful vows, gazes of rapture, flattery and flowers, warmed-up compliments . . .*

*Voice-over from one of the young male performers: And later in Così fan Tutte . . .*

*Don Alfonso: Everyone is down on women. But I forgive her . . .*

'. . . apropos this explosive issue, does not advance our cause or improve our image in the modern world. They complain of the notorious law of *huduq* in Pakistan, which demands that any woman accusing a man of rape should have a minimum of three male witnesses to testify on her behalf. If such fortuitous witnesses are unforthcoming, then the court may accuse her, the victim, of inciting the immorality, of being in fact an adulteress. Faced with the dire sharia penalties for committing adultery, is it any wonder that any woman who is raped, however terribly, however cruelly, in Pakistan, is reluctant to accuse her assailant or assailants? But paradoxes abound. It is also one of the few Muslim countries where a woman, namely Benazir Bhutto, has managed at various times to exert considerable political influence. Some might argue that this anomaly is only as a consequence of her dynastic name, and that her one-time presidency of the Oxford University Union is by the by. But bearing in mind that her father Zulfikar, accused of political assassination, was ingloriously hanged after a bleak and unpleasant incarceration, there seems to be some other force at work. Also, despite the endless litigation against her by past and present political opponents, the accusations of gross corruption and orchestrated violence in the provinces, she has managed remarkably well to stay out of any Pakistani jail. One cannot imagine a female like Benazir Bhutto submitting herself to sharia law with any great alacrity . . .

'So what do these contradictions suggest of the contemporary Islamic world? That we are not as simple as all that and not as black and white as all that? That we are more diffuse and various and subtle and individual than they would give us credit for, those pigeonholing westerners? After all for anyone to have any understanding of any culture, they need first of all to interest themselves a little in that culture. There is scarcely a single intelligent Syrian, Lebanese, Egyptian,

Saudi Arabian who does not have a basic workaday fluency in English. They know it is the lingua franca and the means of advancement in business, science, politics, medicine, literature, the lot. By contrast it is a miracle to meet a single westerner who has even half a dozen phrases of child's Arabic at his or her disposal. Many Arabs will have read a certain amount of Shakespeare for their English examinations but hardly an English person alive could name a single classical Arabic author. Or for that matter a single modern Arabic author. I have met several highly intelligent westerners who think that they speak Lebanese in Lebanon, Syrian in Syria and Moroccan in Morocco, and Egyptian here in Cairo. When I gently point out that we all speak different versions of Arabic, they express a slightly pained amazement rather than a blushing embarrassment. In some cases this is followed by what I can only describe as a facial intimation of worried suspicion. On learning that we all speak the same language, that we Arabs are impertinent enough all to speak Arabic, a certain expression of paranoia steals upon their faces. As if to say, ah you are all of an unsettling conspiratorial sameness after all! Meaning that in their terms we are ganging up linguistically as well as ganging up against them in various other disturbing ways. For even the most, shall we say, forthright and robust of their fellow Christians, the Karadzics and Milosevices who have tried to extirpate the Kosovan Muslims, or the no-nonsense Russian Putin who has a very firm way when it comes to disciplining the Muslim Chechens . . . they all speak their very different tongues, don't they? Serbian and Russian are very different languages, and even though there are plenty of Albanian Roman Catholics and a vigorous Albanian Orthodox Church, the Serbs routinely consider Kosovan Albanian a profoundly mongrel and unpleasantly gypsyish tongue fit only, they might add, for highly suspicious "Arab" types.

'But languages and linguistic affiliations are surely as nothing compared to the business of religious observance.

What I believe shocks westerners more than anything about the world's Muslims, whether they be self-declared moderates or unabashed fundamentalists, is that they all take their religion so seriously. Yes, even the moderates, even the ones who believe in education, liberty and progress for women, in science, in TV and radio and public entertainments, even they take their faith so seriously. Even they practise things that only a relative minority of token Christians, certainly European Christians, would practise. They read their holy book, the Koran, on a daily basis and they take it very seriously. They pray regularly each and every single day, sometimes communally and in public. The mind boggles at the idea of the whole of Stockholm or the whole of Amsterdam or the whole of London or the whole of New York stopping everything to reverently worship their Christian God. Is it conceivable such a thing either now or say five hundred years ago? There are a few exceptions to be sure. There are a few devout Christian cults, tiny agricultural communities as a rule in Europe and America, the Hutterites and the Mennonites and so on, who live a prayerful, secluded and devout life. But they are cults, sociological eccentricities, colourful oddities as far as their secular brethren are concerned. Similarly up until recent years the Roman Catholic Christians in that tiny country Ireland would stop everything for their six o'clock Angelus, perhaps a very majority of the country would stop together and pray together to their God. I gather now that since it has achieved a massive economic boom and is sometimes dubbed as a Celtic Tiger, this kind of public avowal of communal faith is swiftly dwindling.

'It is a very interesting oxymoron though, is it not? A token Christian. I suppose one could talk of a token Muslim, but it would make little sense to most Muslims that I know. Anyone who is truly religious knows that religion involves visible and outward practice, not just an invisible attitude or a mental affiliation. After all, on the most banal analogy, if someone said, I am a joiner or a doctor, but didn't actually do any joinering or doctoring, and didn't actually know much about joinering or doctoring, we would think they were rather pointless idiots, would we not? We would think of them as grossly deluded. Would you trust yourself to a doctor who didn't practise his medicine and who knew very little about the subject? Would you by analogy take seriously a Christian who didn't pray, didn't read the Bible, didn't go to church or chapel? As far as I know the genteel nationalist politician Radovan Karadzic, currently in hiding for his past deeds, is both a psychoanalyst and a failed poet, but I have no knowledge of him assiduously practising his Christian faith. He seems to me to have vigorously flouted one of the Ten Commandments saying, Thou shalt not kill. Perhaps Mr Karadzic, having not read his Bible for a long time, thought that his Old Testament God had actually declared them to the prophet Moses as "The Ten Suggestions"?

'Likewise twelve years ago the Christian world was profoundly astonished when the Muslim world was thrown into turmoil by the business of the notorious book. For the life of them they could not understand why anyone in the Christian year of 1989 should get so upset about a thing as banal as a mere book. I for one have always been against the declaration of the fatwa against the author and his book, for a murder of any kind, judicial or religio-judicial or non-judicial is surely a terrible and irreversible thing. These things, these decisions about spiritual guilt or spiritual innocence, are surely best left to God himself, not to men. After all, given that God has eternity on his side, he has plenty of time on his hands to adjudicate one way or another as his infinite wisdom dictates. But yes the Muslim world took it all very seriously. And the western world, or at any rate the western defenders of the author, said, but no, this is only a book, it is not a bomb! Moreover it is not even a notionally blasphemous tract or work of non-fiction, it is just a story, it is just a novel, it is just a *made-up* thing. This I believe is the tormenting crux of the problem. Aside from the fact most

Muslims, and most Christians for that matter, are not university graduates in literary subjects, and therefore not alive to subtle categorical distinctions about fiction, satire, satirical fiction, non-fiction, satirical non-fiction etcetera . . . the author's allies had failed to understand a very basic principle. That there were not one but *two* books in the explosive equation. There was one book that was written by human hands and another book that came into being, Muslims believe, as a consequence of divinely ordered inspiration.

'And a divinely inspired book, a sacred book, whether it be the Bible or the Koran, is certainly not to be read like one would sit down and read a novel. One does not as a rule read a novel, however great it is, with a spirit of prayerful reverence. This is the nub of the matter and one alas that the western intellectual simply cannot get into his otherwise infinitely elastic and ever-accommodating and ever-tolerant head. The grave mistake of the author and his western allies, and perhaps it was an understandable mistake to make, was to confuse and conflate two different types of knowledge in the philosophical sense. Spiritual knowledge as in the sacred scriptures is one type of inimitable knowledge, one philosophical category, let us call it A. The explosive book, which was theoretically describable as a secular satire or parody or literary allegory or literary fairy tale, was another type of philosophical knowledge, let us call it B. Now there are clearly dozens of different types of philosophical knowledge ranging from the epistemology of falling in love, to the epistemology of drunkenness, to the epistemology of a narcotic experience, to the epistemology of being born, of dying, of being semi-consciousness and so on and so on. Call them C, D, E, F, G, H and so forth. Clearly, some of these categories may be played with and conflated artistically and philosophically and no harm done. But alas if A and B are "playfully" conflated (as opposed to prayerfully kept separate), as they were seen to be conflated in the spring of 1989, then . . .

'Then what, I ask myself?

'Then I am afraid to tell you, puzzled, surprisingly artless, surprisingly childlike, surprisingly unsophisticated, surprisingly disingenuous western brethren (do you see how my adjectives are becoming a parody of the usual attributes a westerner applies to an Arab?), then I am sorry to tell you that you *have* inadvertently produced a bomb as well as a book . . .'

## 636 *(Audio channel)*

Lamentations, 3.20–22

*My soul hath them still in remembrance, and is humbled in me. This I recall to mind, therefore have I hope. It is of the Lord's mercies that we are not consumed, because his compassions fail not.*